THE SPIDER
VS.
THE EMPIRE STATE

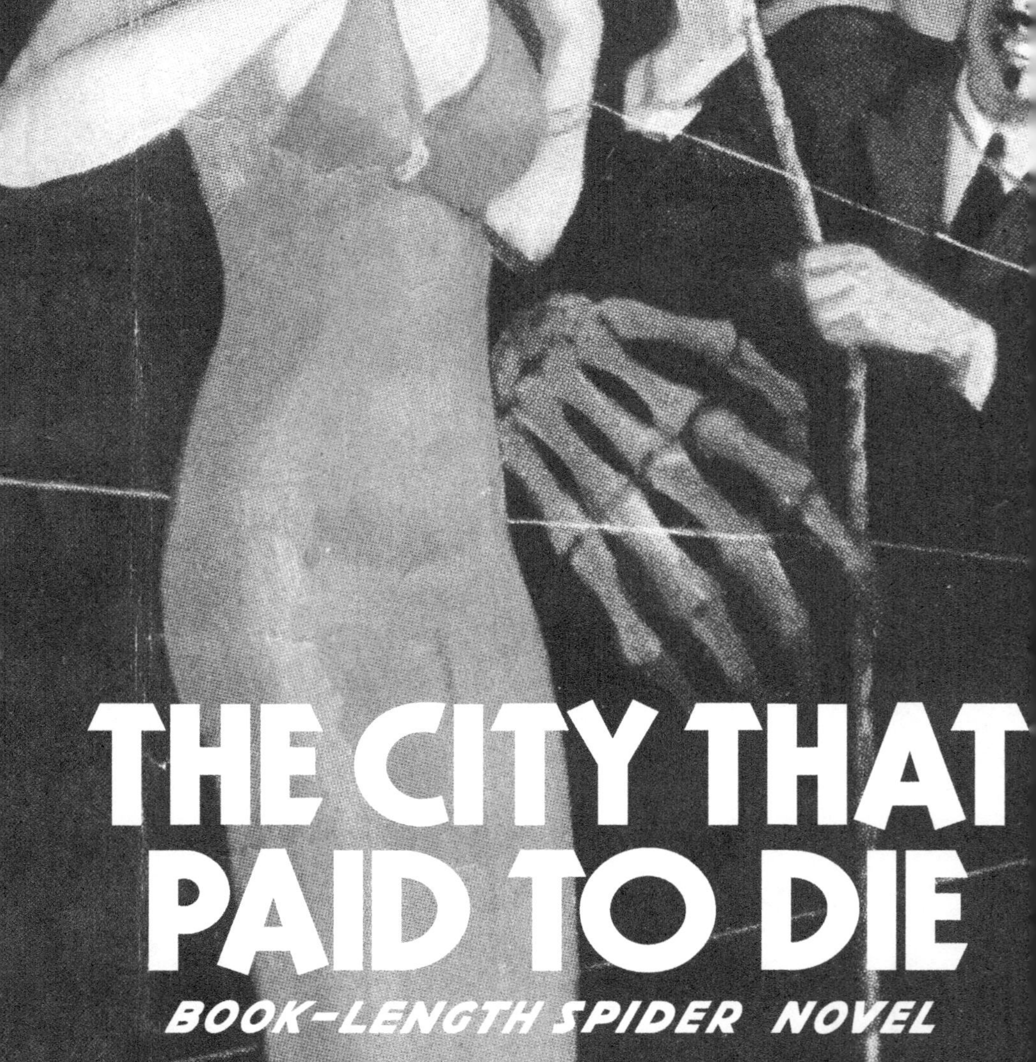
THE CITY THAT
PAID TO DIE
BOOK-LENGTH SPIDER NOVEL

THE SPIDER
AT BAY
BOOK-LENGTH
SPIDER NOVEL

SCOURGE OF THE BLACK LEGIONS

BOOK-LENGTH SPIDER NOVEL

THE SPIDER VS THE EMPIRE STATE

THE COMPLETE BLACK POLICE TRILOGY

BY NORVELL W. PAGE
[WRITING AS GRANT STOCKBRIDGE]

WITH CLASSIC ILLUSTRATIONS BY JOHN FLEMING GOULD AND JOHN NEWTON HOWITT

AGE OF ACES BOOKS   ORCHARD PARK · NY

THE SPIDER VS. THE EMPIRE STATE

The following novels, which appear for the first time in book form, were originally published in the following issues of THE SPIDER magazine:

THE CITY THAT PAID TO DIE, from the September 1938 issue
THE SPIDER AT BAY, from the October 1938 issue
SCOURGE OF THE BLACK LEGIONS, from the November 1938 issue

Published by arrangement with Argosy Communications, Inc.

AN AGE OF ACES BOOK

The original pulp magazine illustrations in this volume have been modified digitally to better fit the layout. Single spot illustrations from the 9/35, 4/36, 1/40 and 9/40 issues have been added to fill out the chapter openings.

Cover illustrations and book design by Chris Kalb • Edited by Bill Mann
Printed on demand by BookSurge Publishing beginning August 2009

The Designer gratefully wishes to acknowledge the contributions of Joel Frieman, David Kalb and Thomas Krabacher in the preparation of this volume.

ISBN: 978-0-9820950-3-4

This edition is dedicated to
THE RESISTANCE FIGHTERS
of the past, present and future

BLACKSHIRTS ON BROADWAY

In 1938 the world was changing, and it changed The Spider. Up until that year *The Spider* magazine—one of the most imaginative and popular pulp fiction magazines of the 1930s—was offering its readers fast-paced action fantasies that featured its title character, The Spider, waging a clandestine war against more or less traditional criminal masterminds and their exotic menaces. The storylines, always melodramatic and often bizarre, provided readers an escape from the uncomfortably real worries of daily life in depression-era America. But, in 1938 with the September to November issues—"The City That Paid to Die," "The Spider at Bay" and "The Scourge of the Black Legions"—the magazine does a dramatic about-face and confronts some of the central political anxieties of its era. These stories are collectively known as The Black Police Trilogy and they offer an allegory for the totalitarianism that was then occurring abroad and a cautionary tale for what many feared could happen here.

To appreciate this, it's worth taking a brief look at some of the key events of the 1930s, particularly as seen from the year of the saga's publication, 1938.

IN 1938 Americans were in the ninth year of the Great Depression. By this point, the decade had witnessed the near failure of the nation's banking system on three occasions, massive unemployment as factories closed and industrial production plummeted, and a catastrophic collapse of the country's farm economy. In 1932 the Bonus Army marched on Washington as social unrest seemed to challenge what were thought to have been even the most stable American institutions. Even the natural environment seemed to rebel. Six years of drought in the plains states combined with poor farming practices resulted in the Dust Bowl, which devastated thousands of farming families and climaxed in the Black Sunday dust storm of April 14, 1935, turning day into night across the Great Plains and blanketing much of the country with dust clouds as far east as Washington, DC.

Conditions in 1937 and 1938 continued to batter public morale. Labor unrest and violence plagued the country; in 1937 police fired into a crowd of protesting strikers outside the Republic Steel plant in South Chicago, leaving 90 wounded and 10 dead; this came on the heels of a major confrontation between strikers and national guardsmen less than two years earlier that brought the city of San Francisco to a standstill. Economically, 1938 saw the onset of a recession and a big jump in unemployment that threatened to undo the fragile recovery that had, until then, been underway. The question for many Americans was not just whether American democracy could survive, but whether it even deserved to do so.

But if the devastation of the Great Depression caused Americans to question the foundations of liberal democracy, then what was the alternative? For many the answer was to be found in a dictatorship. It was felt that only a strong leader unhampered by the restrictions of normal government could restore social order and put things right. The appeal of such a seemingly straightforward solution could be seen everywhere. The 1933 film *Gabriel Over the White House* starred Walter Huston as an American president who singlehandedly dissolves Congress, declares martial law, and orders the public execution of his enemies by firing squad at the foot of the Statue of Liberty. The movie was a hit. Political opposites of the era, such as William Randolph Hearst and Walter

Lippmann, doubted that American style democracy was adequate to the task of dealing with the depression and argued that some form of dictator was needed to pull the country back from the edge of disaster. Benito Mussolini, despite his strong-arm tactics in his native Italy, was widely admired in the United States throughout much of the decade as a man who could get things done. As historian Jonathan Alter notes, "throughout the early 1930s, Fascism remained respectable."

The prospects of an American dictatorship were not merely flights of fancy. In 1933, the year of Roosevelt's inauguration, the ultra-conservative American Liberty League, an organization of prominent politicians, business leaders, and financiers, approached a retired army general with the offer of financial backing if he would lead 500,000 veterans in a military coup against the Roosevelt White House. League members had been appalled by the threat the new president's "socialist" policies posed to established wealth and property. The attempt failed when the general, Smedley Butler, indignantly rejected the offer and reported the plot to Congress. Nonetheless, it inspired Sinclair Lewis to write his own 1935 novel of an American dictatorship, *It Can't Happen Here.*

Throughout the decade, the theme of a totalitarian state regularly surfaced in American politics. Populist political figure Huey Long of Louisiana was accused of exerting near dictatorial control over the reins of government in his home state of Louisiana. Populist demagogues Father Charles Coughlin of Michigan and Kansas' Gerald Burton Winrod commanded large followings, particularly among the rural poor and the urban unemployed. At their peak, the radio audience for Coughlin's broadcasts was estimated at 26 million listeners weekly, and right-wing preacher Winrod was reaching 100,000 readers a month with his newspaper, "The Defender." Their common message preached that the average American was the victim of shadowy forces—bankers, Jews, atheists, Bolsheviks—who were responsible for the Great Depression, and only a strong authoritarian leader could free the country from their grip.

Joining these personalities were numerous organizations such as The Christian Front, The Citizen's Protective League, American Patriots,

Inc., the German-American Bund, and Father Coughlin's own National Union for Social Justice, all spreading the same message. As time went on, the agendas of these parties became increasingly right wing and, much to the alarm of observers, began to openly seek their inspiration in the policies of the likes of Mussolini and Hitler.

Which brings us to Europe.

The United States during the 1930s was profoundly isolationist and most Americans wanted nothing to do with Europe. Not only had the depression at home forced the country to turn inward, but it was the consensus of most people that the United States was tricked into entering the Great War by the European powers acting in collusion with the armaments industries. For most, the final straw occurred when America's former European allies refused to pay their war debts. The high water mark of American isolationism came with the renewal of the nation's Neutrality Acts in 1937.

But if Americans wanted nothing to do with Europe, that didn't mean they were unaware of what was taking place there. Magazines such as *Time*, *Harpers*, and *The Atlantic* kept Americans well informed about events on the continent, particularly in Nazi Germany. Americans followed the appointment of Hitler as Chancellor, the creation of a special national police from the ranks of the SS and SA, and the opening of the first concentration camps in 1933. In 1934 readers saw Hitler take on greatly expanded dictatorial powers as he was declared Germany's *Führer*, and in 1935 the Nuremberg Race Laws were decreed. In 1936 the Gestapo was placed above the law, the SS was charged with guarding the concentration camps, and Germany invaded the Rhineland. Finally, 1938 saw the *Anschluss* as Nazi troops entered Austria and, in the late spring of that year, the Czechoslovakian crisis. Over the course of the decade, Americans watched this first with curiosity and then with growing alarm.

1938 was a turning point in the American view of events in Europe. In spring of that year the first transatlantic radio broadcasts took place, bringing the events of the Czech crisis and Neville Chamberlain's "peace in our time" speech directly into American homes. In September Hitler's address at the Nuremberg Rally was carried live in the United

States and the effect was electrifying. As one commentator noted at the time: "Adolph Hitler has spoken and the world has listened."

While some Americans, such as Coughlin and Winrod, openly admired Hitler and the Nazis, most did not. What they began to realize was that Hitler was no longer merely Germany's problem. Just the year before, FDR warned Americans that "the epidemic of world lawlessness is spreading." Hitler's Germany was now increasingly seen by Americans as not just a threat to Europe, but to the world.

In short, by mid-1938 anxiety over conditions both at home and abroad meant that America's nerves were stretched taut. There was no better demonstration of this than the nation's reaction to Orson Welles' "War of the Worlds" broadcast in late October of that year. Americans had come to recognize that totalitarianism posed a serious threat and that there was every possibility they would be drawn into another European war.

It was against this background that the Black Police trilogy arrived in the pages of *The Spider*.

THE SPIDER and the Black Police were, more than anything, the product of two key individuals, Harry Steeger and Norvell W. Page. Steeger was co-founder and publisher of Popular Publications, which, by the late 1930s, had become the largest pulp publishing house in the country. Steeger possessed a shrewd eye for the tastes of his reading public, carefully supervising magazine artwork and regularly reading some if not all of the content of each issue of every magazine they published. *The Spider* was one of their most successful titles.

Equally important, Steeger was also a political progressive. In later years he would become an advisor to the White House on civil rights, the author of a book on the subject, and president of the National Urban League. During the 1930s, having witnessed economic and social conditions at home and in Europe, he was, to use his own words, "very anxious at the time to say something about the depression and the political elements of the world" in the popular fiction he published. He did this primarily in the pages of *Operator 5*, a pulp adventure magazine that dealt on a monthly basis with a seemingly endless series of threats to the very existence of the United States. Steeger would out-line the themes for the lead novel in each issue, which frequently included footnotes and additional explanatory material to add verisimilitude to the events portrayed. While other pulp magazines commonly dealt with individual heroes and villains, the storytelling in *Operator 5*, in Steeger's words, "assumed a broader canvas," dealing with whole nations and armies, frequently linking story elements to contemporary happenings. In 1938, with its Black Police trilogy about the rise of a home-grown police state, *The Spider* moved in this direction as well.

Why this change in *The Spider* at this time? A couple of reasons suggest themselves. First, the stories in *Operator 5* during this period were primarily concerned with foreign threats to the United States. The magazine had only recently concluded its massive thirteen-part Purple Invasion saga that dealt with a protracted struggle against fictional European invaders and was revving up for a similar multi-part series dealing with a thinly disguised invasion by Japan. In other words, that magazine's dance card was full.

Second, throughout the 1930s Steeger displayed a long-standing interest in the threat of home-grown totalitarianism. It was a regular topic in *Operator 5's* Secret Sentinel column, a non-fiction feature that appeared in each issue of the magazine, and he used it as the basis for a cover story in the magazine a few years earlier, May 1935's "Blood Reign of the Dictator," which told of a takeover of the US government by a Huey Long-style dictator. *The Spider*'s Black Police trilogy pre-sented Steeger and Popular Publications with the opportunity to revisit the same theme on a larger canvas, updated in light of current events then underway in Europe.

And Norvell W. Page was just the author to do the job. Originally from Richmond, Virginia, Page was a newspaperman who had turned to pulp writing in 1930 to supplement his income. By the mid-1930s he was writing full-time, producing more than 100,000 words a month. Under the house name of Grant Stockbridge he was the prin-cipal author of the Spider series, having written 42 of the 59 novels that had appeared prior to the Black Police trilogy. By the end of the magazine's run, he would be responsible for a total of 81 of its 118 novels. During the heyday of the magazine between the years 1933-1936, Page did more to define the character of *The Spider* than anyone else, giving it its bizarre plots, white-hot pacing, and emotional intensity, all situated in a vividly imagined nightmare version of New York City. Intriguingly, family accounts suggest that Page may have traveled to Europe in 1936 where he had the opportunity to witness events in Nazi Germany first hand. It has also been suggested that Page, while still a newspaperman, had become acquainted with Varian Fry, the American journalist and ardent anti-Nazi who later founded the Emergency Rescue Committee, a network that ultimately helped several thousand anti-Nazi artists and intellectuals, and Jewish refugees escape Hitler's Europe. None of this has ever been confirmed but, if true, it made the choice of Page to write such a saga all the more ideal.

The result is the trilogy you have in this volume. Briefly, the story recounts how a new political party, the Party of Justice, takes control of New York's state and local governments by sweeping the general elections. The party itself is controlled by criminals, who quickly utilize the apparatus of government to impose their own totalitarian rule. Local police and government officials are puppets under their control. The newly formed Black Police is used to enforce its will. Oppressive taxes are imposed, shopkeepers who won't pay are punished, and those who resist are beaten, arrested, and see their property confiscated. Opponents are branded public enemies and deprived of civil liberties; public executions soon follow. The general populace is cowed. Against such tyranny only Richard Wentworth, alias The Spider, dares resist…

The novels are frantically-paced exercises in non-stop action that leave the reader scarcely any time to catch his or her breath. To be sure, there are pulp elements that test a reader's credulity: the leader of the criminals is a mysterious mastermind known only as the Master who communicates with his minions by appearing as a white face in a trick mirror; the Black Police, 100,000 strong, is composed of criminals released from New York's state prisons by a corrupt governor—this at a time when the *national* prison population was only 146,000; fancy footwork must be employed to explain, not very convincingly, why the federal government simply doesn't step in and clean things up; and ultimately, in the end, when the Black Police are toppled and The Spider stands triumphant, it all happens a bit too conveniently.

Most of the time, however, such niggling questions fade into the background. What Page, and the story, are primarily concerned with is the workings of a modern police state. Considerable time in the first novel, "The City That Paid to Die," is devoted to showcasing the nightmare imposed by the new regime: the strong-arm tactics of tax collection, the beatings, the floggings, the shopkeeper hanged in his shop, all of which are intended to illustrate their effect on ordinary citizens. For Americans in 1938 such things would have seemed uncomfortably familiar since they would have mirrored events from the daily news. For example:

- The Party of Justice is clearly taken from any of a number of the American right-wing organizations, such as the National Union for Social Justice, that flourished at the time. (It's worth noting here that less than two years later, the FBI would shut down Father Coughlin's own Christian Front for plotting to assassinate public figures and create an American police state);

- Huey Long's Louisiana is cited on several occasions as a model for what is happening in the story's New York;

- The Black Police is clearly modeled on the Gestapo and Hitler's SS;

- The term Black Police itself would have resonated with American readers of the time who were familiar with Mussolini's Black Shirts;

- Show trials are staged that mimic the highly-publicized Soviet purges of the same period;

- The harassment, punitive taxation, and declaration of political opponents as "public enemies deprived of basic rights and property" mirror the heightened anti-Jewish activity taking place in Germany in the spring of 1938, about the time when the first of these novels was written.

To combat this, the character of The Spider himself has to change.

Over the course of the Black Police saga we see that Richard Wentworth/The Spider can no longer operate simply as a vigilante justice figure waging a secret war against crime. Here, he is transformed into a public figure, becoming more symbol than individual, as he inspires and leads the people in their resistance to political terror. As noted at the beginning of this introduction, the story ultimately becomes both an allegory and a cautionary tale for the real-world events of its era.

FOR THOSE of you concerned that what you'll be reading here is a social history of the 1930s, you need not worry. After all, these are stories from the pages of *The Spider* and they *were* written by Norvell W. Page. Their primary goal, even at the time, was to entertain and divert the readers, and that they did, with *The Spider*'s usual fast-paced action and fantastic escapades. Still, the Black Police saga demonstrates that for all their escapist elements the pulps could also be more complex, reflecting the events, concerns, and anxieties of their times. A bit distorted, perhaps, by the need to thrill, but nonetheless recognizable even today.

Thomas Krabacher
California State University, Sacramento

THE SPIDER VS THE EMPIRE STATE

SERVICE
DEEPER AND DEEPER NEW YO
CRIMINAL DICTATOR—UNTIL
REGIMENTED BY THE BLACK POLI

D SUNK IN THE GRIP OF A
TIRE POPULATION HAD BEEN
TO A KINGDOM OF CRIME!

EVERYWHERE WENT THE EVIL EMPEROR'S COHORTS, COLLECTING THE TAXES THAT MEANT DEATH! THE LAW WAS LICKED AT LAST.

AMERICA'S GREATEST CITY, WHICH HAD ONCE BEEN CIVILIZATION'S PROUD METROPOLIS, HAD NOW BECOME CRIME'S CHIEF CITADEL.

NOWHERE DID THERE SEEM EITHER HOPE OR HELP.

ED TO JISTI

BUT IN THAT MOMENT OF DESPERATION, WHEN A DOWN-TRODDEN PEOPLE PERISHED IN THE TOILS, CAME A HEAVEN-SENT INSPIRATION.

NOW RICHARD WENTWORTH,
AS THE SPIDER, HAD RESOLVED
AT LAST TO FIGHT THE UNDERWORLD
WITH ITS OWN MERCILESS WEAPONS.

WITH NEW YORK'S OWN POLICE
COMMISSIONER AT HIS SIDE HE
RAISED A FUGITIVE, FIGHTING LEGIO
OF HONEST MEN SWORN TO TAKE T
LAW INTO THEIR OWN HANDS!

COM

THE CITY THAT PAID TO DIE

MASSACRE!

RICHARD WENTWORTH slapped the police commissioner's desk with an emphatic palm. He did not mince words. "Don't be so confoundedly blind, Kirk!" he said vehemently.

Commissioner Stanley Kirkpatrick knuckled his waxed mustache, masking a smile. "This is really quite a compliment, Dick," he said dryly. "You don't usually appeal to the police for help in criminal matters."

A sharp impatience goaded Wentworth, but he held himself rigidly in check. The charges he had come to make were not susceptible of proof. Good God, how could a man prove that a state and city government were in the hands of criminals! But the indications were there, plain at least to Wentworth's keen mind.

He said quietly, "Have your fun while you can, Kirk. You're accusing me again of being the *Spider*. While you delay, more infamies are being planned."

Kirkpatrick's smile persisted. He had long been convinced that Wentworth was the lone wolf of justice who called himself the *Spider*, who fought criminals with a ruthless hand, finding his own verdicts, administering his own executions inexorably—a master of men at once feared and respected. But proof had never fallen into his hands, and Wentworth and Kirkpatrick were warm friends. Not that this fact would swerve Kirkpatrick from the path of duty by a hair's breadth if ever he found evidence.

Wentworth's own lips twisted into a smile that was cold, almost hostile. "I'll tell you this," he said slowly. "If the *Spider* shared my knowledge of the things that have been done by the police in the last thirty days, and if he knew your true nature less thoroughly, there could be only one ending for Police Commissioner Stanley Kirkpatrick!"

Kirkpatrick's smile vanished. "What the hell are you talking about?"

"A little red seal," Wentworth said softly. "A small red seal shaped like a spider which sometimes is found on the foreheads of the criminals the *Spider* brings to justice. I say, if the *Spider* knew what I do, that seal would be found on your forehead—and you would be dead!"

Kirkpatrick snapped to his feet and blood stained his saturnine cheeks darkly. "Wentworth!" he cried. "Are you accusing me of treachery? Why, damn you. . ."

"That's better," Wentworth nodded, his chiseled lips moving in a faint smile. "Now you can hear what I say. You weren't really listening before. What I said was this: The police department is being used to protect and foster crime. This so-called Party of Justice, which swept the city and the state last election, is governed by criminals and used by them for personal profit. And the police. . . Almost anyone else, Kirk, would blame you to the extent of believing you crooked. As it is, I say you're confoundedly blind!"

THE two men confronted each other angrily, both strong, arrogant, dominant. Kirkpatrick was a little older, as the silvering of his temples attested; his face more square cut and stern. Wentworth's lips were shaped for laughter, and there was always mockery in the quirk of his smooth black brows—a face of quick intelligence, of keen determination. Both men were idealists; both leaders. Natural friends. . . or enemies.

The effort Kirkpatrick made at self-control was plain in the white lines that cut about his mouth. He turned abruptly away to the window. Wentworth strode after him, clasped a hand on his shoulder. "I apologize for goading you, Kirk," he said, his voice deepening, "but, believe me, I do not exaggerate. The morals of the force are broken. Your men are slipping up, deliberately, in their duty. Criminals get away with things they would not have dared attempt before."

Kirkpatrick's intonation was still stiff. "You must have reason for what you say, Wentworth. This Party of Justice—?"

"Have you been reappointed commissioner yet, Kirk?" Wentworth interrupted.

Kirkpatrick shook his long head slowly. "I have seen Mayor Culkin twice. He is. . . delaying."

"Delaying, yes. You won't be reappointed, Kirk. Four successive administrations have reappointed you, but not Mayor Culkin. Kirk, you remember how much money was lavished on that campaign? You know the trend of state and city government since then."

Kirkpatrick faced about slowly. "It seems sound enough. Business, industry, and capital have been relieved of many of the taxes. Labor has fallen into line. We're headed for a prosperous era, without a doubt. This talk of criminals. . ."

"Criminals have been used—" Wentworth pounded home his point—"to work the will of the men behind the Party of Justice. They were protected. Now they are getting out of hand. When they are strong enough, they will. . . eliminate the men behind the Party of Justice and take it over for themselves!"

He demanded, "God, Kirk, can't you see the danger? The public officials were put in office as puppets—to take orders. They can be handled and controlled just as readily by criminals as by the financiers who back the Party of Justice. How long do you think it will take criminals to realize that?"

Kirkpatrick's frown made a worried crease between his brows. "You keep referring to the men behind the party. Are there any such men? Do you know?"

"I'll tell you three of them," Wentworth said shortly. "'Legislation has been aimed at the relief of the utilities controlled by Angus Whitfield; of the factories of Malcolm Nicol; the holding companies of Martin Ducamps!"

Kirkpatrick moved a hand impatiently, "That's guess-work," he said shortly. "You have no proof—"

The shrilling of the telephone upon his desk cut short his words, and he reached the instrument in a stride, snapped it to his ear.

"Kirkpatrick speaking," he said, then his eyes whipped to those of Wentworth. "Martin Ducamps is calling!" he repeated blankly.

In a stride, Wentworth had caught up an extension phone in the desk customarily used by Kirkpatrick's secretary. He heard the rasping, dictatorial tones of the financier.

". . . protection at once," he was saying. "We are at conference at my office. Ducamps Building. We have been threatened. I'll give you the details now, in case. . . This fool uses a trick mirror. He appears as a—" Ducamps' voice paused for a moment, went on in a lower tone, almost a whisper—"a white face in the mirror, and in that way he conceals—" Ducamps' voice broke off in a hoarse scream of mortal agony, and over the wire there came the heavy, stuttering thunder of a machine gun. There were other screams, a louder crash and the phone went dead! In a long leap, Wentworth reached Kirkpatrick's desk, slapped open a cam on the annunciator.

"Radio operator!" he said sharply. "Emergency wagon and all nearby patrol cars to Ducamps Building. Ducamps' offices. A wholesale murder. And fast, man, fast! Order the building closed up completely. No one goes in or out. Send reserves from the nearest stationhouse. That is all."

He straightened. "Forgive me, Kirk," he said, "for usurping authority. It saved a few seconds."

Kirkpatrick was on his feet. He whipped a long-barreled .38 revolver from his drawer, thrust it into his belt. "Right," he said curtly. "Order my car—to the front door. Headquarters homicide detail to follow. Every man they've got."

IT WAS while Kirkpatrick and Wentworth strode through the halls, side by side, that the commissioner spoke, almost angrily. "You're right again, Dick," he said sharply, "and I'm wrong. God grant that we're in time at least."

Wentworth's lips were grimly set but he had no such hope. The murderers must have known that Ducamps was talking to police head-quarters, that the alarm would be instantaneous. They would lose no time in escaping from the building. But Wentworth's voice was calm as Kirkpatrick's personal car sirened its way southward through traffic.

"I had time to give you only part of my reasons for suspecting those three men, Ducamps, Nicol and Whitfield. Not that I think they are the only ones. The tax bill that is up at Albany today is an incredible measure. It puts ninety percent of the burden on the lower and middle brackets of income—leaves the big-money men almost tax-free. I have Jackson up there, and he reports that the law carries a rider which would empower tax collectors to seize property of any kind, without waiting for delinquency—unless the tax is paid on demand."

Kirkpatrick said, "My God, Dick. Nothing like that has been printed in the newspapers!"

Wentworth shook his head with a thin smile on his lips. "I think we should add another name to our list, the man who secretly controls most of the newspapers in the state—Howard Soldan. We don't know how many men were in this conference of Ducamps', but God help the people of this state if criminals have seized control from the crooked officials who have been using them for their own purposes."

Kirkpatrick said thickly, "God help them, yes, if He can. Dick, I have been blind. . . blind, I tell you!"

There were a dozen blue-coated police about the Ducamps Building when Kirkpatrick's limousine slid to a halt there. A sergeant saluted.

"Twenty-first floor, Commissioner," he reported. "There's seven men dead up there."

Kirkpatrick nodded curtly. He did not speak, but the thinning of his lips told the shock of those words. Wentworth's swift eyes canvassed the crowd jammed in the lobby of the building by the police. A raft of office workers, clerks and stenographers. Nor was there any reason for suspecting one more than another.

"Upstairs first," Kirkpatrick said.

The directors' room of Ducamps' offices was a shambles. Ducamps' seat had been at the head of the table, and bullets had clawed through the back of the chair, drilled his body in a dozen places. A phone was shattered under his hand. It was plain that the other men had attempted to escape in vain. Wentworth's face went grim at the sight. He was no stranger to death, yet violence could stir him. The very fact of the attack upon these men was proof enough of the things that Wentworth had deduced and reported to Kirkpatrick.

The bullets had come from behind Ducamps. . . Wentworth swore softly under his breath, as his eyes centered on a curious mirror that hung on the wall. From that, his gaze swept over the room, gauging the paths of bullets.

"Kirk," he said softly, "the bullets came from that mirror."

Kirkpatrick's head jerked toward him. "From that mirror?" he said blankly. "How could they?"

Wentworth shook his head, crossed until he could peer into the mirror itself. He could discern no break in its concave surface, but he was sure. It had to be that.

"What was it Ducamps said?" Wentworth asked quietly, and his voice dropped in imitation of the man speaking over the phone. "*White face in the mirror. . .*"

There was a faint clicking sound. Before Wentworth's narrowed, watching eyes, a narrow port irised open in the middle of that concave glass.

"To the floor!" Wentworth shouted. "Flat on the floor, every man!"

He hurled himself in a long, headlong dive at Kirkpatrick's legs and, in the same instant, the furious, deadly stammer of a machine gun thundered into the room!

CHAPTER TWO

MIRROR OF DEATH

ONCE more, as over the telephone, men's dying screams rang terribly through the long, lavish room. Some of the investigators in the room had heeded Wentworth's shouted hoarse command, but others had waited to look about, to find the reason for that call. They never did. The sweeping stream of bullets hosed from that swiveling machine gun scythed them down.

Wentworth's dive drove his shoulder against Kirkpatrick's thighs, hammered him back against the wall and to the floor. Instantly, Wentworth released his hold and, flat on his back, he drew his automatic with the swift, deadly precision for which he was known and dreaded. It blasted in his hand, jerking with the recoil, dropping back into line with the mechanical perfection of a machine, but fast. . . fast. Starred holes were sewn across the mirror, three above, three below that deadly port. The first shot had smashed squarely upon the muzzle. Behind the mirror, there was another muffled blast, and after that the gun fell silent.

In the instant it ceased, Wentworth was on his feet, charging. Behind him screams still shrilled. There were the hoarse angry shouts of frightened men. A second, loaded automatic was in Wentworth's left hand now. It was with the empty in his right that he struck the mirror. It splintered, tinkled in musical shards to the floor, and Wentworth swore harshly, monotonously under his breath. He had uncovered a recess in the wall, a machine gun clamped into a device that still was swinging the shattered muzzle easily from side to side— a murder-trap deadly in its simple efficiency. Quite obviously, it had been started electrically through a sonic device actuated by the words he had uttered in echo of Ducamps' own mortal phrase, "*White face in the mirror. . .*"

Kirkpatrick, shaken and drawn of face, came swiftly to his side. Through a long moment, he stared into the recess, then he strode to the door. "Doctor Elliott!" he called to the medical examiner. "Come quickly. There may be some. . ." He turned back toward the room. The screams had ceased. Among the three policemen who had fallen, there was no sign of life at all.

Wentworth said fiercely, "I'm a blundering fool! I should have guessed. . ."

Kirkpatrick said, heavily. "No blame attaches to you, Dick. You couldn't possibly know. And you saved five lives, not counting my own. Those people on the first floor—"

"It will do no good to question them," Wentworth said shortly. "This trap could have been set a week ago. That's a hundred-shot drum. It was rigged to fire half of those when first those key words were uttered. That would be easy. A magnet to pull back the trigger and hold it there for a stipulated time. It's possible some of the employees here will know who had access to this room. Because of the mirror, I imagine entrance was restricted."

Their questioning revealed that Ducamps allowed no one save himself in the conference chamber, except on days when a conference was held. Once, a week before, Governor Whiting and he had been closeted in there for an hour. Afterward, the governor had worked there alone.

Kirkpatrick and Wentworth stared at each other incredulously. Governor Whiting!

"It's impossible," Kirkpatrick said shortly.

"I agree," Wentworth said softly. "Whiting is only a puppet. Nevertheless, the answer to this puzzle lies in Albany right now. Whoever is behind this massacre will lose no time in asserting his authority over Governor Whiting and the legislature. Kirk. . . could you pretend to play along with Mayor Culkin and the others?"

Kirkpatrick's drawn face was very pale. He dragged a palm down heavily over his eyes. "Pretend? I don't know, Dick. I can try, per-haps. Why?"

Wentworth explained rapidly. There was no doubt that Kirkpatrick was slated for dismissal. Once he was removed, the police would be completely in the hands of the criminals behind Culkin and Governor Whiting—and it would be damnably difficult for Kirkpatrick to regain his position.

"If you could stay in power," Wentworth said swiftly, "and stall for time until we can locate the criminals behind this atrocity, you would be in a position to strike when the moment came."

"Out of office," Kirkpatrick said slowly, "I am only another and less efficient Wentworth. And the *Spider* needs no allies."

Wentworth smiled, thin-lipped. God knew the *Spider* would need all his strength and more to combat an organization as well entrenched as the criminal who, this moment, was seizing control of the state!

"I'll do the best I can, Dick," Kirkpatrick said grimly, "but I'll consent to no criminality!"

Wentworth's hand closed on Kirkpatrick's shoulder. "Good," he said heartily. "If I learn anything, I'll communicate, but not by phone. I'm sure you're watched all the time. Now, if you'll authorize me to go out through your cordon downstairs. . ."

Kirkpatrick strode beside him. "Do you have any plans, Dick? By God, I'd like to go with you! Anything to strike a blow at these damned murderers!"

"Your job is here," Wentworth said slowly, and regretfully. It would be good to have such an ally as Kirkpatrick beside him, for no one realized better than he the incredible proportions of the task ahead. "I'm going to Albany and register a protest again the tax—personally, with Governor Whiting!"

Kirkpatrick held out his hand. "Good luck," he said and his voice was harsh. "God knows, you'll need it!"

WENTWORTH caught a taxi back to his home behind Sutton Place, the walled fortress of a mansion which he had built partly on filled land between two East River piers. His eyes were gloomy with foreboding; and the sunshine that occasionally struck down through the glass roof of the cab, seemed an incongruous thing. The proud skyscrapers were strangely serene against the blue of the sky, the hustling crowds on the street totally unaware of the peril that hung over them. Every man and woman of the multitude would soon feel the weight of criminal depredations unless. . . God in Heaven, what could one man accomplish, even though that man was the *Spider?*

His arms pressed against the accustomed bulge of the automatics beneath his arm. He could kill. His lips twisted ironically. It was his destiny that he who loved humanity so must prove his love by. . . murder. But he had never killed an innocent man. Before those guns could blast, he would find the keystone of the arch of criminal power which imprisoned the state. He must find the guilty men, without fail. That was the real purpose of his trip to Albany. He would protest against the tax, yes, but in a special and dangerous way. As so often before, he would offer his person as a sacrifice, a murder bait for the criminals.

The taxi swerved to the curb on Sutton Place, and Wentworth strode into one of the houses that abutted the street on the East. He walked swiftly through a first-floor apartment, entered a clothes closet and manipulated certain hooks. The floor moved gently downward—a platform elevator—and he was in a narrow concrete corridor. At its far end, he entered another elevator and was whisked up to the third floor of his fortress mansion. He stepped out into a hallway whose marble walls masked armor plate. He had been under periscope observation since he had entered that other apartment. Now, a bronze-covered door flung wide and a turbaned, bearded Sikh greeted him with a low salaam.

"Any further reports from Jackson?" Wentworth asked curtly.

The dark-faced Sikh's voice came out with a strong nasal accent. "*Han, sahib!* It is recorded."

Wentworth strode directly to the recording device and listened to the play-back of the telephone report. The voice of his man, Jackson, stationed in Albany since Wentworth's suspicions had centered on Governor Whiting came to him crisply, but with curt overtones of worry.

"On receipt of news from New York of the deaths of seven wealthy men and three police," Jackson reported, "Governor Whiting took a personal message to the legislature. He proposed to establish a New York Bureau of Investigation to parallel the federal G-men. They would be uniformed and have powers transcending those of local or state police. The bill was passed by both houses as an emergency measure with an appropriation of a million dollars, and Governor Whiting, within thirty minutes, swore in Jervis Strong as commandant of the NYBI. Tax measure passed as reported. Collections already begun. Owners of two stores were flogged into producing money and their stores emptied of all valuable goods. This will not appear in the newspapers."

With a tautening of his entire body, Wentworth heard that succinct and barren report. The anger that he had held in check now swelled through his body. He would be too late to protest the tax, and this police law was damnable. Like the other measures, it was excellent on the face of it. But "transcendent powers," greater than those of the local police, had been granted, and in criminal hands, that was a fearful weapon. The dishonesty behind the measure was plainly evident, too, in Governor Whiting's appointment of the commandant, Jervis Strong!

Damn it! Jervis Strong was a criminal, but for all that, he had no police record. He had been too clever for that, but Wentworth had personal knowledge that the man had been tied in with big-time racketeers during and after prohibition. And now he was to head a powerful police force for a criminal-ruled governor! For one fierce moment, Wentworth considered the expedience of removing these crooked officials—by death!

BUT the *Spider* was no callous executioner. Whiting might be no more than weak and misled, the tool of some more powerful man. He was dangerous. But against such as those the *Spider's* guns were holster-bound. The governor might even be innocent of criminal intent, ill-advised. But Jervis Strong. . . The thought flashed through Wentworth's keen mind that Strong might possibly be the power behind the throne, the man who had plotted this swift subjugation of the state. It was a thing he would investigate. He whipped toward his Sikh servitor.

"Have the radio truck I prepared ready in fifteen minutes," he ordered curtly. "See that the button-hole microphone and other equipment I'll need to broadcast to the truck is in it."

"*Han, sahib.*" The Sikh's dark eyes glowed with eagerness. "Thy servant goes with his master into battle?"

Wentworth smiled faintly. He might flinch from the fires he was forced to extinguish to protect the people, but for Ram Singh all battle was pure pleasure.

"The *missie sahib* must be guarded, my warrior," he said softly. "Here is where the greatest danger lies. Where I go, there will be only words, words."

Ram Singh acknowledged his orders with a low *salaam*, but there was disappointment in his eyes. Wentworth strode to a phone and put through a call to the apartment of the one woman in the world who shared his dangers and his secrets—even the dread secret that could destroy him, his work as the *Spider*. In a space of moments, her warm voice was in his ear.

"Nita, dear," he said, "I would be most happy if you could run over for a few minutes—at once." His language was curiously formal, and it had its special code significance for them both.

It meant that danger overhung them; that Wentworth was going into battle and Nita van Sloan would be in peril, too! Many times, his enemies had struck at him through his love. It was always his precaution that she should be domiciled in his fortress while he fought.

Nita's tones changed, but she said nothing to indicate the danger of which she was instantly aware. Wentworth's phone and her own had been tapped before this.

"You are a most demanding, *fiancé*," she said lightly. "I must drop everything at your lightest command! This one time, I'll humor you!"

Wentworth laughed. "You are too good to me, dear," he said.

That was all, but Wentworth hummed lightly beneath his breath as he went about the swift preparations for his departure. He waited only to tell Nita van Sloan swiftly of the things he feared and suspected, then he entered the truck Ram Singh had prepared for him and sped swiftly away through the city. In an hour, it would be dark. He would lose valuable time driving, instead of flying to Albany, but the radio equipment was essential to his plans. He wore a visored cap, a whipcord uniform, and on the side of the truck was painted the legend—*Amalgamated Parcel Delivery*.

It was a thin disguise, but, with the guns that nestled beneath his arms, Wentworth reinforced it against the criminals. If they should guess his identity and attack. . . Wentworth's lips grew thin with angry determination. God help those who stood in his way, for tonight the *Spider* struck his first blow against the criminal overlords of the state! This damnable forced immediate collection of taxes was a return to medieval ages.

THE state had lost no time in setting tax collectors to work under the new law. There was no time to put an experienced body of workers in the field, but there were more than a score of trained executives on hand, waiting for the law to be passed. Max Boyar went to Poughkeepsie, routed out the local officials and showed his credentials.

"This burg's quota under the new tax is a half million," he told the three men under him, briskly. "'We'll pick up a truck and start the rounds tonight. There's shops open all over town. And listen to me, punks. When I give orders, you hop, see? I'm not giving them twice!"

Jack Wilson was new to his job in the tax office. He'd been there a month, to be precise, and he needed the work and the salary. He nodded slowly, unwillingly, to those strange orders. There couldn't be any doubt about the man's official credentials.

"Why do we need the truck?" he asked

Max Boyar took a quick stride forward and his right hand slid under his coat lapel. "Getting balky already?" he asked softly.

Jack Wilson's head came up and blood stained his cheeks, angry blood. But he needed the job. "No, sir," he said quietly. "Shall I hire the truck?"

"Hire nothing!" Boyar snarled. "Tell 'em it's for the state tax department. Here's a badge." He tossed a glittering nickel shield on the desk. "Hop to it."

Jack Wilson's head came up and blood went out stiffly, without speaking again. There was a vertical frown between his brows. This Boyar was a funny sort of man to be appointed tax collector, he thought. He didn't know Max Boyar was a highly trained expert. Strong-arm men in the rackets have to know how to squeeze money out of reluctant people.

Tony Manteo's grocery was his home, too. There was a curtained door at the rear and, just beyond that, was the living-room. The radio was playing softly. Tony was happy. Tonight, he was honored by a visit from Father Fiorentia—Father Flower. Angela, his motherless daughter, was pouring the red wine for them.

"Angela, she is *bella*, beautiful, no?" Tony laughed. "She will make some man a fine wife, no? Another glass of wine for the good father, Angela *mia*."

Father Flower smiled, and Angela laughed, too. Her dark hair was lustrous and color was dusky in her cheeks. She poured the glass of wine and, in the grocery, a little bell set on a spring above the door made a tinkling note. She pushed through the curtains to attend to the customer.

In the middle of the store. Max Boyar turned slowly on his heel, scanning the shelves, the dangling cheeses and stockfish. At his side,

Jack Wilson still frowned. The others were out in the truck, waiting.

"You want something?" Angela asked.

Jack Wilson said, uncomfortably,

"We're tax collectors. This is Mr. Boyar."

Boyar grunted, "How're ya, babe? You run this dump?"

The girl's dark eyes widened a little. "You will want my father," she said. "Excuse me, I. . ."

"Stick around, babe," Boyar said expansively. "Hey, Tony! Come out here and be damned quick about it."

Angela looked from Boyar's squat, powerful stance to Jack Wilson. Beyond the curtains, Tony's feet made quick, excited sounds on the floor. He batted aside the curtains, then stopped. His eyes, too, swept past Boyar to Jack Wilson. Jack shifted uncomfortably. He explained again, mentioned Boyar's name.

Boyar fixed his small hard eyes on Tony Manteo. "There's a new tax been passed up at Albany," he said. "Your bill is two hundred dollars." He whipped a pad of forms out of his pocket, scribbled on it and shoved it at Tony. "I'll take your check."

Tony Manteo's face was blank with surprise. "Two hundred dollar," he said woodenly. He took the slip of paper. "*Santa Maria!* For why, two hundred dollar? What is this tax? I do not understand."

Boyar said softly, "So you're going to pull that stall, are you?"

Wilson took a quick step forward. "Please, Mr. Boyar," he said anxiously. "Let me explain to them. Mr. Manteo, an emergency law was passed up in Albany today. A special tax for relief. Mr. Boyar has been sent down to take charge of collection and he—he has assessed you for two hundred dollars."

Tony Manteo shook his head. "For why, two hundred dollars?" he cried. Angela moved to his side and held his arm.

In the curtained doorway, Father Flower's black robe showed. He stepped into the room quietly, his round ruddy face still gently smiling. His blue eyes were kindly, even when they rested on Boyar.

Boyar caught Wilson by the shoulder and yanked him back. "All right, Tony," he said shortly. "You've had your explanation. Now shell out!"

Tony's shoulders slumped a little. "If it is the law," he said humbly, "I must pay, yes. When must this tax be paid, please?"

"Right now, punk!"

"Now?" Tony cried. "*Santa Maria*, but I do not have it! What kind of tax is this that I must pay now?"

Angela said, "Surely, there is some mistake. I've never heard of a tax like that."

Father Flower came wholly into the store, "There must be some mistake, surely," he said gently.

"Button your lip!" Boyar snapped at him. He took his hand out of his pocket, and a blackjack dangled from his wrist. "Do you pay, Tony, or do I clean out your store and smash your jaw in the bargain?"

The priest stepped in front of Tony Manteo and his daughter, the smile on his lips. "You are the most peculiar tax collector," he said quietly. "I think I'll have to see your credentials."

"You'll see nothing!" Violently, Boyar thrust the priest aside, slammed him up against the counter. A stack of canned foods tumbled and rolled on the floor.

Wilson's jaw set, "See here, Boyar!" he said sharply.

Boyar grabbed Manteo by the collar and jerked him forward. "Shell out!" he said grimly.

ANGELA darted past him with a movement as lithe as a cat's. She sprang for the door, but Boyar was too quick for her. The blackjack flicked out. It caught the girl just above the ear, and her dark hair swung wildly at the jar. She crumpled in a heap on the floor.

Manteo exploded. He swung awkward fists at Boyar, shouting in Italian. The blackjack came down twice, heavily, on Manteo's shoulders, and his arms went limp at his sides. Twice more the blackjack flicked home, across Manteo's face. Boyar prided himself on being an artist with the blackjack. His blows did not put Manteo out. They only broke his nose and cut open his cheek.

Jack Wilson was stunned by the violence through those swift seconds, but now he sprang forward. His hand clamped on Boyar's shoulder and he swung him about into a chopping right jab that carried all Wilson's weight behind it. Boyar's head snapped up and he pitched to the floor.

Jack took Tony Manteo gently by the arm and led him toward the door. "You go get a policeman right away," he said. "There's something fishy about this whole business. The state couldn't have sent a man like Boyar to collect taxes. It just isn't possible. Hurry! I'll look after Angela."

He swung back into the store. The priest was adjusting his habit. His lips were moving silently. On the floor, Boyar was sitting up slowly. His eyes focused on Jack, and red rage flared in them. With a movement, swift as the strike of a snake, his hand darted beneath his coat lapel and whipped out a revolver.

"Hit me, will you?" he demanded hoarsely. He got slowly to his feet. "Hit me, will you?"

Jack, gazing into the man's twisted, fierce face, knew with sudden certainty that Boyar was going to shoot! He was dazed, incredulous. He saw the gun fall into line on his body and his lips flew open in a gasp of protest, but all his body seemed paralyzed.

"Take it, then, you dumb cluck!" Boyar said venomously. His knuckles whitened from pressure. The hammer of the revolver was rearing back. . . Out of his eye corners, Jack saw the priest's arm move like a black flail. Boyar glimpsed it, too, spun and fired—but too late. One of the fallen cans of foodstuffs caught him in the side of the head and hammered him to the floor!

There was a gentle smile on Father Flower's lips. "The poor misguided man," he said softly. He got down on his knees beside Boyar and stroked the black sprawling hair back from his forehead. "I do think, though, that you'd better take his gun."

Out in the street, Tony Manteo's voice was lifted shrilly. Other voices sounded and the pounding feet of an assembling crowd. Angela was struggling to her feet, a palm pressed to her head. Jack Wilson helped her up.

"It's all right," he said hurriedly. "It's all right now." He put his arms around her and her uncertain head rested for a moment on her shoulder. "Your father's gone to get the police."

Father Flower's lips were moving again, but this time audibly. He was praying for forgiveness for his anger!

Wilson's thoughts were whirling. Boyar's credentials were entirely right, he told himself again, and he remembered that an emergency tax was pending. Damn it! What could such things mean! A state official behaving like a gangster. . .

"It's all right," he said woodenly again to the girl. "It has to be, or else. . ."

His voice broke off, and his head turned toward the door. The police would straighten things out. . . Jack Wilson's eyes widened. These were not Poughkeepsie police—these men in dapper black uniforms with heavy automatics on their hips. The man with sergeant's chevron's glittering in gold upon his arm, strode sharply forward into the store. There were three other men behind him and one of them had his fist twisted into Tony Manteo's collar!

"So you beat up a state official, did you?" said the sergeant. "This will get you about ten years. All right, boys, round up the lot and take them to jail. I'll look after Boyar."

Jack Wilson shook himself out of his befuddlement. "Look here, Sergeant," he said angrily, "they didn't resist Boyar. He took out his blackjack and started beating up Tony Manteo. He hit the priest, knocked the girl down."

The sergeant swung around toward Wilson. "Oh, a traitor, eh?" he sneered. "Lying on your own superior!" He jerked Angela out of Jack's arms and thrust her toward his men. Before Jack realized the sergeant's intention, his gun was out of its holster.

"Just hold that crowd back, boys," the sergeant said softly. "I think I'll have to teach this young punk a lesson before we take him in."

As he finished speaking, the gun whipped over and caught Jack on the temple. He reeled, fell to his knees, and the pistol lifted again like flail. When a gun crashed out, Jack Wilson thought, for a dazed moment, that he had been shot. The sergeant cursed and wrung his suddenly empty gun-hand. From the door a flat, mocking voice rang out.

"I don't think that's a good idea, Sergeant. I really don't!"

Jack saw the sergeant's eyes flare wide, saw his arms fly high as he backed away until his hips caught the counter. His mouth was working, but no words came out. Jack Wilson twisted his head about and saw the reason then.

One of the Black Police lay on the floor, unconscious. The other two were crowded as close to the wall as they could get, hands high. And in the entrance way crouched a figure shrouded in a long black cape; face taut and mocking under the broad brim of a black hat. In his fists were two heavy automatics. Their muzzles quested restlessly, covering the abject police.

The sergeant found his voice, in a whisper. "The *Spider!*" he gasped. "My God, the *Spider!*"

CHAPTER THREE

CRIME'S LEGISLATURE

FURY rowled Wentworth as he confronted the Black Police in the tiny grocery. The gold NYBI badges on their chests were a mockery. These men enforce the law? They were strong-arm racketeers! They should be killed. Wentworth lifted his right gun. Never in his long career of fighting crime had the *Spider* turned his guns against the police, but these men . . .

Wentworth squeezed the trigger. His bullet raked across the sergeant's chest. The badge was ripped free, flew against the wall and fell, a battered, crumpled thing upon the floor. The sergeant's face was grey with terror, but his shaking hands remained high above his head.

"For God's sake, *Spider!*" he whimpered.

The *Spider's* left gun jerked twice and two more shields were bullet-torn from their wearer's chests. His voice came out, flat with menace.

"If I find anyone of you hiding again behind those shields," he said slowly, "I'll pin them to your hearts...

with bullets! Understand? Now unbuckle your gun belts and get out of here. Fast!"

There was need enough for speed. The street was crowded with people. Wentworth was bitterly conscious of them behind his back. Probably they would be friendly, but among them, there might be one who wanted the glory of killing the *Spider*, even by means of a shot in the back. And other police might come. . . "Hurry!" Wentworth snapped again. "And take your carrion with you!"

Actually, the Black Police needed no admonition to haste. Their hands trembled with eagerness to be gone. They caught up Boyar and their unconscious companion and staggered out of the door. Instantly, Wentworth sprang toward the others—toward Jack Wilson, Angela and the wounded grocer, the priest.

"Out the back way," he directed, in a whisper. "We must hurry!"

Each moment they delayed here, his personal peril, and theirs, increased. Wentworth had had no time for thorough disguise after the street crowd had indicated to him that already the myrmidons of the state's criminal rulers were at work here. His cape covered his chauffeur's uniform. The truck was parked on the back street. If they moved fast, they might make good their escape. How soon would the police spread their alarm. . . Jack Wilson pushed himself up groggily from his knees. There was a smear of blood across his temple from the policeman's gun. Angela helped her father toward the curtained door of their living-room, but Father Flower regarded Wentworth with bright, interested eyes.

"I'm afraid, son," the priest said gently, "that you have made only additional trouble for yourself. Tony will be a marked man now."

"For me, it matters little enough, Father," Wentworth smiled as he moved toward the priest, "but we must get these others away. The police will return any moment now. You can no longer expect justice from the law. What would happen to you and these other three would. . . not be pretty. Lead the way, Father."

Father Flower bowed his head, and Wentworth herded them all through the little living-room, where the radio still played, toward the rear door. Jack Wilson hung back.

"I want to thank you, sir," he said. "I think that sergeant intended to kill me. I don't understand why. I don't understand any of this. I'm a tax collector here, deputy. But that man, Boyar, had orders from Albany. You said we could no longer expect justice from the law."

Jack Wilson had a hesitant smile that made his face curiously boyish. "I know, of course, that you're the *Spider*. I've. . . I've read about your wonderful work, and I never quite understood why the police hunted you."

"Later," Wentworth urged kindly. His hand closed on Jack Wilson's shoulder. "There is no time. . ."

Behind them, a man's voice sounded shrilly in the street. "Here come the cops! Beat it!"

"Hurry! There's a truck on the next street! Room for all of us!" Wentworth drove them before him at a shambling run, hurried them into the truck. Tony Manteo he stretched out full length in the aisle between the radio instruments that lined the walls of the back. Angela pillowed his head in her lap. Father Flower stepped back.

"God-speed," he said gravely.

Wentworth spun toward him. In spite of the man's mild exterior, he recognized a steadfast purpose here. The priest knew his danger fully, but preferred to remain where duty dictated, though he must guess the brutality and injustice that threatened. Wentworth flung a glance toward the alleyway from which they had darted. No one there yet, but there were rough shouts in the distance.

"Tony needs you," Wentworth told the priest hurriedly. "I can't doctor him. No time. We don't dare stop for medical attention. His left collarbone is broken."

The priest's eyes were concerned. "You are providing me with an excuse to leave my plain duty," he said. "You are a curious man, *Spider*. I. . ."

The shouting was nearer. There was a shot, a woman's scream. "Hurry, Father!" Wentworth cried. "We won't leave without you." He drew his guns, checked them quietly. "If we remain, men will be killed. You can't sanction that, no matter what they are. And Tony needs you."

With a sigh and a shake of his head, Father Flower climbed into the truck beside Jack Wilson. "It is so difficult to be sure," he said, "and I have sinned already tonight in anger. . ."

The rest of his words were lost in the engine roar as the car leaped forward under the *Spider's* skillful hands. A shot rang out behind and a frosted star gleamed in the window glass beside him. The truck heeled far over as it screamed around a corner with mounting speed.

THE *Spider's* false heavy brows were drawn together in a worried frown, and his grey-blue eyes kept vigilant watch on the road behind. So far no glare of pursuing headlights showed in his rear-vision mirror. Five times he doubled on his trail, heading ever southward. Now, he reversed his direction and sped northward through the outskirts of the city.

It was his hope that the police would think he was fleeing toward New York City. He could not abandon the truck since it was tied in so closely with his plans in Albany. He glanced toward Jack Wilson, seated beside him while Father Flower and Angela worked over Tony. Wilson's young face was drawn into grim lines.

"You asked me about the police and the tax collector, Wilson," Wentworth said quietly. "They are authentic and fully empowered to do what they did. The truth is that criminals have control of the state government."

"Criminals?" Wilson's face sagged with amazement. "But that doesn't seem—"

"No," Wentworth agreed. "But it has happened—legally, so far as can be proved. The federal government has no more basis for intervention than it had when Huey Long controlled Louisiana. Some people said there was criminality there. I don't know. But those Black Police and the tax collector were acting within the limits of the new emergency laws passed at Albany. What I'm leading up to is this: Neither you, nor any of these others, will be safe in Poughkeepsie again. They will make an example of you to show others that they must bow down to the law."

Wilson shook his head. "Then Tony Manteo will lose his store. My job is gone too—"

"You escaped with your lives," Wentworth reminded him grimly. "There is a friend of mine in New York City, Richard Wentworth.

I want you to buy a car with the money I'll give you presently. Take these others to Wentworth's home and stay there. There's a long fight ahead, unless. . . Well, you'll be safer there, and Wentworth will find work for you to do. Better to remain in hiding awhile."

Wilson said heavily, "I suppose there's nothing else to do."

Wentworth laughed sharply. "You're fortunate to have so safe a refuge. What you have seen tonight is only the beginning of the terror that will come!"

A half hour later, he saw Wilson and the others on their way, by a round-about route, toward New York City. Then he sped on, himself, toward Albany. It lacked an hour of midnight when he rolled across the bridge and pulled to a halt near a quick-lunch diner in the riverside district of Albany. When he emerged five minutes later, a broad-shouldered man with a strangely military bearing followed him and climbed into the seat beside him.

"I was beginning to worry, sir," he said quietly. "There's been no new development here except that they seem to have gangsters out to collect the taxes. Some of the things made my blood boil, sir, but your orders wouldn't allow me to interfere."

"You've done good work, Jackson," Wentworth said quietly. He was again in his chauffeur's uniform. "I was delayed in Poughkeepsie by some of that same. . . tax collecting. Where will I find the governor?"

"Sticking pretty close to the legislature, sir," Jackson said steadily. "He has set up an office in the building, and he's delivering a series of personal messages. He might be either place—in his office, or in the legislature."

"More deviltry!" Wentworth said sharply. "You'd think with those tax and police laws, they'd have enough for one day. Take the wheel, Jackson. Drive as near to the legislature as you think safe. I'm going to change my clothing in the back here. After I leave you, rig up this set for short-wave re-broadcast. Run up the telescopic antenna as high as possible and pick a place where you're not apt to get interference."

Jackson took the wheel of the truck. "You're going to use that portable broadcasting outfit, sir?"

Wentworth laughed harshly. "When I call on the governor," he said,

"I'm going to be wired for sound. Every radio that's tuned to a short-wave station will bring in what he says and what I say! There's been too much secrecy. If the people know the truth, perhaps we can accomplish something toward smashing this damnable combine."

"It will be dangerous for you, sir."

Wentworth said, grimly. "It also will be dangerous for the governor—and anybody that gets in my way! Blanket as many wavebands as possible, Jackson. Full power!"

IT still lacked a half hour of midnight when Richard Wentworth, faultlessly tailored and carrying a large dispatch case, walked calmly up to the front steps of the Capitol. Lights blazed in the legislative chambers but, except for squads of Black Police, the corridors were deserted. Wentworth was acutely conscious of the guns beneath his arms, but his clothing had been carefully padded to conceal them. If he were searched. . .

He walked directly to the main doors where one of the police, the gold oak-leaf of a major on his shoulder, stood on braced legs.

"Dispatches for Governor Whiting," Wentworth told him steadily.

The eyes of the major of police were shrewd and there was a brazen egoism in the set of his lips. "Nobody goes in," he said curtly. "Governor's orders."

Wentworth frowned, then shrugged.

"These were for immediate delivery," he said, indicating the dispatch case. "I flew here from New York in twenty minutes to get them in his hands, but if you want to take the responsibility, it's all right with me." He turned carelessly away.

The police major let him reach the bottom of the steps before he called Wentworth back. "I'll call the governor's secretary," he conceded.

"I'm not giving these papers to anybody except the governor," Wentworth told him flatly, but he waited while a policeman hurried away through the echoing corridors to return presently with a small dapper man who dry-washed his hands obsequiously before Wentworth.

"I'll be glad to take charge of the dispatches," he said, in a faint, disinterested voice, "and turn them over to Governor Whiting as soon as he leaves the Senate Chamber. I'm Glass, the Governor's secretary."

Wentworth frowned at the man's fawning manner, the wincing weakness of his small face. This was the sort of official chosen by the puppet masters of the state!

"Sorry," Wentworth said curtly. "My orders were to place these directly in the governor's hands—and at once. I've delivered the message. The rest is up to you."

The secretary sighed and turned away, murmuring something about "seeing the governor." The doors once more were closed and the major resumed his guardian stance before them.

"No skin off my nose now," he said.

Wentworth turned away. "I'll be at the Stadtler if I'm wanted," he said over his shoulder. None of his disappointment showed in his manner. Every minute of delay meant that so many fewer people would be listening when he began his radio broadcast. Added to that was the danger of being detected too soon since now he would be compelled to force his way into the building.

As he strolled toward the hotel, with seeming casualness, his eyes quested over the Capitol. There were many trees, growing barren with the onset of autumn, near the end of the building in which the Senate was meeting. There were also gable windows in the roof. . .

Wentworth smiled slightly, and his pace quickened. He entered the hotel, walked rapidly to a side door and out. He was conscious of an increasing tension within him and well he recognized the sign. To a man who lived in constant danger, as must necessarily be true for the *Spider*, it could mean only one thing. He was followed.

Outside the hotel door, he paused for an instant to light a cigarette. The polished platinum side of his lighter made an excellent mirror and in it he saw one of the Black Police stride up to the registry desk! Strange that they should so quickly take his trail, unless all the governor's dispatch-bearers were known—or unless Wentworth had been recognized! A dozen quick strides took Wentworth to the car he had rented. He laid the dispatch case on the seat beside him, hurled the car forward. His plans had already taken complete form. He whirled the sedan in a tight U-turn and sped back toward the Capitol grounds. The grade was sharp, but the light machine gathered speed rapidly.

A single glance sufficed to spot the tree Wentworth had selected for his daring entry into the state building—a drooping elm with a crotch not too far from the ground. A shout rang out behind him, then a police whistle laid its shrill hysteria across the night! Down the steps of the Capitol, a dozen black-clad police poured in extended order. Guns glinted in their fists. Wentworth's lips were parted in silent laughter. He wrenched over the steering-wheel, hurled the curb and sent the sedan charging straight for the police! A gun crashed from the head of the steps. Wentworth did not hear the lead strike, but instantly other police opened fire. Wentworth steered carefully to the right of the tree he had chosen. He caught up the briefcase and, as the car rushed on— its headlight dazzle full in the eyes of the police—he flung himself out in the shelter of the tall elm.

The guns made a furious racket in the quiet night, but the fire was all concentrated on the wildly racing car—and all eyes would be on it, too. Without an instant's delay, Wentworth sprang upward and lodged the dispatch case in the tree's fork. With that as a hand-hold, he drew himself up the thick trunk.

When the sedan struck the Capitol steps with a splintering crash, Wentworth was already twenty feet above the ground and scrambling rapidly up the branch that arched out over the building's roof. The sedan charged half up the broad steps of the Capitol before its wheels wrenched about and sent it skittering across them. A wheel struck a column and the car reared like a stunting motorcycle, then somersaulted to a shuddering halt. The police charged in with flaming guns. Under cover of the confusion, Wentworth dangled by his hands and dropped lightly to the roof. An instant later, he had driven a foot through one of the gable windows and was in the dusty, airless attic of the Capitol itself!

Wentworth straightened with a small, triumphant smile on his lips, adjusted his clothing and threw the narrow beam of a special pocket flashlight about him, spotted a door. He was within ten feet of it when the door was flung wide open and two of the Black Police confronted him, guns in hand!

GOVERNOR DEATH!

WENTWORTH had not more than a half second's warning of that door's opening. In that time he could have whipped out both automatics and been ready to blast when his enemies came in sight. The advantage was his. The flashlight had accustomed his eyes to light, and the two police were gazing into a half-dark room, themselves strongly silhouetted. It was not the fact that they were police which held the *Spider* in check this time. He had made his own judgment of the Black Police. No doubt that they were wholly enlisted from the Underworld, or that they were ready to kill and rob on order. It was a far simpler reason that caused Wentworth to fling both hands high and call out his surrender.

He didn't want to betray his whereabouts to any more of the Black Police—and gun shots would bring them running!

Wentworth put a smile on his lips and walked toward the two police.

"You boys were smart to spot my hide-out," he said

equably, "but my orders are to get to the governor quickly, and I've got to do it!"

Wentworth was clear of the threshold now and already he had made his estimate of the chances. The hallway was narrow, consisting merely of a small platform at the head of a flight of iron steps which doubled on itself to the corridor of the floor below. Behind the policemen was only this flight of steps and the low railing that guarded the stairwell. Overhead, there was a single, glaring light.

"Take me to the governor."

The gun hands of the policemen relaxed a little. "Hell, if that's all it is," one said to the other, "why in hell make all this fuss about it?"

"I can't answer that one," Wentworth smiled. "They wouldn't let me see the governor, and I have to do it."

The first policeman half-turned to the other. "What do you think, Joe?" His gun sagged to his side.

Joe never answered, for this was the chance Wentworth had awaited. He seized it without a moment's preliminary bracing to betray his purpose. He hurled himself straight at the two men. His shoulder rammed into the chest of the man called Joe. The dispatch case, swung at shoulder height with the full sweep of his arm, slammed in under the chin of the second man and its metal-reinforced edge struck squarely on the larynx. He took a stumbling step backward. His hands plucked futilely at this throat, his face purpling. His larynx was paralyzed, crushed. The steps were just behind him. His body made a long arc and crumpled on the platform.

The man called Joe let out a single harsh oath as Wentworth's shoulder drove into his chest. He reeled off-balance, and the *Spider* checked his rush and struck a blow as solid as an ax biting into oak. The low railing caught Joe's thighs and he toppled backward, stiffly as a tree falling. His legs pointed straight up. The crunching violence of his landing on the steps, fifteen feet below, made the steel sound a deep, ringing note. Afterward, there was utter silence in the hallway.

Wentworth stood, motionless, his chest lifting a little more quickly with excitement.

No sound of alarm within the building; only the distant outdoor uproar of the police around the car.

Wentworth ran lightly down the steps. It was death he had dealt in this sharp struggle, and he paused beside the body on the platform, fingered out his platinum cigarette lighter. For an instant he hesitated in a grim weighing of perils—then he shrugged and stooped over the dead man. He thumbed open the base of the lighter, ground it down on the paling flesh of the dead policeman's forehead. When he removed it, there was a glittering vermilion insignia upon his prey, a figure of sprawling hairy legs and poison fangs—the seal of the *Spider!* Once more, beside the other policeman, Wentworth paused to imprint his seal—then hurried on.

Wentworth admitted, as he sped down the steps, that he had taken a major risk in thus branding the dead men as the *Spider's* victims. If he had been recognized in his own identity. . . He shook his head. Justice was gone from the state. If ever he were hauled before a court, accused as the *Spider*, the verdict would be death regardless of proof. It was well to warn the Black Police and their masters that there was a justice which still could reach them—the justice of the *Spider!*

More immediate perils harassed him now. Had the two men who accosted him, seen his ascent of the tree—or had they been sent by a superior? If the latter were true, there would soon be an investigation! Before then, he must be well hidden. Useless now to hope for an interview with Governor Whiting unless the *Spider* stole upon him in the night. But the Senate was in session. . .

WENTWORTH knew his way about the building thoroughly from the days when Stanley Kirkpatrick had been governor. He went directly to the locked doors of the Senate gallery and, from a leather girdle about his waist, slipped out a lock pick made of surgical steel. In a matter of seconds, he was inside. He locked the door behind him, and moved on soft feet across the darkened gallery until he could peer down upon the brightly lighted pit of the Senate floor itself!

Immediately, he spotted Governor Whiting's leonine head. The state's chief executive stood beside the president's rostrum and read from a paper before him. Wentworth's lips twisted in a grim smile. He opened the big dispatch case and, in a few moments, rigged the super-sensitive microphone he had brought. It was only necessary for him to whisper into it.

"Ladies and gentlemen, citizens of New York State," he said, "I bring you the speech of Governor Whiting delivered before a secret session of the State Senate tonight. Your state is in the hands of criminals. Governor Whiting is their tool. Listen to him. . ."

He aimed the microphone, with its telescopic focusing tube, like a long gun—and Governor Whiting was obliging. He thundered out his speech.

"You have already given me two powerful weapons, gentlemen," said the governor. "The new system of immediate and forcible collection of taxes will fill our coffers. The New York Bureau of Investigation, with its plenipotentiary uniformed force, will insure obedience from stubborn local authorities. They have already given proof of that!"

He paused, and there was general laughter among the legislators. Plainly, there had been some incident during the day in which the Black Police had proved themselves—for their criminal masters! Wentworth was surprised and infuriated at the openness of the tyranny expressed. He had expected the usual hypocrisy—that he would have to interpolate explanations to the radio audience. But it was apparent Governor Whiting considered himself too powerful to require such subterfuge. Heaven knew what he said required no interpretation.

"Gentlemen," he was resuming, "I ask you for one more weapon. It has excellent precedent and harks back to dear old England—to our own frontier days. It has proved its efficacy against lawless elements—and against enemies of the government." Once more laughter interrupted his speech, but Whiting pressed on, lifting his voice. "I say it has proved its value too well to require much debate. I want you to vest in me the power to declare conspicuous criminals to be public enemies."

He explained.

"That is our own more modern term. In olden times, they had another name for them—outlaws."

Now he laughed. "I do not think the terminology need trouble us, but in New York State, the phrase 'public enemy' will have a special significance. If the governor proclaims that a man is a public enemy, it will immediately deprive the man of all civil rights, including the right to own property. A ten-thousand-dollar reward will be posted for him, dead or alive, and no questions asked if he is brought in dead!"

He went on. "There is one other little thing this new law will provide. In olden times, the crown immediately confiscated all the property of an outlaw. I'm afraid our constitution won't permit that, but we can do this. When a man is declared a public enemy, his property will be seized and placed in escrow pending capture. If he's brought in dead. . ."

Fury swept over Wentworth at the full realization of the thing that was proposed. Its villainy was so obvious, and it was plain that the legislature would do immediately what the governor requested. It would be a terrific weapon in criminal hands. If any man lifted his hand against the authorities, or dared to protest against injustice, he would be outlawed and all his property seized. There would be scores of bounty hunters on his trail at once for his body would immediately become worth ten thousand dollars—and no questions asked! Governor Whiting already was reeling off a glib explanation for the confiscation.

"Obviously, it is a criminal's ill-gotten wealth which permits him to checkmate the law," he said. "We take that weapon away from him as we would deprive him of a knife or a gun!"

WENTWORTH straightened slowly where he crouched behind the railing. He had come here tonight to broadcast the infamy of officials, it was true, but he had another deeper, and more perilous purpose. He wanted to offer himself as bait with the intention of forcing into the open whoever was behind Governor Whiting. The very idea Whiting voiced now was much too clever to have sprung from his own brain. Wentworth focused the microphone to pick up his own voice, sprang upon the balustrade and shouted his challenge!

"Governor Whiting," he cried, "you are a traitor to the state and to the people who elected you! You and these whipped curs chosen to represent the people—every one of you is in the pay of criminals! You are turning the state government into a racket, into a plaything for gangsters and killers!"

Wentworth's thundered words cut short the governor's speech. Whiting's pale face turned up toward the gallery, but there was no challenge in the lift of his leonine head—only amazement and fear.

"This is my warning to you!" Wentworth cried, his voice deep and ringing. "Criminals always fail. You will be destroyed with all your hireling thugs and killers and the master who rules you—destroyed by the people you have betrayed!"

The doors of the Senate chamber whipped open and several of the black-clad police darted in. Governor Whiting lifted a long arm and leveled it at Wentworth like a gun.

"*Kill that man!*" he screamed.

A score more of the Black Police jammed into the doorways. In moments, too, they would be at the doors of the gallery. Wentworth laughed and dropped behind the balustrade an instant before the guns crashed out. But he was not through. While he drew two tear-gas bombs from the dispatch case, and lobbed them down into the pit of the Senate Chamber, he was talking rapidly into the microphone.

"You have heard the governor's message," he said, "and the danger to every citizen in his plan is too clear for me to have to explain. You heard the governor order me killed when I challenged him, and you can hear the guns as the criminal Black Police try to carry out his orders. I must go now before they succeed! But think well on what you have heard. When the call comes, be ready to act." He paused, and then threw his laughter into the microphone, the flat mocking laughter of the *Spider*. He whispered, "*The Spider has spoken!*"

FROM the dispatch case, Wentworth took out a silk, goggled mask and crouched, waiting, until the blasting of the guns gave way to panic shouts and strangling coughs with the spreading of the gas. There was a pounding at the gallery doors now. Wentworth lifted his head, cautiously. The legislators were streaming toward the exits, carrying the police before them as they fled from the torture of the tear-gas.

Wentworth slipped on the mask, left the radio equipment and climbed over the railing. The drop was not too high. Moments later, he fled from the Senate Chamber among a dozen coughing, terrified men. Their flight had swept away all the guards. Wentworth whipped off the mask, coughed rackingly.

"Whoever did that," he gasped to his nearest neighbor, "ought to be hung now!" It was easy then to detach himself from the stampede and make his way presently to the office of Governor Whiting in the building. It was deserted, locked, but doors offered no barriers to the skill of the *Spider*. Presently Wentworth was gazing, narrow-eyed, at a concave mirror set into the wall of Whiting's private office. It exactly matched that mirror which had vomited machine-gun death in the Ducamps Building. What secret this one hid he did not know, but he thought that presently Governor Whiting would solve that for him!

The private office boasted a fireplace in which a grate of channel coals threw out grateful warmth. Wentworth settled himself before it in a wing-chair, poured a drink, softly turned on the radio at his right hand. He forced himself to relax. It required all Wentworth's will-power to affect this because of the anger that burned through his veins. As Kirkpatrick had charged, Wentworth had been merely guessing about a criminal overlord for governor and legislature. The things he had heard this night had gone far beyond even his fears.

It was plain that the people no longer could look to the government of the state for protection. Henceforth, they were victims to be robbed of whatever wealth they possessed, maltreated by the police; ruthlessly slaughtered, and legally—through this new outlaw-proclamation system—if they so much as dared to protest. And this gang was being careful to allow no loophole by which the Federal officials could step into the picture. Criminal law, with certain notable exceptions, was a matter for state enforcement. So long as they fought clear of any Federal protected organization, they were safe on that score.

Wentworth swore under his breath, moved restlessly in the chair. He would force some truth from Whiting, if he had to kidnap the man and torture him! Public officials who betrayed their trust deserved no mercy—and would receive none from the *Spider*!

His attention swung sharply toward the radio over which now came the voice of a news commentator.

"Mayor Culkin, of New York City, tonight declared that the police department had mutinied against his authority," the man said rapidly. "He charged that the commissioner, Stanley Kirkpatrick, had refused to accept his orders and was leading a small squad of men in resistance to state officials who were attempting to collect the new tax voted at Albany today. According to the mayor, Kirkpatrick refused to give any explanation of his actions and other men, loyal to him, have barricaded police headquarters against the mayor and other city officials. Mayor Culkin threatened to ask Governor Whiting to dispatch companies of the National Guard, unless Kirkpatrick surrendered his office within the hour."

A slight bitter smile moved Wentworth's lips. He needed no more details to guess what really had happened. Some of the thugs of the Black Police had invaded New York City and attempted to enforce their racketeering tax as they had in Poughkeepsie. Kirkpatrick, with his stern sense of justice, had gone to battle for the people. It was a gallant gesture, but a foolish one. Kirkpatrick was finished now. Certainly, he would not fight the National Guard, though the veteran police were well able to hold their own against civilian soldiery. Much wiser to have dissembled, bided his time. But Kirkpatrick was incapable of such deceptions. Wentworth's heart contracted with fear for his friend. If only he could reach him, warn him. . .

Wentworth's hand snapped to the radio and clicked it into silence. He thrust himself more deeply into the shadows of the chair which was large enough to conceal him entirely in the half-light. He had heard the metallic rasp of a key in the outer door. Even as he settled himself, Governor Whiting fairly ran into the inner office. He closed and locked the door.

A THIN smile brushed Wentworth's lips. He slid an automatic from its holster—and then sat rigidly still. For Whiting did not even wait to turn on the lights. He ran directly to the mirror set in the wall, took his stand immediately before it. His voice came out, huskily, anxious.

"White face in the mirror," he whispered. "White face in the mirror."

Wentworth slid quietly from the chair and, crouching in its shadow, watched the governor. Even in the half-light from the fire, it was plain that Whiting was trembling. He mopped his forehead, repeated the phrase again. Then Wentworth smothered a curse, for in the heart of the mirror—lights began to glow, lights that gradually took form and became. . . *a white face*! Its lips moved and a deep, solemn voice spoke from the mirror!

"Why do you summon me?" it demanded.

Governor Whiting babbled out the happenings in the Senate chamber. Wentworth's narrowed gaze concentrated on that face in the mirror. Quite obviously, it was a creation of lights in that concave surface. Some such sonic-operated device as had, in Ducamps office, discharged the machine gun, could be employed. But Wentworth had a sharp certainty that this was a man's actual face upon which he was gazing. If not the face itself, then a reflection of a man's face worked by some sort of *camera obscura*. His gun lifted slowly in his hand. The voice in the mirror was speaking again. . .

"The man in the Senate chamber," it said, "was Richard Wentworth, the friend of Stanley Kirkpatrick. He broadcast your speech on outlawry, by short-wave radio. Outlaw both Wentworth and Kirkpatrick. Hurry those pardons to the prisons."

Governor Whiting stammered, "Yes, yes. Of course."

Wentworth's lips parted in soundless laughter. In a long bound, he reached Whiting's side. His gun barrel flicked against the governor's head, drove him unconscious to the floor. In the next instant, Wentworth smashed the mirror to fragments. He flung the beam of his flashlight into the recess it revealed—not a recess, but a narrow corridor!

A cry of triumph sprang softly from Wentworth's lips. In an instant, he was clambering into the secret corridor he had revealed; which he had guessed must be there. If that face could answer a direct question, which could not have been anticipated, then it was the voice of an actual man. And that man must be somewhere along this corridor!

His questing light revealed a narrow, twisting flight of steps that led downward and Wentworth bounded to them, sped light-footedly on his quest. Governor Whiting would remain unconscious for a half hour or more. He was locked in his office, and outside interference was unlikely. The *Spider's* back was protected and ahead, somewhere, was the key to the mystery, to the criminal who held in his greedy hands the reins of the state government!

The spiral of steps was steep and led straight down, without a side opening, for a full thirty feet. Abruptly, Wentworth seized the railing and jerked himself to a halt—but not quite in time. He turned his shoulder and caught his weight as he ran full-tilt into a brick wall! Wentworth stared in amazement, flung the beam of his light upward. He was in a narrow well, precisely the size of the stairway, and its end was a blank wall!

Plainly, there was some secret doorway on the stairs, either here at its base or somewhere along its thirty-foot length. Wentworth tapped sharply on the bricks with the muzzle of his automatic, but the sound was solid as earth itself. Probably the hidden exit was somewhere above. A soft, metallic sound over his head jerked Wentworth's head upward, and a harsh curse sprang to his lips. A steel grating had slid into place. He was a prisoner here in the bottom of the shaft!

Even as Wentworth's eyes took in that fact, he became aware of another thing. His lips were dry and there was odd heat in his blood. He felt as if he were burning up with fever! He clapped a hand on the railing of the stairway and it was cold to his touch. The walls were cold, too. He laid his forehead against the bricks. His lips were parted and his breath was coming more rapidly.

For the first time then, he knew a touch of fear. Fever in his blood. . . God, he knew the answer to that! Science had devised a way of inducing artificial fever by means of ultra-short wave currents of electricity. He was in the focus of such a machine. Already weakness was coursing through him. His brain felt swollen, light, A few minutes more and he would be delirious, and after that. . . after that, *death!*

CHAPTER FIVE

TAXES AND TERROR

IN Wentworth's New York home, Nita van Sloan paced the long third-floor drawing-room with worry in her violet eyes. She had heard Dick's broadcast from the legislature, heard his voice fade out amid the crashing of hostile guns. Yet that alone should not bring her such terror. Dick had fought his way through a hundred gun battles without serious harm. But terror walked with her, nonetheless.

From the refugees Wentworth had sent to her, she had heard the story of the fight in Poughkeepsie. It was like Dick to send Jack Wilson and the old priest, Tony Manteo and Angela, to his own home for protection, but it was also a dangerous thing. It would give the police an excuse to smash their way in, if they learned of the presence of the four. And it added little to the strength of the fortress—even if Jack Wilson walked the guard rounds with Ram Singh.

Nita's thoughts were harassed. She could not help but feel that there was some salient point in the situation which she should have grasped, and yet missed.

She sent her mind questing over the developments of the night. The newspapers and radio commentators had been strangely silent on events in New York State. There was a bare mention of the emergency tax, of the new police force created "because of the breakdown in local enforcement." Then had come Dick's startling broadcast, and the governor's demand for power to issue outlawry proclamations. No doubt that his request would be granted by the subservient legislature. . . Nita stopped her pacing abruptly. Dick had told her that he intended to allow himself to be identified, to bait the real leader of the criminals into the open!

Surely, the next step was obvious. Wentworth would be outlawed, his property confiscated! Heavens! The order might already have been issued! Could she defend the mansion against the police? It might be possible with the powerful armament Wentworth had devised and with the proper garrison of men. But what would that accomplish? In the end, the fortress would be forced. . .

Ram Singh glided into the doorway.

"Kirkpatrick *sahib* asks for you, *missie sahib*." Ram Singh cupped his hands to his forehead in a *salaam* only a little less reverent than that he gave his master. He had fought under Nita's orders, too, and knew her power and her strength.

Nita crossed rapidly to a phone and caught it up. "No, Stanley," she said presently, "I haven't heard from Dick. The broadcast? But that was the *Spider*—didn't you hear?"

Kirkpatrick's voice came to her with restrained urgency. "If he calls you, Nita, for God's sake have him get in touch with me at once! Tell him I'll be fortunate if I can hold out one more day as commissioner. Tell him I'll fight beside him from now on! The things that have happened tonight are damnable. The Black Police have moved into New York. I saw a woman flogged because she resisted the taxes. A man was hanged in his shop."

Nita drew in her breath, shakily, "I'll tell Dick—if he calls," she said.

"Do that." Kirkpatrick hesitated a moment longer. "I. . . I need his help."

Nita was more shaken than she dared admit to herself when she hung up the phone. When Kirkpatrick called on the *Spider* for help—when a man to whom duty and the law were sacred, volunteered to follow the *Spider*—things must indeed be desperate. But even while Nita had talked to him, a resolution was taking form in her mind. If Dick was to be outlawed, and she had no doubt of that, only one course was open to her. She must gather such weapons as she could, assemble all his available cash, and flee to some hiding place until such time as she could unite with Dick, himself. Already, the house might be under surveillance. . .

Nita struck her hands sharply together, and Ram Singh was instantly in the doorway. Nita beckoned the faithful Sikh toward her, swiftly outlined her fears and their plan of action.

"Only this remains," she finished. "Where can we hide? The *sahib* has places to which he, himself, can retreat, but we have others to protect. It must be somewhere we can find weapons and wealth."

Ram Singh's eyes held a fierce light. "There are countrymen of mine who will serve until death!" he cried.

Nita shook her head. "They would be immediately suspected because of you. Think further, Ram Singh." Abruptly she turned toward him. "Chei Hwang-yo!" she cried softly. "The *sahib* did him a great service once. He slew the monster who was taking Chinatown away from Chei Hwang-yo and destroying it. Do you know how to reach him?"

Ram Singh's teeth flashed white through his thick beard. "There is a way, from the river," he said.

NITA rapidly laid her plans, and called every person in the house, except the injured Tony Manteo, into service. Weapons were carried in staggering loads to the library on the first floor. This entire room actually was an elevator that would drop them to the level of the secret hangar and boathouse underneath the piers between which the house was built. The aged butler, Jenkyns, who had served Wentworth's father before him, was bewildered at the threatened change, but adjusted himself quickly. When Nita had loaded the last of the weapons into the room, he was busy preparing a midnight lunch for them.

Nita issued her orders to them then. "Jenkyns will operate the elevator," she said. "Load all this equipment in the motorboat he will show you. Keep this door locked regardless of what happens. Mr. Wilson, you will be in command. I'll be back within a half, or three-quarters of an hour. You must be sure to be ready then."

Outside the door, she faced Ram Singh, resolutely. "The *sahib* keeps a hundred thousand dollars in cash in each of two safety-deposit boxes, on opposite sides of the city, for emergencies like this. I have access, and we must get it. The cash that he keeps on hand here will not suffice if there is a long siege. Get out the Daimler. See that the automatics and machine guns are ready for immediate use. And, Ram Singh—*hurry!*"

Once inside the bullet-proof car, and hurrying toward the all-night safety-deposit box vaults, Nita felt less frightened. If she were wrong in her expectations—if Wentworth were not outlawed—no harm had been done. But she had no doubts, really. There was another fear at the back of her mind which she dared not admit even to herself. All of this was futile, useless, if anything had happened to Dick!

There was no trouble at either of the banks. Three times, patrols of Black Police crossed their path, but Ram Singh swung wide about them. Once Nita heard a woman screaming, terribly, and she clutched the sub-machine gun across her lap while her heart contracted. But she could not help there. It was so much more important for Dick to have the means to fight against these tyrants. He would smash them, if only. . . Nita resolutely closed her mind on the thought of harm befalling Dick. She thought, instead, of his strength and his keen brain and the unfailing accuracy of his guns. If she could have known that at this very moment Wentworth lay, half-fainting, a prisoner at the bottom of that hellish well!

Ram Singh's abrupt application of brakes pulled her forward on the seat, both hands clutching the gun across her lap.

"What is it?" she cried softly, but even as she spoke, she saw the reason he had halted. A motorcycle crawled past the cross-street with its siren shrilling and one of the Black Police in the saddle. Immediately behind it was another, and another, and Nita heard a cry that soared even above the moan of the sirens—a man's scream!

Ram Singh cut off the lights, let the car drift to the curb and they remained there like that while a slow procession filed across the end of the street. Immediately behind the siren-shrieking police rolled a truck. Nita's breath caught in her throat, as she saw that three men were lashed to the tailgate by their wrists. Behind them walked two of the Black Police with heavy whips. At regular intervals, one of them swung the lash viciously across the naked backs of the men!

Along the side of the truck ran a sign on which crude red letters had been painted. It read—*They Didn't Pay the Poor Tax.*

That truck was only the first of the procession, and the screams that came to Nita's ears now were women's voices! Her hand flew to the catch of the door, the gun ready across her lap—then she checked. What could she possibly accomplish? There wasn't a chance that, charging that line of police, she could free those poor victims. Nita cried out, herself, as the third truck in that cruel line rolled past. The whip man whirled his lash high and brought it down across the naked back of a woman. With a scream of utter agony, she sagged in her lashings. The truck did not stop, though the woman dangled by her lashed wrists, half her beaten body dragging on the paved street!

Nita heard curses rumble from Ram Singh's throat. If she but spoke the word. . . Abruptly, a motorcycle whirled into the street and rushed toward them!

Nita's voice came out harshly. "Is your knife ready, Ram Singh?" she asked coldly.

Ram Singh laughed sharply once, an explosive sound. The motorcycle slued to a halt beside them, and the policeman had his gun in his hand—a Black policeman with the face of a killer, of a criminal, beneath his visor.

"We need this car!" he shouted. "Swing into line. Swing in, damn you, or somebody else will drive, and you'll walk behind, under the whip."

R AM SINGH slowly cranked down the window and looked at the officer, through a long moment. He said, quite clearly. "*Pig!*" At the same instant, his hand whipped over. There was a minute gleam of silvery steel, then the policeman pitched backward into the street, kicking, plucking at the hilt that protruded from his throat.

Nita swallowed. "An excellent throw, Ram Singh," she said flatly.

The Sikh slid to the pavement and regained his knife. His teeth showed white through his beard as he moved back again. "*Wah, missie sahib!*" he said, his deep voice rumbling, "these are not men. They are snakes and their heads are easily crushed."

Nita's anger burst out ringingly. "We'll crush a few snakes, Ram Singh!" she cried.

The end of the procession was passing the street corner now. She made a swift estimate of the number of police in the procession. . . Not more than twenty. She leaned forward and unhooked a second, machine gun from the rack, held it out to Ram Singh. Nita's was a woman's heart, and merciful. She had always deplored the lives that had sped at Wentworth's hands. But anger was on her now—anger at injustice, the strong, implacable fury which she had glimpsed on Wentworth's face. . . and trembled to see. But these were not men. They were beasts of prey!

"Quickly, Ram Singh," she ordered, "before they miss their fellow-snake. Roll up the right-hand side of the street past the procession. There are three trucks besides the motorcycles in front. I'll take the first truck. Be sure you don't kill the drivers. Wound them so that they'll have to stop the trucks."

Ram Singh threw back his head and laughed, "*Wah!*" he cried. "Thou art one worthy to be the mate of the *sahib!*"

The great car lunged forward. Nita leaned forward and opened a narrow port in the left-hand window. The machine gun rested on her lap. In her right hand was an automatic pistol. She was glad that Wentworth had taught her how to shoot!

The Daimler rounded the corner and rolled toward the last of the trucks. The two whip men paid no attention until too late. They were too intent on torturing their victims. As the brute of a man nearest her lifted the whip again to lay it across cut and bleeding flesh, Nita drew a careful bead and squeezed the trigger. The gun sound inside of the closed limousine was terribly loud, but she knew its blast would not carry far outside. The truck engines were too noisy.

The man she had shot lurched sideways, almost tripped his companion. The second flogger twisted about a white, amazed face. He clawed for his gun. Nita waited for a long moment, her gun level and ready. When he had his hand on the butt of his revolver, she fired again. It was only when Nita had her automatic ready to fire at the truck's driver that she realized the mistake she had made. She could not shoot him lest the lunging truck crush those poor helpless women tied to the tail of the machine ahead. She should have struck the leading truck first. It was too late now!

Even as Nita hesitated. Ram Singh opened fire on the police around the truck ahead. Nita had waited too long. The truck driver saw her and, in desperation, whirled the heavy truck straight toward the creeping Daimler! The crash hurled Nita to the floor. Her head struck the door frame, leaving her dazed. Through a fog of whirling blackness, she heard the crash of guns. She forced herself upward, just in time. A gun muzzle was thrust into the gun port she had opened!

Nita's automatic spoke almost before she was aware of aiming. The muzzle vanished from the port, and a man's scream soared horribly. Then Nita was on her knees, peering out at the scene. The truck ahead had been jammed across the street to block any possible escape. From its cover, bullets rained on the bullet-proof glass, the armored sides of the Daimler. Already the windshield was frosted over so that it was almost impossible to see through it. How could it withstand this pounding of the bullets of the Black Police!

Ram Singh's sub-machine gun was stammering in short, vicious bursts and already a half dozen uniformed bodies spotted the street.

"Can you back the car?" Nita asked, quietly. "I'll hold them in check."

Ram Singh shook his head, "I am a fool, *missie sahib*," he said. "I allowed them to wreck the steering gear. I allowed you to make this attack, and the master put thy life into my hands! They shall not have thee while I live, *missie sahib!*"

A section of the windshield crumpled and thudded to the floor, and the triumphant shouts of the police reached Nita's ears. She twisted, her head about. She could see the men at the rear of the truck, the prisoners. They were crouching low under the tail to keep clear of bullets, but she could see their wrists and the rope that bound them—a single rope that stretched from side to side. Nita laughed softly. Poor reinforcements, but better than none!

She drew careful bead with her automatic and fired. Three shots were necessary before the rope was severed.

"To me!" she called clearly then. "I have guns for you!"

A man's head lifted slowly above the tail-gate. His face was drawn with suffering, but there was a hard set to the jaw. He tugged at the severed rope, freed his hands. Nita opened the window beside her more widely and tossed a fully loaded automatic to the man. He ducked out of sight again and, presently, she heard the automatic blast out. She saw one of the skulking police throw up his hands and pitch to the pavement, and Nita *laughed!* She armed the other two men. "Get in the truck!" she called. "Back it away and charge them!"

AS if the police sensed the turn in the tide of battle, they launched a furious charge. Ram Singh shouted his challenge, and the submachine gun swung a crisp deadly arc. Nita's own weapon was sputtering now. She scarcely noticed when the truck wrenched away from the car, but she saw it loom across her sights and released the trigger.

With the cessation of her fire, a great ringing stillness descended on the streets. Her ears ached with it and, through a long moment, it puzzled her. Then she realized that the police who remained alive had fled! She had won!

Dimly, a siren began to sound. Its shriek swelled rapidly.

"Quickly, Ram Singh!" she cried. "Well take one of those motorcycles! Tell those men in the truck to free the others and to drive to Chatham Square. If we win through, we'll care for them! They'll make allies in this battle!"

Minutes later, with the sirens almost upon them, the truck load of tortured creatures rumbled off down a side street. Ram Singh wheeled over a motorcycle and Nita mounted the saddle with the Sikh clinging behind her. The machine gathered speed, swept without lights eastward toward the fortress mansion.

As long as she was dodging the police, excitement held Nita up, but the reaction set in swiftly once the steel gates of the fortress clanged behind her. Her mouth corners twitched and there was a coldness through all her body. She had killed!

"Quickly," she gasped to Ram Singh, "to the boat. They'll identify the limousine."

She stumbled through the hallway toward the library, used her key. The last of the weapons had been cleared away. She thrust the money into Ram Singh's hands. "To the boat," she ordered, panting. "I must get off a radio message to Jackson, if I can—to warn the *sahib* in time."

Ram Singh bowed, and Nita whipped open the door of a closet in the hall, released a secret panel there and began to pound out a message on the wireless key. She must hint, rather than tell where they were going, and hope that Dick would understand. Too many could hear the wireless—for her to risk the truth. . .

Swiftly her wrist bobbed with the movements of the key. Swiftly. . . almost in her ear, the gun crashed out. The sending set was smashed by the bullet. She spun around, realizing that she had thrown aside her weapon in the library; realizing, too, that she was alone in the house. The others were all aboard the boat, waiting for her.

She turned, and looked into the muzzle of a revolver held by one of the Black Police. His grin was wolfish, cruel.

"We'll have to work out something new to punish you," he said. "Death, of course, is the end. . ."

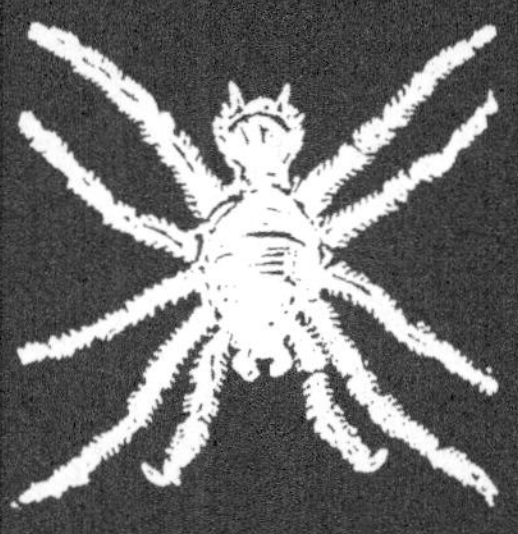

CHAPTER SIX

FUGITIVE FROM FURY

AND in Albany, imprisoned in the well, Wentworth battled frantically against the fever in his brain, trying to force coherent thought. All his senses felt deadened. His ears rang. He had been staring at the grill which, closing off the stairs above him, held him captive. For several long moments, in the thin light of his flash, he had actually seemed to see the gleaming metal bars. If he could move those. . . The idea was preposterous and yet Wentworth moved up toward the grill, clinging to the railing, draining his flagging strength to reach the bars. He reached up a tentative hand, while his eyes ran along the grill toward the brick wall from which the steel spikes thrust out separately. And he didn't touch the bars. Something stopped him, and it was other long moments before he realized the truth. Dimly, then, he knew that each of the rods was insulated from the bricks through which they passed. That meant they carried electricity. . .

Foggily, the idea penetrated to his dulled brain.

Somewhere in this newfound knowledge was a solution, if only he could arrive at it. It still seemed to him that his body had an independent intelligence—that it went about tasks before his brain knew why. His hands moved with a fumbling slowness that was torture. Everything depended on speed. He knew that. He ripped off a shoe and, using the lace, he bound one of his automatics at right angle across the toe. Leather would not conduct electricity—not so well as his gun.

It seemed to take hours to stretch out his arm, gripping the heel of the shoe. He knew now what he intended to do. He would form a solid contact between the grilling and the wall, using the automatic to short-circuit the hookup that was draining him of strength and killing him. The wall seemed to drift away from his out-reaching hand. He was leaning far out over the railing. . .

Blinding, blue-white flame seemed to strike him in the face. Wentworth felt himself hurled backward but managed to bow his head and protect it from concussion. The flashlight was gone from his hand, but he had no need of it. The sputter of electric fire still filled the well with eerie light and the fresh, energizing odor of ozone stung his nostrils. The arcing of the current had welded the automatic's muzzle against the steel bar, held the butt rigidly against the wall. The bar was glowing red hot at the point of contact—and the fever was gone from him.

With a violent effort, he forced himself erect. Hot steel could be bent! His brain was clearing, though a numb weakness still gripped him. He inspected the bar, then, fumbling, removed his coat, slipped a sleeve over the bar and threw all his weight upon it. The odor of scorching cloth closed his nostrils, strangled him—but the bar yielded!

A few moments of strenuous effort, and he had bent the bar sufficiently to be able to squeeze his body through. He fought his way weakly up the stairs, dragging his coat, one shoe missing. His face still wore the high flush of fever and his forehead was wet with the perspiration of weakness. The single gun he still carried seemed almost too heavy to be borne. Somewhere nearby, he knew, was the secret chamber from which these mechanisms had operated, but Wentworth was too spent to solve the problem now. Even his clothing was an intolerable burden as he fought his way up the incalculable miles of steps toward the faint light that showed overhead.

At last, he stood swaying in the opening where the governor's mirror had been. The office was empty. Either Whiting had recovered or been carried out. Everything else was exactly as before—the soft warmth of the fire, the amber glow of whisky in a decanter. Nothing out of place except for the glittering shards of mirror on the floor.

WENTWORTH took a stiff drink, and it brought back some of his strength. He fought for clarity of thought. To be so close to the nub of the mystery and then to fail. . . His eyes swung to the opening in the wall, and grimness tautened his cheeks. He hefted the automatic in his fist. He felt better able to use it now. He took a single stride forward, then checked, listening. Footsteps in the outer office, a stampede of them! That would be the Black Police hurrying to the kill! For an instant Wentworth paused, on the brink of battle. He swore under his breath. No way of telling how many of the police were out there, but the sound of shots would bring scores more. Even so, Wentworth might have stayed to fight, if he could have hoped for any profit from the skirmish. Well he knew that, long before he could rout the killers, and search out the hiding place of the *"White Face in the Mirror,"* the criminal—whose trap he had so narrowly escaped— would have fled.

No, his only recourse was flight. In a swift stride, Wentworth reached the window and whipped it open. On the ledge, he paused long enough to close it before he jumped to the earth a few feet below—the noise the police made covered the sound—then he was limping off into the shadows. He had again drawn on his coat with its scorched sleeve. The ground was cold beneath his shoeless foot, but the chill of the autumn night stimulated him and his stride lengthened. The weakness of the fever was still upon him. It was his will that drove him on—his will and his furious anger at himself.

It was true that he had accomplished the two things for which he had come to Albany, but he knew now they would avail nothing. His most pessimistic imaginings had never pictured such absolute criminal control of the government as he had uncovered. True, also, he had succeeded in getting a broadcast past the control which Whiting and his underlings already had established over press and radio. Such people as had heard it must be convinced of the things he had declared. But the plain truth was that, even with that knowledge, they would be helpless. Short of armed revolt, which would destroy the governor, his legislators and the infamous Black Police, what else would suffice?

His foray undoubtedly would delay Whiting for a brief while in his plans. But it was unlikely the governor would wait for the passage of the law to hurl the full force of his "public enemy" proclamation against Wentworth and Kirkpatrick. Why, damn it, unless he moved swiftly he would be without even funds to battle against the criminals! He must get word to Nita van Sloan, to Kirkpatrick, and meantime he must evade capture. Fortunately, the city streets were nearly deserted, for he was a marked man with his one shoe and his torn coat

GRIMLY, Wentworth forced himself to the decision which alone could help him in his warfare. He must turn his back on Albany where the criminal undoubtedly was for the present—must flee to New York and assemble reinforcements. Wentworth paused in a darkened recess of a store entrance and gazed back at the Capitol. In this brief while, it had been turned into a fortress.

There were sand-bag barricades at the main doors and the glint of machine guns behind it. As he watched, armored trucks rolled up. Their blazing searchlights began to play over the grounds while squads of Black Police marched and countermarched in their search for the man who had defied them! Wentworth had escaped only just in time.

God, what could one man hope to accomplish against that armed might! He had succeeded only in arming Governor Whiting and his subordinates. Yet he must reach them before he could penetrate beyond to the true identity of the White Face in the Mirror. Until the Master was destroyed, the lopping off of limbs would accomplish little. A feeling of despair flooded Wentworth. For once, he had met a combination which all the cleverness of the *Spider* could not conquer single-handed. Beyond any doubt, he must have reinforcements. . .

Wentworth glanced at his watch. It was time for Jackson to meet him at their rendezvous. Wentworth slid along, close in the shadows of dark buildings, toward the spot. Patrol trucks were beginning to roll through the streets with questing searchlights, with machine-gun armed men. Governor Whiting would make very sure that there were no hostile gatherings on his doorstep!

One thing was immediately apparent to Wentworth, as he raced on across Albany, dodging into the shadows whenever a patrol truck came near. Whiting and the Master must find recruits for their Black Police, men who would obey their orders without scruple—criminals ready to kill at a moment's notice. . .

"Good God!" Wentworth stopped, suddenly remembering. When Governor Whiting had stood before the White Face in the Mirror, to receive instructions for outlawing Kirkpatrick and Wentworth, there had been an additional order. The Master had said, *"Hurry those pardons to the prisons!"*

No need to wonder now about his meaning. Recruits for the Black Police would come from the prisons of the state. Hardened criminals who would go through hell for their liberators, under the threat of return to narrow cells—and the promise of rich loot! The curse that rose to Wentworth's lips was almost a sob. He broke into a sloping run, checked suddenly to the sound of guns. It came from straight ahead—from the spot of the rendezvous! Wentworth gripped his automatic and plunged forward again, whirled a corner, then flung himself prone. His fears were too well justified. The radio truck which Jackson had operated was wrecked against an apartment building. From behind the armored sides of a truck, a half dozen men were pouring deadly fire into the car. One of the Black Police had now spotted Wentworth and his bullets scored the concrete on which he lay!

In desperation, Wentworth crawled back around the corner and put the protection of a brick wall between himself and those killers. He was in front of a low building, formerly a private home which now had a "Vacancy" sign for roomers in the window. In three strides, he had reached the door, and once more the lock pick came into play.

Moments later, he was bounding up the steps toward the roof. But when he peered down into the street, it was swarming with Black Police. Three other trucks had stopped there. He saw them drag Jackson's limp body from the wrecked radio car and his automatic dropped into line of its own accord. . .

But the *Spider* did not fire. He could not battle fifty men single-handed, with any hope of success. He did not even know if the loyal Jackson still lived. Even so, Wentworth would have chanced that battle. . . But a graver duty called. The *Spider* had no right to risk his life in this purely personal affray. With what he knew and had guessed, it might be possible to form an alliance with Kirkpatrick which could weaken and then smash this oligarchy of crime.

Regretfully, Wentworth thrust the automatic into its holster and resumed once more his flight across the city. He masked his face, held up and bound the night man at a garage; took his shoes and one of the stored cars. He delayed long enough to put through a telephone call to his home in New York City. It seemed hours that he waited in the tight, smelly office of the garage, listening to the murmur along the wires. He heard the bell buzz on and on—on and on in his home.

"Your party does not answer," the operator reported.

Wentworth felt fear choking him. "There must be someone there!" he cried.

The formality of the operator's voice was maddening. "I'll ring your party again, sir."

More ringing; more silence. Wentworth swore and slammed up the receiver. In God's name what had happened to Nita! Even if she had left the house against his orders, Jenkyns should still be there. . . unless the Black Police already had struck!

WENTWORTH hurled himself from the garage office like a madman. No need to speculate on what had happened in New York. Somehow, the Black Police, or other emissaries of the Master, had found their way into his home and now Nita. . . Wentworth realized that he had bitten through his lower lip.

Twice on his mad race across Albany, Wentworth was intercepted by flying squadrons of Black Police. They couldn't stop him. There was a frenzy on him that not even bullets would break. Each time, he fired just one shot at the pursuing cars. The first time, he killed the driver outright. The second time, he shot off a front tire. The chase ended like that. Fifteen minutes after he had slammed up the useless phone, Wentworth was on the flying field. There were police there, too. The hangar was closed and the men in black ringed it against invasion.

A semblance of sanity returned to Wentworth then—and the knowledge that no matter how soon he reached New York City, he would be too late to help Nita. But not too late to strike at the Master and his men! Kirkpatrick still remained to be saved. Afterward, there would be a reckoning. His decision was made in the same instant that he recognized the impossibility of storming the hangar.

He swung the wheel of the car over as the Black Police opened fire and jammed in behind the administration building. Another tight turn, and he was headed straight for the broad door. Wentworth braced himself rigidly against steering wheel and dashboard and the car crashed, stalled. In low gear, he pushed it on. He could hear shouts and more shouts now above the hammer of the engine, but he paid no heed. The spinning wheels gripped. There was a rending of wood and metal and the car burst through into the main hall of the building. It was the work of an instant to jump out, to fire a shot through the gasoline tank.

Two minutes later, when the charging Black Police reached the building, gasoline-fed flames were leaping high, sweeping the walls, crawling hungrily across the floor. In the luridly lit interior, Wentworth crouched behind a partition with a ready gun. He opened his lips with a scream that tore with pure agony. He kept that up for thirty seconds or more, and then the gasoline tank of the car let go.

The Black Police were milling around the collapsed door. Wentworth watched his opportunity and slipped out the opposite side. There were no guards around the hangar, naturally. These men were not disciplined forces. His lips twisted in a thin smile, he sprinted for the building where the planes were stored. He managed to enter it without being detected. A speedy sport monoplane was poised behind the doors. Wentworth started the motor before he sprang to the wide hangar doors. Fortunately, they were counter-balanced, easy to operate. A thrust sent them sliding upward, and he leaped to the wing of the monoplane, to the cockpit.

HE set the brakes, eased the throttle gradually wider. The cold motor spluttered, faltered, roared for a moment—missed again. Through the widening arch of the door. Wentworth peered toward the burning building. The police had spotted him now all right. Several of them were sprinting toward him, guns crashing. A cold smile moved Wentworth's lips. He jockeyed the throttle even wider, then lifted his automatic. There was a thought in his brain that almost became spoken words. . .

"For Nita!" His lifted automatic fell implacably in line, and he squeezed the trigger. He did that three times, as deliberately as at target practice, and three men fell to the ground. The fourth turned and fled. Wentworth lined his automatic, then held his fire—not in mercy. He might need his cartridges presently.

Headlights were streaming along the road from Albany, more Black Police.

They could stop him all right with a car. Cold as the spluttering motor was, he would have to risk a take-off. He eased the brakes, let the plane trundle down the ramp to the field. Police were firing on him from the cover of the administration building. A bullet snicked through the fabric close by his shoulder. Wentworth yanked the throttle wide, heard the motor choke, falter, then pick up. The plane began to roll faster, faster. . . a car swerved wildly out on the field, endeavoring to cut across his path. With lips grimly set, Wentworth held his course true.

Gently, he tried the stick, levered the plane's tail off the ground. The automobile was dangerously close now. Guns blazed. Angrily, Wentworth leveled his automatic, fired. He had missed! No time for another shot. Savagely, Wentworth yanked back the stick, felt the sluggish lift of the ship. If the motor faltered now. . . Five, ten feet he gained—fifteen. Wentworth thrust the stick forward again, felt his momentum pick up. Just as the wheels were skimming the ground, headed for a certain crackup with the car, he used his increasing speed to zoom.

Men were screaming below him. He caught their voices in a brief gust of sound, then they were left behind and the plane was climbing in a steady long slant toward the southeast, toward New York City. He was safe now. His burning of the administration building served more than one purpose. He had destroyed telephone communication from the field. Before the police could reach other instruments and have guards sent out to New York fields, he would have landed. . .

His landing would be safe enough, but after that. . . Wentworth's lips twisted bitterly. He must try to find and warn Kirkpatrick and then—prepare for battle! A coldness that had nothing to do with the bite of the upper air crept over him. He had battled before against desperate odds, but never before against a monster who ruled an entire state—where even the supposed forces of law and order fought on the side of crime!

CHAPTER SEVEN

DISASTER!

THE lights of New York City soon lifted above the horizon, the buildings looking like a black, crowded badlands against the dirty grey of the first dawn. Soon the smokes of a thousand furnaces would blot it out, but at present the silhouette was clear and strong, a man-created beauty that never failed to stir Wentworth. It was grief that moved him now. Men could create, but men could destroy, too, and it was the destructive element that held reign over his city.

It was not often that doubt or hesitancy shook Wentworth. He had chosen the path of service long ago when shaken by a too young discovery of the injustices which dominated the world of men. He had never regretted it for himself, but no man could live alone. He had dragged others into the maw of warfare through their affection for him. Brave Jackson, a prisoner or dead in Albany; Nita. . . gone. Men had died in his service before this, in the thankless task of championing people who, in the mass, would turn on him for the rewards offered for his life.

Wentworth's firmly chiseled mouth set awry in a bitter smile. The thought was not new but it came with special poignancy in this grey dawn when, close to exhaustion and bereft, he pressed on into the battle. Despite his careful strategems in Albany, the bullets of the Black Police might well be waiting for him at the air fields of New York. Even when he had braved them, he could not speed then to the help of those toward whom his heart yearned. His duty, self-imposed though it was, bade him speed to warn Kirkpatrick—to find fresh battles. Only afterward could he even think of Nita and Jackson.

The city was sweeping toward him, and Wentworth made his decision. Rather than risk the landing fields, he would risk the half-dark, the early mists that obscured the earth and attempt to set the plane down in Central Park. He swept in a wide circle and, flinchingly, gazed down at his fortress home on the East River. Its iron gates stood wide. That was proof enough that it was no longer guarded—that Nita and the rest had fallen prey to the Master's raiders.

Wentworth's eyes were hard and bitter as he turned back to the task of making a safe landing. He chose the sports field in the center of the park and slanted steeply in. It would have to be swiftly done. Police cars were on constant patrol of the park, and they would speed to investigate. They might be Kirkpatrick's men and loyal to him; or they might be taking orders from Kirkpatrick's successor. He had no way of telling.

The white, rising mists of dawn shredded out before the plane. The motor's rhythm was subdued so that the whine of wind on the struts came through to his ears. He cast a final glance toward the roadways, but failed to spot any police cars; then all his attention was concentrated on landing. The plane took the ground gently under his masterly handling, stopping within a few feet of the trees that girdled the field. Wentworth cut the ignition, sprang to the ground and darted to their cover. His deadened ears picked up the hammer of an automobile engine from the west driveway of the park and he turned to the east and drove his weary body into a lope.

The high windows of buildings were red with the first rays of the sun when, slowing to a walk, he strode out into Fifth Avenue. He found a taxi presently and sped southward. He debated a telephone call to Kirkpatrick and discarded the idea. Such a call might precipitate action against the commissioner, if he still were safe. No question but that it would be intercepted. He could ascertain if Kirkpatrick was in his office. . . He stopped the cab presently and, from a booth in an all-night restaurant, phoned headquarters. The instant he heard his friend's crisp voice over the instrument, Wentworth hung up. It took will-power to do that. So easy then to blurt out his warning, but it might be fatal to Kirkpatrick. Wentworth raced back to the taxi and sent it speeding toward Centre Street. The sound of Kirkpatrick's confident voice, harassed though it was, buoyed his hopes. He had failed everywhere else. Perhaps, this time, he could strike a successful blow. . .

WENTWORTH'S lips were set bitterly as he hastened toward headquarters. He had decided to risk an open invasion. He could not know to what extent Kirkpatrick still held the reins, but probably no one would try to block his entrance. Unobtrusively, he loosened his single remaining automatic in its holster though it was useless against the legitimate police. The *Spider* did not harm honest officers. That added to his risk. His eyes glinted coldly. He peered alertly ahead as the cab swung into Centre Street. A curse leaped to his lips.

"Don't stop," he ordered. "Go right on by and turn the corner two blocks down."

A squad of police stood guard over the entrance, but they were not the familiar blue-clad men of Kirkpatrick. They were the Black Police! Was he already too late then? Wentworth damned himself for failing to chance the phone warning, but dared not try again. When the cab pulled to a halt, Wentworth leaned forward.

"I'm a secret-service agent," he told the driver. "I've got to get into police headquarters without being seen. I'm going to fire some shots into the air. As soon as I have, speed for the corner, double back and pass behind headquarters. Here's twenty dollars."

The driver winked, "Okay, chief," he said. "You want I should stick around afterward?"

Wentworth shook his head with a slight smile. If he succeeded, there would be no need and if he failed, he would have no chance to flee! "No. Get away as fast as you can, for your own safety," he directed quietly.

He lifted his automatic then and fired it into the air—two shots, a pause and a third; then three more as rapidly as possible. The cab leaped forward like a racehorse from the barrier, and, brief seconds later, Wentworth dropped from it within a half block of police headquarters' rear. His reloaded automatic was back in its holster. He slipped quietly along in the half-light of the street. An emergency truck, loaded with police, slammed out of its garage, and Wentworth ducked into a doorway. As soon as it spun the corner, he darted into the garage.

One policeman was on guard. He swung around. . . and looked into the muzzle of Wentworth's automatic.

"You're taking me to the second floor of headquarters," Wentworth ordered, "as if I were your prisoner."

The man stared at Wentworth with wide eyes, then said falteringly, "I don't get it, Mr. Wentworth. I'll do it, sure—but why?"

Wentworth laughed. This was better luck than he had hoped for. It was one of the regulars who knew him and his friendship for Kirkpatrick.

"The commissioner is in danger," he said curtly. "Those new state police are on guard at the front door. Maybe all over the building—I don't know. I've got to reach Commissioner Kirkpatrick right away."

The man cursed. "Those damned Black Police," he said. "Sure. Let's go."

Despite the officer's apparent willingness, Wentworth watched him warily as they took the iron stairway that led to sleeping-quarters over the garage. From there, a covered bridge went directly to the second floor of police headquarters. At its entrance, Wentworth faced the policeman and held out his hand.

"From here on, I'd better go alone," he said quietly. "If I fail, I don't want to involve you."

The cop wrinkled his forehead. "What the hell is this?" he said gruffly. "Are them Blackies trying to put anything over on the commissioner?"

Wentworth smiled faintly. If only it were no more than that! "Something like it," he agreed. "Go back to your post and, if you have a car, get it ready for immediate flight. Have the engine running."

"Right." The cop started to salute, then grinned. "Anything for the commissioner." He went rapidly down the stairs and Wentworth faced toward the headquarters building, presently was peering furtively up the broad corridor before Kirkpatrick's office. An entire squad of the Black Police was on guard there! God, had they already made Kirkpatrick a prisoner!

IN HIS office, Stanley Kirkpatrick, commissioner of police, stood at bay behind his desk. It was not that he was physically cornered. Only one man, besides himself, stood in the square box of an office which had a barren, military aspect. But the mutual hostility of the men was apparent in the angry blood that tinged their faces.

"I've already given you my answer, Mayor Culkin." Kirkpatrick bit off his words almost fiercely. "I will not surrender this office to any crooked hireling of yours!"

Culkin was a pompous man, more used to underhand maneuverings than this open battle. He puffed, attempted an amiable smile.

"I really can't understand such defiance, Kirkpatrick," he said slowly. "You have no legal right to the office, you know. I haven't reappointed you. If necessary, I can have you ejected forcibly!"

Kirkpatrick shook his head slowly. He was standing very stiffly, his arms folded, chin pulled in. Those who knew him best were a little apprehensive when he assumed that pose. They knew then that he was fighting to hold his temper in check. They knew what happened when his anger burst loose.

"Not without a court order, my dear Mayor," he said flatly. "If you attempt it, there will be. . . *resistance*."

Culkin lost patience. "What in the hell can you hope to accomplish by this?" he shouted. "A few days more in office at most! You are destroying discipline! Promoting crookedness among the police!"

Kirkpatrick leaned across his desk, laid a palm down gently on its top. "Let's understand each other, Culkin," he said. "You want to eject me so that you can put a crook in my position. You and the Black Police—Governor Whiting, himself—are taking orders from criminals and I know it. Very well, as long as I can prevent it, you shall not have complete control of my men. Now, if you want to call in your Black Police, go ahead!" He laid a hand on a board of push-buttons on his desk. "I will sound the alarm and bring every man of mine in the building to fight them!"

Culkin laughed. "Go right ahead," he said softly. "Every man of yours is under guard!" He turned toward the door, swaggering, his fat shoulders pulled back as far as they could go.

The window glass broke inward with a tinkle that lay strangely across the hostile silence that had fallen in the room, and Richard Wentworth sprang lightly to the floor, his automatic leveled at Mayor Culkin.

"Stay right there, Culkin," Wentworth ordered softly, "or I'll embroider a pattern on that fat stomach of yours—with bullets!"

Mayor Culkin's jowls quivered. He got his shoulders against the door and stood there, gasping. "Kirkpatrick," he said hoarsely, "arrest that man! He's a public enemy!"

Kirkpatrick's face was stern as he swung toward Wentworth. "Put that gun away, Dick!" he ordered coldly.

"Stay where you are, Kirk," Wentworth answered quietly, "and listen to me!" His gun swung impartially from Kirkpatrick to Mayor Culkin. "Kirk, you heard the mayor call me a public enemy, but you don't know what that means yet. Tell him, Mayor Culkin! *Talk, damn you!*"

Culkin started violently; his words came stammering out. "The governor outlawed him," he said rapidly to Kirkpatrick. "All his property has been confiscated. There's a reward of ten thousand dollars for him, dead or alive."

Kirkpatrick stared at Mayor Culkin in amazement, "What the hell are you talking about?" he demanded.

Wentworth laughed softly. "It's the latest device of our friend, the White Face in the Mirror," he said and saw Culkin's countenance grow pale. "By it, he can assure the destruction of anyone who opposes him.

The legislature gave the power to Governor Whiting, and he can use it at his discretion. But you left out one thing, Mayor. If a public enemy is brought in dead, the reward is paid. . . *and no questions asked!*"

Kirkpatrick's face was dark with anger. "But that's damnable!" he cried. "That's something out of the Middle Ages! It's murder!"

"Yes, murder," Wentworth agreed softly. "Kirk, the governor has made you a public enemy, too. There's ten thousand dollars on your head!"

"Yes!" Culkin's voice rose shrilly with defiance. "You're a public enemy, Kirkpatrick! That's why you must surrender this office at once!"

Kirkpatrick took a long stride toward Culkin, then checked himself. "That is why he's so anxious to get me out of office," he said harshly. "He doesn't want to proscribe me while I'm the police commissioner. But as soon as I'm out. . . Culkin, I think you're a public enemy. I think you should have your neck wrung right now!"

Culkin squealed in terror. He turned awkwardly toward the door and beat on it with his fists. The ground-glass panel crashed outward to the floor. "Help! Help!" Culkin cried. "They're killing me!"

Wentworth took a long leap forward, but it was too late. Culkin whipped open the door and ran, waddling, toward the hallway where the Black Police stood guard.

"Kill them!" he was screaming now. "Kill them. They're both public enemies, and there's ten thousand dollars to the man who kills them!"

WENTWORTH twisted aside from his race toward the door and threw himself at Kirkpatrick. Together they slammed against the side wall of the office—and not a moment too soon. The volley from the corridor sent a hurricane of screaming lead through the doorway. The inkwell on Kirkpatrick's desk exploded, and a dozen bullets powdered the plaster of the wall. White dust floated into the air as the fusillade continued.

Kirkpatrick stared at Wentworth and his face was dead white. He said, with difficulty, "It seems that I owe you my life again, Dick."

Wentworth threw a quick glance toward the window. They were cut off from it by gunfire, trapped against the wall. He swore under his breath. He should have had more foresight! But that was foolish. He had saved Kirkpatrick in the only way he could. Any delay for strategy would have meant the commissioner's death.

"We've got to leave here at once," he said curtly. "The building is overrun with Black Police. If we can reach the window, there's a narrow ledge we can walk to the end office, then into the emergency-wagon garage. There's one of your men there and he'll have his car ready, with the motor running."

Kirkpatrick pulled out his long-barreled revolver, "I'm not leaving!" he said grimly.

Wentworth's own automatic was in his fist, and together they kept alert watch on that doorway. Two guns were still firing, fanning the opening with bullets. That meant the rest was creeping nearer for a rush.

"It's no use, Kirk," Wentworth said rapidly. "You can't hold onto the commissionership any longer. I tell you the Black Police have taken over! You're not a citizen of this state any longer. You're an outlaw, with no rights, except the right to die! There won't even be an investigation if you're killed! Ten thousand dollars reward—and no questions asked! We've got to get away."

Kirkpatrick's face was cut with harsh lines and Wentworth knew well the struggle that went on within him. Kirkpatrick had given years of his life to build the New York police into the strongest and most loyally efficient force in the country. To lose them now, with the certainty that all his good work would be destroyed—that criminality and protection would become the duty of his men instead of a thing they fought—was the bitterest blow that could strike Kirkpatrick. Added to that was the knowledge that he would be a fugitive criminal himself; that from now on his hand must be turned against the men he had taught and loved. Wentworth saw his mouth set grimly and he spoke harshly.

"Kirk, if you take a step toward that door, I'll knock you cold! Getting yourself killed won't help. It's selfish! The people need you now more than they ever had! We'll defeat this combination in time. When that's done, the force will need you to restore its strength. Listen to me. Kirk!"

Kirkpatrick smiled thinly. "It's no use, Dick. I'm finished anyway. I can't live your sort of life. If I could help you do the *Spider's* work, I would. But—" he shrugged—"I can at least create a diversion while you escape. And maybe I can destroy Culkin!"

"I won't leave you," Wentworth threw at him. "If you die here, I do, too! Come on, we'll be fools together!"

Abruptly, the gunfire from outside the door ceased and there was a pounding rush of feet! The Black Police were charging in for the kill— an entire squad of them against two men. Twenty thousand dollars on their heads—and no questions asked of their murderers!

FIGHT TO A FINISH!

WITH a violent thrust, Wentworth hurled Kirkpatrick toward the wall beside the door. That would be the most protected spot. For himself, Wentworth wanted no protection other than his gun. He could use its swift, unerring bullets like a sword blade against the thrusts of the enemy. There was a fierce anger in him and no fear at all. He threw his mocking laughter in their faces and his automatic was ready in his fist. There were seven cartridges—seven messengers of death!

Two men came through the door together. They dove headlong like tumblers, close to the floor, wrenching their guns about to fire while they still were in the air. Wentworth's automatic seemed to swing almost leisurely. He didn't fire first. Only super-trained gunmen could shoot accurately in the middle of such a charge. Wentworth's automatic crashed out twice, and the two Black Police struck the floor limply, already dead. Wentworth dropped to a knee and scooped up one of the revolvers, and his laughter rang out once more.

Kirkpatrick's revolver crashed and outside the door, a man screamed. Three more were jammed in the opening, fighting to get through. Wentworth helped them. His shot caught the middle man in the forehead, wrenched him backward. The other two pumped out frantic bullets as rapidly as they could, without aiming, screaming in their fear. Wentworth's two guns and Kirkpatrick's hammered out together, and the combined blast rocked the office. The doorway was cleared.

Kirkpatrick twisted a white, distorted face toward Wentworth, then abruptly whipped up his revolver and fired! Wentworth's lips cut short a cry that welled to them. The bullet hissed past so close that his temple felt the hot wind of its passage. For a mad moment, he thought Kirkpatrick had lost his mind, was firing upon him. . . and then he heard the scream. He twisted his head about.

One of the Black Police, leg hooked over the windowsill behind Wentworth, cradled a sub-machine gun in his arms. Its muzzle began to flicker with powder flame—but too late. Already the man, still screaming, was arching backward. The gun kicked higher, higher in his arms, then man and gun were gone. They popped out of sight, plunged downward. In the sudden aching silence of the room, the sound of the killer's landing made a sodden thud.

Kirkpatrick staggered, a palm grinding to his forehead, and Wentworth leaped to his side. "Are you hit?" he gasped. "God, man, that machine gun. . ."

Kirkpatrick's hand dropped like a stick. "Hit? Not by bullets, no, Dick," he said thickly. His stern eyes had become, in brief moments, unbelievably sunken in his head, and there were dark shadows beneath them. He looked old, broken. "Take me out of here, Dick—" his voice died to a whisper "—before I have to kill. . . my own men."

Wentworth threw a glance at the window. Men were shouting in the street. Silence within here, except for Kirkpatrick's deep struggling breath that was close to sobs. Were the Black Police all slain? It must be chanced.

Wentworth caught Kirkpatrick's wrist and charged through the door, his own body before that of his friend. He saw then where the sub-machine gun bullets had struck. The two remaining Black Police had been prepared to charge in. They were driven back, pinned blood-ily against the wall of the outer office. But more would come from below unless they were fast. So far, the entire battle could not have lasted more than two minutes.

Wentworth swung left and raced along the corridor, dragging the stumbling Kirkpatrick behind him. They whirled into the covered bridge, and Wentworth's gun swung up. Only at the last moment did he manage to stay the shot that threatened. It was the policeman who had helped him before.

"God, sir," he whispered. "God, sir, you almost. . ."

"The car!" Wentworth snapped. "Your orders were to stay with it!"

The man wheeled and ran drunkenly before them, half-fell down the iron stairway.

Moments later, Wentworth hurled Kirkpatrick into the rear of the sedan and sprang to the wheel. Before he could prevent it, the police-man had thrown himself in beside him.

"I'm with you, sir," he said. "Anyway, my life wouldn't be worth a cent. They'd know you escaped where I was on guard." He grinned whitely, freckles standing out with an almost painful contrast across his cheekbones. "I stay with the commissioner."

THERE was no time to stop and put the man out. Wentworth wrenched the wheel about and bore the accelerator to the floor. The light car jack-rabbited toward the corner and, behind him, the guns of the Black Police began to hammer again. Wentworth's brows were knotted in a tight frown.

Where was he going to hide? For himself, there was always escape in disguise if he could reach certain of his hideouts in the Underworld. But Kirkpatrick was too forthright a man, too unbending in his pur-poses and concepts, to utilize masquerade. The policeman was an added responsibility. His fortress home obviously had been swept clean by the Black Police. They would have guards there and traps, await-ing his return. It would be suicide to go there. It would be equally impossible, without preparation, to escape from the city. The plane in Central Park would not carry three men even if it could be wrested from the guard that undoubtedly had been placed over it.

No, there was no choice for it. Somewhere in New York, they must find a hiding place. Without thinking, Wentworth was doubling and redoubling on his trail, dodging the pursuit at top speed. It would take the police a few moments to organize. Before that time, he must be far away from the neighborhood of the headquarters. The car was roaring now down the Bowery, the clatter of elevated trains overhead. Store fronts were still dark and only a few tattered remnants of humanity walked the pavements. Ahead was Chatham Square and Chinatown. . .

"Master!" a man's voice cried out from the darkness. *"Sahib!"*

Wentworth ground down on the brakes. He knew Ram Singh's voice instantly, and where Ram Singh was, there would be Nita also! The car wrenched wildly as he fought it to a stop and, from the shadows of a doorway, a fleet, tall figure sprinted toward him. Wentworth flung wide the door.

"Get in!" he ordered, as Ram Singh darted up. "We're pursued. Where is the *missie sahib?*"

"Pursued?" Ram Singh threw a swift glance up the street. "Here is safety—in the stronghold of Chei Hwang-yo."

Wentworth laughed aloud. Of course! He would have remembered Chei Hwang-yo presently. They had sworn friendship to him, those Chinese who owed Chei Hwang-yo allegiance—and there were many of them. In the old Chinese's home, they would be safe for a while. He sprang to the pavement.

"There is an entrance near here?" he demanded while he gestured to Kirkpatrick and the policeman to leave the car.

Ram Singh rushed out directions while he was climbing in behind the wheel. He knew his task without being told. He must take the car away from this neighborhood. His dark eyes turned hauntingly on his master's face.

"The *missie sahib*," he said brokenly. "On my head be it, master. She is. . . gone."

"Gone where?"

Rapidly, Ram Singh outlined the things that had happened in his mansion fortress. "While thy servant was loading the boat, as the *missie sahib* had ordered, I heard her cry out. The elevator was slow, slow. When I reached the spot where the *missie sahib* had been, she was gone! There were police in black uniforms. They did not escape! But the *missie sahib*, I do not know!"

Wentworth's heart was leaden within him. He had recognized Nita's planning, in the instant Ram Singh had mentioned the Chinese—had hoped to hold her in his arms again, no matter for how brief a while. But now. . .

"What could be done, you did, my warrior, I know," he said heavily. "Go now, and return swiftly. There is work."

Kirkpatrick's hand was on his arm. "They have taken Nita?" he asked curtly. "Then, by God, I am glad I did what I did! Lead on, Dick."

WENTWORTH heard the whooping of sirens, and Ram Singh whipped the car from the curb and sent it rocketing straight ahead down the Bowery. He would do that until he was sighted. No, his bravery could not be questioned, but Nita. . . Wentworth led the way heavily toward the shadows and into the sour, slattern entrance of a tenement down the cellar stairs. The steps were boarded in with tongue-and-groove planking. There was a great deal such boarding in Chinatown. Its frequent joints made it easier to conceal hidden doorways. He found the knothole Ram Singh had mentioned, thrust his finger through and found a loop of string. A pull and a section of the boarding swung free. He led through it and they were in a low tunnel that paralleled the cellar wall. The way led presently downward, into an iron gallery along a great storm sewer.

Wentworth moved like a man in a trance. He had known Nita was a prisoner or worse, but the sight of Ram Singh—the knowledge that it was Nita's planning that made him safe now with Kirkpatrick and the policeman—lent an added weight of sadness. They were groping their way in utter darkness, but Wentworth scarcely noticed the fact. His hand glided along the brick wall on his left. He felt the beginning of a bend.

"Wait here." he said dully and his voice echoed off through the arch of the sewer. "I must go ahead and prepare for you."

Ten slow paces, he took and then he stood and sent his voice before him in the darkness. "One comes seeking," he said. It was the pass-word he had from Ram Singh.

Instantly, a yellow light bloomed in the blackness and, in its glow, Wentworth could presently see a powerfully built Chinese, standing with folded arms, hands tucked into his sleeves. There would be guns here, Wentworth knew.

"Say to your master, the thrice honorable Chei Hwang-yo," Wentworth lapsed into the Mandarin dialect, the Chinese as spoken in Peking, "that one whom he honored with the unworthy title of friend craves the privilege of speech."

"Wentworth *san*," the Chinese answered, "my master waits. He bade me say that his unworthy and wretched home is yours."

"I bring two friends."

"Shall a man not bring friends into his own home?"

Wentworth felt his heart swell with gratitude toward the old Chinese. Too few white men would do so much in the name of friend-ship! Wentworth bowed over his clasped hands, then called Kirkpatrick and the policeman forward.

"A friend of mine makes us welcome," he said quietly.

Wentworth followed the Chinese guard through other series of tun-nels and cellar-ways and they came presently into a broad room where a dozen white men and women were stretched upon rude couches. The scent of antiseptic was strong in the chamber and, when he entered, he saw the black-robed figure of the old priest from Poughkeepsie. A smile touched the man's face.

"Ah, my son." he said gently, "I am glad you come in safety."

From the far shadows of the place, two other figures hurried for-ward, the girl Angela Manteo and the young tax collector, Jack Wilson. There was a smile on Wilson's face, despite the pallor of his cheeks.

"Sir." he said, "when you go to fight those Black Police, take me with you! These people are their victims, rescued by Miss van Sloan. And we let those damned police capture her!"

A man lifted himself on his elbow from one of the couches—a gaunt, powerfully built man, weakened now by pain. He lifted his other hand in a clenched fist!

"Lead us against those damned police!" he cried. "Lead us!"

His cry echoed through the room and other figures stirred and lifted themselves; men's voices picked up the words. Wentworth's throat closed on the things he wished to say. Despair had drowned him. The *Spider* who was accustomed to hopeless battle against great odds. But there was no despair here, though these men were crippled with pain, though they had been stripped of everything that was dear to them. Instead they cried out for a leader in the battle against their oppressors. New strength flooded Wentworth.

"You shall be led," he said, his voice choked. "You shall have the chance to strike back! With men like you, we shall overthrow these criminals who rule the state! *I swear it!*"

A ragged cheer answered him, and Wentworth passed on, his head lifted again, renewed with courage. He would find Nita and free her. He would destroy the Black Police and their Master. . . Wentworth's lips twisted a little. That was madness and well he knew it. A dozen men, broken in body, hidden beneath the earth lest they be slain, and with them, he hoped to overthrow the powerful organization that in a few days had destroyed the state? Self-mockery tortured him. But who else was there to fight? Not the police, with Kirkpatrick driven from office, outlawed with a price on his head. Regardless of the odds, he must succeed.

IT WAS in that moment of despair that, Wentworth's plan was born. The Master was a nebulous figure who appeared only to his lieutenants as a white, ghostly face in a mirror, but his minions were everywhere. His organization must be destroyed first of all, crippled through its main strength, which was stolen wealth. Once his coffers were emptied, the Black Police, the thousand subordinates, would rebel. Such criminals could be held loyal only through money and fear. Wentworth would build a greater fear, and strip them of money!

Well he recognized how great a task lay ahead, but there were tens of thousands of honest men in the state. They would hear the brunt of the crime-madness of the Master. More and more, they would be oppressed and from among them, Wentworth could muster a secret army. They would have to be armed and trained. Very well, the state should supply them with money! They would strike from a hundred coverts against the oppressors and, in the end, they would triumph. *They must!*

There were untold obstacles to be overcome, but with courage and perseverance. . .

Wentworth realized that he had been ushered into the presence of Chei Hwang-yo. The aged Chinese was smiling at him, his face cut with a thousand wrinkles.

"My son," he said in his perfect, even pedantic English, "you have come to me in your trouble as I came to you in mine. I am proud to serve you. My house and all that I have is yours!"

Wentworth was aware of his overwhelming weariness, as he sank upon the cushions Chei Hwang-yo indicated. The relief of sanctuary, after so many hours of flight and battle, loosened his muscles like a drug. He made his formal response to the Chinese, but, in spite of himself, his head nodded.

Chei Hwang-yo laughed. "You do me too much honor, friend," he said softly. "Now you must rest."

Sleep struck Wentworth like a thunderbolt and it seemed only seconds later that a hand, laid gently on his arm, awakened him. Chei Hwang-yo's face was no longer smiling, but gravely lined.

"My son," he said. "I could wish that I had other words for you than I must voice. At sunset tonight, at Union Square, there is to be a public execution of what the state is pleased to call traitors."

Wentworth shook the sleep from his brain and started up. "What time is it now?" he asked quickly.

Chei Hwang-yo gravely indicated a clock whose hands pointed to four o'clock. "I have just received the word, and there is more, my friend."

Wentworth felt all his body grow taut. Somehow, he knew the answer even before he heard the Chinese speak. He drew himself slowly erect and his eyes tightened with pain.

"Tell me," he said slowly.

Chei Hwang-yo nodded. "It is as you have guessed. The first of those to die will be the woman to whom you have given your heart— *Nita van Sloan.*"

CHAPTER NINE

GALLOWS FEAST

BY A violent effort, Wentworth controlled the anger that surged through him. His voice was almost steady as he shot out rapid inquiries. He learned that Ram Singh had at last managed to make his way back to the hideout, bringing word of Nita's doom. The news was being broadcast throughout the city by the newspapers and by Black Police who, mounted in armored cars, stopped at street corners to cry out the news. The Master was preparing to show the people the cost of disobedience to his orders. No doubt of that, or that he hoped, by the threat to Nita, to lure Wentworth into a trap!

Well, he would have that opportunity! Wentworth made the resolution, silently. If he allowed the Master to perform his executions, the reign of terror would be complete. This was the course he must follow, to harass the Master at all times; to give the people hope and the courage to fight.

To Chei Hwang-yo Wentworth said only, "I understand many of my possessions have been brought here.

I shall need some of them."

The Chinese eyed him impassively. "My men shall take your orders, Wentworth *san*." he said. "The gallows has been erected on the north side of the square and two companies of the Black Police are there already."

Wentworth shook his head slowly. "You already have done too much for me. This is my own battle!"

To reach the room where his possessions were stored, Wentworth had to pass through the chamber where the men Nita had rescued were being doctored. He hesitated there. These men would follow him to rescue the woman who had saved them!

Then he shook his head. It could not be. They were too few to attack in force; and now one or two men could accomplish more. He and Ram Singh. . . the *Spider!*

Wentworth paused beside the couch were Kirkpatrick slept. It would be best that Kirkpatrick knew the plans he had formed in case anything should happen to him in the battle that lay ahead. But if he aroused him, Kirkpatrick would insist on participating in the venture. Wentworth hurried on, and began to search among the things that Nita had brought. Ram Singh presently joined him.

"What are my master's orders?" he asked, gravely. "It is thy servant's hope that he may be permitted to offer his poor life in recompense for his failure."

Wentworth set his hands on the Sikh's broad shoulders. "Both of us may die," he said quietly, "but there is to be no sacrifice. No blame rests upon you. I have made certain plans. Here are grenades, rifles, automatics and ample ammunition, thanks to the *missie sahib*. This is what we will do. . ."

THEN the sunset lay red as blood across the city, there were twenty thousand people packed into the plaza on the north side of Union Square. Many had come of their own volition, drawn by horror; many thousands of others had been herded there by Black Police on horseback who stopped throngs in the street and drove them toward the square like cattle.

They moved restlessly, and the mutter of their voices was like a gathering storm. Scores of mounted Black Police hemmed them in and, on the southern edge of the plaza where they stood, there was a solid phalanx of horsemen. They stood guard before the colonnaded grandstand. It was on top of this that the gallows had been rigged.

Hurriedly erected of great timbers, it was no trap-platform that had been built. Two uprights had been braced into place and, across their top—fifteen feet above the level of the roof—there was a cross-piece, like the lintel of a giant's doorway. Over that, dangling ropes had been tossed. Plainly, the victims were to be hoisted by the hang noose and allowed to strangle slowly, their struggles a lesson for the assembled thousands in the square!

Presently, a slow procession turned from Broadway into the midst of the crowd. Before them, Black Police rode with rearing horses, striking out to open a path. There were three limousines and, behind them, flanked by more of the mounted police, was an open truck in which seven people stood, their hands lashed to the sides. One of them was a woman, and of the six who were men, three of them were heavily bandaged and one had his arm in a sling. A mutter like rising wind swept through the crowd. These were the gallows' prey—those who were about to die.

It was strange that, of all those who rode in this new and cruel tumbrel, only the woman kept her head erect. Her lips even managed to move in a smile as she looked down upon the people who gazed upon her. Nita's chestnut curls were loose to the wind and they stirred about her face. If the sight of that brutal gallows shook her, she showed no sign. Instead, she looked beyond them, up at the fiery brilliance of the sky—the jut of buildings that shouldered against it. She had no hope of rescue, did not even know that Richard Wentworth had returned to New York.

She had no regret for the things she had done, nor for the life she had chosen to share with Dick. But it would be hard to die without seeing him once more, without knowing whether he had escaped the traps set for him in Albany. She turned to the man bound beside her.

"It will soon be over now, Jackson," she said quietly.

Jackson turned his soldier's impassive face toward her. He it was who wore his arm in a sling. "If *he's* alive, Miss Nita," he said harshly, "they won't get away with it. Don't you give up hoping, Miss Nita, even when—when they get busy."

Nita smiled then. "It's brave of you, to encourage me," she said simply. "Thank you, Jackson. But even if he's safe—even if he knew about this—what could he do?" Her nod indicated the jammed thousands before the gallows, the close lines of mounted police, a machine gun mounted in the speaker's stand. "Better to hope that he doesn't know!"

They fell silent then as the truck maneuvered and backed up against a flight of steps that led to the roof and the gallows. There was a continuous shouting from the people now. A troop of the police drew their revolvers and fired shots into the air. Nita turned her eyes toward the gallows and the roof. One man there in civilian clothing, the others were high officials of the Black Police, a half dozen in all. Over on the far side of the crowd, a single horseman was pushing his way forward. For a moment Nita's heart leaped with hope and fear. There was something familiar about the erect, masterful way the man sat his horse. . . but he wore the uniform of the Black Police, an officer of some sort from the glitter of gold at shoulder and sleeve.

ROUGH hands seized Nita. Her bonds were slashed loose and she was thrust up the steps toward the gallows, alone. Below, the other prisoners stared upward after her with gaunt and terrified faces. Something close to panic seized Nita, as she was brought to a halt beneath those dangling ropes. Her hands were wrenched around behind, tied again; the rough hemp of the rope rasped her white throat.

Nita bit her lip and lifted her face to pray, but above her was the brutal black line of the gallows against the red of the sky. She choked down a sob. If only she could have seen Dick once more. She thought again of that lone horseman off there in the crowd, but she could no longer see him. The civilian, flanked by the police, had stepped to the edge of the gallows platform, and was lifting his voice. It boomed out over the assembled crowd and a thick, waiting silence fell.

"This woman," he thundered, "rebelled against the constituted authorities of the state, the men you elected to serve you. She was responsible for the deaths of five policemen! She has been duly tried by the state courts and condemned to be hanged, publicly, as a lesson and an example to others who may contemplate lawlessness. This woman is a traitor to the state. She—"

There was the thud of a blow, and the speaker catapulted queerly backward to the roof. He struck so violently that his feet lifted and then clumped down again. They drummed on the metal and the sound that they made was terribly loud in the abrupt quiet. Nita stared at him with her eyes strained wide in a white, frightened face. Between the man's eyes was a bullet hole!

Even as Nita recognized the import of the thing that had happened, the black-clad police officers were falling. Three of them were down, and there still had been no sound of a shot.

The fourth struggled to pull his revolver. A shout that might have been the beginning of an order rose in his throat, but got no farther. A bullet drove him back against the side post of the gallows and he clung there, his face working terribly, through a long moment before he fell. The one remaining officer ran to the edge of the roof and leaped out into space, but, even as he jumped, death was upon him. His body jerked, arms and legs went limp, and he struck the earth as insentiently as a shovel full of dirt.

From the ladder by which she had mounted to the gallows, a man's voice spoke with harsh authority. "Bring the prisoner here. At once. It's an attempt to rescue her. Hurry, you fools, before you're killed, too!"

The rope was snatched from Nita's neck and the two executioners thrust her across the roof. A crescendo of pistol shots burst out, but none of them flew near. Nita was staring at the Black Police officer upon the ladder, the man who wore the silver eagle of a colonel upon his shoulder. A cry rose in her throat, but she choked it down.

"Hurry!" the man rasped.

Nita was thrust down the ladder into his arms and the two executioners leaped for safety. Nita's hands were bound behind her, but she gazed up into the face of the colonel of police with eyes that were at once incredulous and laughing.

"Dick!" she whispered. "Oh, Dick. . . I knew you'd come!"

Wentworth thrust her into the back of the truck, without a word, then mounted to his horse. "Driver!" he shouted. "Take the prisoners away! Fast! It's an attempt to rescue them!" He flashed a sword from its scabbard, flicked it toward the mounted men. "You men surround the truck! Make an opening through the crowd there! Hurry before the attack begins in full force!"

The crowd already was in flight, and the horsemen easily opened a path for the fleeing truck. Wentworth spurred up beside the driver and around the truck, horsemen began to pitch from their saddles. Bullets whined out of the air from nowhere at all, without a sound except the hiss of their passage, and one after another, the mounted police pitched to the pavement. Long before they reached the verge of the crowd, they were panic-stricken. They put the spurs to their horses and fled, leaving the truck to trundle on with only Wentworth riding beside the cab.

P RESENTLY, he stepped to the running-board of the truck, jerked open the door and ordered the driver to move over. He took the wheel himself and, an instant later, his automatic's muzzle cracked against the man's skull. Slowly then, as Wentworth tooled the truck through the last fleeing remnants of the crowd, he began to smile. There was a tap on the window in the back of the cabin and he turned, slid the glass aside and looked into Nita's lovely eyes.

"I've cut all the prisoners loose, Colonel," Nita said gaily, "and I have them lying on the bottom of the truck. Any further orders, Colonel?"

Wentworth laughed. "None for the present, Captain," he replied, "but when I stop this truck presently. . ." He caught her hand to his lips and kissed it and there was a pain in his throat at the remembrance of Nita, so brave and pitiful, with that rope about her sweet neck. There had been a while when he had feared he would not arrive in time. It had been no easy matter to find a high officer of the Black Police in such a position that he could be overpowered and robbed of his uniform. There had been a time, too, when he had been afraid Ram Singh, hidden on a roof with a silenced rifle, would not be able to shoot swiftly enough to prevent Nita's death. But now. . . Nita laughed at him, at his kiss upon her hand. She waved her narrow white hand until he kissed it again, "Is that strictly according to military code, Colonel?" she asked.

THE evening in the underground warrens, to which Wentworth took Nita and the other prisoners, was strangely gay; perhaps the more so because of the horror they all knew ranged the streets above. Wentworth knew that it was a moment stolen before the months of perilous labor to come. Before the dinner Chei Hwang-yo set before them was fairly over, he was summoning the men he had hidden into conference. There he laid before them the plans he had made.

"It will be impossible for us to hide here indefinitely," he said. "Kirkpatrick is going to take a group of you to the Catskill Mountains where both of us have summer camps. There we will prepare a hide-out for the army we must train before we can hope to defeat these criminals. Don't worry about arms or money. The state will supply them to you—the state and the Black Police!"

There were muffled cheers in response to that, but Wentworth silenced them quickly. "I am going to call for volunteers to remain in hiding here with me and fight the Black Police and their masters. It will be perilous. Some of us will be killed. But it is necessary. We must keep up the spirits of the people so that, when we can strike, they will rise to help us. We must prevent the collecting of taxes. That entire criminal crew is held together by the hope of loot. If we keep them from getting it, we will do more than any other thing to wreck their morale!"

He went on. "Before you answer, there is one more thing to tell you. Word has just been brought to me that the Black Police have evolved a new weapon. Those who lift their hands against the police, but are not important enough to be outlawed, are being driven into concentration camps. They are herded through the streets like animals, men and women and children. Those of you who served in the war will know what such camps are like, barbed-wire fences and leaky, cold ram-shackle buildings, too little food—a dozen people jammed into a space where two could not live healthily. Within a few weeks, there will be disease, a dozen deaths a day.

"These are the people I am asking you to defend at the risk of your own lives. Those who will volunteer. . ."

A spontaneous shout rang out from all the assembled men. Wentworth laughed, but there were tears in his eyes. With men like these, he could destroy a hundred such criminal governments! He lifted his hands.

"We will divide up the forces this way," he decreed. "Those who are disabled will go with Kirkpatrick, to prepare for the day when we can smash the concentration camps and send the people to hide in the mountains. The rest will stay and fight!"

The crash of the door being thrown open was like a gun-blast. A Chinese ran in and prostrated himself before Chei Hwang-yo where he sat beside Wentworth, and the words poured from his lips in broken sobs.

Wentworth caught his phrases and faced the men before him. "You will have a chance to fight for liberty sooner than I had thought," he said crisply. "Jackson, Ram Singh, open that door and distribute guns and ammunition, while Kirkpatrick and Chei Hwang-yo plan for our defense.

"The Black Police have tracked us here, and are already breaking down the doors!"

BATTLE IN THE DARK

NOTHING of the despair that swept him showed in Wentworth's firmly lined face. The men cheered as they rushed for the arms that Ram Singh and Jackson were distributing. "Shame be upon my head," Wentworth said to Chei Hwang-yo. "I have brought destruction upon you!"

The Chinese smiled slightly. "The way to the river is still open," he said quietly. "Do you and your friends fly that way while my men hold back the enemy. They are at the doors, but it will be long before they reach here. I have taken certain necessary precautions long ago."

"The way to the river," Wentworth echoed softly. Suddenly, he laughed aloud. "Chei *san*, honorable father," he said, "this place would not long have been safe for you with the human rats who burrow toward us now. It will be safe again as soon as we have wiped them out. We must retreat by way of the river! We move sooner, instead of later, to the fastnesses of the mountains! Let them follow us there if they dare!"

Kirkpatrick and the aged Chinese stared at him. Nita's hand closed on his arm and clung there, while Wentworth raced on.

"We can operate from a base there, strike equally well at Albany or New York," he cried. "Within a few days, we can be fortified so strongly that they cannot drive us out! Nita, set the men to carrying arms and ammunition to the river passage. Fasten them in bundles that men can sling over their shoulders! Ram Singh, take five men and fight as rearguard against these Black Police until we are clear."

"My son forgets," said the Chinese slowly. "We cannot run through the city streets with arms on our backs. Even if we could find enough cars, they would be stopped by the armored trucks and machine guns of the police."

Wentworth laughed aloud, in triumph. "That is the easiest part of all," he cried. "Near the place where your river door opens, there is a fire-boat, which keeps steam up all the time. There is only a small crew on board, the rest on shore in the firehouse. If we strike fast, we can seize it before an alarm is given. . . And fire boats are speedy—they have to be!"

Kirkpatrick's lips parted in a wide smile. "Give me three men. Dick, and we'll bring that fire-boat to the river door."

Chei Hwang-yo lifted a hand that trembled a little and removed his glasses, symbol of his age and wisdom. He bowed.

"You are my elder brother," he told Wentworth, then he turned and his voice crackled with orders. Within moments, Chinese were scuttling everywhere, salvaging treasure and arms, trotting off along the way toward the river. Somewhere a man screamed, hoarsely, terribly. Chei Hwang-yo smiled a little. "My arrangements. . . still fight for us," he said gently. "We have plenty of time."

Within ten minutes, everything that could be moved had been fastened into bundles for men's backs and was being sped toward the river door. Ram Singh's party was shooting now, the crash of their guns echoing through the dark caverns below the city streets. Nita ran to Wentworth's side.

"The boat has left the dock!" she cried. "The men are waiting to leap aboard. Call Ram Singh in."

"It is time," Chei Hwang-yo agreed. "Even when we have left, my arrangements will fight for us. You need not fear pursuit from these men, my elder brother!"

Wentworth had fought his way through the warrens of hostile Chinese before this, and he had some knowledge of the horrors that lay in wait for the Black Police. It was not his way of fighting, but he could feel no sympathy for those criminal cohorts, most of them recruited from the penitentiaries whose doors the crooked governor had thrown wide. Together, the aged Chinese, Nita and Wentworth made their way along the storm sewer that led to what Chei Hwang-yo called his 'river door.' Ram Singh and his men closed in behind them, a great metal barrier slid down behind them in rubber-sealed grooves. It dimmed the sounds behind, but even so Wentworth could hear thin, rising screams. They did not continue for long. . .

Nita's face was pale when, at the mouth of the sewer, he handed her up a ladder thrown over side from the fire-boat. Kirkpatrick called down cautiously from the wheelhouse.

"We'll have to hurry," he said. "They might send my own men after us."

Wentworth's voice cracked out, hurrying the last of the men aboard. No, they could not fight the regular police. They were honest men, and fearless, a different breed from these renegade Blacks. Moments later, the fire-boat swung out into the stream. The tide was setting in, and they sped northward with the double drive of current and engines. Fortunately, the night was black. Let them at once distance pursuit and gain the wide reaches of the Sound. Until daylight, they would be safe enough.

WENTWORTH hurried up to the wheelhouse and found there one of the men he had saved from the gallows—a red-faced, broad-shouldered fellow who seemed utterly at home where he was. He grinned, touched his forelock.

"You don't need to worry as long as Sailor Joe is at the wheel, Mr. Wentworth," he said, with a wink. "I know these waters like the palms of my hands."

"Good!" Wentworth nodded. "Take her into the Sound, Joe. Keep well out from both shores and give all boats a wide berth." He remained for a moment beside the wheel and watched the competent movements of the man's blunt-fingered weathered hands. He glanced out the windows, then uttered a startled exclamation.

"One of your police boats, Kirk!" he cried. "It's overtaking us fast!"

Kirkpatrick swore under his breath. "We can't fire on them!" he said resolutely. "They're honest men, Dick, not scoundrels like those black uniformed killers."

"You're right," Wentworth agreed swiftly, "but I have a plan. You talk with them when they come within hail, Kirk. They won't open fire on you." As Kirkpatrick hurried out, Wentworth turned to the helmsman. "Joe, listen for my hail. When you hear it, stop the engines. When I shout again, full speed ahead. And stop for nothing!"

The man winked his cheerful blue eyes again. "Aye, aye, sir," he agreed. "Stop the engines at the first hail; full speed ahead at the second, and stop for nothing!"

Wentworth raced out of the wheelhouse and shouted for Jackson and Ram Singh. The police boat was drawing rapidly nearer now and Kirkpatrick stood at the rail, facing it. A pistol shot rang out.

"Aboard the fire-boat!" The hail came from the police launch. "Heave to!"

Wentworth sent a low-voiced hail to the wheelhouse, felt the pulse of the engine die, then raced toward the bow. Ram Singh was clambering to the roof of the wheelhouse, Jackson slipping to the stern. Far down in the hull, machinery began to throb as Wentworth signaled the engine room. The firemen operators were still aboard, under guard of his men. Assured of safety, and early release by Wentworth, they had agreed to work the boat and they had responded promptly.

Kirkpatrick answered the police hail, "I'm Commissioner Kirkpatrick," he called crisply. "I've commandeered this boat. Sheer off and convoy us."

The hail that came back was respectful. "Sorry, Mr. Kirkpatrick, our orders are to arrest you and everyone with you. Unless you surrender, we'll be compelled to open fire!"

Forward, Wentworth was swiveling the hose-nozzle of the bow water-gun toward the approaching boat which was running close under the rail now. Atop the pilot-house and in the stern, Ram Singh and Jackson were doing the same. These guns could hurl a three-inch column of water a hundred and fifty feet into the air, and the police launch was less than fifty feet away, drawing closer. Kirkpatrick was haranguing the men.

Cautiously, Wentworth reached out and tapped a single light peal from the watch-bell forward. At the same instant, he wrenched open the valve of the water-gun; Jackson and Ram Singh did the same. The converging columns of water struck the launch with fierce force. Wentworth's stream smashed the glass from the pilothouse, drove the helmsman in a backward somersault into the cockpit. Ram Singh's water-gun, depressed from the roof, beat the sergeant to the floor and the combined wash hammered the police relentlessly about in the bottom of the cockpit.

For nearly a minute, while the men scrambled to get to their feet and loose their gunfire on him, Wentworth continued to deluge the launch. Only when he heard the launch's motor splutter and die as it was drowned out by the flood did he shout to Sailor Joe in the wheelhouse. The fire-boat had not lost way entirely and quickly picked up speed, while the water-guns continued to play over the launch until it dropped out of range. It was the only challenge to their escape. Apparently, no other boat was near enough to reach them before they charged through Hell Gate and out into the black reach of the Sound.

As soon as he was sure they were out of immediate danger, Wentworth called a conference in the cabin, outlined his plans.

"BEGINNING at midnight," he told the assembled men, "we'll land small parties at various points near Connecticut towns. You'll carry your quota of arms and supplies and be given expense money. Each of you will be under charge of two leaders, one of whom will remain in hiding with the men. The other will make his way into the nearest town and, as soon as possible, buy a second-hand truck.

You will then proceed to certain rendezvous in the Berkshire Hills. The routes will be marked out for you.

"I will arrange for each group to be met then and guided to the hideout. Once we are established there, not even the Black Police will be able to destroy us. And we need not worry about food or supplies—for the Black Police will finance us, too! Get what sleep you can now."

The men gave Wentworth a brief, muffled cheer and filed out. Their morale was good. Wentworth was glad to see. The facility of the rescue from the gallows, the escape from the underground trap and the defeat of the police launch had given them faith in his leadership.

Wentworth, with Kirkpatrick and Nita, worked swiftly through the night, deciding on leadership and routes. Dawn was scarcely arrived when it was time to begin disembarking the groups.

There were two rowboats and with these the landings on deserted shores were accomplished. It was necessary to move warily to avoid possible police patrols. The radio brought news of rioting throughout New York and of planes questing for the stolen fire-boat.

Wentworth had no fear of being spotted by the planes during the blackness of the overcast night, but he knew that with the dawn, their safety would be at an end. Nevertheless, the east was rosy-colored with the rising of the sun when the last group of men was put ashore near Bridgeport—and for him the most desperate part of the venture now began. He had waited until last, and Nita insisted on remaining. The last man ashore, and Nita at the wheel. Wentworth took command of the engine-room, gun in hand. He sent the fire-boat speeding southeastward toward the Long Island shore.

It was necessary to delay, as long as possible, any pursuit in Connecticut, for it would be impossible for the men to make purchases of trucks and cars until nine o'clock or later. License plates must afterward be bought, and then the long trek into the hills begun. Kirkpatrick would take charge there until Wentworth's arrival. But meantime. . . Wentworth started at the shrill whistling of the speaking-tube and bent toward it to hear Nita's terse voice.

"Two planes coming this way," she reported. "I think they're New York police ships."

Wentworth glanced at his watch. It was eight o'clock, and they were in mid-Sound. The police had one amphibian plane and might attempt a landing; probably they would content themselves with radioing New York for police launches. Abruptly, a smile stirred Wentworth's lips. He eyed the three men in the engine-room, then set swiftly to work. He ordered one man to bind the other two.

"You'll be free in a few moments," he reassured them. "The police planes are coming now."

He stopped the boat's engines, called up the speaking-tube to Nita to keep out of sight until he was ready. Then he faced the third fireman and, emptying the cartridges from a revolver, handed the weapon to him.

"You're going to take me a prisoner, up on the deck." he said, "and signal to those planes. Put on your uniform cap."

The man grinned wryly. "You're going to fix it so I'll be kicked out of the department," he said. "Pension gone and all the rest of it. That's a hell of a note, Mr. Wentworth."

Wentworth nodded somberly. "I'm sincerely sorry," he said. "I could offer you money, but that would be bribery. I can only tell you this. Sooner or later, the crooked regime that has control of the state will be thrown out of office. When it does, I'll see that you get your job back. If I'm not still around, then Commissioner Kirkpatrick will attend to it. That goes for all of you men. If you're honest, you know that criminals have seized control of the government. Because Kirkpatrick opposed them, they've made him an outlaw with a ten-thousand-dollar price on his head." He nodded to the man who had protested. "Your name? Frank Connors? All right, Connors. On deck."

Wentworth led the way to the deck, the empty gun pointed at his back, careful not to allow Connors to come close enough to strike. He lined up against the railing then, hands lifted.

"When the plane comes near enough," he directed, "hail them. They probably won't be able to hear you, but point to the engine-room, then to me. Hold up your fingers, spread out, and try to indicate to them that you have fifteen prisoners there and need help."

Connors' face was pale, "I'll try, sir, but if those are Black Police, they're going to kill me when you're gone. You want them to land so that you can take the plane?"

Wentworth nodded, eyes keenly on Connors' face. It was an honest face, though deeply lined now with worry.

"Look, Mr. Wentworth," he hurried on, "let me go with you! I hate these crooks as much as you do! I'll be glad to fight them! I know you have no reason to trust me, but if Mr. Kirkpatrick is in with you, then, damn it, I am too!"

Wentworth smiled slowly, "I'd shake your hand for that, Connors, if they couldn't see us. It's a deal! But remember, it's a long fight that lies ahead of us. There will be death for some of us."

"I'm not afraid of death, sir, if it's honorable!"

Wentworth nodded again and his heart was more buoyant for the faith that the man expressed. Criminals couldn't continue to rule, when honest men felt that way. They needed only a leader and, heaven helping, he would lead them! The two police planes were swooping near now and Connors began to wave his hands frantically at them, shouting and gesturing as Wentworth had ordered. The land plane swung in a wide circle, then sped back toward New York. The amphibian swooped nearer, motor cut and struts whining with the wind, as it swept past the fire boat.

"Prisoners!" Connors shouted. "Ten prisoners. I'm alone!"

THE plane picked up and circled again while Connors continued to gesture despairingly. Abruptly, Wentworth leaped toward Connors and wrested the gun from him, pretending to strike him over the head.

"Lie quietly," he said sharply. He darted toward the wheelhouse, with a backward-flung glance toward the plane. This time, he had accomplished his purpose. The amphibian was slanting swiftly to a landing. He heard the popping of police guns faintly, and lead whined past his head—but he made the pilothouse.

"As soon as the plane lands," he told Nita rapidly, "get to a water-gun and bring it to bear. Don't loose it unless I tell you. We need that plane!"

He darted out then and ran back toward the engine-room, and

bullets began to plunk into the bulkhead in his path. He pretended to be frightened, dodged back. The amphibian took the water easily and plowed straight toward the fire-boat. For the first time, Wentworth could make out the uniforms of the two men in the cockpit, and his lips thinned. *Black Police!* He flung himself prone on the deck and held his automatic ready. Bullets gouged splinters from the deck, and one sliced across his cheek.

Wentworth sent three shots, carefully wide of the mark, toward the men in the plane. When next they fired, he cried out hoarsely and slumped limply to the deck. The Black Police raised a triumphant shout and continued to pump bullets toward him as the ship slued around and one man climbed out on the wing. He poised then for the final shot that would make certain Wentworth was dead.

Wentworth started to jerk up his gun, but, before he could fire, the Black killer's bullet drove down through his right shoulder. Numbness raced through his side, his hand relaxed about his gun. Desperately, he shifted it to his left hand. The policeman was laughing, taking his time with a final, murderous shot. . .

The crack of the gun came from far forward, where Nita had taken her stand—and her aim was true. The Black Policeman pitched backward off the wing. His hands clawed frantically for a moment at the fuselage and then he hit the water with a violent splash. He went straight down. Wentworth pushed himself to his knees, leveled his automatic at the pilot of the plane.

"Surrender!" he cried.

The man's answer was a hoarsely shouted challenge and the crash of his gun, as he grabbed for the throttle. He never reached it. Wentworth's gun jerked in his hand. He slipped and almost fell, but the bullet sped true. The pilot reared out of his seat and slumped over the edge of the cockpit, instantly dead. For a moment, Wentworth stared toward the man. Then, fumblingly, he pushed himself to his feet, lips shut grimly against the tearing agony that was beginning to run through his shoulder and down his back. Wentworth gestured with the automatic, "Make the plane fast to us," he ordered Connors, and watched while the man did the job. He showed no inclination to hold back, or to attack him. Nita's feet beat swiftly along the deck.

Then she stopped.

"Dick!" she cried. "Dick, you're wounded! Is it—"

"Cracked my shoulder blade, I think," Wentworth told her slowly. "Tie me up the best way you can, and we'll get away from here. You can pilot the plane. You know where to go. . ."

Minutes dragged past, while Nita worked over his shoulder. "The bullet went straight through," she said, with relief. "But your shoulder blade does seem to be fractured."

Connors stood white-faced before Wentworth, his lips taut, "What do you want me to do, sir?" he asked quietly. "You made it possible for me to stay aboard by attacking me like that. Is that what you want?"

Wentworth nodded, fighting for clarity of thought against the pain that was racking him. "It would be better. Smash the radio. Head the boat for New York. Delay your report as long as possible, without drawing suspicion to yourself. They should give you a medal. Tell them you wounded me."

Connors said slowly, "I'd prefer to go with you, but if I can serve you better this way, then I will. At least, I can gather information in New York City for you."

Wentworth held out his left hand and gripped that of Connors. "You won't lose by this, I promise you," he said.

It was laborious for him to climb along the wing and into the cockpit, but Nita's bandages had stopped the bleeding. As soon as he was seated, she climbed in and eased the throttle of the still idling plane, sent it skimming over the water. Wentworth glanced at his watch. It lacked only a few minutes of nine o'clock, and satisfaction lighted his eyes. Within the next half hour, the last of his men should have started for the hills. It would be a great deal longer than that before the police got the truth from Connors.

He turned his head toward Nita, and smiled. There was a smile on her lips, too. The wind tossed curls about her face, and her mouth shaped soundless words, "We'll win now!"

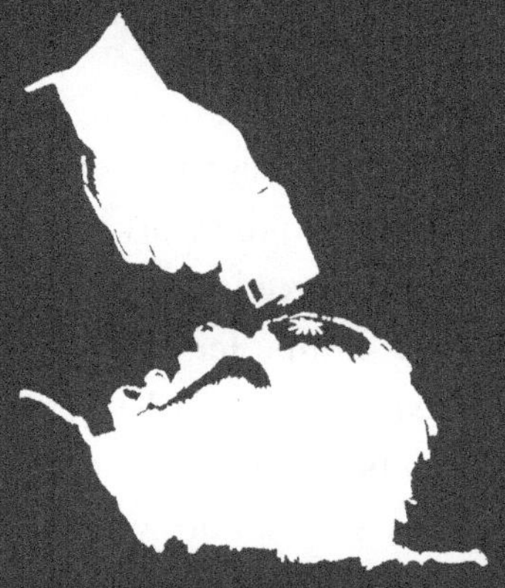

CHAPTER ELEVEN

THE GROWING TERROR

NITA guided the plane with consummate skill to a landing on the lake near Wentworth's Catskill camp. Kirkpatrick arrived soon afterward and helped her get Wentworth into bed. It was twenty-four hours before the last contingent of men reached the hideout, though only one party ran into difficulties. They had been forced to shoot their way clear, but none of the police had been killed. Even after that arduous flight, there could be no rest

Wentworth found himself with a band of forty men and women hidden out in the mountain fastnesses. There were crowded sleeping accommodations for all in the large hunting lodge, but food was an immediate problem as was the ever-present danger that they would be spotted by the Black Police. Of these forty, twelve were Chinese who had come with Chei Hwang-yo, nine of them servants, three others good fighting men. Of the white men, the nine Nita had saved from the floggings of the Black Police, and the six Wentworth had snatched from the gallows, were all partly crippled by the mistreatment they had undergone. But none hung back on that account from the work.

Though Wentworth was forced by Kirkpatrick to remain in bed, he swiftly organized the camp. Jack Wilson and the policeman, Cassidy, who had elected to flee with Kirkpatrick, were dispatched with one of the trucks to buy foodstuffs at some remote point; Ram Singh and the three Chinese warriors were posted as sentries. The women, of whom there were three besides Nita and Angela Manteo, took over the operation of the house. The remaining men set to work to build shelters for the trucks, hidden in the woods from airplane observation; to cut firewood and enlarge quarters; to erect barricades for defense in case of attack. Even the diminutive priest, Father Flower, swung an ax with the rest, and the men sang as they worked.

When these things had been arranged. Wentworth could think for a moment of the future. They were reasonably safe here from a concerted attack by the Black Police—so long as they were content to remain here and keep hands off the oppressors. But that was far from the *Spider's* intention. He had the nucleus of a strong fighting force and a fair armament for them. Nita had carried off a small arsenal from his home; Chei Hwang-yo had contributed other guns. There were a dozen rifles already in the hunting lodge and, in addition, two submachine guns. With discipline established, and the men trained in marksmanship, they should be able to defend themselves adequately.

But all that would take time. Meanwhile the oppressors were gaining in strength, the criminal Master was cementing his power in the cities and people were being tortured, stripped of their meager wealth. With the urgency of his thoughts, Wentworth stirred restlessly in the bunk to which the weakness of his wound confined him. As soon as he could regain his strength, he must leave this organization and fortification to others, to Kirkpatrick. For himself, he must push on with the ceaseless warfare to which he had eternally dedicated himself. He must find and destroy the Master. He must snatch their victims from the Black Police.

Already he was convinced that no single, sharp blow could smash the swiftly waxing power of the criminals. Here, in these fastnesses, they would assemble an army that would end by destroying Whiting and Culkin and their murderous Black Police!

Nita's voice called to him cheerfully, and he rolled his head to see her entering with a great armload of spruce with which she began to decorate the barren, rough hewn logs of the walls. The fresh cold of the high altitudes, against which a fire blazed on the field-stone hearth, had brought warm color to Nita's cheeks.

"I think the people are completely happy," she called to him. "It's like something out of the past—Robin Hood in the green forest of Sherwood." She crossed to him. "Only, Robin is wounded and out of the battle."

A smile softened Wentworth's lips, but grimness lay darkly in his eyes. "The feudal lords of those days never mistreated the serfs any more cruelly than the Black Police do in these days," he said somberly. "I'm afraid our task is more difficult, too. Robin Hood at least knew whom he had to defeat. It won't accomplish much to battle against the Black Police, unless we can learn the identity of the Master and crush him. And this confounded shoulder of mine. . ."

Nita bent toward him. "The work doesn't need to stop, Dick," she said urgently. "You can accomplish a thousand times more by remaining here in the hills until you get your strength. You can plan for the men, send out spies. I'll go myself."

Wentworth moved impatiently. It must be so, until he could recover from this wound.

BUT the days that followed were torture for him. News began to trickle in, from the men they sent out and over the circumscribed press broadcasts of the radio. Three big concentration camps had been established by the Black Police and already were jammed to overflowing. The suffering of the people aroused Wentworth to fury. But he could do nothing, nothing, until his magnificent body had mended itself.

The fireman, Frank Connors, was sending a constant stream of information through the contact Wentworth had established.

Under the stringent new tax laws, the people were being drained of their resources, tortured and beaten when they resisted. And Mayor

Culkin had devised a new means of extorting money. Wentworth heard his oily voice over the radio as he proclaimed the "Save-a-Life Relief Fund," with a goal of ten million dollars!

"This state takes care of its own unemployed and poverty-stricken," Mayor Culkin intoned. "Its citizens are generous—very. In raising this great fund, there will be no solicitation of the people, no canvassers. We are sure that will not be necessary. Instead, we invite those who wish to make gifts to come to City Hall Square and turn in their contributions in person. To each person will be given the Order of the Purple Cross, a medal which we are going to ask all donors to wear prominently. On the back of each medal will be stamped the amount of each man's gift. . ."

Wentworth swore harshly as the mayor's smooth voice rolled on. "That's the most diabolical thing I ever heard," he said sharply. "You see what he intends? His Black Police will patrol the town, and every person who doesn't wear that Purple Cross will be persecuted! Furthermore, they'll be afraid to make small contributions because the amount is to be stamped on the medal! And all very neat and within the law. Mayor Culkin, the Black Police, and the Master, will have ten million dollars to play with!"

Kirkpatrick's own lips were grimly set. "It's time we took some action, Dick," he said. "Though, I'll admit, I don't see what we can hope to accomplish against Mayor Culkin and his Purple Cross campaign!"

Wentworth stood and deliberately loosened the sling from his right arm. His face went white with pain as he lowered it to his side.

"Not you, Dick!" Kirkpatrick said sharply. "You're not strong enough for it yet."

Wentworth's pallor came from more than pain. His voice was strained, subdued. "I'm afraid you're right," he said, "but no more can you make an attack in force on Culkin and the Black Police. We aren't ready yet. I have the beginning of a plan. We'll need money, arms, more men. . . and by heavens, the Black Police shall supply us with what we need—the arms and money. For the men, there are the concentration camps!"

The men grouped about the fire in the big main room of the camp had fallen silent, but at Wentworth's words they broke into a cheer. Wentworth smiled at them, turned to Kirkpatrick.

"We've been idle too long," he said, in an undertone. "We've information here we can work on. The monthly payroll of the Black Police will be assembled in Albany tomorrow. We'll steal that—and use it to defeat them! There has been a police arsenal assembled in New York City. We'll loot that! Then smash open the concentration camp nearest the city, arm the men. . ."

"And seize control of the city government!" Kirkpatrick cried.

Wentworth shook his head. "Useless, unless we can identify the Master and eliminate him," he said. "Governor Whiting would send the national guard against us. We couldn't fight them. They're not criminals like the Black Police. They're honest men like your own cops, doing their duty."

Kirkpatrick frowned heavily. "Then what can we accomplish, aside from harassing them?"

Wentworth smiled, leaned closer, "The loss of their loot will do more to disrupt the Black Police than any amount of sniping we can do!" he said. "What we'll do is to seize that ten million and give it back to the people from whom it was stolen!"

THANKS to the men he had sent out as spies, Wentworth had a very complete picture of the handling of the Black Police monthly payroll. It was distributed from Albany. Each substation of the police sent two men to the capital and it was their job to return the money to the stations. For the work, Wentworth chose the men who had been snatched from the gallows and some of those who had been flogged. He addressed them privately.

"I am choosing men who know the true nature of those we fight," he told the ten he had chosen, "for this reason. When we reach Albany, we will scatter. It will be each man's job to get a Black Police uniform. Any of you who has scruples against. . . attacking one of the Black Police may be excused now."

Wentworth's keen eyes swept the faces of the men assembled before him and the grimness of them gave him his answer, even without the low, angry murmur of assent.

"Very well," he agreed. "We are going in one truck. If police stop us, that will reduce the labor of our search for uniforms by so much."

Sailor Joe was one of those Wentworth had chosen, and he threw back his head in a deep-throated laugh. "I like the talk of you, sir. I'll vow I do!"

Wentworth laughed with him. "You are brave men," he said finally. "You have suffered. Tonight, you will have a chance to avenge yourselves somewhat. But remember this. I must have obedience, complete and absolute. I do not threaten you. But I warn you this: The slightest delay in following a command may doom us all." In spite of the necessity of carrying his arm in a sling, Wentworth was determined to lead this first foray against the enemy himself, both for the sake of the morale of the men and to be sure that nothing went wrong. If they failed in this first attempt, it would seriously damage the spirit of the whole group. He had trained the men as carefully as possible. They had been drilled like soldiers by Jackson and Kirkpatrick and trained to shoot with deadly accuracy.

Wentworth rode in the cab beside the driver as the truck trundled off toward Albany, and it was already twilight when they began to roll into the city's outskirts. Wentworth stopped the truck then, spoke briefly to the men.

"As soon as you get uniforms, put them on," he ordered. "I'll expect you all to meet me in one hour at the place you know. If any is delayed longer than that, he will have to make his way back to the camp as best he can. We cannot wait."

There was a low murmur of assent from the men and they scattered into the early dusk except for Sailor Joe who would remain with Wentworth. At Wentworth's signal, the driver of the truck turned about and headed back for the hills. Watching it go, Wentworth knew a curious sense of desertion. That was the last link that bound them to the safety of their mountain encampment. From this point, they were on their own.

Sailor Joe growled, "Orders, sir?"

"Find some of the Black Police!"

Side by side, they walked rapidly toward the center of the city. Once, an armored truck patrol passed at high speed, and they had a glimpse of black uniforms within. Sailor Joe swore under his breath, but Wentworth shook his head. This was not at all what they were looking for.

It was a half dozen blocks farther on that they heard a woman scream, and Wentworth's left hand closed on Sailor Joe's arm.

"I think we've found our quota of Black Police!" he said softly.

They rounded a corner toward the sound, and Wentworth spotted the armored truck parked before an elaborate residence. The woman cried out again in hysterical pleading. The door of the house stood open and light laid in a yellow trapezoid on the stone steps. A black-uniformed guard lounged in the doorway and there was another on the truck.

"Four inside the house," Wentworth said softly. "Joe, you go straight ahead along this side of the street and double up behind the truck. Take the driver without shooting if you can. I'll handle the man in the door. . ."

"And then, sir?"

Wentworth smiled thinly, "I think we'll pay a surprise visit to the gentlemen inside!"

Sailor Joe's voice was hearty. "Aye sir!"

THEY separated, and Wentworth walked steadily toward the house. A man screamed tearingly, and the woman's broken pleading went on and on. Wentworth felt his lips tightening. He had to force himself to a slower pace. He must give Sailor Joe time to reach the truck unobserved. So far, the Black Police guard had paid no attention to his approach. It told, more plainly than any words, how little they had to fear from most of the citizenry.

Wentworth was within twenty feet of the steps to the house before the guard spotted him. "Hey, you!" he called out roughly. "What you doing sneaking up in the dark?"

"I didn't mean to sneak." Wentworth said humbly. "I was just walking by."

"Walking by, huh?" the man snarled. "You come up here and give an account of yourself!"

That suited Wentworth exactly, but the continued cries from within were drawing his nerves taut. He could hear the sickening sound of a whip striking flesh. He went up the steps slowly, cringingly. Up his left sleeve, he carried a blackjack with its loop about his wrist. If he could get close enough. . . Out of his eye corners, he saw the driver of the armored truck peering toward him. That was fine for Sailor Joe. If they could only time their attack together. . .

"Hurry up, you!" the guard said raspingly. He knotted his fist threateningly. "How much money you got?"

"None at all," Wentworth said with what sounded like abject fright. "The tax collector was at my house today. . ."

He caught the sound of a deadened blow in the direction of the truck. The guard whipped his head that way and, in the same instant, Wentworth sprang forward. The blackjack slid out of his sleeve and its weight across his palm was good. The guard uttered a startled shout, grabbed for his holstered gun and Wentworth drove the blackjack home to his skull.

Wentworth glanced up, and Sailor Joe's round, ruddy face was grinning at him from the cab of the truck. "Nice work, sir!" he whispered. "This bird won't bother nobody again!"

"Into the truck," Wentworth snapped. "Quickly." He seized the collar of the guard and dragged him forward. Sailor Joe caught up the body and heaved it callously into the back of the truck. "And he won't bother nobody neither. Well, there's our two uniforms."

Wentworth was already facing toward the house. "Yes," he said softly. "But some of our men may not be so. fortunate. I think there are four men who shouldn't be needing their uniforms much longer!"

Wentworth slid his automatic into his left hand, for he still carried his right in a sling. "Just follow me," he said, and led the way silently into the house. The man's voice broke out in a sudden, broken cry. "In God's name, leave my wife alone! I've given you my last cent! I swear there's not another penny. . . Ooh!" It was a gasp of agony, and it echoed the meaty thud of the whip.

Wentworth was in the main hallway of the house and the sound came from a lighted doorway to the rear. He moved toward it softly; Sailor Joe whispered oaths at his elbow. A moment later, he was peering cautiously into the room, and the thing he saw ripped from him all thought of caution.

A woman, stripped of her clothing, was dangling unconscious from ropes that, bound to her thumbs, had been looped over a door. Her back was laced with crimson whip welts. The man was on his knees before an officer of the Black Police who gripped a stained whip. There was blood on the man's face and on his back. Three other police lounged in evident enjoyment in chairs tipped back against the wall.

"I'll rip the skin off her back, if you don't cough up," the officer said. He drew back the whip again. . . and it was then Wentworth acted.

He sprang into the room and fired in the same instant. The heavy bullet smashed between the officer's eyes and blew him kicking against the wall. Simultaneously, Sailor Joe opened fire. There was a brief thunderous crashing of guns, and then Sailor Joe was lifting the woman tenderly down from her torture rack.

"I'm afraid, sir," he said hoarsely, "that I ruined one of them uniforms!"

The man looked up with dazed eyes, "In God's, name," he whispered. "What have you done? They'll murder us now!"

Wentworth's lips were tight with fury. "Have you a car?" he asked harshly. "Can you drive?"

The man shook his head. "I could drive, yes, but I have no car. Nothing."

"Doctor her up as best you can," Wentworth told him gently. "Get yourself a car and drive to Numbersville. Here's money to buy the car, but make it fast. Take these men's guns with you."

The man stared at the money, took it slowly. "Thank you. Oh, thank you!" he sobbed. "But I don't understand!"

Wentworth forced his lips to relax in a smile. "I'm Richard Wentworth," he said. "There will be safety for you in Numbersville. My men will come for you. Joe, cart out these uniforms. Leave the bodies here."

When the three had gone from the room, Wentworth fingered out a cigarette lighter from his pocket. If these people ever talked, the thing he was about to do would doom him. But the Black Police must feel terror, too—the terror of reprisals! He would frame some story to cover it. He stooped rapidly beside the dead men and, on the forehead of each, he imprinted the burning red seal of the *Spider*!

Swiftly, then he hurried from the house. Sailor Joe was at the wheel of the truck, clad in one of the uniforms and Wentworth swiftly donned another of them.

H E KNEW it was madness to tempt the fates further in this town overridden by brutal forces who had, at their command, all the strength of the law. But the scene he had just witnessed, drove Wentworth beyond caution.

Further examples of the police brutality were not far to seek. They had not driven a dozen blocks before, once more, cries and the vicious thwack of whips caught Wentworth's ear. They turned a corner and, two hundred yards away, caught sight of a piteous procession. A dozen men and women, fastened together in single file with chains about their necks, were being herded along the street by three Black Police on horseback. The first man in the chained procession was being forced to carry a placard on which a small attached light was focused. As Wentworth sent the truck toward them, he made out the legend upon it, painted in fiery red letters, *We didn't pay the tax. We are going to the slackers' camp.*

"The concentration camp." Sailor Joe mumbled. "That's where they're going. Do we take them, sir?"

As Wentworth hesitated, one of the Black Police deliberately spurred his horse against that marching line and rode one of the men to the ground. Two others were dragged down by their chains and, at once, one of the other two police leaped to the ground and began to belabor them with his whip until the victims staggered to their feet.

"Yes," said Wentworth harshly, "We take them! Show them the same mercy they show those poor wretches. As soon as you are along-side of them, stop the truck and shoot. I don't imagine gunshots in this town attract much attention. If they do—well, we are the Black Police!"

A few seconds later, Sailor Joe pulled the truck to a halt. He fired once; Wentworth twice. The chained prisoners stared at them with frightened eyes. Wentworth hurriedly searched the Black Police who wore a sergeant's chevrons and found the keys to their shackles, freed the leading man.

"Unlock the others," he ordered curtly. "Here is money. We'll leave you these men's guns. Get hold of cars and go to Numbersville. You will be protected. If anyone asks who freed you, tell them what you saw."

Wentworth stooped and, on the forehead of the dead sergeant, ground in the seal of the *Spider*!

"The *Spider*!" the man gabbled. "The *Spider*! Oh, thank God. We have needed a leader—"

"*Hurry!*" Wentworth ordered. When he turned back to the truck, Sailor Joe had already stripped off two of the uniforms and loaded them aboard. He stared at Wentworth with a half-frightened look in his usually cheerful eyes.

"The *Spider*?" he said slowly. "You. . . the *Spider*?"

"I know the *Spider*," Wentworth told him quietly. "He has given me the right to use his seal. It is something the Black Police can under-stand. Soon, you will be given the right to use that seal, too. Every man I can trust shall have that seal! We'll put the fear of God in these Black Police!"

Sailor Joe chuckled, though its note was a little uncertain. "Fear of God, huh? I'd call it the fear of sudden death and the *Spider*!"

Wentworth's lips felt as if they would never again relax in a smile. He said curtly, "We have three minutes to make the rendezvous. And there is still the police payroll to be seized!"

CHAPTER TWELVE

DISCIPLES OF HELL

O F THE eight men who had set out to acquire uniforms of the Black Police, six came to the rendezvous with their loot. The seventh reported to Wentworth, his face white and drawn.

"We got our men all right, sir," he said, "then an armored car came up. Martin was killed. I managed to escape—but without the uniform."

Wentworth's lips drew out thinly. "I'm sorry for that," he said quietly. "Martin will be avenged within the hour! You'll find an extra uniform in the back of the car. Hurry. Our time is drawing short!"

If the courage of any of the men was shaken by the casualty, they did not show it. Rather, they were more grimly determined than before. Wentworth hurried them all into the body of the armored truck and, Sailor Joe at the wheel, they sped toward the payoff headquarters of the Black Police. Wentworth entered the back with them.

"This should be simple," he said quietly, "but there is a fair chance that some of us will be shot, so play it cautiously. We will go into the headquarters in a body. As I understand the layout, there are two offices connected by a wicket through which the payrolls of the various stations are passed. The bulk of men will be in the outer room. Five of you, under Sailor Joe, will guard that room, from outside. Shoot anyone who tries to get out. I'll take the other three men and force the door on the payroll room. It will be better not to leave anyone in the truck, but, at the first shot, Sailor Joe will send a man to start the engine."

He looked slowly from face to face then but failed to detect any sign of weakness. A smile moved his stern lips. "You'll do," he said. "If anyone is hit, he is to be carried by the others to the truck. The chief risk will be for the three men who go with me. I'll ask for volunteers. Just raise your hands."

If there was any disparity in time among the unanimous lifting of hands, Wentworth failed to spot it. He nodded his approval and made his choice just as the truck slowed at the entrance of a barracks-like brick building. One of the Black Police was lolling in the door, smoking. No one else was in sight, but through a window, Wentworth saw a dozen uniformed men lolling about a large room. He frowned at that. Their getaway would be in plain sight through that window. It couldn't be helped now.

As he swung to the ground, he stopped to speak to Sailor Joe. "Take that man at the door," he said shortly. "Post one of your men in his place. He is to shoot anyone who shows at that window after we begin our attack."

Sailor Joe nodded calmly and the men climbed down leisurely from the truck

Wentworth moved ahead, stopping to light a cigarette before he went toward the entrance. He nodded to the guard at the door.

"Getting cold," he remarked and went on past.

The guard grunted. "Damn cold, if you have to stand out here." He turned to glance at Wentworth and that was the moment Sailor Joe struck.

"Tuck this in the bushes," he said shortly to two of his men. "It won't be waking up any time soon." He singled out the man whose partner had been killed. "You stick right here and play guard. After the shooting starts, you nail anybody who tries to get through that window. Remember what they did to Martin!"

Wentworth was relieved to find the corridor empty and went straight toward the door which led into the paymaster's office. The three men he had chosen were at his heels and bunched behind him as he bent to the keyhole with his lock pick. It revolved silently and, hand on the knob, Wentworth lifted his head and looked about him. His three men were ready, guns in hand. Sailor Joe and the three men with him were alert by the entrance to the main room.

"All right," Wentworth said quietly. "Here we go. Don't shoot unless you have to. But don't hesitate if someone yells or goes for a gun. And shoot straight."

HE OPENED the door and stepped into the paymaster's office. Three men were busy counting out money at a long table while an armed guard leaned against the far wall. Wentworth reached him in a long stride and slammed his automatic against the man's head. He went down without a sound, and Wentworth wheeled toward the others. His men had followed suit and two of the pay-counters were down. The fourth man, the paymaster, shouted out a startled oath and snatched at an under-arm gun. Wentworth threw his automatic, accurately, and, as the paymaster slumped to the floor, Wentworth brushed some silver money to the floor.

"Damn you!" he shouted in a hoarse imitation of the paymaster's voice. "Look what you're doing. Now, pick up every cent of that money!"

Someone rapped imperatively at the wicket, and Wentworth caught up his automatic and reached the window in a bound, slammed it up. With his body, he blocked the view of the room beyond where his men were scooping the money into sacks.

"Don't be so damned impatient!" Wentworth snarled at the Black Policeman who had rapped at the window. "You'll get your money. It's a pity they wouldn't give me somebody who could do this kind of work, instead of punks who knock all the money on the floor!"

The Black officer backed up, lifting his hands. "All right, all right." he said. "I thought I heard somebody yell!"

"I yelled!" Wentworth snapped at him. "One of those damned fools dropped the money!" He slammed down the window, turned to his men. "*Quickly!*" he whispered. "This is going too smoothly. Something…"

Like an exclamation point to his words, a gun crashed out in the hallway. The last of the money was being thrust into the sacks. Wentworth reached the door in a bound. More guns were hammering out there now, the corridor full of their crashing thunder. In the front room, men were shouting and their feet stamped hard as they rushed for the door. Wentworth peered out. Sailor Joe and another man were standing back to each side of the door, guns ready, silent and waiting.

"Fire through the door," Wentworth called, "but don't empty your guns!"

Sailor Joe nodded, and began a deliberate fire.

A hand touched Wentworth on the shoulder, "All ready here, sir."

"Good!" Wentworth stepped out into the hall. "Each of you fire three shots through the door as you go past, but go past there fast!"

He raced along the hallway. "Outside, Joe, and cover that window. Man at the truck?"

Sailor Joe nodded and leaped for the door. Wentworth took up his post, and the money carriers leaped past, guns in hand.

Their bullets sieved the door. But the police inside were firing now. The last man, leaping past, stumbled and staggered against the wall. His gun dropped from his hand, but he reeled on, clutching the money bag. His right arm dangled. Wentworth caught up the weapon and kept his post, firing at deliberate intervals until his piercing glance showed that all save himself and Sailor Joe were on the truck. Then he sprang for the steps, slammed the main doors of the building behind him.

"*Fast, Joe!*" he snapped. "On the truck there! Fire at the window!"

A DISTANT siren was beginning to wail, but under the cover of the gunfire from the truck, Wentworth and Joe made good their escape. The moment they were aboard, the armored truck leaped forward. Once out of the immediate neighborhood, they would be safe.

The survivors of that ripping gunfire would know only that men in their own uniform had committed the robbery. It would be hours before they learned that their own men were not responsible, and by that time this little band would be safe in the hills!

Sailor Joe squatted stolidly beside him. "Sorry about that shooting, Mr. Wentworth. Couldn't be helped, sir. Four of them got suspicious after that yell and were trying to sneak out the door. We blew them back."

The other men laughed, and even the youngster with the broken arm managed a smile. When they roared clear of the city limits and began the race for the hills, they began to sing softly. Wentworth gathered the money together.

"This will buy a lot of arms to fight the Black Police," he said gravely, "and help many a poor soul the Black Police have robbed. And about that next raid, Joe. . ."

The singing stopped and the men were instantly listening. Wentworth could feel their waiting. He smiled and there was pride in his eyes—pride in the loyalty of these men who were eager to risk their lives in his service.

"I don't exactly approve of these concentration camps," Wentworth said softly. "I was thinking we might smash one open and turn the people free."

For a moment after he finished speaking, there was absolute silence, then Sailor Joe threw back his head in a mighty laughter. The others joined heartily and raised a ragged cheer.

"*We'll fight the Black Police off the map!*" they cried.

IT WAS after midnight when, rolling up the mountain road toward the camp, they were challenged by the alert sentries. Wentworth's call lifted a cheer of welcome and, when they reached the camp, they found an elaborate table spread in the main drawing-room and the entire group assembled. And yet a tension held the room, waiting as the men filed in one after another. Wentworth walked straight to the head of the table and poured a glass of wine which he lifted. "To a hero who died in line of duty," he said quietly. "To Martin."

They drank that toast in silence, and Wentworth shattered the glass on the table's edge and set the broken stem upon the mantel above the great stone fireplace. "Five thousand dollars will be given to Martin's heirs," he said then. "Dugan was wounded. A five-hundred-dollar bonus to him. Martin did not go unavenged. We will probably never know the casualty list of the Black Police for tonight. They won't be eager to publicize it, but at least a dozen of them died!"

Sailor Joe walked up to the table with his rolling stride, picked up a glass. "By your leave, sir," he said. "Here's another toast. I'm giving you, pals. . . the next man to die for the cause! And if it's me—hell, just split the five thousand among you and drink her up. Sailor Joe'll be drinking with you!"

They laughed then and thronged to the table, and not until then did Nita come to Wentworth's side. Her hand clung to his. Kirkpatrick crossed and laid a hand on his shoulder.

"Now what?" he asked quietly.

"Double the guards," Wentworth said grimly. "It's time to set up those lookouts on the surrounding hills with signal fires ready to light, in case of invasion. We must send a truck to Numbersville. I sent fourteen victims of the Black Police there. And I think our best defense will be to press on with our attacks. A raid on the police armory in Burnton is in order. We must smash open a concentration camp, arm the prisoners and turn them loose to harass the Black Police. From now on, we must be doubly careful about admitting any new recruit to the camp. And a week from today. . . we'll take that ten million away from the Black Police in New York City. On the last day of their 'Save-a-Life' drive."

"It's an ambitious campaign," Kirkpatrick said slowly. "What about the Master?"

Wentworth shook his head. "When we have disrupted the Black Police, I hope he will be forced into the open. And when he is. . ." Wentworth's eyes met those of Kirkpatrick and the smiles that touched their faces were curiously alike, bitter with the promise of death.

KIRKPATRICK handled the raid on the arsenal in Burnton successfully. He returned with three trucks loaded with revolvers, rifles and sub-machine guns, together with ammunition. But three broken glasses were added to the one that stood on the stone mantel.

Wentworth conducted the raid on the concentration camp. He mounted himself, Sailor Joe and Jackson upon horses and they took with them a dozen men, all veterans of their previous battles. They walked ahead of the horses, shackled together like weary prisoners, but the locks of their chains were not fastened and, under his clothing, each man carried two revolvers and extra ammunition. A truck followed behind with a hundred guns and ammunition for those Wentworth expected to free.

Twice on the way to the camp they ran into roving patrols of Black Police but they escaped suspicion and marched up to the barbed-wire barriers of the slattern camp in late afternoon. Wentworth had spied out the territory with great care. He knew that there were twenty Black Police stationed here to watch over three hundred prisoners, but only a third of them would be on guard at a time. It was the mounted machine guns, lifted on wooden towers outside the fences, which gave them control.

There was a perilous moment at the gates when the two guards stationed there started forward to search the new prisoners. Wentworth and Sailor Joe drove their horses up so that they blocked out the view of the machine gunners and leveled their automatics at the guards.

"Keep your mouth shut," Wentworth ordered harshly, "or you die!"

Jackson swung down off his horse and disarmed them, thrust their guns out of sight under his coat. At his orders, the two guards marched inside the barrier with the twelve "prisoners"—and left the gate unlocked.

Wentworth dared not wait for the results there. Jackson had his orders. He was to take the two Black Police inside the nearest building and there they would be overpowered and bound. Wentworth wheeled his horse toward the headquarters building, outside the barrier, and Sailor Joe followed. They had timed their arrival carefully for a few minutes before the change of the guard. Already the armored truck, with the two extra men Wentworth needed for his plans, was trundling into sight from the woods road a few hundred yards away.

At the door, Wentworth and Sailor Joe swung from their horses and moved carelessly toward the entrance. There should be not more than eight men in the main wardroom; the others should be off-guard and asleep in the adjoining bunk-house. Wentworth stole a single glance toward the prisoners' barricade. Jackson and two other men in Black Police uniform were moving toward the gates. That would be two of Wentworth's men in the clothing of the overpowered guards. So far, everything was moving smoothly.

Wentworth pushed open the door and went in, with Sailor Joe close behind him. Instantly, he whipped out his automatic and covered the eight men. Three of them were just pulling on coats for the guard change. The others were ready, but lounging carelessly about, and they were taken completely by surprise.

"The first man who moves gets his head blown off," Wentworth said crisply. "Your entire camp is surrounded with my men. *The Spider speaking!*"

Sailor Joe was already in action. He reached the side of the officer-in-command, in two strides, and cracked his gun against the man's skull. "If you want the same medicine, punks," he said, "just wiggle a finger. That's all, just wiggle a finger!" He snatched down shackles from pegs on the wall and rapidly linked the men together, gagged them. In the midst of the work, the truck snorted to a halt outside and Wentworth's two extra men came in with Jackson just behind them. "Into the bunkhouse, fast!" Wentworth snapped. "No time to tie them up. We've got to change the guard on time. Slug them. Hurry!"

Jackson and the two men darted through the door into the next room. There was a slight scuffling noise, a single muted cry, and then they were hurrying back. Wentworth looked them over quickly, nodded.

"All right," he said. "There's no formality about guard change here. You four men just saunter out and go toward the four machine-gun towers. Usually, the men on watch start to climb down before you reach them. Keep an eye on each other. As soon as all four men have started down, shoot them! Jackson is in command. All of you wait for his shot as a signal. Make sure you don't need a second shot. If one of them manages to reach his machine gun, there'll be more broken glasses on the mantel. All right. *March!*"

WENTWORTH watched them file carelessly out of the door, then drew his automatic and stood near a window where he could watch the four towers. Two of the guards already had started down from their machine-gun towers, but the other two were slow. Wentworth saw Jackson and Sailor Joe quicken their stride toward those two. This was the dangerous moment. The guards would know their relief men and, once Wentworth's men approached closely enough to be recognized, the trick would be discovered. And still the two guards remained in their towers! Wentworth could see one of them dimly through the side window, and he slowly lifted his automatic. The first two men had reached the ground and were turning toward their relief. Jackson broke into a run, reached the foot of the tower for which he was heading. Without a moment's pause, he whipped out his automatic and fired straight up into the tower!

Wentworth nodded and, at the same instant, fired on the one guard that he could see—the one toward whom Sailor Joe was racing. There was a brief burst of shots, then silence. Wentworth threw a quick, comprehensive glance over the scene. The two guards who had descended their towers were prone on the ground. Jackson signaled with a wave of his hand that his man was taken care of. Sailor Joe was swarming up toward his objective and, a moment later, signaled also. Wentworth's shot had sped true.

On the instant, the men Wentworth had planted within the stockade, burst out of hiding and the work of freeing the prisoners began. It was furious, frantic labor. Wentworth and his men must be back in the hills before a report of this was made and the patrols took the roads. When the prisoners all had been assembled outside the gate, Wentworth mounted to the truck and addressed them.

"I have weapons here for a hundred of you," he said briskly. "You will know how to use them! Each of you will be given fifty dollars. Scatter as quickly as possible. I ask only one thing of you, in return for this. Fight the Black Police wherever you go. Some of you will fight your way across the borders of the state. Spread word as to what was done to you. And one other thing. . . Help each other. If you see someone oppressed by the Black Police, and can help him, do it. If a man comes to you from me, help him!"

Wentworth paused and a murmur ran over the prisoners, became a shout, a cheer.

"You will always know my men," Wentworth went on, more slowly, "for each one will carry with him a token—like this." He reached behind him into the truck and held up a scroll which he unfurled. On it was emblazoned the scarlet seal of the *Spider*!

The cheer that rose then echoed against the surrounding hills.

His men sprang swiftly to work.

The crowd was shaped into two long files to which, as they passed the tailgate of the truck, money and guns and ammunition were handed out. Others of Wentworth's men were swiftly dismounting the machine guns, assembling ammunition and supplies. Two hours after the first shot had been fired, they were heading toward the hills and comparative safety. Behind them, the released fugitives were already scattering. Some would undoubtedly be recaptured, and Wentworth dreaded to think of their fate. But more would break free.

They were within a half hour of the camp when the radio brought them news that the delivery at the camp had been discovered.

"Governor Whiting has announced a new reward for the outlaw, Richard Wentworth, who calls himself the *Spider*," the announcer said. "To the ten thousand dollars already offered for his capture, dead or alive, the governor himself will add an additional fifty thousand dollars—dead or alive."

The announcer went in. "In the emergency, and because of numerous depredations by armed men, Governor Whiting has declared the state under martial law. Hereafter, any man carrying arms without proper permit, or found in possession of arms, shall be considered in armed rebellion against the state. The penalty for armed rebellion is death!"

A grim silence settled over the men in the truck, but Sailor Joe merely chuckled. "The way that guy says it," he said, "you'd think that was something new. Hell, the way I look at it, they can't do no more than kill us! And they've been trying that plenty already! My glass ain't broken yet!"

Laughter rippled over the men then and it was a singing, once more happy squad of men who tramped into the late dinner table in the camp that night. Only Nita's violet eyes were worried.

"Sixty thousand dollars on your head, Dick," she whispered. "Men have forgotten loyalty and gratitude before this for that amount." Her eyes searched and weighed the half hundred men gathered in the hall. "Oh, Dick, where will all this end?"

CHAPTER THIRTEEN

MASTER OF MURDER!

ALTHOUGH Wentworth smiled at Nita's fears of possible betrayal by his own men for the sake of the reward money, he knew the heavy temptation it represented. As long as they were winning, the danger was probably slight, but let the Black Police gain ascendancy for a day or a week, and the situation would be reversed.

During the days that followed, when Wentworth was preparing for the attack upon New York City itself, he kept the men busy improving their quarters and strengthening the fortifications he had thrown up about the camp. A half dozen times, planes cruised low over the hills. At such times, all activity ceased and men remained utterly motionless in the forests. Apparently, they escaped observation.

The radio brought an increasing budget of disorders. The men Wentworth had freed from the concentration camp were striking on all sides. Black Police were waylaid in the course of their duty; a chain gang of prisoners was freed; a sergeant was hanged on the main street of Poughkeepsie. There were reprisals, too. Some of the raiders were captured and hanged. A group of ten was seized in a quarry hide-out near Peekskill and taken to New York City for execution in the public square. Their hanging was announced for the very day Wentworth had set for his raid upon the extorted contributions in City Hall Square. He was determined that they be rescued.

Early on the morning of that day, Wentworth assembled his men in the great main chamber of the camp. His fighting force numbered forty now and all of them had been tested in at least one excursion against the enemy. They presented the appearance of perfectly trained troops, their demeanor quiet and determined. Wentworth felt pride swell within him, and the confidence of his bearing increased. They were a pitiful handful against the ranks of the Black Police, but their morale, the deadly accuracy of their gunfire, made them picked soldiers.

"We will draw lots—" Wentworth began his talk—"for five men to remain in the camp and supplement the Chinese defenders. The rest will be divided in this way. I want five men to carry rifles. It will be their job to mount various roofs and prevent the execution of the ten men scheduled to be hanged. Five more, scattered through the crowd, will attempt to start a riot."

He explained. "The diversion they create will be the signal for our attack upon the guard placed around the money. Concerning the distribution of the remaining twenty-five men, I will give more detailed orders later. A rendezvous will be fixed on the northern boundaries of the city. If any man fails to make that rendezvous on time, there will be a secondary rendezvous and a car hidden for their escape. Any questions?"

None of the men stirred or spoke and Wentworth smiled grimly down upon them from his stand on the steps.

"If we succeed today," he went on quietly, "we will have struck a powerful blow against the Black Police—and won a thousand friends among the people. We will have laid the groundwork for over-throwing the entire crooked government. And you will have a chance soon to return to your homes. Remember that when we meet the enemy this afternoon!"

The cheer that went up was tense and subdued, not through fear, Wentworth knew, but because it was the restrained eagerness of men before battle. When they were loosed upon the enemy, they would strike terribly!

THE hanging of the ten raiders was set for five o'clock in the afternoon and a new gallows had been built upon a platform at the south end of City Hall Square—a long gallows on which ten dying men could swing at one time! It was not accident that the gallows had been built near the collection booth into which the intimidated citizens filed to make their extorted donations to the "Save-A-Life Fund" and receive the telltale Purple Cross which had the amount of each man's "gift" stamped upon its back.

The campaign had all the outward trappings of a charity drive and, silhouetted against that grim gallows, was a representation of a thermometer, twenty feet high, whose high point registered ten million dollars! Every hour, a man in the uniform of the Black Police would mount a ladder beside that thermometer and paint the level of the "mercury" a little higher, creeping up now toward the ten million mark.

All day a long queue of men had shuffled slowly toward the collection booth. With the lateness of the afternoon, that line increased and there were hundreds, thousands of others crowded into the square, watching in sullen silence the slow rising of the thermometer that marked the enormity of the fund wrested from them by intimidation and coercion. It was a cold, blustery day, with thickening clouds overhead and, a little while after four o'clock, a thin scattering of snowflakes began to drift down. At that time, too, a hangman arrived and draped ten ropes over the gallows.

In that thickening crowd, no one would notice the arrival of twenty men in pairs, not remark particularly that they all worked their way slowly toward the collection booth where the thousands of dollars, turned in that day, was kept—and the new-built concrete building behind it where the entire contribution, running now well over nine million dollars, was stored under guard. The men waiting sullenly in line to make their contributions did not resist when two men silently wedged their way into the queue ahead of them. They were in no hurry to surrender their money in exchange for that hateful tin medal which alone could gain them temporary surcease from persecution. If these two fools were in a hurry, let them go first!

Wentworth had calculated his place in the queue to a nicety. He wanted to move into the booth at the same time his men opened fire on the gallows guards. It would not be long now. Already, the usual guard of mounted Black Police was assembling. At sight of them, an angry murmur ran through the crowd, but it was soon muted. Terror rode the people of the city too sternly. Wentworth had difficulty in maintaining the stooping, cringing posture he had assumed. Jackson, behind him, muttered an oath.

"Our time will come later," Wentworth reminded him softly. "Do you know if everyone is here?"

Jackson shook his head. "I've spotted a few people we know," he said, referring cryptically to their assembling force.

Wentworth let his eyes sweep the crowd. He heard a renewed murmur and saw the tumbrel of this new revolution trundling down Broadway toward the gallows. Time was drawing short. Within ten minutes at most, his men would open fire from the roofs of surrounding buildings—unless his plans had miscarried. It had been necessary to separate his force into units of two, send them to the city separately. But he could count on his men.

His mind returned fleetingly to Nita's warning of a few days before—the temptation of the sixty thousand dollars that had been placed on his head. He had given any of the men an ideal opportunity to betray him today. But he had no real fear. There was no reason for this nervous restlessness that goaded him, except the anxiety for battle. That was what Wentworth told himself, but there was a coldness that dragged intermittently up his spine.

He was glad that Jackson stood guard on his back.

The tumbrel had reached the gallows now and the ten captives were visible, their faces pale blurs against the gathering dusk. Abruptly, a brilliant light blazed over the gallows and Wentworth smiled grimly. The Black Police were determined that the crowd should miss no atom of this reprisal, but they would be sealing their own death warrant! From the loud-speaker attachment in the collection booth, from which exhortations to greater gifts had been voiced from time to time, a man began to tell of the crimes of the ten prisoners. He was driving home the penalty for armed resistance to the authorities.

WENTWORTH watched the faces of the crowd. Anger there, but it was sullen. They were terrified. The hangings would have their effect. . . if they were carried out. Wentworth's eyes quested beyond the crowd toward the street and, abruptly, he stiffened. Wasn't that one of his men with the Black Police hurrying along beside the queue of waiting citizens? Jackson's hand closed on his arm from behind.

"The reward," he whispered. "That's Megley there with the Black Police!"

Wentworth swore under his breath. The speaker was talking on and on, and the queue was not moving at all. Over there by the gallows, everything was at a standstill until the speech was finished. He did not want to start the raid until the diversion at the gallows had been begun.

Jackson said, "I'll attend to this!" Before Wentworth could protest, Jackson had slipped from his place in the line and was starting toward the tall thermometer. Within seconds, he was scaling the ladder beside it. Men's faces turned white and questioning up toward him, but Jackson's eyes were focused beyond them. He had a clear view now of the Black Police—and the traitor with them.

"*Megley!*" Jackson called sharply.

For a moment the man froze amid his guardian force of Black Police. That was what Jackson wanted. On the instant, his gun blasted in his hand—three swift shots. Megley's scream rose hoarsely into the dusk, and Jackson slid down the ladder, darted away into the crowd toward the gallows. The bullets of the Black Police sang toward the spot where he had been, but they were seconds late. A series of black smears that were bullet holes marked the bright new paint of the thermometer.

The speaker in the collection booth had stopped abruptly. Fear ran its trembling course through the crowd. Men began to shrink back. On the outskirts, a few began to run away. They had learned by experience what reprisals the Black Police could inflict. Wentworth held his place in the line. . . and then he heard the faint, whip-like crack of a distant rifle and over there on the gallows platform, the hangman collapsed with a bullet through his breast!

Black Police were violently pursuing Jackson. A squadron of the mounted officers urged their horses forward into the crowd in an attempt to locate him. But the distant rifles were making a steady crepitation now. Among the mounted gallows guard, men were dropping from their saddles. Part of the group guarding the collection booth, broke into a dogtrot for the gallows, striking callously through the waiting crowd, hurling men from their paths.

It was the moment for which Wentworth had waited. He left his place in line and walked quietly toward the collection booth. Attention was centered on the gallows and the confusion around it, and Wentworth reached the door of the booth without being noticed.

He peered inside, cautiously. Five men there, all of them crowded against the rear window to peer toward the gallows and the excitement. Wentworth sprang inside with two automatics in his fists and began to fire. Only one of the men managed to pull his gun, and his bullet went wide as Wentworth slammed lead into his chest. Outside the booth, other guns were blasting now. A glance showed Wentworth that ten of his men were closing in on the concrete storehouse which was a mere projection of the one in which he stood. Three of his men sprang in through the doors.

"Orders, sir?" snapped a cheerful voice, and Wentworth could have cheered at the matter-of-fact manner of Sailor Joe.

"Scoop up the money," he ordered swiftly. "Get other boys in here to go through into the storehouse. Grab all currency. Ignore anything else. The guard set outside?"

Sailor Joe nodded, winked. "Me and another lad had to crimp one of these nosey Black Police. It just happened he carried a sub-machine gun. If those Black Police rush us, a lot of them won't never rush again!"

Wentworth sprang to the loud-speaker and switched it on. "Your money is being taken away from the Black Police!" he said swiftly, and his voice went booming out over the crowd. "It will be returned to you, on the evidence of your medals within a week or two at most— and in a way that the Black Police cannot trace! Rise against your oppressors! Attack the Black Police on sight! They must be overthrown or our state will perish!"

He told them, "We must fly now! Your money is going to be given back to you instead of wasted upon the Black Police and their criminal masters. *The Spider swears it!*"

FOR a moment after he had finished, there was absolute silence outside where the crowd huddled fearfully in the smother of falling snow, then a cheer started. It was feeble at first, then it roared out irresistibly. It swelled until its volume shook the night and drowned out even the harsh hammer of blasting guns. More of Wentworth's men were darting inside the collection hut now, into the concrete chamber behind—and fleeing, moments later, with a heavy bag of money swung; over their own shoulders. "Cars on the east side of the park," Wentworth snapped, as they fled past him. "Shoot any man who tries to stop you! Quickly now!"

Wentworth crouched by the rear window. The shouting crowd was milling in the path of Black Police who were attempting to charge through the mob with their horses. One of them was pulled from his saddle, and his scream rose thin and piercing even above the mob roar. The rifles were still at their work, for man after man pitched from his saddle. The gallows platform was empty now and, as Wentworth watched, he saw the tumbrel lurch into motion. Men swarmed swiftly into the rear of the truck with guns blasting in their hands—and they did not wear the uniforms of the Black Police!

A touch on Wentworth's arm wheeled him about. "The money's out, sir," Sailor Joe reported. "Better go now, sir."

Wentworth nodded. "Call off the guard outside. If necessary, they are to throw away their guns and mingle with the crowd. They know the rendezvous." He turned toward the door and a choked cry rose in his throat. A man in the uniform of a Black Policeman, his face smeared with blood, swayed on the sill. In his hands, he clenched a sub-machine gun.

"Freeze, damn you," he whispered. "Don't try to move. There's sixty thousand dollars on your head and, by God, I'm claiming it."

Wentworth had holstered his gun; his men were gone. And that gaping muzzle that could spit bloody death was centered squarely on his body. A single slight pressure on the trigger and he would be riddled with bullets.

Wentworth smiled slowly. "Go ahead and shoot," he said quietly. He was playing desperately for time, without hope, without any real plan. Sailor Joe, beside him, was tense. "Don't try it, Joe." Wentworth said. "We're licked. But remember this, copper. Killing me won't stop anything. The people have found out how to beat you now, by organization, and. . ."

His voice died in his throat. Over the policeman's shoulder, he glimpsed the face of Governor Whiting's cringing secretary, Glass. The man was smiling widely.

"Got you, Wentworth!" he said. "Now, we'll smash your band of criminals overnight. Go ahead, man, and shoot! This means sixty thousand dollars in your pockets!"

"Glass!" Wentworth whispered. "By God, I see it now. I should have seen it long ago—at the Capitol. You met me at the door and sent me away and, moments later, the Black Police came after me. Then, when the face spoke from the mirror—the face of the Master—he knew my identity! And yet you were the only one who had seen my face. Glass. . . you are the Master! You are the head of this entire government, this bunch of criminals. You're a great man, Glass!"

Wentworth could see the tautening of the man with the machine gun, confident now that the high command of the state was behind him. His eyes flickered a little, but Wentworth did not move.

"Shall I shoot now, sir?" the man asked hesitantly, and this time he half turned his head away.

It was the moment Wentworth had waited for. His draw was a blur of motion and the automatic blasted in the same instant it cleared the holster. The bullet drove the policeman backward, and Glass was carried with him. Wentworth lunged forward, firing as he went, and gun flame answered him from the darkness. It seemed to explode within his very skull, and then all consciousness blotted out.

WHEN Wentworth recovered consciousness, he realized that he was in an automobile speeding through a black night which was thick with falling snow. Sailor Joe was beside him, and at the wheel was Jackson. Wentworth pushed himself up, violently.

"Glass!" Wentworth whispered. "Glass, what happened to him? If he got away. . ."

"He got away all right, sir," Sailor Joe said cheerfully. "But we got you away safely, too, and that was a close thing. Also, we got away with the ten million!"

"Damn the money!" Wentworth snapped. "Don't you realize that man, Glass, is the head of the whole damned thing! If we killed him. . ."

Sailor Joe chuckled, "Well, sir, we did sort of kill him. We chased him to an automobile and then we wrecked the automobile. But when we got inside of it, there was nobody there. Only some clothes Glass had worn, and this note."

He handed the note over and Wentworth read it by the uncertain light of the dash.

My dear Wentworth:

If you survived my bullet, which I sincerely hope you did not, allow me to compliment you on your strategy. You will never see Glass again, my friend. It is a role which has outworn its usefulness, but the Master—the White Face in the Mirror—is still at hand. No later than tomorrow, we will locate and destroy your puny band. Adios.

The message was unsigned, but Wentworth needed no signature. His lips drew taut with anger. Obviously, the identity of Glass was a mere disguise for the Master. His real identity remained hidden. And tomorrow, the Black Police would attack. . .

Sailor Joe laughed again, "Plucky devil, ain't he?" he grunted. "But he don't know where our camp is, and he'll have his hands full in New York after the licking we handed them. Jackson, here, has recruited them gallows birds. They're driving their execution truck to Numbersville. We won all along the line, and we're going to keep on winning, you can bet!"

Wentworth smiled faintly, sinking back against the cushions. He lifted a tentative hand to his bandaged head. He had the Master to thank for that. What Sailor Joe said was, to a large extent, true. Rebellious mobs would keep the Black Police busy in New York, and if the *Spider* struck again, swiftly, they might drive the criminals out! With such loyalty as Sailor Joe and the rest gave, the *Spider* could not be defeated! They had won greatly. Even the Master had been forced into flight. . .

"I'll find the Master again," Wentworth said softly, "and when I do. . ."

"When we do," Sailor Joe growled, "there won't be a spot of skin left on him big enough to put a Spider seal on! You can bet your bottom dollar on that!"

NEW YORK WAS POWERLESS IN
THE HANDS OF THE BLACK POLICE
AND ITS MADDENED MASTER.

EVEN THE FEDERAL GOVERNMENT, WHICH HAD STEPPED IN TO HOLD A NEW DEAL FOR MANHATTAN, FOUND ITSELF HOPELESSLY DEFEATED!

WHEN MEN DARED OPPOSE THIS RED REGIME, THEY WERE STRUCK DOWN BY A FRIGHTFUL PLAGUE!

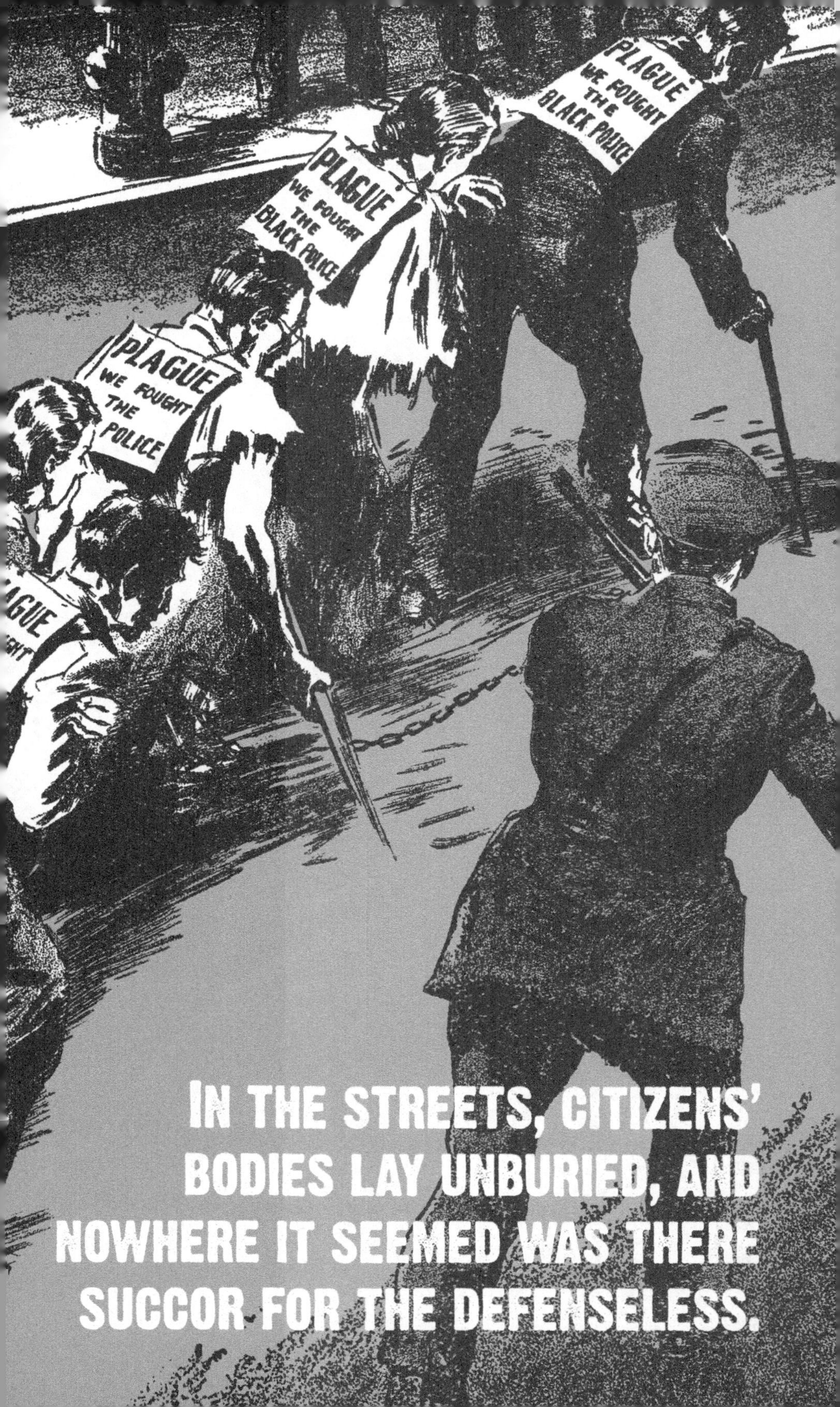

PLAGUE
WE FOUGHT
THE
BLACK POLICE

PLAGUE
WE FOUGHT
THE
BLACK POLICE

PLAGUE
WE FOUGHT
THE
POLICE

PLAGUE
WE FOUGHT

PLAGUE
WE FOUGHT
THE
BLACK POLICE

IN THE STREETS, CITIZENS' BODIES LAY UNBURIED, AND NOWHERE IT SEEMED WAS THERE SUCCOR FOR THE DEFENSELESS.

IN THIS MOMENT
OF BLACK DESPAIR,
RICHARD WENTWORTH
HAD COME FROM HIS
MOUNTAIN RETREAT.

WITH HIM WAS A GALLANT LEGION OF HONEST FIGHTING MEN WHO WOULD FIGHT FIRE WITH FIRE!

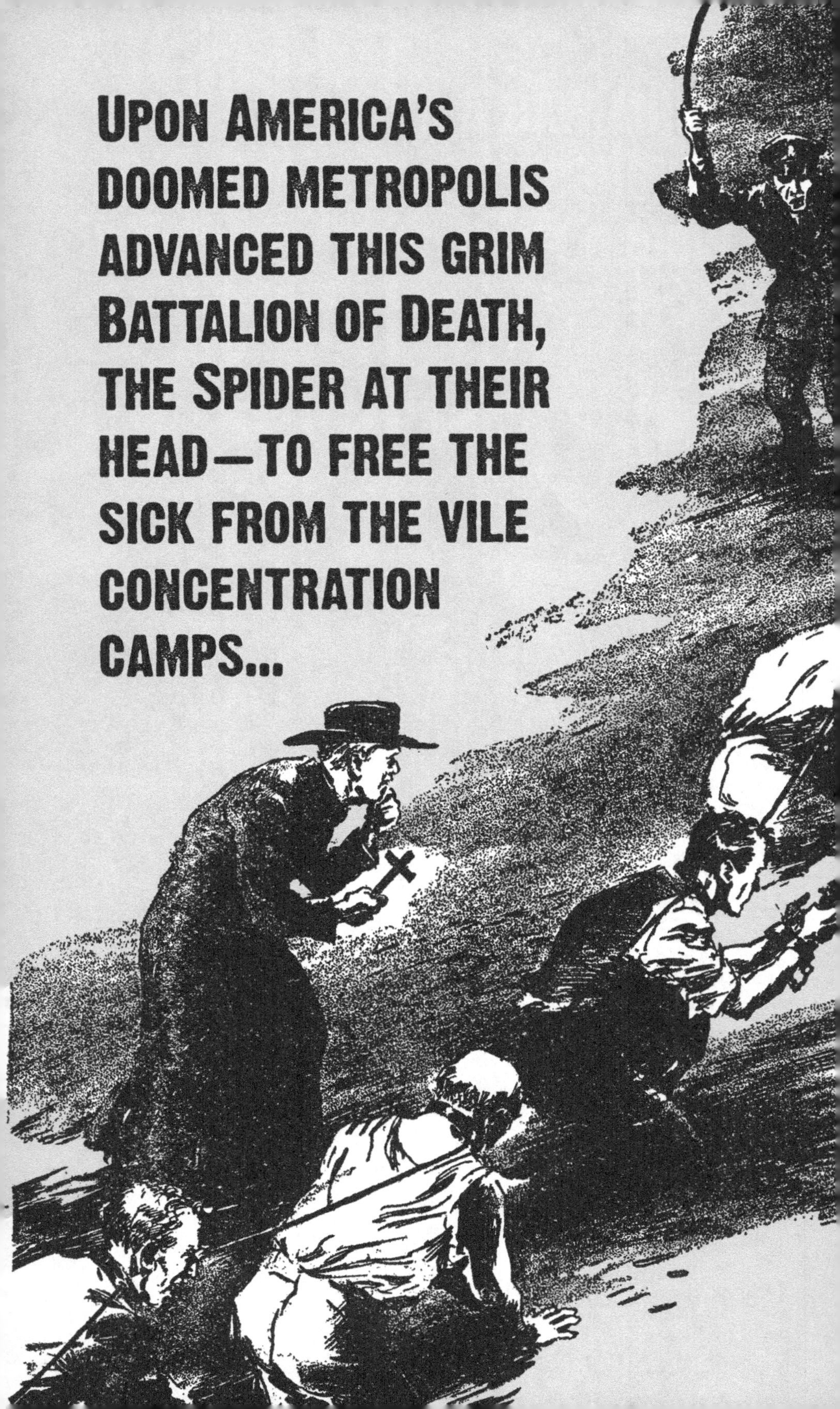

UPON AMERICA'S DOOMED METROPOLIS ADVANCED THIS GRIM BATTALION OF DEATH, THE SPIDER AT THEIR HEAD—TO FREE THE SICK FROM THE VILE CONCENTRATION CAMPS...

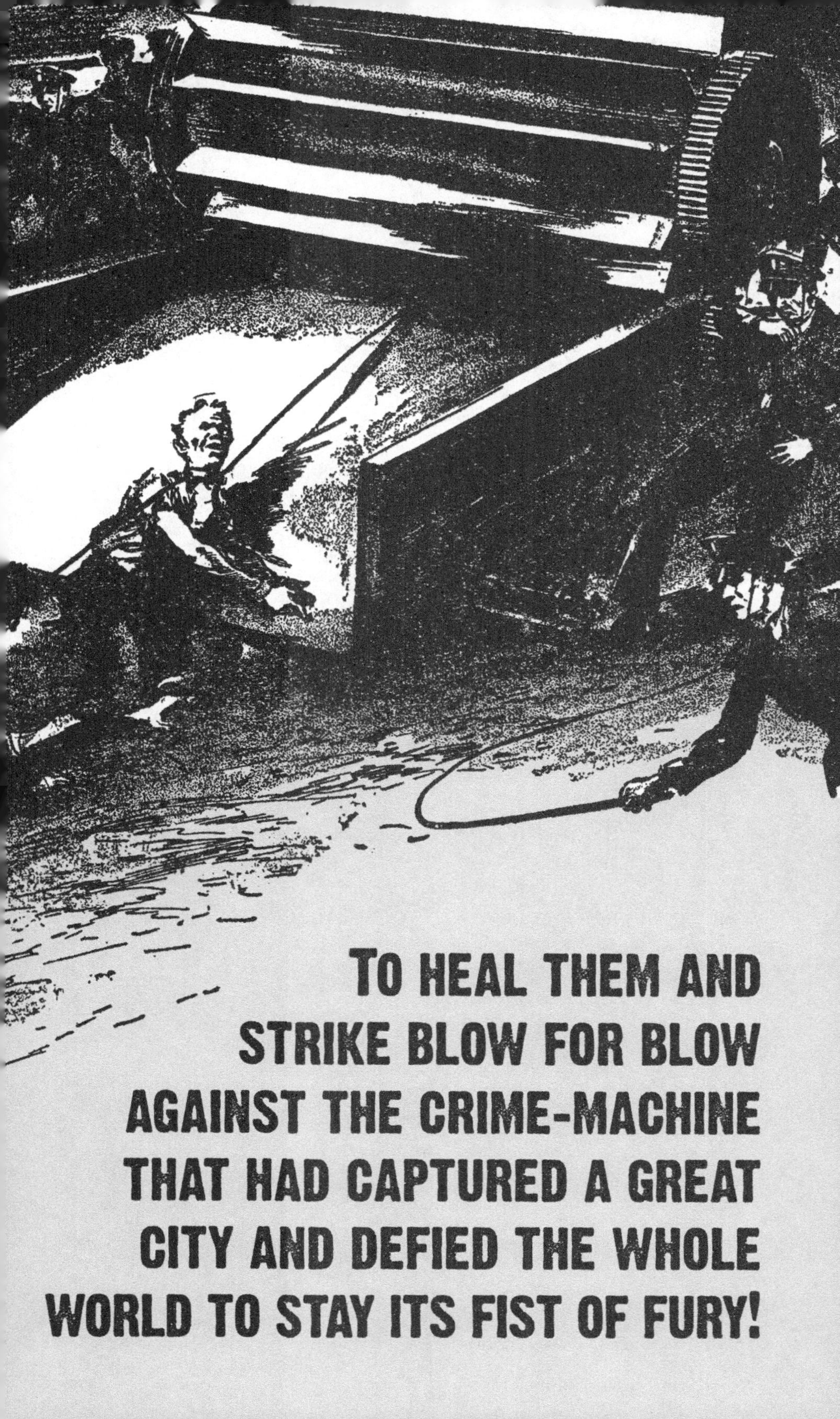
TO HEAL THEM AND STRIKE BLOW FOR BLOW AGAINST THE CRIME-MACHINE THAT HAD CAPTURED A GREAT CITY AND DEFIED THE WHOLE WORLD TO STAY ITS FIST OF FURY!

THE SPIDER AT BAY

INTO THE TRAP!

RACING the stolen police car along the twisting mountain road, Richard Wentworth kept a sharp lookout on his back trail. Twice, in the long dash from Albany, he had been sure the pursuit of the Black Police was shaken off. But each time their headlights, menacing as the fierce eyes of some wild beast, appeared once more, doggedly ferreting out his flight. They were no more than a mile behind now and, despite the wide-open roar, of Wentworth's engine, they were creeping closer.

Wentworth turned his keen, bitterly intelligent eyes to the road ahead. He was within five miles of safety, but it was a sanctuary he dared not claim unless he first shook off these minions of the organized criminals who, in these mad days, controlled the state government. Many brave men, whole families of fugitives from the tyranny and cruelty of the Black Police, were quartered in this hideout. If he fled there, they would be betrayed.

Once more, Wentworth flung a glance backward.

That pursuing car was much closer. His lips straightened in a thin line. It was always like this now when he made his forays against the tyrants. There must be fully a hundred thousand of the Black Police under arms and ceaselessly patrolling roads and city streets. The people were frantic—terrified. They had been stripped of their wealth, even the poor of their stern necessities, by tax collectors who used the extortion methods of racketeers. . .

Wentworth laughed harshly. His own wealth had been figured in millions, long since dedicated to the service of the people, as his own life had been since youth. He had risked everything a hundred times in battles against the underworld, but now the situation was reversed. The underworld was on top. It was in the saddle, in complete control of state and city machinery. And, ironically, it had been the people themselves who had put the criminals in power! The election had been legitimate enough despite the lavish expenditure of campaign funds, and for that reason the Federal government had been powerless to intercede. All this crime was committed with the full sanction of the law and the courts!

Take Wentworth's own case. Charged with being the *Spider*—that was the identity under which, through the years, he had fought the underworld, but not always within the law—Wentworth had been declared a public enemy, an outlaw. Under a new state law, his entire wealth had been impounded, pending trial. On the surface, only that had happened. Actually, Wentworth knew, his wealth had long since flowed into criminal coffers!

But he dared not face trial. Those judges who refused to obey the mandates of the new government had been rapidly disposed of— within the law. One by one, they had been impeached by subservient legislators. And there was no redress, save in the way Wentworth had chosen, the furtive raids in the black of night, the recourse of men who were outlawed because they were honest!

PERHAPS it was because of his bitter thoughts that Wentworth had no warning of the trap into which he drove. It had been carefully set. He rounded the sharp curve of the hill road where a shoulder of

Old Baldy Mountain crowded it close against the brawling waters of Rocky River. As his headlights jerked back to the roadway, he saw the barricade, not fifty feet away. Built solidly of tree trunks, it blocked the entire passage between rocky wall and the brawling cataract. Even as he spotted the trap, he was blinded by the broad, intense beams of military searchlights blazing into his eyes. But before that he had caught the steely glint of leveled rifles!

There was no time for thought, scarcely time to act, but the *Spider* had not survived a thousand battles with the underworld by sluggish reaction to danger. His reflexes were acutely attuned. Despite the drain of sleepless nights and constant exertion, his body was in perfect physical condition, his brain razor keen. In that split-second, he had estimated his chances and made his choice.

Even as the dazzling light struck him like a violent blow, he wrenched the auto from the road and sent it lunging toward the turbulent river. With the same movement, he flung himself crouching, flat on the floor, putting the maximum protection between his body and those lean-snouted rifles.

Instantly, the night was torn apart by a crashing volley of the rifles and, louder than their blast, riding it as thunder rides a storm, the chattering fury of a machine gun rolled out. The storm of lead struck the car with the violence of a suddenly released hurricane. It shuddered, swerved in its course. Glass pelted down upon Wentworth's back and bullets struck on the metal body like a titan's drum roll. If there had been time for a second volley, nothing could have saved Wentworth. But the speed of his car had been terrific. As the bullets struck, the front wheels crashed the rocks on the river's margin and it leaped like a heart-shot deer and crashed down into the dark flood.

Wentworth felt the upward, lurching surge of the car as it left the bank, and his hand leaped to the door at his head. An instant later, he was tumbling through space, then the icy water swallowed him. Swimming was out of the question. Half-stunned by the violence of the plunge, his muscles contracted by the knifing cold, Wentworth was swept brutally down the stream. A rock sledged against his ribs. Then he was sinking in the deep pool at the bottom of the cataract, sinking and racing on with the swift, mountain current which flowed deep and fiercely at this point.

Even half-conscious as he was, Wentworth's keen brain was working. The Black Police would not be content with hoping that he had been killed in that crash. Within moments, they would be streaming along the river's banks with ready guns! Wentworth fought the paralysis of the cold, which already was cramping his limbs; and struggled against the numbing effect of the shock. Slowly, he forced himself to movement. The rapid thrust of the river already had carried him nearly a quarter of a mile below the barricade. At intervals, he managed to bob his head above water long enough to breathe, but he realized he was nearly spent.

A dark shadow, slanting out from the bank, indicated a fallen tree, and Wentworth managed to maneuver so that his weary body collided with it. Minutes seemed to pass before he could drag himself, with its help, to the bank and clamber ashore. He staggered into the woods that grew close, at this point, to the river. Behind him, men were shouting. He could hear the crashing of their progress through the underbrush as they searched the banks for him. Wentworth braced himself against a tree, removed the twin automatics from their clips beneath his arms, reloaded them with fresh bullets from a water-tight packet in his pocket—then he pushed on.

THERE was the sharp crease of a frown between his arched brows. He knew now why the car, which apparently he had lost, had been able to reappear on his trail. Obviously, he had been followed on his other trips into the mountains. The barricade proved that the Black Police had known the course he would take. He stopped abruptly, alarm tingling his brain. If they already knew his course, they must also know the location of the cavern sanctuary in the hills!

With that thought, new resolution put strength into Wentworth's body. Even the biting cold of the thin mountain air scarcely chilled him. He had to reach the camp at once, evacuate the people there. . . Wentworth checked his retreat and peered about to get his bearings. Against the star-glittering sky, he could make out the shoulder hunch of Old Baldy. The sanctuary was beyond that, five miles. If it were not already too late, he would soon get there—in one of the Black Police cars from beyond the barricade! It was sound strategy. Whatever those ambushers might expect, they would certainly not look for him to attack!

The automatics balanced in his hands, Wentworth moved softly to meet the men who were hunting him down. The mouth that could be so kind was now pressed into a harsh gash strangely like that of the *Spider's* accustomed disguise.

There would be no mercy for these Black Police when his guns spoke. They had been recruited from the cells of prisons, from the dregs of the underworld. Too often, Wentworth had seen them torturing helpless citizens who happened to oppose them. Wentworth froze and shrank against the black bole of a tree. The gleam of a flashlight had shone through the shrubbery and two of the Black Police, automatics in hand, plodded along the bank of Rocky River.

"He won't come up till doom's day!" one of them said, and laughed roughly. "We put enough lead in his carcass to sink him clear through the bottom to China!"

"Maybe," the other one grunted. "Gawd knows I hope so. But the chief said not to take no chances."

Wentworth waited until they were nearly opposite the place where he crouched, then he stole toward them. If he could capture them soundlessly. . . But it was necessary to move too fast for absolute quiet. One of the two police cursed and whirled toward him. In a single, lithe leap, Wentworth reached the man's side, and the automatic in his left hand swung in a chopping, blurred arc. The sound of its striking was solid as an ax biting into oak.

The second man flung up his gun and fired wildly. Wentworth's catapulting dive drove his shoulder against the man's chest in the next instant, sent him hurtling backward into the river. A choked cry, a splash swiftly smoothed by the fast-moving current, and the policeman was gone. Wentworth bent over the man he had slugged and swiftly changed garments with him.

Afterward, he tossed the body, clad in his own clothing, into the river. It was not murder. Wentworth's heavy blow with the automatic had crushed out his life instantly. . . One uniformed man, automatic in hand, stood guard over the three police cars parked in the woods road just beyond the barricade. He lounged against a tree, smoking. Abruptly, he snapped to the alert.

"Stop right there," he snarled. "Who in the hell are you?"

Clad in police clothes, Wentworth stepped from the darkness. "Pipe down," he returned in the same tone. "Who'd you think it was, Governor Whiting?"

The guard relaxed—and that was a mistake. The next instant, a fist was buried in his solar plexus and another clicked home against his jaw. Wentworth stood frowning down at the guard, shook his head. He had no time to bind the man—and those blows had been solid.

He swung to the police car nearest the road, set it rolling downgrade with its motor dead, presently let out the clutch so that the engine caught without the whirring of the starter. Throttling along dead slow, he crept away from the barricade. But presently he moved more rapidly. Usually, he left the road and walked the last mile to the sanctuary, but tonight, there was no time. He might already be too late. If he were, he would be rushing into another ambuscade. . .

WENTWORTH wrenched the car into an opening in the close underbrush of the woods, rolled through a fringe of trees and across an open pasture. A shallow stream, carefully cleared of boulders, made him a roadway for a half mile, then he swung the car up a steep climb, began to wind between forest trees. The road here was well defined. Abruptly, men burst from the underbrush on each ride. Light blazed into his face, and there were glittering guns.

Relief made laughter pump from Wentworth's throat. "Thank God I'm in time!"

"It's the commander!" one of the men in the darkness cried. "Hey, send the word! The commander is here!"

Wentworth thrust from the car and eyed a powerful man. Now that the lights were out, the high glitter of the stars limned him fairly, broadshouldered, bearded, his head surmounted by a clean turban.

"The *missie sahib* said you would come, *sahib*," he whispered. "We have waited the feast."

Wentworth's lips relaxed a little from their battle grimness. The Hindu warrior who walked beside him was his own personal servitor in normal days, and had now been set as a guard over Wentworth's fiancée, Nita van Sloan. She had been forced into hiding also, for the Black Police did not scruple to attack a man through his loved ones. She had been expecting him.

"The feast?" he said curiously. "I don't understand, Ram Singh."

Ram Singh's deep voice was quiet, contented now that his master was beside him. "It is the feast you call Thanksgiving, *sahib*."

A startled exclamation was surprised from Wentworth. Had it really been three months since they had been forced to flee into the hills? It was already Thanksgiving. He smiled faintly. There would be no feast tonight. A hurried meal, then flight. . . At the carefully muffled entrance of the cave, Nita van Sloan ran into his arms and he caught her fiercely to him. Their meetings had been all too few in these perilous months.

"I knew you'd come if you could," she said. "Oh, Dick!"

In the central cavern, which they reached after a quarter mile scramble through narrow ways, a fire blazed on a great central hearth, its fumes sucked upward through a ceiling vent. There were a hundred men and women about the chamber, and they sprang to their feet at the sight of him. A cheer rang through the vaults. Wentworth lifted his hand for silence.

"I bring you bad news," he said quietly. "I'm sorry that it falls out so tonight. I was ambushed by the Black Police five miles from here, just above where the road crosses Rocky River. It can only mean that they have located our hideout!"

A stocky man with a weather-reddened face strode forward, his shoulders rocking with the roll of a seaman.

"We can fight them off, sir," he said, deep-voiced. "Just give me five men and go on with the dinner."

Wentworth smiled. "I don't doubt it, Sailor Joe," he said quietly, "but the value of any one of our encampments obviously is lost when it's discovered. I want a volunteer group of men. A dozen will be enough. . .

Before he had finished speaking, every man in the chamber was on his feet, volunteering even before they knew the task that lay ahead of them. Wentworth paused for their shouting to die before he could speak, but there was pride in him. A few short weeks before, these men had been grocers, clerks, skilled workmen. Discipline and work had turned them into a closely-knit corps of fighting men, more efficient by far than the sloppy criminal Black Police.

Not one of them but owed his life and the lives of his loved ones to Wentworth and the men he captained. How could men such as these long be defeated by criminal tyranny, Wentworth asked himself—and not for the first time. Nowhere in the world were men so free, so liberty-loving as here in his native America. Nowhere would they fight so fiercely for justice and right. Yet they were failing. Three months now they had tried without success to track down and destroy the Master behind the criminals. A few successful raids, yes, but criminals still ruled. . . Wentworth shook the thought from his mind.

"Sailor Joe," he said, "choose a dozen men and. . . eliminate the Black Police who ambushed me. It's barely possible they're the only ones who have tracked us this far. Bring the bodies and all supplies back here."

Sailor Joe touched his forelock, grinning. "Aye, aye, sir," he growled. "Landing party this way! All right, you volunteers!"

"Joe," Wentworth called, "they have rifles, at least one machine gun and Army searchlights."

Sailor Joe rubbed his grizzled jaw. "And we could use another machine gun," he said. "Hey, you lubbers. The Black Police are donating another machine gun!" The party he had chosen filed out through the narrow entrance of the cavern and the echoes of their footsteps died out. Wentworth turned to Nita.

"I think I've got a cracked rib," he said. "If you'll get some bandages. . ." He turned to the assembled crowd. "Go on with your meal," he said. "We won't have long."

HE WALKED off with Nita. "The safest measure is to evacuate at once. We can leave a watch behind to find out if this place is discovered. Later, perhaps we can return."

"Any luck in Albany?" Nita asked quietly while she prepared bandages.

Wentworth frowned. "I think I've figured out a way to get hold of Governor Whiting. I know he's not the brain behind this thing, but perhaps he can be forced to talk if we brought him here. . . or to one of the other camps. How did the rebellion in Titustown come off?"

Nita's face was pale as she inspected the bruise on Wentworth's side and her cool fingers prodded to find the extent of the injury.

Wentworth winced, and Nita looked up at him apprehensively. Her cheeks were tanned from the out-of-door life to which she had been driven, but the soft violet depths of her eyes were the same and the chestnut curb clustered about her oval face. Wentworth looked into her eyes, and she glanced away.

"It's just a fracture," she said. "No actual separation. Some adhesive. . ."

Wentworth cupped her chin in his hand, "Things went badly in Titustown?" he asked quietly.

Nita smiled faintly at him. "Very badly, Dick," she said. "There was a slipup, or a leak. The Black Police raided the arms depots an hour before the rebellion, and crushed it"

Wentworth swore softly. "I knew I should have gone myself!" he cried. "What about Kirkpatrick?"

Nita shook her head. "There's no word of him."

Wentworth jumped to his feet, but Nita forced him to a seat again while she strapped up his injured side. She knew how close was the friendship of the two men, Wentworth and Stanley Kirkpatrick, who had been ousted from the police commissionership of New York City after years of faithful service.

They had often been on different sides of the law, Wentworth and Kirkpatrick, but always they had struggled toward the same goal—the protection of the people from criminals. Kirkpatrick had long been convinced that Wentworth was the *Spider*, whose swift justice struck where the law could not reach. It was fortunate that he had never been able to assemble the evidence to prove it, for Kirkpatrick would never have swerved from the course of absolute duty—even for such a friend as Wentworth. And now, Kirkpatrick, too, was outside the law, branded a public enemy by the criminal courts, his property confiscated. There was a ten-thousand-dollar reward on his head for capture, dead or alive.

"Wait, Dick," Nita pleaded. "Wait until I have finished with the bandage."

"There must be some word," Wentworth said quickly. "Nita, what are you holding back? If you knew the revolt failed. . ."

"Wait," Nita urged again, and would not speak until she had finished the job. Then she stood quietly before Wentworth, with her violet eyes on his. "There is nothing anyone can do now," she said. "The Black Police have taken over the entire city. They are going to make an example of it. More than fifty executions, half the population shifted to concentration camps and a fine of two million dollars on the business men."

Wentworth sprang to his feet. "They can't be allowed to do that!" he cried fiercely. "I'll go myself. . ."

"Please, Dick," Nita urged. "You can't. . . There's more bad news."

"More!"

Nita nodded slowly. "Some horrible disease has broken out in Titustown. Some awful thing like leprosy, but it kills quickly, terribly."

"The Black Police," Wentworth whispered the words fiercely. "They're behind it! They're bound to be. New diseases don't develop overnight. God, if I could get my hands on the Master!"

"But it's too late, Dick!" Nita pleaded. "The whole city is surrounded. In the morning, the executions and the evacuation starts. Besides, you have to get these people to safety. And that disease. . ." Wentworth smiled and clasped her shoulders in his hands. "I can't desert them, Nita," he said. "Don't forget, I urged them to revolt!"

"But, Dick, the state needs you! No one else can hold the men together, make the plans! Kirkpatrick will do everything that can be done in Titustown!"

"I'm going," Wentworth said. "And I'll go alone. We have enough men there for any work. No use endangering more lives. You take charge of the evacuation here. Heavy arms and equipment must be hidden and hidden well. Disband the group and scatter it. They must make their way to the Catskill camp."

Nita was silent for a long moment, then she forced a smile to her lips. "I knew you'd go, Dick," she said, "but I hoped you could stay for a little while. . . I'm not really a coward, Dick!"

"You're brave, dear," Wentworth told her. He caught her fiercely into his arms, then strode to the crowded fireside again. "I leave Miss van Sloan in charge," he cried. "You must evacuate at once."

He started toward the entrance of the chamber, and men cried out to stop him. "Stay with us, commander! We'll fight them off!"

Wentworth paused for a moment in the exit. The firelight was warm on his stern lined, pleasant face, showed the tired lines about his compressed lips. But his shoulders were erect and his grey eyes showed their rigid and inflexible purpose. A tall man, with a deceptive slightness of build that did not reveal the whipcord strength of that finely trained body. Command sat easily on his shoulders, and it was plain why men would follow him, even into practically certain death—a master of men.

"I have another duty," he told the men quietly. "You can serve best by getting yourselves to safety, not wasting strength in purposeless battles. The revolt in Titustown failed. I go to save our people there."

He turned then, as precisely as a soldier, and marched off into the darkness. Silence followed him at first, then a ringing cheer. Nita's hand clasped his. Her hand was cold. It clung. . . but there was no trembling there.

CHAPTER TWO

CITY OF DOOM

TITUSTOWN was cupped in the hills, a rich valley that Dutch farmers had made fertile with their work. Industry had crept in and studded the banks of the broad, hurrying Carson River with factories. Now fifty thousand people lived there and from the crest of the surrounding hills, Titustown showed a neat pattern of corner street lights that extended for over a mile along the river and ran in precise lines up toward the piedmont slopes. It's glow reached up toward the black sky, borne on the smoke from a thousand chimneys, from homes. It was doomed.

Around it, the Black Police had thrown a circle of steel. Every road that led from the valley was guarded, and the open fields that stretched from outskirts to the down-reaching tongues of woodland, were commanded by machine guns and powerful searchlights. Across their prying beams patrols of armed men marched. Their shadows stretched, black and ominous, for hundreds of yards across the stricken land.

Fugitives had been stopped. Some were flogged back toward the city, but most of them lay where they had been halted, by bullets.

Through the streets of Titustown rolled armored trucks in which patrols of Black Police quartered back and forth. Squads of men marched on foot, too, and where they moved cries of pain and terror arose. The whole city was being routed into the streets, crowded into central squares as the work of punishment went on.

One man in twenty-five would be shot. Of the remaining group, twelve would be marched into a concentration camp. Already, the first thin line of doomed people was filing out of the limits of the city toward the north. Their destination was fifty miles away. The night was cold and there were women and children mingled with the men. Already, some of them had felt the bite of the whips that drove on the laggards, or those who were too weak to keep the pace. Fifty miles like that. . .

Five miles away, a police roadster was roaring along the highway toward the city. A picket stopped it in the first gap of the hills and challenged the man in the uniform of the Black Police who drove it. The man's steely grey-blue eyes regarded the picket impassively, but a hand, below the side of the car, gripped an automatic

"Password be damned," said the man in the car. "Your orders are to stop people coming out, not going in. I'm carrying messages."

The picket grinned. "You're right, at that," he said. "But don't think you can leave without the countersign."

The man in the car smiled thinly as he sent the machine racing forward again. No, there would not be much trouble getting into the city of Titustown, but getting out would be a different matter. There was one countersign that opened all gates. The man touched his hand again to the automatic in his lap. . .

Then he went on.

In Titus Square, a still, huddled crowd of citizens had been herded together by the Black Police. There was a bandstand in its middle and it was against this that the men chosen to die were lined. Most of them were young; a few were brave. They stood unflinchingly before the lifting muzzles of the firing-squad. Others cowered on their knees and two were praying. The voices of the crowd were a babble of pleas, of indignation, of despair. Then the firing squad officer's whistle piped, and he called "Ready!" Silence fell over the packed square—comparative silence. Somewhere, a child still whimpered and a man's pattering prayer lifted. *"Aim!"*

Along the verge of the park rolled a police car with a single man behind the wheel, a hunch-shouldered man in a black cape. The car checked suddenly and, from its dark interior, the bright yellow flame of gunpowder lashed out! The firing squad officer pitched against the nearest rifleman, but the gun continued to speak from the automobile, hammering death into that stiff line of executioners. Even the whimpering of the child was stilled now, the silence unbroken save for those shattering gun blasts. There were other police on guard, but for seconds while those guns hammered, they were frozen, without comprehension.

Then a voice thundered from the car, *"Seize those rifles and fight! The Spider has come to save you!"*

Instantly, the police car with its sinister, black-caped driver leaped forward, whipped around a corner. The Black Police had awakened from their daze now and their guns began to speak, but the crowd had also snapped from the lethargy of terror. The men, a moment before certain of death, sprang to the weapons of the slain police.

"The Spider!" voices cried. *"The Spider has come!"*

It was a rallying cry. The prisoners no longer were passive under the threat of death and horror. Guns slammed, but the men who fired were pulled down and their weapons torn from them. Presently, sirens began to wail and motors roared heavily as reinforcements rushed to the scene.

A half block from the police headquarters, the *Spider* dropped the cape and was revealed once more in the black uniform of the tyrants. Reserves were rushing out. Truck loads of men in black uniforms were rolling toward Titus Square. The crashing of guns was continuous and the muttering roar of many voices, of a mob rocked by fierce anger, mingled with it.

The disguised *Spider* went bounding up the steps of police headquarters and into the hallway. "Where's the chief?" he demanded of the guard in the foyer. The guard stared at him, gestured toward the steps.

"What's happened?" he cried, but the *Spider* already was sprinting up the steps.

The building was ancient and the steps were wooden. The jail building was behind it and connected by a covered bridge. Another guard stood there, but to him the man in police uniform appeared a comrade. If he caught the steely glint of the grey-blue beneath the visor, it did not help to identify the man. How could he know that, racing toward him, was Richard Wentworth, the *Spider!*

Wentworth sent his voice vibrantly ahead of him, "Quick!" he snapped. "Into the jail! We've got to keep them locked in!"

The guard turned across the covered bridge, and Wentworth struck once swiftly as he overtook the man. He clanged shut the steel doors that separated the headquarters of the police from the jail, and raced on.

There were three men in the guardroom as Wentworth sprang inside. They were lounging about a table strewn with playing cards. Wentworth did not hesitate. He had, suddenly, a gun in each fist and he was striking with them before the men knew that he was attacking. He felled two men. The third skittered backward from the table, clawing for his gun. Wentworth swore, seized and flung a chair in the same movement, and went across the table in a long dive. The man's voice, lifted in a startled yell, broke short as the breath was driven from him. He crashed to the floor and Wentworth's swift-striking gun accounted for him also.

Wentworth heaved to his feet. His breath was coming in long, slow exhalations. His position was relaxed, ready, but his ears were tautly attuned. Had the sounds of his attack raised an alarm? No matter. There was no time for delay. The chances were it would be overlooked in the louder bedlam from outside. All the guards would be concentrating on that.

Wentworth bent over the unconscious men and swiftly thrust their guns into the waistband of his trousers. A coat hanging on a wall peg had gold-laced chevrons on the sleeves. Swiftly, Wentworth exchanged it for his own. Then, deliberately, he strode into the corridors beyond.

As in most old-fashioned jails, the main hallway was closed by two iron gratings and a man sat usually at a desk between them. Now, one of the gratings stood open, and it was clear that the guard was one of those Wentworth already had struck down. He moved calmly through the open grating and peered beyond.

THE jail was in darkness, but from it came the mutter of many voices. Wentworth found a switch, closed it, and brilliant light sprang up in the tiered cells beyond. Then he swore softly under his breath. Every cell, made for two men, now contained eight and ten. They were jammed in so that it was impossible for anyone to lie down. Faces stared whitely at him between the bars.

Without the loss of a moment, Wentworth snatched open the locking lever of the cell doors, caught up the ring of keys and dashed for the first cell. It was the work of an instant to unlock it. He thrust the ring of keys at the first man to come out.

"Unlock all the cells," he ordered swiftly, then he sprang to a central position where he could be seen from all tiers. Swiftly, he whipped his silken cape from beneath his coat and flung it about his shoulders.

"Silence, men!" he called softly. "The *Spider* has come to rescue you!"

Despite his admonition, a muffled cheer went up, but it died quickly. Already, two more cells had been unlocked.

"I've created a diversion," he said, "I started a riot that has drawn most of the police from headquarters. If we are fast, we'll be able to seize their entire arsenal! Kirkpatrick, are you here?"

"Right above you, Dick!"

Wentworth peered upward, saw for the first time a cage of steel bars suspended near the ceiling. It was too small either to lie in or sit down, and Kirkpatrick's gaunt height was painfully contorted, in his narrow prison. A cry burst from Wentworth's lips. His eyes swiftly followed the rope that suspended his friend and, in moments, he had freed him. Kirkpatrick reeled, braced himself against the torture cage.

"I knew you'd come, Dick," he said quietly. "What are the orders?"

With fumbling hands, he began to set his clothing in order and, irresistibly, a smile tugged at Wentworth's mouth corners. Even in this tense moment, Kirkpatrick would think of his appearance! His usually dapper clothing was ruined.

But there was no time for pleasantries. Wentworth thrust the captured guns into his hands.

"Seize arms, Kirk," Wentworth snapped. "Take as many men as you can gather and rush to Titus Square. I started a riot there and if you make a flank attack on the Black Police, I think we'll have the bulk of their force within the city trapped. I'll follow as soon as the rest are freed!"

Kirkpatrick looked swiftly about him while he still exercised his gaunt body to restore the circulation of blood after his long, cramped confinement. His voice had the old crispness as he called out names and orders briskly. These were men Kirkpatrick knew. He had organized them for revolt and there was no hesitancy, no delay in the swift obedience to orders. A dozen men followed him.

While Wentworth made a swift estimate of the cells, he whipped a small packet from a pocket of the cape and hung a metal mirror on the bars of a cell. The light from overhead was brilliant, and he set deftly to work. He brushed his cheeks with liquid from a vial and the skin sallowed, drew taut across the bones. His lips vanished and his mouth became a sinister gash. It was the work of seconds then to change, with putty, his chiseled nose into a hawk-like, predatory beak. Thick bushy eyebrows covered his own and a lank, black wig hung about his nape. He drew on a black slouch hat, and, under the cape, his shoulders assumed a hunched and ominous aspect. In those few moments, the *Spider* had sprung alive again.

Wentworth turned to find men staring at him with wide, half-frightened eyes. He sent the flat, mocking laughter of the *Spider* at them, abruptly switched to his normal tone of voice.

"You'd almost think I was the *Spider*, wouldn't you," he laughed. "It will give the people courage to think they are led by the *Spider*. For you it will be enough to know it is your commander!"

The cheer of the men was spontaneous. There was burning enthusiasm in their eyes, a determination that he knew would carry them successfully against terrific odds. He had fully three hundred men. If he could arm them. . . Wentworth dispatched another squad to follow Kirkpatrick and to hold the arsenal when Kirkpatrick left to reinforce the fighting citizens.

"Hurry with unlocking those cells," Wentworth ordered. "We must be out of here in three minutes! Men, form in a column of squads here, quickly. Move slowly out through those gateways, but don't cross the bridge until we're all ready! I'm going ahead. Keep your ranks. We can move more swiftly that way when the time comes!"

Wentworth raced along the corridor. From ahead, a gun blasted out three times, then was silent. Wentworth tugged open the steel door that closed the bridge, then breathed deeply with relief. A half dozen of the Black Police were lined up against the wall under the guns of two of the liberated prisoners. One of the police lay dead upon the floor and, from the police arsenal, a line of grim rebels already was filing out. Kirkpatrick stood by the street door.

"Hurry, men!" Kirkpatrick barked. "At the double! Your families are fighting the Black Police for you!"

His squad tumbled down the steps, armed with rifles and revolvers. It was ten minutes before Wentworth's heavier column could form in the street in front of headquarters and follow. As they swung along at double time, the rapid crepitation of the battle in Titus Square came back to Wentworth. He flung a glance along the line of men. They seemed well disciplined. Kirkpatrick had done a good job. Wentworth checked while the column filed past and flung swift instructions in a low voice, raced back to his position at their head.

In an incredibly short time, the flood-lights of Titus Square showed ahead. Instantly, Wentworth flung the column, divided, both ways from the corner. They spread out, paused.

"Charge!" Wentworth shouted. *"Death to the Black Police! The Spider leads you!"*

Wentworth's swift eye had spotted the scattered line of the police, ringing the square. Kirkpatrick had attacked at a point two blocks away, and already the mob of penned prisoners was streaming out through the breach he had made. At Wentworth's attack, there were a few scattered shots, then the Black Police broke and ran.

"Marksmen," Wentworth called sharply. "Pick them off!"

The rout was complete, a skirmish had been won, but the main battle remained ahead. Wentworth sprang upon an abandoned police truck and sent his voice reaching across the multitude.

"All armed men to me!" he cried.

FIVE minutes later, he had started the column of jubilant people marching toward the city's edge under guard of a third of his augmented force. Their orders were to halt short of the machine-gun barricades which Wentworth knew were laid in ambush.

Rapidly he outlined his plans. Groups of the armed men were sent racing over the city in captured automobiles with orders to attack the Black Police wherever found; refugees were to be sent toward the exit of the city that Wentworth had chosen—the road by which he had entered. In that direction, within a dozen miles, lay the sanctuary of the hills. The people could not remain in their city, for, after this revolt, the Black Police would strike with the ruthlessness of which they were so fearfully capable. Artillery, airplane bombs. . . Only in flight, in scattering the people was there any safety.

With himself, Wentworth kept a group of ten men. At his orders, they swiftly stripped police uniforms from the bodies of the dead. Mounted on an armored truck then, they sped past the straggling column of refugees. Theirs was the task of opening the way. Kirkpatrick and Wentworth were wedged in beside the driver.

"I understand the necessity of flight, Dick," Kirkpatrick said slowly, his saturnine face more grave than usual, "but these multitudes will be found as easily in the hills as in a city. And how in the name of God will they be fed?"

Wentworth shook his head. "That's an impossibility," he said. "As soon as we have broken a way through, we'll go back to the city, seize every car we can find. As rapidly as the cars are loaded, the people will have to scatter over the state. The fighting men you have organized well, take into the hills. They will be proscribed wherever they go. But the others won't be identifiable."

The driver said, quietly, "Picket just ahead, sir."

"Stop, when they challenge," Wentworth ordered. "Kirk, we'll have to take out the sentries, and without noise if possible. We have to pass two more before we're behind the machine-gun barricades. After that, we can attack on their flanks—and the road will be open!"

The sentry's challenge rang out, and, at Wentworth's order, one of the uniformed men swung to the pavement as the truck halted. "All right, sentry," he called. "I have a pass."

The man came toward the truck. When he was within reach, Wentworth sprang. It was over in an instant—the man bound and thrust out of sight in the roadside ditch. The truck rolled on. The third sentry managed to get out a choked cry before he was silenced, but apparently no alarm was given and, moments later, Wentworth and Kirkpatrick led the silent file of men in a flank attack upon the machine-gun emplacements. A single shot was fired there, but the lack of discipline among the Black Police prevented further trouble. Instead of investigating, nearby posts of police contented themselves with shouted inquiries. Wentworth called back something about an accident, and they were satisfied!

One by one, then, the other emplacements fell. There was a pitched battle at the fourth, and Wentworth lost two men when the operators managed to swing their machine-gun about. That was the end. Wentworth left guards at the machine-guns, sent for reinforcements, and he and Kirkpatrick hurried back to the city to begin the work of scattering the refugees.

It was a frantic, heart-breaking task. Women wailed over leaving their homes; men were grim-faced and some were stubborn and slow to obey orders. There was, too, the ever present danger that a column of Black Police might be on its way from some other point to quell the rebellion. Wentworth had tried to prevent an alarm from being sent out by severing communications but he could not be sure he had succeeded. Guards were thrown out to keep watch and, an hour after sunup when the harassing job was finally completed, no enemy had been sighted. But with daylight their danger increased from airplane patrols!

The city was deserted now save for skulkers and the few who had flatly refused to leave. Wentworth's three hundred men had been augmented by another fifty—and there was no transportation for them. The city had been swept bare of motor vehicles of any kind. They could not delay their departure. It would be impossible to hold Titustown against any sizable attack with his worn out men. They must take flight to the hills, twelve miles away, and the trip must be made on foot!

AFTER a hurried meal on canned goods, taken from an already looted store, the march got under way. Wentworth threw out men ahead of the column and on the flanks to guard against surprise attacks. Kirkpatrick and himself walked at the head of the line and set the pace. Despite the weariness of the night's labor, the men were jubilant. A heavy blow had been struck at the morale of the Black Police and families delivered from a savage vengeance. They marched behind leaders whom they admired and trusted. Someone started a low-voiced song and soon the whole column was singing:

> *"Oh, the Black Police, they think they're tough,*
>   *Parley vous.*
> *The Black Police, they think they're rough,*
>   *Parley vous.*
> *But when they found we wouldn't bluff,*
> *They were glad, by God, to yell enough.*
> *Hinky-dinky parley vous!*

Kirkpatrick's grim face relaxed in a slight smile as he nodded to Wentworth, beside whom he marched. "They're in good spirits, right now," he said. "I'd stack them against three times their number of Black Police."

"We may have to," Wentworth told him flatly, and explained about the ambush and evacuation of the cavern hideaway.

"The devil!" Kirkpatrick muttered. "And the nearest camp, aside from that one, is a hundred miles or more! We're heading for the cavern anyway?"

"There's no choice," Wentworth said quietly. "There are supplies hidden there.

It's just possible that our attack wiped out all the men who knew about it, but we won't work on that assumption." Abruptly, he stopped. Two shots from the advanced guard had sounded. He whirled toward his men. "Airplane coming!" he shouted. "Off the road and scatter! Lie flat!"

The song broke off short, and the men scattered into the fields and thin woods. Wentworth found himself prone beside Kirkpatrick while he lifted field-glasses to scan the skies to westward. The roar of the airplane engine came rapidly nearer and Wentworth finally brought it in focus.

"Police machine all right," he said quietly.

It swept over and on toward Titustown, slanted down to a landing. Wentworth piped shrilly on a police whistle, and the men quickly formed into a column again, went at double-time up the slow grade toward the surrounding hills. When the plane took the air again, the men had reached the cover of the woods near the ridges, but Wentworth's forehead was set in a frown.

"That means trouble all the way to the hills," he said quietly. "Perhaps a fight when we get there. Kirk, we'll never put an end to those devils in Albany and New York by any such tactics as this."

Kirkpatrick agreed moodily. The men were no longer singing. They needed breath for marching, and Wentworth set them a hard pace. Once an hour, they would rest for ten minutes, then swing on. There was need for haste, because open country lay between them and the sanctuary of the hills. There was a single town on their path, two miles ahead. If they could reach that. . .

"Dick, you have any new theories as to the identity of the man behind all this—the Master, the Face in the Mirror—whatever you want to call him?"

Wentworth shook his head briefly, and there was a hard glint in his grey-blue eyes. "It's only clear that he must be someone who has easy access to the Governor and the Mayor of New York.

"That face in the mirror is an obvious trick, but it makes it necessary for him to be at that spot occasionally. Some of his messages are undoubtedly phonographic. He's clever at disguise, too, apparently.

For a time, he posed as Whiting's secretary, and I'm convinced not even Whiting knew the man was really the Master. When we tracked him down in that disguise, he simply discarded it and fled."

"Then you have no new evidence?" Kirkpatrick's voice was heavy. "You were going to Albany. . ."

"I found out nothing there that might point to the Master," Wentworth said, "but I think I have devised a way in which we can kidnap Governor Whiting. If we could get him to one of our camps, we might be able to make him talk. . . if he knows anything. At least, we might force the Master out into the open. With Whiting gone, he might be compelled to take active control. That, at least, is what I'm hoping. But first this column must be placed in safety, and. . ."

Once more, from the advance guard came the two shots which signaled the approach of an airplane and Wentworth shouted his orders. There was no cover this time, only the open fields to each side.

"They'll be looking for us this trip," Wentworth said quietly to Kirkpatrick. "That town is still a mile ahead. If we can reach that, we'll commandeer automobiles."

The plane droned rapidly nearer and swung in a wide circle over the scattered column of men. Wentworth swore under his breath, lifted his voice.

"Two squads of men to me!" he called sharply, and indicated the men he wanted. When they were close about him, he organized them into a compact group, kneeling, rifles at ready.

"At my order," he said quietly, "we will fire a volley. Lead the plane by two yards. The idea is to throw up a wall of lead into which he will dive. We'll fire as a squad—ready, aim, and fire. Understood?" He turned to Kirkpatrick. "It would be much more effective with the entire company, but there isn't time to organize them, and. . ."

"I'll form a squad across the road," Kirkpatrick said quickly, and darted to the other side of the highway.

THE plane was swinging lower now and a dark speck plummeted down from beneath it. . . a bomb! Wentworth followed its course with narrow eyes, but it struck wide. The concussion rolled across the fields. A second bomb followed, but it was also wide. A taut smile moved Wentworth's lips. The plane would come lower now, to make sure of its target and when it did. . .

"Kirk!" he called softly. "Have your men fire at my command also!"

His call was just in time. The pilot of the plane, encouraged by the lack of resistance, swung in a wide bank and dived down over the road. A bomb rocketed downward, striking the concrete two hundred yards away. The concussion was shattering, and fragments of metal and stone whined hoarsely through the air. A man screamed on a rising pitch, was still.

"Ready!" Wentworth called steadily. "Aim."

The plane was roaring toward them.

It's machine guns began to hammer, and above its chattering and the heavy thunder of the engine, Wentworth's voice rang out clearly.

"Fire!"

The combined blast of the rifles beat down the plane's racket, and Wentworth called out again, sped a second volley at the ship. There was a ragged cheer from the men as the plane wavered, zoomed in a steep climb. Two hundred, three hundred feet it soared until it seemed virtually to hang on its propeller. Then it slid off in a stall. An instant later, it struck the earth and its remaining bombs exploded together. The plane was torn to bits. Fragments of it were hurled high into the air.

Everywhere, Wentworth's men were on their feet, cheering madly. But there was no time for delay. Wentworth's whistle shrilled imperatively, and he sent the column at double-time toward the village. He stood watching them hurry past and, abruptly, a worried light appeared in his eyes. Most of the men ran well, with cheerful faces, but there were others who staggered in their pace. Their eyes were dull and their heads swung. One stumbled and pitched heavily to his face, and it was a long moment before he began to push himself to his feet.

Wentworth hurried to his side, helped him up. The man's eyes were bright with fever, but there was a curious, almost lustrous whiteness to his skin. He held his gun against his side by the pressure of his forearm and his hands were claw-like.

"What's the matter?" Wentworth asked quietly. "Are you sick?"

The man's face twitched. "Sick, yes," he said thickly. "It's got me—the White Face sickness."

"Nonsense, man!" Wentworth said sharply. "What are you talking about?"

The man threw back his head and his voice came out hoarsely, with obvious effort. "It gets you if you fight the Black Police. They warned us, and. . ." His gun slipped out from under his arm. "My arms are going dead, too. No feeling in my hands or feet."

He held his clawed hand up before him, struck his fists together violently. The end joint of one of his fingers broke off, but there was no blood, and apparently he felt no pain. He stared at it, and screaming laughter began to pump from his lips. He tore from Wentworth's grip and began to run wildly across the field! The tail of the column had passed now, but Wentworth was aware of faces twisted about, staring palely back. The sick man had fallen again and seemed unable to push himself off the ground. Wentworth ran to him, saw the man struggling toward his knees. Even as Wentworth reached him, it was too late. With convulsive effort, the man had driven a knife into his breast!

Horror shook Wentworth, and his mind flashed back to the warning Nita had given him long ago. . . God, it was only last night! *Some horrible new disease, like leprosy. . ."*

A shudder racked Wentworth, but he could not stay here. The column was already three hundred yards away. He could help the dead man no longer. He swung about and began to lope steadily after the men. The village was drawing closer, but he would have to rest the column first. This sickness was a new and insidious complication.

If that thought, which the sick man had voiced—that the White Face sickness attacked those who fought the Black Police—was widely circulated, it would utterly subdue the people of the state. Here was an end of all revolt. . . Wentworth swore bitterly. *If* it were circulated? The Black Police would strew the state with propaganda! Here was a weapon more powerful than any armed force. The Master was clever!

WENTWORTH halted the column for two minutes to rest. While the panting men flung themselves down, he moved swiftly along the line and, as inconspicuously as possible, inspected their condition. As he moved, his horror increased. Fully a dozen of them showed the symptoms of the White Face disease! They were not as well marked as in the man who had died. One was stamping his feet as if they were numb; another was curiously working his fingers. In the eyes of all of them was that curious fever brightness accompanied by a contrasting pallor of their cheeks.

"Fall out," Wentworth ordered them curtly, and added, with a brief smile, "We must throw out a rear guard to watch against pursuit from Titustown."

He could not afford to have panic spread through the line, nor could he risk contagion. In this way, he could isolate the men and, being behind the column, their ultimate collapse would not spread panic He had no intention of abandoning the men. Once they reached camp, he must devise some treatment. There were injections which would cure leprosy in its early stages. . . *chalmoogra* oil.

Wentworth hurried on to the head of the column. They were now close to the environs of the city and could slow their pace a little. Once they acquired automobiles. . . Toward them, along the road, a car was speeding. As Wentworth reached Kirkpatrick's side, the machine halted and a man hurried toward them. Fright was in his face.

"We have to ask you to detour around the town," the man said.

Wentworth regarded the man impassively.

This was a new development. He had found most people eager to help him against the Black Police. They had regarded Wentworth and his men as their protectors. But now. . .

The man hurried on. "I'm sorry, sir, but that's the way it is. You have the White Face plague in your blood. You're bound to! You've been fighting the Black Police."

Wentworth stared at the man incredulously. So that damnable propaganda already was at work! God, the Master fought with shrewd weapons! There might be some slight danger of contagion, but he could hold his men together in the village and push on rapidly. They had to enter, to obtain transportation and food. Without these necessities, his whole column would be doomed. Even as he confronted the man, Wentworth heard once more the signal shots of his lookouts which meant another airplane, perhaps a group of them, was headed this way!

"You are mad, man!" Wentworth said sharply. "No one in your town will be harmed." He lifted his voice. "Forward. . . *march!*"

The column swung on, and the townsman leaped from the road. "I've warned you!" he cried violently. "We're not going to have the White Face plague in our town! Every man in there is ready for you with guns. That tree—" he pointed to a twisted oak no more than a hundred yards ahead of the column—"that oak tree is the deadline. The minute your men pass that point, *we open fire!*"

CHAPTER THREE

CAMP DESPAIR

WENTWORTH confronted the man, who wore a sheriff's badge on his coat, and cold anger surged through him. Were they to be stopped by this man's stupidity when safety was so close? But he could not order his men to fight against the citizens of the town. It was to defend such as these that he had taken the field of battle against the Black Police and their white-faced Master. Now, the people for whom he fought were opposing him. . . He threw a quick glance at the skies. There were three airplanes this time. The column had almost reached the tree. . .

Wentworth blew a shrill blast on his whistle. "Two files to each side of the road—as skirmishers. But wait for the order to open fire!"

He turned to the sheriff. "My troops could crush your two-penny defense in a few minutes," he said patiently, "but I prefer to avert bloodshed."

The sheriff was white-faced, shaken. He had anticipated no such hostile answer to his challenge.

Wentworth's friendship, his desire to help the people was too well known. The man wet his lips with a furtive tongue.

"Really, sir," he said hoarsely. "You do not wish to infect us with the plague."

"That is arrant nonsense!" Wentworth told him sharply, "but I will humor you on one condition. You will either lend me fifteen large trucks or four times that number of automobiles, or we will march into town and take them. It is for you to say!" Wentworth lifted his voice. "Kirkpatrick! Try some volleys at those planes!"

The ships were swooping very close now. Wentworth turned imperturbably back to the sheriff. "Well, which will it be, man?" he demanded. "Will you bring out the trucks and cars at once—or shall we take them?"

A volley crashed out, was echoed by the heavy blast of a bomb. The sheriff trembled; glanced over his shoulder. A dozen of his armed men were running frantically back along the street, away from the scene of battle.

"You shall have the trucks and cars at once," he whispered. "They'll be returned, I hope, sir?"

"Report them stolen," Wentworth said carelessly. "No doubt, your friends, the Black Police, will return them to you. Now, hurry! I'll give you five minutes to get the machines here. Your own will do for a starter!"

Another airplane bomb burst nearer at hand, and fragments of metal whined overhead. The concussion sucked at Wentworth's clothing. The sheriff turned and ran back toward the town. He was fat and fled awkwardly. He kept glancing up at the swooping planes.

The three were diving in formation now, and Kirkpatrick had the entire company organized, ready to fire upward. Wentworth saw his arm raised, the whistle between his lips. A bomb burst at the far end of the ragged line of skirmishers and two men were blown, tumbling, through the air. Then the whistle skirled, the guns crashed together. The leading plane wavered and slid off to the right, recovered. Its engine began to misfire and black smoke belched from under the motor cowling. Another ship was towering like a wounded bird. A second volley crashed out, but the third plane slanted low and went, hedge-hopping, at frantic speed toward the cover of the hills.

The men were cheering again. Flames had followed the gout of smoke from the cowling of the first ship. Its pilot sprang over side, but he was too close to the ground and struck before his 'chute could open. The second ship was spinning, out of control, toward the earth. A geyser of earth blasted upward when it struck with its load of bombs.

"Hold your line, Kirk!" Wentworth called. "We're having a bit of trouble with these villagers."

Even as he spoke, a first automobile was rolling out of the town. Its driver parked it on the road, took one glance toward Wentworth and ran heavily back toward the protection of the buildings. Wentworth moved toward Kirkpatrick.

"We can't look for any more luck like that," Kirkpatrick said quietly. "After that escaping plane has given warning, they'll fly high and drop their bombs from a distance. The Black Police will probably send a motorized car after us."

Wentworth nodded and repeated his conversation with the sheriff.

"What the hell did he mean—White Face plague?" Kirkpatrick asked sharply. When he had heard of the infected men within the ranks of the company, his face became stern and sharply lined. "We have no weapons against such callous slaughter as that," he said harshly. "If the people turn against us, too. . . We'd better get some of the men started, don't you think?"

"I'm not sure the sheriff will perform, if we weaken our threat of invasion," Wentworth told him wearily. "I'm afraid we'll have to wait. Send messengers to call in the flankers and the rear guard, if any of the latter are left alive. It looks like leprosy, Kirk. We'll have to send a raiding party to one of the New York laboratories and try to get hold of *chalmoogra* oil for injections."

"We can thank the Master for this!" Kirkpatrick said violently. "By God, if I could get my hands on him, I'd strangle him!"

Wentworth smiled faintly. "Without due process of law, Kirk?"

Kirkpatrick's face remained grim. "This is once when the *Spider's* methods would be justified! Why not throw aside pretense, Dick, and appear in your own right as the *Spider*? It would hearten the men. It's all right for you to say you're only using the *Spider*'s seal and identity because it will help terrify your enemies. But the other role would be stronger." "No doubt it would," Wentworth agreed quietly, "I wish the *Spider* would join forces with us."

KIRKPATRICK turned impatiently away to the men. Kirkpatrick had long been convinced that Wentworth was the *Spider*, but there could be no confession. Someday, Wentworth hoped to reinstate his friend as Commissioner of New York Police. He was invaluable in his service to the people that way. If he knew that Wentworth was the *Spider*—Wentworth shook his head. No, the present method would have to serve. Frankly assuming the *Spider*'s identity would not increase his men's loyalty. He had told them only that the *Spider* was his friend—that he had the right to use the seal and he had given to a few of them that right also. It was a potent weapon against the Black Police. . .

It was a half hour before Wentworth could finally load his men into the assembled automobiles and push on through the town toward the retreat in the hills. This way, the retreat would take no more than half an hour. . . When the motorcade neared the spot at which he had been ambushed, Wentworth halted and sent men ahead on foot. The barricade had been swept away. Hope sprang up in his heart. At top speed, he pushed on toward the hidden woods lane that led to the camp. When he reached it, fear began to run coldly through his veins. The bushes were trampled and beaten down and there were the tire marks of many cars. Surely, Sailor Joe and Nita would not have been as careless as that, even though they were abandoning the camp. Both had known that the evacuation was only precautionary.

He could see from the stiffening of Kirkpatrick's body that the same thought had flashed into his mind. If there had been a raid, and the Black Police were still here. . . Swiftly, Wentworth got the men out of their cars and organized them into a thin column. Rapidly, he surveyed them and despair ran through him. Once more, he saw the tell-tale symptoms of the plague. Men stumbled in their stride, or fumbled their guns with numb fingers, and the fever was in their eyes—ten, fifteen, a score of his diminishing force. But it would be useless now to separate them from the others. He strode to the fore of his line of men and led the way cautiously on through the woods, across the fields beyond and over the creek.

The way rose sharply from that point and heavy glacial boulders made a natural fortress about the cavern's mouth. But it was not the frowning menace of the trap that might have been set among them that brought Wentworth to a sharp, incredulous halt. A score of bodies dangled limply against the face of those rocks, the bodies of dead men. No need to guess what had happened. The Black Police had arrived in force before the cavern could be evacuated—and had turned that rocky fortress face into a giant gallows tree! Such defenders as had been captured alive had been hanged out of hand by the ruthless forces of the Master.

With a frantic cry rising in his throat, Wentworth started to hurl himself forward. . . and didn't. Those murders might well be bait for a trap, to induce whatever force came to dash in unwarily. His voice shaken with fury, Wentworth ordered men to climb to points of vantage and reconnoiter. It was only when they had reported the way was clear that Wentworth pushed on.

THE scene inside the barrier was appalling with its proof of cruelty. Men and women had been tortured here. Their pitiful bodies still bore the marks of fiery torment, and the cavern itself was a shambles. His face rigid as stone, Wentworth made himself move slowly about his quest, for Nita van Sloan had been here. They would be sure to single her out. . . He stopped abruptly as he caught the faint signs of life in one of the tortured victims. He knelt beside the man whose eyelids had fluttered.

"Torture," the man whispered. "Water!"

Wentworth gave him whisky from a flask, and the man revived a little—and with it came renewal of his pain. His limbs were crushed and horribly twisted beneath him. His hands. . . Wentworth fought down the strong shudder that tugged at his nerves.

"Miss van Sloan. . . prisoner," the man whispered. "Sailor Joe. . . Albany."

"Taken to Albany?" Wentworth snapped.

The man nodded feebly. Tortured them there. . . information. I. . . I had to live until. . ." His body jerked and, with a final gasping breath, the life went out of him.

Wentworth rose stiffly to his feet and peered around once more. His force of men stood in dejected, exhausted attitudes. They had fought through a long night, marched rapidly for miles—only to find death and slaughter at the end. The plague. . . Wentworth's eyes sharpened as he glanced over the wavering line of men. God! *Fully half of them were stricken with the White Face horror!*

Even while he stood watching them, one of the men let fall his gun and stared, with bulging eyes, at his clawed hands. A hoarse scream tore from his throat

"My hands!" he cried. "My hands. I. . . I can't feel them!"

Wentworth sprang forward. "You're sick," he said. "Lie down there in the shade. All of you rest. Well arrange for food and medicine. *At once!*"

The man who had screamed was staring at him piteously. "God!" he whispered. "It's true! We fought the Black Police and. . . and we've got the plague!"

"Silence!" Wentworth snapped. "If you are ill, it is because someone had fed you germs or injected a virus into your veins. It has nothing to do with fighting the police. . ."

The man subsided, lay down in the shade as Wentworth had ordered, but it was plain that the fear which had brushed him laid its cold hand upon the rest. Wentworth stepped to Kirkpatrick's side.

"I think most of our force is infected," he said softly. "There's only one thing to do. We have to send a raiding party to seize supplies from some hospital. Albany will be our best bet. If we can't get any action, we'll have to capture some of the Black Police and. . . question them!"

Kirkpatrick nodded stiffly. "I'll stay here and do what I can for them, Dick," he said. "You go to Albany. And for God's sake, get Nita out of those mad men's hands!"

Wentworth's face was drawn and pale. He could not allow himself to think of Nita in the hands of the Black Police, but he must. His inclination was to send Kirkpatrick on that errand, to remain here where the peril of the plague was greatest. . . but Kirkpatrick was right. Wentworth was more skilful in such raids.

Wentworth nodded curtly. "Very well, Kirk. You still have about a hundred effectives here. I'm going on alone. No, it's better that way. We have a few allies in Albany. I'll go to them, or else to the Catskill camp. If I took men with me, they might only. . . spread the plague!" Kirkpatrick nodded, held out his hand. The two men shook hands with a strong clasp, but neither of them spoke the things that were in their hearts. Each knew that they might never meet again, that death would be lying in wait at every turn of the road. And the power of the Black Police was waxing hourly. The stroke of loosing this plague, with its propaganda, would rob Wentworth's pitifully small band of every ally. The attack on the cavern had destroyed a third of his men. There were only two other camps—the main one in the Catskills, another hidden nearer New York City in the vicinity of Peekskill and if they. . . Abruptly, Wentworth whipped about at a startled cry behind him. A man he recognized as a messenger from the Catskill camp had just entered the fortress. He came rapidly forward.

"Commander," he said hurriedly in an undertone. "Jackson, commanding at Catskill, sent me with news. Jackson has sent out another man to try to get your message through to Washington. The first one was caught and. . . hanged!"

"Surely," Kirkpatrick put in, "Washington doesn't need a message from you to know what is going on here!"

Wentworth shook his head. His voice came out dully "Everything is legal on the surface, Kirk," he said. "Washington won't know of such things as happened here. If they found out, we would be classed as armed rebels against the government. Things were almost as bad as this in the South, you remember, until an assassin managed to shoot the dictator there. And the government could do nothing. They'll step in fast enough, if there is basis, but until they have the evidence. . . If this second messenger fails, I'll go myself!"

"There's more news, sir," the messenger hurried on. "The state has been put under quarantine because of the plague. The border guards have been strengthened!"

Wentworth nodded again in acknowledgement. "Kirk, I'll send back medical supplies at the first possible moment" While be spoke he was rapidly stripping off the *Spider* disguise and once more was a Black Police official. He turned to the messenger. "Your name?"

"Perrin," the man saluted. He was a chubby, cheerful man. "Very well, Perrin. Come with me."

THE men raised a ragged cheer as Wentworth went out through the narrow entrance to the fortress, but it was pitifully weak. It hurt something inside of Wentworth. As long as men could cheer, there was perhaps some hope. Perhaps. . .

When Wentworth reached the line of cars in which they had fled, men sent by Kirkpatrick already were hurrying after him to drive them to the encampment. Wentworth entered a small, swift car, and Perrin slid in quickly behind the wheel.

"Where to, sir?" he asked cheerfully.

"Albany," Wentworth ordered quietly.

"It's under, martial law, sir!" Perrin urged. "I had to skirt it when I came up here."

Wentworth's lips tightened in grimness, but there was no help for the course he must follow. "Very well," he agreed. "Stop five miles short of Albany, and we'll lay plans. I'm going to catch a nap. Wake me, then."

Wentworth relaxed against the cushions then, forced his eyes to close—drove despair, all thoughts, from his mind. It took an enormous concentration of will to accomplish that, for his tired brain raced with fears and conjectures. He was realizing now that it had been more than twenty-four hours since he had slept or rested. Weariness swept over him like a weakening fever. He slept. . . It was this remarkable ability to force sleep upon himself at need that enabled Wentworth to keep going long after most other men would have succumbed to fatigue. He awoke presently at Perin's touch on his arm, instantly in full possession of his senses and enormously refreshed. He glanced sharply around him.

The sun was slanting toward the west and there was a chill on the November air which meant the night would be cold. The car was parked beside a narrow asphalt road that wound through trees ahead. Beyond the crest of the next hill, Wentworth could see the smoke smudge of a city against the sky.

"Albany?" he asked quietly.

Perrin assented, "Have you any orders, sir?"

"None as yet," Wentworth replied quietly. "Military law was established after I left Albany yesterday. Do you have an idea how stringent it is?"

"The word is, sir, that it was set up to prevent spread of the plague."

The plague was damnably convenient! It gave the state government excuse for the most rigid measures of control—and it would account for any deaths that the Black Police might wish to inflict secretly or in their concentration camps. Also it would make neighboring states anxious to assist them in preventing anyone's escape across the border. Yes, the plague was convenient as more than a weapon of propaganda and subjugation! To Wentworth, it was inconceivable, however, that so shrewd a man as the Master would release wholesale contagion upon the state—unless he possessed the means of controlling it!

Either the White Face plague was not contagious at all, but was spread by germs being fed or injected into the veins of the intended victims—all the victims had come from the group who had been in jail—or all of the Black Police had been rendered immune by injections. There must be an antitoxin if this were not a true leprosy, or else large quantities of the *chalmoogra* oil specific, and surely Albany would have a supply. . . Thus Wentworth drove himself first of all to the errand of mercy he must perform for those brave men he had left stricken behind him. All his soul cried out that he strike immediately to free those who were being tortured for information, Nita and the rest. But. . .

"Our headquarters first," Wentworth directed. "Drive openly into the city. This uniform of the Black Police should still serve to get me past the guards. I've commandeered your car."

Perrin nodded, though his full face for once was grave, and sent the car speeding ahead. Presently, he swung out into a main highway. Wentworth was apprehensive over the guard, but they passed him quickly. They were not the Black Police, but men of the National Guard in khaki uniforms, and Wentworth swore under his breath as Perrin wove the car dexterously through Albany streets. If soldiers had displaced the Black Police in Albany, it would make his task doubly difficult. He had no scruples about using firearms against the tyrant and criminal police, but against these men his guns were holster-bound. The *Spider* did not harm the innocent!

ONLY two of his men were present in the Albany spy headquarters, a small side-street restaurant, when Wentworth entered there, but they gave him valuable information. The Black Police still stood guard over the governor's offices and home, but the rest of the city was under control of the troops under Colonel Roscoe Rice.

"Colonel Rice!" Wentworth exclaimed softly. "In God's name, what can a man of Rice's quality be doing as the ally of these crooks!"

The man in charge of the restaurant, an oldish former army man named Brace, laughed shortly. "The odor of sanctity, sir!" he told Wentworth. "They are getting a little worried about Washington after catching your messenger."

In the back room of the restaurant, Wentworth paced the floor for a few minutes in deep concentration. "This may be a fortunate break for us," he said finally. "These are the orders. Two men to the hospital to seize supplies of antitoxin or whatever injections they employ, by any means possible and rush it to the Cavern. The rest of you, with Perrin to help, will seize a group of officials. Brace, you'll know the ones to select, which will be easy to find and capture. They must be men allied to the Master and the Black Police. Blindfold them and take them to the Catskill camp. If my efforts fail, we'll use them as hostages for the safe return of our companions who are being held by the police. Understood?"

Brace nodded briskly, "Of course, sir. And you? You'll go directly to the camp, won't you, sir? This town is dangerous for you. A great many of the men stationed here know you by sight. We can't afford to have anything happen to you, commander."

Wentworth smiled and clapped a hand on Brace's bowed, but still sturdy shoulder. "What I'm going to do," he said, "is a job I couldn't assign to anyone else. I'm calling on Colonel Rice. I'm going to persuade him to desert the Master, enlist under me and turn over all his prisoners."

In spite of Brace's army training, his jaw sagged at that announcement, but Wentworth cut him short; set him to work to gather all his men and begin the raids at once. Wentworth sprang to the steps that led to the living quarters above and there rapidly threw off the garb of the Black Police.

When, a few moments later, he hurried to the street, he was completely in his own identity. He wore the neat dark tweeds of which he was so fond and a light topcoat, a soft brown felt drawn low upon his black brows. He was taking his life in his hands, but the soldier guards were not apt to recognize him. Colonel Rice would, for Wentworth knew him personally. That was in accordance with his plans!

DUSK was blue in the city streets when Wentworth made his way toward the armory headquarters and there was a refreshing briskness in the air. The day after Thanksgiving. . . The thought was ironic. There was little for which the people of New York State could be grateful. The fact that they were alive, perhaps, but even that was a mixed blessing.

At the entrance of the armory, a sentry challenged Wentworth.

"I bring an official message," Wentworth told him curtly. "Take me at once to Colonel Rice."

The crisp authority of his voice accomplished more than his words, and he was passed rapidly to the sergeant of the guard, then to the anteroom of Colonel Rice. His adjutant was a man Wentworth did not know, but he wasted no time with him, insisted that his message was for Colonel Rice alone. When the adjutant rose to show him to the inner office, Wentworth stepped close and struck with a chopping punch of his right fist behind the ear. It was not the method he would have chosen, but there was no help for it. Colonel Rice would recognize him instantly and might very well order his arrest before he had a chance to talk at all. Rapidly strapping the adjutant's wrists with his own belt, Wentworth heaved the man to his shoulder, opened the door of the inner office and walked in. He had an automatic in his fist.

"I'll trouble you not to call the guard, Colonel Rice!" he said crisply.

Behind his desk, Colonel Rice sprang to his feet. He had a fighter's jaw, and his eyes were cold and arbitrary beneath bushy iron-grey brows.

"What the hell do you mean? Adjutant!"

Wentworth deposited the adjutant on the floor and moved quickly to the desk, removing his hat. Colonel Rice stared at him.

"Wentworth!" he rasped. "Major Wentworth! What does this conduct mean? Damn it, man, there are a dozen warrants out for your arrest. I'm have you in irons. . ."

Wentworth thrust his automatic into the holster. Colonel Rice had not called the guard. He didn't think the officer would until he had opportunity to speak. If he did. . .

"I came to ask you a question, Colonel," he said shortly. "How long have you been taking orders from murderers and thieves?"

Colonel Rice's jaw dropped, then angry blood surged into his throat "What the hell do you mean?"

Wentworth leaned across the desk. "Don't you realize, Rice," he demanded, "that the state government is in the hands of criminals? Governor Whiting is no more than a puppet who jumps at the orders of a crook. But you take orders from him! You police this city for him! You hold prisoners who are being tortured at this moment. Tortured, sir! One of them is my fiancée, Nita van Sloan. I think you know her, Rice."

"You're mad!" Rice sank heavily into his seat "Torturing. . . Miss Van Sloan?"

"You haven't answered my question," Wentworth pointed out sharply. "Don't you realize you are being used as a tool by criminals?"

Colonel Rice's short-cut hair bristled. "Confound you, Wentworth," he said, "don't be a fool! I'm a soldier! When the governor issues orders, I obey!"

Wentworth smiled faintly. "When the Federal government takes over here, I'm afraid they won't recognize your innocence, Colonel Rice. They're apt to hang you as high as Governor Whiting."

Rice sat still through a silent moment, but in those few seconds, a subtle change crept over his face. It was no longer belligerent and angry. It was suddenly very tired.

"You knew all that," Wentworth said quietly, "and you don't approve, Colonel Rice. That was why you didn't order me arrested the moment I came in here. There's an incomparable opportunity here for you. Muster your men and declare Governor Whiting for what he is— a criminal! You could seize the government and, in a few days, we would cleanse this state of all the criminals who rule it now!"

Colonel Rice stared at him incredulously. "Armed rebellion against the state?" he gasped. "Damn it sir, that's mutiny! Whiting was legally elected. He's my commanding officer!"

"Not at all," Wentworth said quietly. "Governor Whiting is betraying the people who elected him. Even if he is your superior officer, he is subject to arrest by you as a traitor! The people would support you overwhelmingly! Damn it, Whiting has released this plague on the people who oppose him!"

Colonel Rice shook his head. "It sounds splendid," he said. His anger was gone now, but he was quiet assured. "What you don't realize is that I am absolutely helpless. I am surrounded by spies. No doubt your arrival is already being reported to the Black Police. And I don't have a regiment here, only two companies of comparatively undisciplined and unskilled men—no machine guns. The Black Police are in force all about the governor and the capitol, and fully prepared for any such attack. It would be just about hopeless."

"But you'll permit me to take away those prisoners!" Wentworth urged. "Surely, you can't countenance torture!"

"They shall not be tortured, if I can prevent it!" Colonel Rice assured him, "but I'm not at all sure I can prevent it. In precisely one minute, I'm going to call the guard and have you put under arrest,

Wentworth. One minute." He shot his cuff and looked at his watch.

Wentworth drew a deep breath, "I hate to do this, Colonel Rice," he said, "but if you lift your voice, I'll shoot!"

The eyes of the two men met fiercely and there was no wavering in either. "You have thirty seconds left," Colonel Rice said flatly.

Wentworth laughed and holstered his automatic.

In a long stride, he reached the adjutant's side and whipped his sword from its sheath. "You have your sword, Colonel Rice!" he cried. "*Draw!* I'll fight you to see whether I surrender or you enlist under me for the duration of the war against Governor Whiting! But I warn you, the only way you can win is by cutting me down!"

For a moment longer, the eyes of the two men held, then Colonel Rice said shortly, "Done! I promise that if you surrender, you'll have a fair trial if it takes my entire two companies to guarantee it. If I lose, and am able, I'll send my resignation to the governor and go with you! After I resign, what you accomplish in the direction of freeing prisoners will rest on my subordinate."

Colonel Rice came lithely around the desk, his movements light and sure. He swung the saber hissing through the air, flexed his wrist. "I warn you," he said grimly, "I was fencing champion at WestPoint!"

Wentworth laughed again. "On guard, Colonel Rice! It will be a pleasure to have a man like you fighting from now on at my side!"

The sabers leveled, and the two men glided toward each other until the steel dashed lightly. Then Colonel Rice attacked with the sudden fury of an electric storm.

The fight began.

FATE'S SWORDSMEN

WENTWORTH had a set plan in mind before their sabers clashed in the first slash and parry. He intended to disarm Colonel Rice and enlist him in the battle against the Master of the criminals. Besides the prestige his force would gain from the desertion, he would acquire a clever leader for armed men. Wentworth had no illusions about the future.

Not that an easy task lay ahead of him. Colonel Rice's saber was a darting, steel serpent and it was plain that he was in excellent condition, and practice. Adding to Wentworth's difficulty was the fact that he did not want to wound the colonel—and there was constant danger of interruption from other men. It was true the door was locked, yet. . .

Wentworth was forced to drive all divergent thoughts from his mind and concentrate on the saber duel. A lightning thrust with the edge had been averted only by an utterly unorthodox parry which threw Wentworth's saber completely out of line. Before

Colonel Rice could take advantage of the fact, Wentworth leaped in so close that the sabers could not be brought to bear. When he sprang back again, he was on guard.

A grim smile moved Colonel Rice's lips. "Do you wish to surrender?" he demanded. "I have the honor of first blood."

It was not until he spoke that Wentworth realized the slight stinging burn in his cheek had come from the bite of his opponent's saber. The thrust had been even closer than he thought!

Wentworth laughed. "I warned you, Colonel," he said lightly. "I won't surrender while I can still lift the saber!"

Colonel Rice was pressing his fancied advantage. His saber whirled in a powerful head cut, spun and slashed at the legs. Wentworth sprang back and an oath of dismay forced itself out. He had forgotten the adjutant might have recovered consciousness. As he leaped, the adjutant struck out with both feet. They caught Wentworth behind the knees and he pitched backward, staggering, brought up hard against the wall. His saber was jarred out of his hand. . . but Colonel Rice stepped back, dropped his point. His face was flushed with anger.

"Confound you, Smithers," he snapped at his adjutant "Is that the kind of fair play they taught you at West Point!"

Wentworth had his saber again and flashed it in salute. "Sir," he said, "It is a pleasure to meet so honorable an opponent!"

Rice shook his head sharply. "I don't strike unarmed men!" he said flatly. "On guard!"

Once more the sabers clashed and now, gradually, Wentworth began to take the offensive. Colonel Rice was a little over-confident. On a parry, he left himself open to a shoulder cut, but Wentworth instead swung his saber from the wrist and his edge caught the colonel's blade just above the hilt; it was a powerful and smoothly executed blow, and Rice stepped back—his saber rang on the floor.

Wentworth smiled, caught up the sword and presented it hilt first. "On guard, Colonel Rice," he said. "Honors are evening up."

Rice caught the saber, saluted, and Wentworth sprang into a dazzling attack. His sword was everywhere. A button leaped from the colonel's coat; the fabric was slashed on the shoulder, but so lightly that the flesh was not touched. Then once more the saber was driven from his hand. Both men were panting, heavily. Perspiration made little crooked traces down from their temples. The force of his breathing made Wentworth's mouth corners tight, drew them back slightly from his teeth. Colonel Rice accepted his sword once more. There were no words this time, only the formal flash of the blades in salute, then once more the whir and dash of tempered steel.

A moment later, the sword of Colonel Rice flew high into the air, crashed against the wall and thudded to the floor. He was flat against the wall with the point of Wentworth's saber to his chest

"I don't wish to hurt you, Colonel Rice," Wentworth said hoarsely. "You are outpointed, sir. Will you surrender?" Rice's blue eyes were blazing and muscles knotted along his jaw. "I have never surrendered yet," he said thickly.

"We are not enemies," Wentworth urged. "We are on the same side, the side of honor and justice and the law! There was a bargain. We need such men as you!"

He dropped his sword point, tossed the weapon to the desk and held out has hand. For moments longer, the eyes of the two men held, then a smile strained Colonel Rice's lips. He clasped Wentworth's hand warmly.

"You are the better man, Wentworth," he said simply. "It will be a pleasure to serve under you! I'll phone my resignation, confirm it by a letter left here. But I will not be a traitor to my commander!" Wentworth bowed. "I ask no more, and you won't regret the decision. Be at. . ." He leaned close and whispered into the colonel's ear the place of rendezvous. "Either I or my men will meet you there."

He pivoted toward the door, unlocked it. A dozen men in khaki stood outside, bayonets fixed. They stared in amazement at Wentworth and beyond him to the colonel. Rice's voice reached out to them crisply.

"Release all prisoners into Major Wentworth's custody at once," he ordered. He closed the door then.

Amazement held Wentworth in his tracks for a moment. It was more than he had dared to hope, but he took instant advantage of the order.

"Sergeant," he said briskly. "Form your men. You will escort the prisoners to one of your armored trucks. . . You have one? Good. At once, please. I will want four men as a guard to the city limits. I'll wait here."

The sergeant saluted, though his eyes rested curiously on the saber cut on Wentworth's cheek, and briskly marched his men along the long corridor and to a flight of steel steps.

FIVE minutes dragged past while Wentworth waited casually outside the colonel's door. He lighted a cigarette, sucked the smoke deep into his lungs. Technically, of course, the colonel could not resign while on active duty. He would be called on to turn his command over to his junior, probably. Seconds were precious, but an attempt to hurry the freeing of the prisoners would increase the obvious suspicions of the men and probably excite immediate action. But Wentworth's ears were keenly attuned to sounds below and, presently, he caught the measured tread, of marching men. His eyes strained down the hall, and he caught a deep breath of relief.

They were bringing the prisoners and, foremost among them, marched Nita van Sloan and Sailor Joe! Ten prisoners, some of them with crudely bandaged wounds. Joe had a bloody cloth about his head but, though the eyes of the ten clung to him, none of them spoke. Wentworth's eyes met Nita's but he said nothing. Moments later, they were crowded, standing, into a truck. One soldier took the wheel, the others took their posts at the rear. Wentworth entered the cab and gave quiet directions to the driver.

A fraction of a second after the truck had swung around the first corner, motorcycles sirened their way to a halt behind them. Wentworth suddenly noticed the driver's eyes regarding him covertly, as the truck trundled too slowly along the street. Wentworth acted instantly. With a deft movement, he whipped the man's automatic from its holster.

"Stop the truck!" he ordered.

The man stared, mouth sagging, into the leveled muzzle of the gun and obeyed instantly. As the brakes took hold, Wentworth jabbed stiff, merciful fingers against nerve centers in the man's throat. He slumped, instantly unconscious, behind the wheel. It was the work of a moment to drag him from behind the wheel and start the truck on its way again.

Wentworth jammed the accelerator to the floor, twisted around the first corner, sped wildly through the dark streets. He was frowning with hard concentration. It looked very much as if Rice had been trapped before he could leave the armory. If that were so, he would have to send men to free the colonel.

He peered over his shoulder. There was a glass panel in the rear of the cab and, pressed against it, was the face of Sailor Joe! Wentworth motioned him back and, with a backhanded blow of the automatic, smashed out the glass.

"Overpower those men!" he snapped.

Sailor Joe winked a cheerful blue eye. "Begging the skipper's pardon," he said with a grin. "It's already done."

Wentworth laughed. It was good to have subordinates like Sailor Joe! But it was probably Nita who had ordered that it be done. A swift question revealed that four of the men besides Sailor Joe were in condition for active duty.

"When I check at the next corner, you five drop out," Wentworth ordered briskly. "Take the soldier's arms and uniforms, go back and make sure that Colonel Rice gets away. He has enlisted for the duration of the war—with us! You know the rendezvous. Here's another prisoner in the cab."

When he checked the truck again, Nita ran forward and slid into the cab beside him. "All ready, Dick," she said quietly. "Sailor Joe is on his way."

Wentworth sent the truck surging forward again, and Nita's hand rested for an instant on his where it gripped the wheel. "I knew you'd get us free, Dick, if you were. . . if you were spared. We were ready to march out of the cavern camp, when the Black Police struck. We didn't have much chance. It was. . . horrible."

Wentworth flung a quick smile toward her. "They've already been paid in full for that—at Titustown," he said quietly, "if there's any satisfaction in that. The Master keeps us so busy defending ourselves, we have small opportunity to plan to find and remove him. It's good strategy."

His words were light, but his voice was grave and there was a heavy weight about his heart. His status, and that of the outlawed men he captained, was becoming increasingly precarious. If they had found the cavern, well hidden as it was, they might easily discover the Catskill and Peekskill encampments. After that, the end would not be far away. This was not a battle which could be fought by one man alone as so often the *Spider* had done before. It called for detailed organization, strong forces of quick-moving men.

Nita spoke hesitantly. "The other camps—they are safe?"

"At last reports, an hour ago," Wentworth told her, "but the messenger I started for Washington was caught and hanged. We've dispatched another, but God knows whether he'll get through."

Nita said quickly, "Washington is investigating, I know that! A man disguised as one of the Black Police came to our cell an hour ago. He had a G-man's credentials, and his name was Miller. He wanted to get a message through to you."

"What did you tell him!"

Nita shook her head. "Nothing at all, of course. The papers were all right—his credentials I mean—but we were afraid to take a chance."

"G-man Miller," Wentworth mused. "I hope to God Washington is taking up our battle! I'm afraid that escaping from the state to carry information there will be almost impossible. The entire state is doubly guarded, under quarantine because of the plague. . ."

The words died on his lips. Along the street ahead of him marched a dragging file of men and women. Each of them carried a tiny bell which he rang incessantly and on their backs were placards which read:

PLAGUE
WE FOUGHT THE BLACK POLICE.

Their guard of Black Police marched a half block behind and ahead of them, armed with rifles, although flight was impossible for the prisoners. They were chained together. Wentworth's foot hovered over the brake. . . But what could he do against the plague? Those poor victims would soon be beyond fear or danger from the criminals! His anger hardened in his breast. It was cowardly to flee to the safety of the hills while the Black Police rode roughshod over the people!

By a rigid effort, he controlled himself. He did not have sufficient men necessary to sweep the Black Police and the Master from power. Failing in that, it would be suicidal to attempt a minor foray. But there would be retribution! Tonight was not the time. The entire city would be in arms within a short while—probably already the Black Police were organizing a search for their vanished prisoners. They must flee now, but tomorrow, another night, he would return. . .

WENTWORTH braked the truck, whipped up a side street and from that into the entrance of a warehouse. The door thundered shut behind him, and Wentworth threw open the door. The bent figure of the old soldier, Brace, hurried toward him.

"Congratulations, commander," he said quietly, "but we knew you'd do it. Sailor Joe phoned they were successful and were on their way here with Colonel Rice. Perrin already has left with antitoxin for the cavern. And we have a few prisoners for you. Two captains of the Black Police, whose records we can give you, and the judge who condemned two senators to death on false evidence!"

"Excellent," Wentworth replied. "Keep up the raids. I'll send you ten more men who are not known to the police. Destroy this truck. Well make the rest of the trip in passenger cars, with the prisoners. I'll give you an order on Jackson, commander at Catskill—for the men. We're going to Peekskill." He started to turn toward Nita, but something grave in Brace's face stopped him. He faced the old soldier. "Something else to report, Brace?" he asked quietly.

Brace nodded heavily. "It's news I hate to give, sir. There was a phone call a few minutes ago. Peekskill has been raided by the Black Police. Our people succeeded in fighting the raid off, but the losses were terrible. They abandoned the camp, took to the hills. And. . . there's plague among them."

Wentworth ripped out a harsh oath. "Antitoxin. . ." he began.

Brace nodded. "We divided the supply, sir, and I took the liberty of sending a batch down there, but there's not nearly enough though we cleaned out the hospital. And, sir, there's more ill news."

Wentworth swung heavily down from the truck and felt Nita's hand come to rest on his arm. They had faced many defeats together, but this was worse than all the others. Two of his camps destroyed. God alone knew if the third was threatened. If that went, too. . . He braced his shoulders with an effort. If only they could get word through to Washington and win Federal intervention. But he was not too hopeful of that. As yet, the state authorities had been careful to provide no opening for Federal action—had covered their violence well.

"The rest of your news, Brace?" he said harshly.

"The second messenger to Washington was caught, too, sir. Secret agents overtook him in Delaware and. . . and killed him." The man's grey head came up suddenly. "I was sure he'd get through for you, sir. I drilled him well."

"You, Brace?"

Brace said, dully, "He was my son, sir."

Nita uttered a little cry of sympathy and moved to Brace's side. "Oh, I'm so terribly sorry. Those scoundrels in the Capitol! Oh, Dick— we're beaten! There's nothing left except to break through the state borders and flee this terrible place before we're all killed or stricken with the plague."

Her eyes pleaded with him, but the steely glint in Brace's gaze was inflexible. Wentworth put his hand on the man's shoulder. "Vengeance is a feeble thing to replace a son," he said, "but you shall have that, at least. And you shall have your reward when this state is made clean again. But I can't ask any more men to make that try at Washington." He drew in a slow breath. "Send word to Kirkpatrick at the cavern," he went on, his voice crisping. "Sailor Joe will relieve him there and Kirkpatrick will join Jackson at Catskill, and take command in my place. Brace, you shall have fifty men for raids—instead of ten. Nita, Catskill for you, too. Hold all prisoners there until I return to try them for their crimes." "Return?" Nita cried. "Oh, Dick. . ." Wentworth's lips drew thinly together. "I'm going to Washington," he said quietly

WENTWORTH met opposition from his own men in his determination. Sailor Joe volunteered to make the effort, but in the end Wentworth had his way. It already had been proved that ordinary methods would not serve to escape from the state. Even if that were achieved, there was still the peril of the secret agents of the Master, now apparently spread over the entire East. It was not the first time that men outside of New York had been found by the vengeful agents of the Black Police. If Washington could be persuaded to act, it would mean a sudden cessation of the tyranny. Wentworth knew that to achieve the same thing independently might require months, if indeed it could be accomplished at all.

It was midnight when, all arrangements made, Wentworth left the rendezvous and drove alone toward the Albany airport. Ships there undoubtedly would be under strong guard, but it was his best bet. Ordinarily, he would have chosen to try one of the smaller fields scattered over the state, but the Black Police long since had concentrated ships at a few central points. The Master had early recognized the danger they might constitute in the wrong hands.

Wentworth made a wide circuit of the airport district and approached the field itself through a woods, on foot. There was small chance that he could force the hangars single-handed, but he had other plans. He had chosen the down-wind end of the field. Any ships that took off would have to taxi to a point near him before making their up-wind run. There would be a few moments, while the plane was maneuvering a turn, when the pilot's attention was entirely centered in his craft—and when it would be comparatively easy to overcome him. So Wentworth hoped. . .

For two hours, Wentworth waited in his covert for the chance. Several planes landed, and one took off, but at a point too remote to make an attack feasible. Wentworth had almost determined to attempt a raid on the hangar when a small-winged, swift craft was rolled out and the engine started on its warm-up.

Outlined against the hangar fights, Wentworth could see the pilot, clad in the uniform of the Black Police, as he shouldered parachute straps and pulled on a helmet. Grimly, Wentworth gathered himself in the shadows. His hand moved tentatively to an automatic, but he waited.

After a long dragging while, the pilot climbed into the cockpit of the plane and sent it trundling down the field. If this chance also failed. . . but it must not! Wentworth rose to his feet. The plane obviously was not coming as close as he had hoped. No matter—it must serve. The ship was almost opposite him now and better than a hundred yards away. In a moment, the pilot would throw the tail around and take off.

Wentworth sprang from his cover, like a sprinter from the mark, and raced toward the ship. It would take him eleven, perhaps twelve seconds to reach the plane. . .

Wentworth's eyes held steadily on the pilot. If the man should spot him. . . The plane was handled expertly and a quick roar of the motors, a kick at the rudder threw it nose-on to the wind. Wentworth was still fifty yards from the ship when the field floodlights blazed on. He was fully revealed in that instant, and saw the pilot's head whip toward him. In the next moment, gun flame lanced toward Wentworth! The ship began to trundle slowly forward!

Wentworth whipped his automatic from its holster and, in the same instant, checked his forward race. He squeezed off a single shot, then was sprinting forward again. The plane still rolled on, but no more gun-flame spewed toward him. The pilot's head had disappeared below the edge. Was it trickery, or had the bullet sped true? Deliberately, as he darted after the slowly moving ship, Wentworth threw another bullet through the fabric of the fuselage at the cockpit.

The pilot ranged into sight. His cry echoed hoarsely, a strange lorn sound across the beat of the engine. Other guns were spitting now from the hangars. A motorcycle was racing toward Wentworth. He threw all his strength into a final effort and reached the wing of the plane. When he threw his weight upon it, the ship slewed in its course, wavered for a moment and almost ground-looped.

Then Wentworth was beside the cockpit. He seized the pilot by the shoulders, heaved and tossed him to the ground. He flung himself into the pilot's seat, wrenched the throttle wide.

Guns were still smashing out near the hangar. The motorcycle was racing to intercept him and he caught the glitter of a mounted machine gun on its side-car!

Wentworth leaned wide over the side and pumped out three bullets from his automatic. He thought he heard lead *ping* on his propeller, but couldn't be sure. He saw the operator of the motorcycle bullet-hammered from his saddle. The machine slewed wildly and, just short of it, Wentworth wrenched the plane into the air. Moments later, he began a swift climbing spiral toward the black sky.

Twice, he circled the field. Already, they were running out a ship to pursue him, but he knew it would be minutes before the motor could be warmed. By that time. . . A chill of alarm touched Wentworth. Surely, there was something wrong with his engine!

He listened more acutely and spotted the trouble. He had not been wrong about a bullet striking the propeller. Its vibration was uneven. Already, he could feel the tremor of the ship. Impossible to estimate how long it would last, but he knew the vibration would increase rapidly as the wind of its rotation tore at the warped and punctured propeller. The end would come suddenly. A wrench as the propeller tore loose, a wild engine ripping loose from its mountings—and he wore no parachute!

CHAPTER FIVE

THE LONG BLACK ARM

THE certainty of disaster heavy upon him, Wentworth studied the night-black skies and tried to make plans. Already the pursuing plane was preparing to take off from the Albany field. A battle with the pilot and headlong flight were equally out of the question. By throttling the motor down, Wentworth still had a chance to keep the ship in the air until the state border was passed. But that meant disaster, as surely as did the damaged propeller. He would be overtaken, shot down . . .

As the only alternative, Wentworth held the plane at a steep climb. He would soar as high as the steadily increasing vibration would permit. When it became too great, he would have to cut his motor, and glide with a dead stick toward the border—hope against hope that he would succeed in passing the guards. If the pursuit managed to keep him in sight and climbed more rapidly . . . Wentworth lifted his shoulders in a slight shrug. It was not fatalism, but grim readiness to meet whatever blows destiny might deal to him, when they befell, and to the best of his ability.

Gripping the stick between his knees, Wentworth made sure his automatics were fully loaded and ready. Afterward he divided his attention between the laboring motor and the pursuit. The floodlights below blacked out—the other ship was in the air! At the same moment, Wentworth realized that be must cut the speed of the engine, or rip his plane to bits. Reluctantly, be eased the throttle. It was the first step toward failure. He would be compelled to repeat that action with mounting frequency until finally the engine would sustain the plane no more. Then. . . flight's end.

Abruptly, Wentworth formed a resolution. Without lights in this black sky, he could be spotted only by the flame of his exhaust. He dared not kill his motor, but he throttled it so low it barely turned over. His altimeter showed three thousand feet. He could glide for a mile, perhaps five, according to the wind. By that time, pursuit should have swept past. Then he could open the throttle, climb again—and repeat the process as long as the racked motor held together.

It was a desperate chance Wentworth took, with the absolute certainty of death if he were spotted by the high-flying machine-gun-armed police plane behind him. The only thing in his favor was that the other pilot would expect headlong flight. . . Minutes dragged past while the plane slid through the air, the prop barely turning, the whine of wind among the struts clearly audible above the muffled engine. Presently, Wentworth's straining ears caught the sound for which he waited—the bellowing roar of a plane driven at full speed. It flashed past two thousand feet overhead, its exhaust a scarlet gash, a blazing comet's tail against the sky.

Wentworth held the glide as long as he dared, until the up-reaching tops of trees seemed to brush the fuselage, then cracked the throttle again. The motor faltered a little before it picked up, and a crack-up was perilously close before Wentworth dared once more to pull up the ship's nose. He put the plane into a slow climb, the motor very little above stalling speed. The least fluke of the wind might throw him into a spin from which he could not escape because the ground was so close. But even at this reduced pace, the engine labored and the vibration of the distorted prop threatened dissolution.

Seeming hours dragged past while Wentworth fought the logy plane slowly higher. There would be air patrols, searchlights at the state's border. Even as the thought crossed Wentworth's mind, he saw the focused blue-white beams lick out at the sky. They were like monster legs, crossing, kicking apart in a soundless, stately tap-dance—or like groping fingers combing the blackness of the sky. Now and again they prodded an insect-plane of the patrol into sight, clung to it an instant for identification, then flicked carelessly on.

Altitude was Wentworth's only chance, and he could not hope to climb high enough to evade those lights. Once he was spotted, the killer planes would converge upon him. Wentworth's glance flicked to his altimeter which registered five thousand feet. The chart showed the Delaware River a bare mile beyond the border here.

Swiftly, Wentworth made his decision. Instantly, he put the nose of the plane down and cut the motor, killed it. He dived steeply. A mile to the border and, a mile beyond that, was the Delaware River. No motor sound at all now—only the whistle of the wind-revolved propeller, the whining struts. There was a bare possibility that, nearly silent, he might glide across the border undetected—except if a light struck him. His dive should give him a speed of nearly two hundred miles an hour, even with the motor dead. It wouldn't take long, after he crossed the border, to reach the river. But if he were spotted, during that brief hop to the river, he would be a dead, helpless target for the machine-guns!

Nearer and nearer swept the lights. As if they knew of his approach, they seemed to sweep in more furious pirouettes across the sky— already in a dance of savage triumph. Wentworth's lips drew thin and cold against his teeth. He hunched forward, then smiled mirthlessly and forced himself to relax. He touched his automatic briefly. . . A hundred yards away, a thousand feet below, the eye of a searchlight abruptly winked directly into his dazzled gaze!

WENTWORTH held his plane steadily on its way. He had no choice with that dead motor. The light pinned him for a long second, then another flashed across the sky, and another. He was embraced in a thousand broken nettles of light, thrusting up past the wings, finding tiny apertures in the floor of the fuselage. It seemed to Wentworth that they were tangibly gripping, holding the plane. He heard the heavy, slow stammer of high-caliber machine guns on the earth and, like a bird of prey's scream, the high whine of a diving plane behind him.

Frantically, Wentworth thrust down the nose of his ship and broke the glide in which he had swept across the border. His only escape from those lights lay close to the earth where they could not follow. He kicked the rudder and, numbly, heard the drumbeat of machine-gun bullets on the taut fabric of the left wing. Then, abruptly, he was in darkness. Two swords of the lights crossed over his head. His eyes were blinded, and he peered desperately toward the earth. How far below was it now? For long seconds, he could see nothing. Then, incredibly close, the tossing green top of a tree made itself visible below him. It was stirring with the wind of his passage!

Desperately, Wentworth used some of the force of his dive in a powerless zoom, banked off to the right and straightened out once more on the course for the river. A parachute flare blossomed into chemical brilliance overhead. The shadows of the trees were black shifting canyons among highlighted green. Ahead, a deeper, blacker canyon loomed— the river! But the planes were diving again, machine guns perforating the high shout of the wind. Wentworth's speed was wasted, the ship moving dead slowly. In swift despair, Wentworth thrust forward the stick and swept down toward the trees! It was not the completely mad, blind maneuver it seemed. Through the trees, he had caught the glint of water where a creek tumbled down a ravine toward the nearby river. If he could strike through that, even though wings were snapped off, the ship should catapult through to the deeper water of the river itself. He hoped. . . Machine-gun bullets plucked across the fuselage behind him. The instrument board shivered to bits. The whole plane shuddered under the assault of the lead. In frantic pantomime, Wentworth surged upward in the cockpit, then drooped forward limply as if the flying steel had pierced him through.

An instant later, the plane swept into the black canyon of the ravine.

Limbs tagged the undercarriage, the wings threshed against saplings. With precise, deliberate fingers, Wentworth unbuckled his safety belt. In the dying light of the flare, he could see the black, ominous breast of the river a hundred feet ahead. The right wing struck a tree, and the plane started to loop. Another tree caught the left wing. The weighted fuselage lunged on, glanced off the soft earth of the embankment and made a frantic leap, turned it into a dive as the motor dragged it down.

Wentworth saw the river reach up for the plane. Dazedly, he tensed his legs beneath him and, in the instant before the motor clove the water, he flung himself out into space. Wentworth tried to steady himself in the brief moment of his passage through the air—strove to strike feet-first. He was only partly successful. The surface reached up and struck him like a sledge-hammer. It drove the wind from him, hammered his senses into numbness. Paralyzed, he sluiced down through water into icy coldness sword-sharp.

Somehow he got his hands above his head, planed along below the surface. His heels scraped jarringly along the bottom, his legs bent and his whole body slammed down with the force of a rough parachute landing. . . but it was no more than that. Dazedly, Wentworth knew that he had escaped serious injury. But his muscles still refused to obey the summons of his will.

The swift current already had caught him up and the natural buoyancy of his body was floating him upward. Feebly, he achieved a kick—a faltering stroke with his arms. After an eternity, his head burst out into the air.

He drew a sobbing breath and let the water carry him. He could do little more. The paralysis of the cold seized him when shock began to recede. . . He drifted. . .

THERE was a period when things went completely dark in his brain. When, finally, memory began to function again, he was half out of the jostling river and clinging to an exposed root of a tree. Feebly, he dragged himself ashore.

He drove himself to his feet, with the help of a fragment of a dead tree branch, and, with that for support, fought his way through thick woods. Gradually, as he struggled on, his limbs began to move more freely. It was close to dawn when he spotted a ramshackle hay barn and managed to push out of sight in its welcome warmth. Then exhaustion claimed him.

It was dark again when Wentworth dragged himself out of the barn. He was sore, weak from hunger and exposure, but he had made good his escape. . . it seemed. Wentworth stumbled presently upon a farmhouse and managed to persuade the family to feed him. More than that he dared not risk, lest they suspect that he was other than his unshaven cheeks and ruined clothing indicated—a tramp.

It was hours later that he reached a railroad, and other hours before he reached a siding where he could steal aboard a freight train. He continued the role he had assumed, for it seemed to Wentworth less dangerous than an attempt to purchase new clothing and rehabilitate his appearance.

Without doubt, the Master had many spies in Washington, and they would be alert and watching for him. The Master would not permit his apparent death to be taken for granted!

WITH that in mind, Wentworth, in the two days that followed, made steady progress to the west and south until he had circled Washington and could enter from the south. Only then did he dare to enter a barber shop and purchase new clothing.

He delayed overnight to buy a second-hand car and license plates in a town in the Valley of Virginia, and then struck out again for Washington. But his task was only half completed when he actually had entered the city. The strongest guards would be thrown about the very offices to which he must penetrate, if he were to gain official help against the Master and the Black Police. For that, only one thing would serve: Wentworth must somehow get through to the President himself!

In his own identity, that would not be too difficult. He had rendered signal services to the government in some of his many battles against the underworld, but. . . Wentworth dared not announce himself! The instant he did, the Master's entire spy system would be at work to track him down and prevent the interview! The capture and execution of Brace's son, beyond the boundaries of New York State, showed the efficacy of their organization.

As he drove steadily through the streets of Washington, Wentworth could not escape a feeling of bitterness. On these thoroughfares, people walked and rode in freedom. Men stood laughing in corner groups. Their shoulders and heads were carried erectly.

Until he saw them, Wentworth had not realized completely the pall the Master had laid upon New York. There men moved always with a certain furtiveness or, if they were allies of the Black Police, walked with a conscious and oppressive swagger. What smiles came to men's lips were arrogant or fawning, and of healthy laughter, there was none at all. And on top of that had come this foul and man-created plague. . .

The goading demand for instant and radical action against the powers that could so oppress the people Wentworth loved rode him cruelly and it was with difficulty that he forced himself once more to patience. He registered at a small hotel under a false name and bought a newspaper before he went to his room to make his plans. He had hoped to learn from the paper no more than the President's plans for the day but abruptly be was startled by the black headlines. They concerned a trial in New York State. . .

FOUR POLICE CONFESS
SPIDER BRIBED THEM

OFFICERS BROUGHT TO TRIAL
BY GOVERNOR—PUT BLAME
FOR OUTRAGES IN STATE
UPON OUTLAWED CRIMINAL

For a long moment, Wentworth could not tear his eyes from those headlines, then he skimmed through the story and a slow rage ate its hot way through his veins.

Several high officials of the Black Police had been brought to trial in a "purge" that was a replica of the wholesale executions of the Soviets. Well Wentworth knew the machinery of such travesties of justice. Through threats to their families, through torture, men were compelled to say on the witness stand whatever the government wished. In this case, the intention was clear enough. The Master was going to lay the blame for the lawless plundering of the state squarely on Wentworth's shoulders! He ran through the list of the crimes confessed by the men "in betrayal of the public trust and of the oath sworn before the governor." One and all were blamed directly upon the orders of the *Spider!*

With hands that shook a little, in spite of his iron control, Wentworth slowly folded the paper and placed it carefully upon the desk. He had to make himself do these routine things slowly lest his anger burst beyond his control!

He needed no explanation of the reasons that had actuated the Master. This was a deliberate attempt to discredit in advance anything Wentworth might manage to communicate to Washington! Wentworth had spoken truly when he had said that the Master struck so rapidly and shrewdly that the outlaws had time for little except defense! According to the newspaper, Governor Whiting had issued a personal appeal to the people to destroy their malefactor, the *Spider*, and the co-operation of all neighboring states was requested in apprehending him. . .

ABRUPTLY, Wentworth whipped toward the door. There was no reason for footsteps in this hallway to be so soft and furtive. He had heard the muted tread of several men. His constantly attuned senses told him that they stood motionless, listening now, just outside his door. A small and pursed smile touched his lips. Briefly, his hands touched the automatics beneath his arms. They had tracked him very quickly, these spies of the Master!

He shook his head sharply. He was leaping too rapidly to conclusions! What was much more likely was that the secret police of the Master had traced him—and then demanded federal help in his arrest.

All this flashed through Wentworth's mind in the pregnant moment between the cessation of sounds in the hallway and the first, commanding knuckle-rap upon the door. It caused him to whip his hand from his gun and spring to the window. He saw instantly that there was no escape that way. He darted into the bathroom and swiftly crouched before the inter-connecting door which led to the next room. A steel implement in his fingers moved swiftly, and the lock gave. Behind him, a man knocked more loudly.

Wentworth shouted from the doorway, "Wait a minute!"

He opened the faucets in the tab and, while water poured noisily into it, he slid through into the next room. It was fortunately empty. He reached the hall door in two strides and opened it, stepped outside. There were four Washington city police and a plainclothesman outside the door of his own room. Wentworth stared at them with well-feigned curiosity.

"Who you pinching?" he asked in a hoarse whisper.

One of the cops swung toward him, "Beat it!" he ordered, whispering, too. "There may be lead flying here in a minute!"

"Yeah? Who you pinching?" Wentworth repeated.

The cop took a threatening step toward him, and Wentworth scuttled along the hallway, but kept staring back until he reached the steps. He went down them rapidly, it wouldn't take them many seconds after their entrance to figure his mode of escape. . . If he had needed any substantiation of the danger he underwent, it had been provided!

Wentworth hurried to a sight-seeing tour center and bought a ticket for a two hour trip around the city. Then he settled himself on the bus to make plans. As a result, when the sight-seeing tour finally entered the White House grounds, Wentworth managed to separate himself and remain concealed among the shrubbery. It was the last trip of the day, but even so Wentworth had an hour's wait for darkness.

The grounds were patrolled and the house closely guarded, but Wentworth had broken into more difficult places than this. Dinner was being prepared in the kitchen and many people moved back and forth, so the door was not locked. Wentworth merely walked openly and purposefully through the service hall. He nodded absently when one of the servants glanced toward him, feigned preoccupation as he moved on. If Wentworth had hesitated or appeared in the least uncertain, he would have been challenged. As it was, the servant went back to his work, and Wentworth was within the sacred precincts of the White House.

He knew his way thoroughly—as he always did when once he had been a guest in a house—and made his way without hesitation to the office in which the President was wont to work after dinner. He was waiting there when the President entered. . .

"I'm Richard Wentworth, Mr. President," he said quietly, and rose with a deliberate bow.

THE President's intelligent eyes swept Wentworth's face with a quick, comprehensive scrutiny. A lesser man might have challenged even a personal acquaintance who had forced his way into this sanctum, unannounced, but the President, after that single look, moved deliberately to his chair behind the desk.

"It's slightly irregular," he said with his quick, pleasant smile, "but you undoubtedly have your reasons, Mr. Wentworth. I have had occasion to be grateful to you on one or two occasions."

Wentworth had not been aware until that moment that he was holding his breath. He let it out softly. "Thank you, sir," he said, quietly, "I won't waste time. I don't know how much time I have. How familiar are you with affairs in New York State?"

The President, now seated, was openly studying him. "I'm not sure," he said. "I have had reports, but they are contradictory. I was contemplating a request that Governor Whiting visit me here, when these trials started. They are strangely reminiscent of Moscow. On the other hand, Mr. Wentworth, my reports say that you have openly used the seal of the *Spider*. To the *Spider*, on occasion, the government has owed much. Frankly, you have placed me in a very difficult position by coming here."

"That is one reason I came as I did, sir," Wentworth said swiftly. "The other reason, that I did not simply request an interview. . ."

"Yes?" the President prompted, as Wentworth hesitated.

"I'll be frank, too, sir," Wentworth said steadily. "I was not sure whether the criminals who control New York State would not intercept that message—and reach me first!"

A slight weariness touched the President's face. "Yes, you may be right," he conceded. "I've lost many people I used to lean upon. Tell me now about your state."

He leaned back in his chair, closed his eyes, while Wentworth crisply recounted the oppressions inflicted upon the people—torture, murder, extortion. He told how the few people, who dared to oppose the Black Police, had banded together under his leadership—and he also told of the coming of the plague.

"Two men I dispatched to you, sir, with messages," Wentworth concluded, "were killed out of hand. It became necessary for me to come in person. I've been three nights and three days getting here. . ."

The President opened his eyes. His face was stern and deep lines curved downward about his mouth. "It is infamous!" he cried ringingly. "Short of armed intervention, it would seem almost impossible to overthrow such a combine! If I were to order a regiment there. . ."

"You would be impeached overnight," Wentworth supplied softly. "I know, sir! If any rumors of affairs there have been leaking out, as they must have, these trials and 'confessions' will put the sole blame on my shoulders. As long as federal prerogatives are not interfered with, you cannot act. And they are very careful about those. But if you could send federal agents there to investigate, to make a report to Congress?"

"My cross!" The President smiled faintly. "Yes, something might be accomplished that way. This is what I am going to do, Mr. Wentworth. I will try to compel a new election in New York State and I'll order some navy ships to the Hudson for 'maneuvers'. It would be possible to warn Governor Whiting that, unless lawlessness is stamped out, we will be compelled to take some action to protect our leading port."

Wentworth sprang to his feet, "It's more than I had dared to hope for, Mr. President!"

The President said dryly, "It may be more than I can accomplish. I'll try!

Now. . ."

Abruptly, the door of the President's office was thrown wide, and three armed White House guards jammed into the entrance. Their guns covered Wentworth.

"Your pardon, Mr. President," the leader said. "One of the cooks reported seeing a fellow come in. Put up your hands, man. We'll shoot, if you stir!"

Wentworth lifted his hands slowly. Under his breath, he whispered to the President, "Denounce me, sir! Say I held a gun on you! You can't permit your political enemies to say you allowed me here—a criminal and murderer!"

The leading guard was moving warily toward Wentworth, gun ready, and Wentworth was forced to cut his whisper short.

"You came just in time," he said harshly. "You slaves of tyranny! Another thirty seconds, and I would have fixed this blood-sucking capitalist so he couldn't oppress the people any longer!"

CHAPTER SIX

VOTE DOWN THE PLAGUE!

IT WAS incredible, under the circumstances, to hear the President break into a deep and hearty laugh! The heads of the guards swung toward him in amazement and, for an instant, Wentworth hovered on the brink of leaping upon them. But it might endanger the President's life, and God knew the nation needed him as never before in these days.

"I appreciate your zealous work, Marlowe," the President said pleasantly to the leader of the guards, "and it's true that Mr. Wentworth was somewhat informal in his manner of calling. No, no, put away your guns. Mr. Wentworth will have his little joke."

He turned to Wentworth, and his face was grave, "I appreciate your intention, but, if my willingness to hear complaints against tyranny is ammunition against me, then let my enemies use it! To the best of my ability, Mr. Wentworth, I'll fulfill my promise!" He held out his hand.

Wentworth felt a deep reverence for the President's courage, though, under the circumstances, he considered it foolhardy. He grasped the hand warmly.

"Thank you, sir," he said. "I'm going back now."

"It's a task I don't envy you," the President said, "but I admire your respect for your duty—the more since it is self-imposed. Marlowe, place a car and a guard at Mr. Wentworth's disposal. Good night, sir, and thank you."

Wentworth carried his elation with him for a full five minutes. Then he discovered that the sedan in which he left the White House was trailed by another car. His lips settled into a grim mold then, but his hope refused to be crushed. Even with the unfair tactics which the Master would employ, any election called in New York State should sweep Governor Whiting and the Black Police out of power. There was some question of whether the President would be able to enforce his will—considerable question. But the mere threat of federal interference should do a great deal to alleviate conditions for the people of New York. . .

Wentworth's head whipped about and his hand half-lifted to his automatic as the trailing limousine sped past. There were five men in the car, and their glares concentrated on him. Wentworth laughed softly and lifted his hat to them. He had no immediate fears. Even the minions of the Master would scarcely dare to attack a Presidential car. It would be unwise. . .

At the airport to which Wentworth directed the car, he made immediate arrangements to charter a plane for Albany. There was some demur, because of the plague, but finally the deal was completed. . . and the trailing crew of gunmen did not interfere. Their reason was plain enough. Things could be handled so much more satisfactorily in Albany, from their point of view!

Within five minutes of the take-off, Wentworth was aware of another ship, powerfully motored, which kept pace with them across the night sky. Five miles across the border of New York State, Wentworth lost them by the simple process of leaping over the side, and plunging without opening his parachute until dangerously close to the ground.

It was a repetition of his flight across country to Washington—except for two things. Here the Black Police patrolled constantly and therefore were on the look-out for him. But the people also knew the *Spider* for their friend and were eager to help him. A farmer got out his milk truck and drove Wentworth forty miles to a city where his men had a spy headquarters. When Wentworth entered the tiny magazine shop, the operator fell on his knees and tears trickled unashamed down his cheeks.

"The commander!" the man stammered. "The commander! They told us you were dead. Oh, thank God!"

WENTWORTH commandeered a motorcycle and drove it to within ten miles of the Catskill camp, where he abandoned the machine for a horse and pushed on through the back-lanes of the hills. He did not know how thoroughly the Black Police patrolled the district, but he would run no risk of capture. The news he bore was too heart-filling. Why, if the President achieved his promise, they were within a few weeks of freedom again! One thing could make victory sure—if they discovered the identity of the Master and destroyed him! No one else, Wentworth was sure, had the intelligence to defeat them at the polls. . .

With his thoughts to spur him, Wentworth pushed the horse at a steady pace into the hills. He paused presently in a night-black ravine and drew out a whistle on which he blew three shrill blasts. The embankments picked up the sound and sent it echoing ahead, and, moments later, a searchlight blazed down the cut. Then a man's almost inarticulate shout of joy sounded.

"The commander! It's the commander!"

His voice echoed and other voices picked it up, sent the news winging ahead as sentry after sentry relayed the news back to camp. A small grave smile tugged at Wentworth's lips. It was humbling to be so hailed. He had achieved so little in his ceaseless warfare. It seemed to him that only failure lay behind, but with such loyal men. . . Wentworth spurred up the glade and past sentries whose faces creased in smiles of welcome. Their voices bore him along. . .

"Thank God you're back, commander!"

"They spread the word you were dead, commander!"

"We knew they couldn't kill you, commander!"

No lights could be shown within the fortress itself, but in the darkness men ran and called eagerly beside him. He was lifted from his horse and borne on their shoulders until he came to the porch of the log cabin headquarters. Two men met him there, and Wentworth clasped hands with Kirkpatrick and with Colonel Rice. Jackson stepped forward from the darkness to salute.

Wentworth turned to the white glimmer of upturned faces before the porch and called to them softly. "I have seen the President," he said quietly. "He has promised to help in every way he can. Tomorrow, I will have plans for you."

He turned to Kirkpatrick. "The time has come to make our biggest play," he said. "We must kidnap Governor Whiting and force him to tell the identity of the Master!"

Kirkpatrick's lips curved in a faint smile, "We're one up on you, Dick," he said quietly. "We have the governor a prisoner here. But he either doesn't know who the Master is or else is too terrified to tell."

Wentworth's laugh was startled from him. "It's a good omen!" he cried. "Now I believe in victory again."

While he spoke, his eyes were questing in the darkness. It was inconceivable that Nita van Sloan should not meet him if she were here, and he knew a sharp moment of fear. Nothing had happened to her. It couldn't now, when so much that was good offered. Kirkpatrick understood that glance and the suppressed anxiety behind it.

"Our headquarters in New York was destroyed," he said quietly. "Nita went to set up a new place. We couldn't stop her. Sailor Joe and Ram Singh went with her."

Wentworth nodded wordlessly, though his heart leaped with anxiety for Nita. She should be well protected by those two men. "I think," he said softly, "that an interview with Governor Whiting is indicated."

He led the way then into the log cabin and, within blanketed windows, lights were turned on again. A man in a priest's black robe rose from beside the open fire and came toward him—a small man with a gentle face. "We have missed you," he said simply "And I have missed you," Wentworth told him. He sucked in a chest-filling breath. "It's good to be back if only for a few hours."

Father Flower shook his head. "We have done evil things since you have been gone," he said. "Evil things though they were necessary. We have hanged fourteen men."

"Not our men!" Wentworth cried. Colonel Rice's bluff, curt voice cut in. "Black Police. Prisoners. They were duly tried. Kirkpatrick defended them. Convicted, hanged. . . with the *Spider*'s web. And delivered back to the towns in which they sinned. Every man we hanged was a murderer a half-dozen times over."

Wentworth frowned. He could not say it was ill done. It was such a course as he himself might have followed, though he had never yet killed a man who did not have opportunity to defend himself. It was completely just. But it was unfortunate at this time. It might make intercession by the President difficult.

"A forceful answer to their crimes," he said slowly, "but I think we should discontinue such punishments now if we are to get federal help." Briefly then he told of his interview with the President. "We must concentrate our attention on finding the Master. He can cancel out all our work unless we are rid of him before the election. I'd like to see the governor now."

JACKSON nodded and, heaving up a trapdoor in the floor, called an order. Presently Governor Whiting was thrust up the steps by two armed men, each handcuffed to one of Whiting's wrists. The governor was a man of leonine mold and inclined to bluster but the strength was gone out of him now. His lips trembled and his eyes only touched Wentworth's in passing before they sank again to the floor.

"I protest against this outrage," he said weakly. "The state of New York will not tolerate this. I am the governor, sir!"

Wentworth allowed a slight, cold smile to move his lips. "You *were* the governor," he said. "Now you are a prisoner before a just court. Can you advance any reason why we shouldn't hang you as we have fourteen of your underlings? If they were guilty, you are separately guilty for each of them. They were appointed by you. They took your orders!"

Governor Whiting sagged to his knees.

"As God is my witness," he whispered, "I have never ordered a human being harmed or killed! Please, you won't harm me? I've only taken orders myself, from a man I don't know—but who threatened to kill me, horribly, if I didn't obey. You can't kill for me for that. Not just because I was afraid! For God's sake, say you won't kill me! Anything but that! I'll be your slave—"

"Shut him up!" Wentworth said curtly. He felt sickened. This cowardly groveling creature had been elected governor of the state and had surrendered it to criminals. Death? Yes, certainly he deserved death a hundred times over. He had wrought the deaths of many, better men. There was no need now for the guards to shut him up. Whiting closed his trembling lips, but his eyes begged for him.

"One thing can save you," Wentworth said coldly. "If you speak again, tell us the name of the man you serve—the Master! Otherwise…"

Jackson caught Wentworth's brief gesture and dropped a noose about Whiting's neck. He started like a bee-stung horse and an inarticulate cry rose in his throat. "No, no!" he gasped. "If I knew I would tell! I swear I would. I only see a white face in a mirror!" There was disgust on the faces of Kirkpatrick and Colonel Rice, and Wentworth knew that his own mirrored their expression. He said heavily, "I suppose he's telling the truth."

Kirkpatrick and Rice nodded deliberately. The colonel said crisply, "He's no more good to us, or to the state. I vote for death! Such a coward doesn't deserve to live!"

Abruptly, the door of the cabin flung open and a sentry burst in, stiffened to salute. "Commander! Party of our men coming with a blindfolded prisoner. Says he's G-man Miller and has a message for you!" Wentworth's eyes narrowed at the news. He remembered that Nita, when he had freed her from the Black Police, had mentioned a federal agent of that name. It was possible, of course, that he brought word from Washington.

"In five minutes," he agreed shortly, and turned back to Governor Whiting. "Trial adjourned. We will discuss your fate later. I would advise you, Whiting, to improve your memory a little. If you could think of any little thing that would help us to find the Master, we may be more inclined to leniency. Take him below."

He turned his back on the wretched man's babblings and moved to
a table where he dropped into chair. Kirkpatrick and Colonel Rice
joined him at his gesture of invitation.

"I'm afraid we'll have to devise some other way of discovering the
Master," he said heavily. "Whiting will have to go free, of course."

Kirkpatrick nodded gravely, but Colonel Rice set his lips in disap-
proval. "Only way to win this war," he said, "is to kill them off from
the top. At least hold them as hostages."

Wentworth's brain gave an involuntary assent to Rice's words but
it was a policy to which he could not subscribe. This fight could be
won only by the destruction of the Master. As long as he lived, he could
find fresh puppets to do his bidding. Whiting was no more than that. . .

"Bring in Miller," Wentworth directed Jackson.

A few moments later, a stocky, square-shouldered man was led in,
blindfolded. He seemed in no way incommoded by not being able to
see. He stepped out with a strong confidence that showed his courage
and his solid lips had a quiet smile.

"I've come a devilish long and inconvenient way to see you,
Wentworth," he said. "I hope I am going to see you?"

"Of course," Wentworth agreed and, at his gesture, the blindfold
was removed.

His steady grey-blue eyes studied the face that was revealed. It was
square and determined, the brows horizontal above direct blue eyes. As
soon as he was again accustomed to the light, Miller unbuttoned his
vest and, from an inner pocket, produced his credentials.

"You'll want to see these, of course," he said, "but I think my message will convince you more than the papers. The President has
arranged for an election to be held ten days from tomorrow in the
form of a recall election on Governor Whiting. It is conditional on
your surrendering Governor Whiting into my hands for immediate
return to Albany!"

RELEASE of Governor Whiting accorded well with Wentworth's
plans. Nothing was to be gained by his longer incarceration since
there seemed no doubt that he knew nothing of the Master's identity.

In himself, the man was unimportant. His destruction might merely allow another, actively criminal, man to take his place. So, when Wentworth had satisfied himself of the authenticity of the credentials submitted by Miller, he allowed him to depart with Governor Whiting, blindfolded as they had come.

Instantly, Wentworth began to organize his election campaign. Ten days allowed little enough time, but there could be no question that the bulk of the people were hostile to Whiting. Their opinions did not need to be swayed—what was needed was the mass courage to vote their convictions. And instilling the necessary strength into the electorate was an even bigger task. More than any other single thing, the capture of the Master would help, but months of work, had failed to uncover him. There was small hope that the next ten days would be much more fruitful.

Wentworth must send his men everywhere to encourage the people, to fight against the tyrannies of the Black Police and give the voters at least the illusion of protection. Against one thing, however, Wentworth was powerless—the plague. Of those among his followers who had been stricken, only the ones who had received the injection showed any improvement. The others were dying by a slow process of living disintegration. If they failed at the polls, it would be the plague which defeated them!

The victims were everywhere. In little abject bands they roamed the countryside with the placards ordered by the state placed upon their backs, with small mournful bells jangling constantly to their shuffling walk. If the mass of the people believed that the plague fought on the side of the criminals—that to oppose the Black Police was sufficient to bring on the plague—Wentworth's task became practically impossible. Against that, his only weapon could be the free dispensing of the anti-plague injections. Therefore he organized a series of raids on various scattered hospitals.

The task Wentworth had chosen for himself was at once the most important and most dangerous. With swift skill, he assembled a powerful portable radio broadcaster and set out on a tour of the state. He had to make brief, pungent speeches, while the radio car sped along the road, but his talks could run for but a few minutes only. Well he knew that the Black Police would be listening in and, by means of swiftly organized triangulation, locate his position. Thus it was speak, then flight across the back roads and presently speak again from a position fifty miles away.

Twice the racing cars of the Black Police converged so rapidly that he escaped only after a running gunfight. After that, Kirkpatrick insisted on organizing a guard under Colonel Rice—a half dozen armed men in an enclosed truck which would pace the radio car. To Wentworth this seemed a mistake because it hampered mobility and increased the likelihood of attracting suspicion. However, on the insistence of his men, he gave in.

The radio work must not stop, for the whispers of menace from the plague spread daily. Wherever the men of the *Spider* gained some transient advantage, the plague was sure to strike more terribly than ever. The fears of the people were so increased that, twice, the *Spider*'s men had been driven from towns. The citizens preferred to submit to tyrannies and robberies rather than face the certainty of the plague!

It was on the second day after Wentworth accepted a guard, and a bare three days before the election, that the *Spider* had actually to force himself to make his daily patrol in the radio car. He had an overwhelming sense of disaster—a curious coldness in his breast that he recognized from many similar experiences. It was the warning of his subconscious against danger. He paid it no heed other than to ask of Colonel Rice special alertness.

"Call it a hunch," Wentworth said somberly, "perhaps only a feeling of depression of spirits because things have been going so badly for us. I find it wise not to ignore hunches."

Colonel Rice nodded his blunt head and his eyes were anxious. "I've been worried, too. Perhaps it would be better not to go today."

Wentworth's lips closed grimly. "If we relax the fight, we lose what small chance of victory we have. I'm laying plans for a raid that I hope may turn the tables. We'll talk it over tonight."

THE roads over which Wentworth sped that day were strangely deserted. Not once in an hour did they pass another machine. In the towns, too, few persons were in sight, save for the melancholy bands of the plague-stricken. The sight of them shook Wentworth with a helpless fury. The Master and the Black Police had turned back civilization a thousand years!

As the car left the limits of the town, Wentworth began to speak. Beside him, his driver kept a sharp outlook. He was a young chap named Forrester whose father had been murdered by the Black Police and Wentworth had chosen him deliberately for his skill—and his loyalty. As Wentworth finished his speech, Forrester jerked his head angrily.

"These empty roads have got me worried," he muttered. "Looks almost as if they were barricaded—even if we ain't found any yet."

The words had scarcely left his lips when the trumpet horn of the patrol truck, which had rounded a curve ahead, rang out in a triple-blast which signaled an attack! Before its last note had sounded, machine guns began to hammer.

Forrester slammed on brakes. "A barricade!" he snapped.

"Go on!" Wentworth ordered. "That truck should be able to smash through!"

The car picked up speed again, eased around the curve—and the truck was motionless in the road. Guns crashed out from its loopholes, but none of the men who manned the auto barricade fell under that fire. The attackers leaped out with their guns in their hands and, with a soft oath, Wentworth guessed the reason for that ineffective fire! These were not the Black Police, but National Guardsmen in khaki! Colonel Rice could not bring himself to fire on them!

Well, that was in accordance with Wentworth's desires, too. Never, even at the risk of his life, had he hurt innocent men and, though these guardsmen fought the battle of the Master, they were only obeying orders from the governor, as they were sworn to do. "Back!" Wentworth ordered. Forrester was already fighting the car around. Bullets began to slam against the car. Wentworth twisted about and stared down the road behind. Side by side, two trucks filled with men in khaki, were trundling up the road. That way, too, was blocked!

Desperately, Wentworth's eyes searched the woods that crowded the road. On one side, the hill climbed steeply; on the other, a sharp declivity dipped toward a valley, but the trees were timber.

Steadily, Wentworth ordered Forrester to drive from the road and attempt to thread a way through the trees. The driver nodded with quick comprehension, his eyes sharp and eager. The car lurched across the ditch, smashed through a fringe of underbrush and rocketed down the slope. A stump blocked their path, and Forrester swerved around it, scraped off a fender against a tree—but roared on.

Wentworth's eyes swept the way ahead. By following a zig-zag path, there seemed every chance that they would manage to make the open field below the woods. A half mile away was a farmhouse, and there would be a road there to the highway beyond. Hope began to rise again in Wentworth's breast. He peered behind. The troops had been thrown from the trucks and were lined up for volley fire, their rifles snouting perilously down the steep grade.

"Down!" Wentworth snapped to Forrester. "Stop and duck!"

Instead, Forrester wrenched the wheel violently. The car made a skidding turn around a thick-boled maple, turned again and drove down the grade. . . and the rifles crashed out in a single, heavy concussion of volley fire. The windshield dissolved in slashing, silvery fragments. Forrester uttered a choked cry and was driven forward across the wheel, slain instantly. By some miracle unhurt, Wentworth made a frantic grab for the wheel. Too late. The car, like a thing possessed, hurled itself squarely against a tree!

Wentworth felt himself plucked from his seat by the giant's hand of momentum and pitched through the air. He had a whirling glimpse of barren tree limbs overhead, then dazzling light and utter blackness struck him in one agonizing blow.

As his senses flickered and went out, he had a single despairing thought. If he were not killed, he would be captured—and the Black Police would see to it that, if he regained consciousness at all, it would be only to dangle at the end of a rope! This was the end—and that end was triumph for the Master!

CHAPTER SEVEN

VOTES FOR MURDER!

THERE was no need for outlaw spies to carry the word of disaster to the Catskill camp or to Nita in her hideout in New York City. Within a half hour of Wentworth's capture, unhurt except for superficial lacerations and a concussion, the news was broadcast from every state-controlled radio. They calculated on the effect of that announcement to smash the final opposition to Governor Whiting and turn the election overwhelmingly in his favor—the election that was only three days away. . .

But the Master was not content with that. Wentworth was ordered, as the *Spider*, to immediate trial in Albany on multiple charges of murder. The radio carried more announcements that members of Wentworth's band had confessed their complicity and that many of the Black Police were in his pay; and that Wentworth and Wentworth alone was responsible for the spread of the plague. His men had stolen experimental virus from the hospitals, it was charged, and, under the guise of administering antitoxin, had infected fresh hundreds with the dread White-Face Plague!

Such a trial could have only one end and Nita, hearing the news in her New York City hideout, was brought, pale-faced and terrified, to her feet.

Her impulse was to dash madly to Albany to Wentworth's side to share whatever fate was to be his, but she fought down that madness. She must play a much more desperate role than that. She must fly to the Catskill camp and help organize Wentworth's rescue. Kirkpatrick would be there, but such furtive attempts were not his strong point. No one could be better at leading men, or in an open attack, but no such means would succeed in this case. The Black Police would be ready for a frontal attack.

Within a few minutes after the announcement had come over the air, Nita was in action. She recalled Sailor Joe and Ram Singh from the tasks to which they had been assigned and laid her plan before them.

"You two will put on Black Police uniforms," Nita ordered, "and commandeer a plane to fly me, as a prisoner, to Albany. We must get there at once before any foolish frontal attack is organized and our manpower wasted."

Ram Singh drew himself to his full, powerful height. "*Wah, missie sahib!*" he cried. "I will myself fly to Albany. I will break into the governor's home and my knife. . ." His hand went to the heavy hilt, half-concealed at his waist.

"You will have your chance to use those knives!" Nita said and her voice was cold and fierce. "But tonight is not the time."

Sailor Joe tugged his forelock. "You're giving the orders, skipper. Me and Whiskers here will trail along."

Ram Singh's eyes flashed toward the broad-shouldered, red-faced man, but he recognized that no affront had been offered to his dignity. They had fought side by side before this! He bowed to Nita, cupping his palms to his forehead.

"Yours to command, *missie sahib!*" he said, gutturally. "There is a thing I have learned today, *missie sahib*. All the supplies of antitoxin for the plague are being brought to New York City and placed under heavy guard in the Sixty-Ninth Regiment Armory. It is to stop the raids of our men."

Nita nodded, scarcely conscious of what the Sikh said. Dick needed her help. That was her only thought now. "Hurry!" she ordered. "The Black Police uniforms!"

She kneeled and opened a secret section of the baseboard and removed the uniforms, tossed them at the men. She drew out also some forged official forms such as the Black Police used and skillfully, with her hand trained in drawing and painting, forged a warrant for herself and an order to commandeer an airplane. When she had finished, Sailor Joe and Ram Singh strode back into the room. "I keep telling him he ought to shave off them whiskers," Sailor Joe said. "They'll spot us sure."

Nita smiled. "Sikhs never shave," she said quietly. "It is a part of their religion. . ."

Ram Singh said harshly, "Yours to order, *missie sahib*. If these miserable hairs endanger you and the master, they shall come off!"

Nita shook her head, though tears touched her eyes. She realized the sacrifice Ram Singh offered to the cause. In his own eyes, he would be eternally disgraced if he removed his beard, shorn of his birthright as a Singh, a lion of warriors. "If you have escaped detection in New York City in the work you have been doing," she said, "you'll be safe enough tonight. Come, we must hurry!"

The papers Nita had forged got them their plane and, within the hour, they were in the air and speeding toward the Catskill camp. The flight was brief and, presently they slanted to a landing in a pasture. The plane was rapidly wheeled into the cover of the woods and a car, hidden for that purpose in a nearby deserted barn, sped them on their way to the camp. They switched presently to horses and, after what seemed to Nita an interminable time, the hails of sentries stopped them, then heralded them to the camp.

Nita was stricken afresh by the camp. Usually, there was a supporting buoyancy, a brisk and hopeful tone to the very voices of the men. Today, there was a forlorn and despairing droop to men's shoulders. Their challenges and cries were listless. Overhead, the skies were leaden and seemed to sag to the very hilltops. As Nita entered the stockade before the tree-masked cabins, a cold rain began to lash downward. The wind made a deep mourning in the barren trees.

NITA found the main cabin packed with fully fifty men and, standing on a chair at one end, was Kirkpatrick addressing them. "Our spies," he was saying, "have brought us word that tonight, the commander will be held in the Black Hole concentration camp and taken some time during the night or tomorrow morning to Albany for trial. That is our chance. . ." He broke off at sight of Nita, stepped down to greet her.

Kirkpatrick's lean face had grown more dour and drawn since last she had seen him. In his eyes, too, there was hopelessness—as if he knew in advance that what he proposed was foredoomed to fail.

The men were all staring at her, Nita realized, and they even raised a muffled cheer. It was not that they distrusted Kirkpatrick, but all their loyalty was given to Wentworth. It was the reflection of that whole-hearted service to the *Spider* which made them turn to Nita now. It was a weapon she could use to forestall the madness of the thing Kirkpatrick was planning. It was plain that he had no specific information as to time and route, or even the method by which Wentworth would be taken to Albany. Their strength was too slight to risk on so long a chance.

"I bring a message from Dick," Nita told Kirkpatrick, her voice low, but her eyes direct as she told the lie. "One of my spies managed to get near him."

Kirkpatrick's face brightened. "Splendid!" he cried and swung to the men. "Miss van Sloan brings a message from the commander!"

Nita's conscience troubled her at the way in which her lie was whole-heartedly accepted. She was lifted to the chair where a moment before Kirkpatrick had stood.

"The commander says," Nita's voice rang clearly, "to carry on the election campaign! He has a plan for his own release and the capture of the Master! He will communicate when the time is ripe!"

There was nothing half-hearted about the cheer that was raised this time. Harassment left their faces as if by magic and Nita put a gay smile on her own lips.

"I'm not sure," she said lightly, "but it almost seems that the commander intended himself to be captured, but wouldn't tell you about

it because he knew you would not want him to run that risk for you.
He says, 'Keep on fighting!' He says, 'Our day is near!' He says, 'I will
send you word!' Dismiss and spread the message!"

The men trooped out and, when they were gone, Nita's shoulders
drooped in spite of her strongest efforts. Kirkpatrick hurried toward
her eagerly. From a distant corner of the room, a small man in a priest's
black robe came toward her. He had a rueful smile on his gentle face.

"It was gallantly done, daughter," he said, "but why need you lie
to these men?"

Nita held out her hands to the priest, "Father Flower!" she cried
gladly. "You can ask that? Didn't you see how much stronger they
were! How much more bravely they went out!"

Kirkpatrick's face was dazed. "You lied?" he repeated. "You. . .
lied? Then Dick has no plan? What madness is this, Nita?"

Nita spun on him. "It is madness to make an attempt to save Dick
when you don't know the plans! How do you know they won't fly
Dick to Albany, and send out a machine-gun company in trucks to
trap you? We have too few men to risk them that way with Dick's life,
and the fate of the whole state in the balance!"

For a moment, stern anger darkened Kirkpatrick's face, but slowly
it faded. "You are right," he said, almost humbly. "If you, who loves
Dick so, dare to wait, then it is not for me to order immediate action.
Do you have any plan?"

"Only one," Nita said quietly. "Wait—and send spies to learn the
truth. Our best chance will come during the trial in Albany. When that
day comes, Stanley, one of us must wear the robes of the *Spider*. In a
fair court, that might convince them that Dick was not guilty. Aside
from that, with the *Spider* to lead them—and remember that the men
know Dick is only using the *Spider*'s identity and name to strengthen
the cause—the men will fight each with a dozen men's strength."

Kirkpatrick's face was pale, but there was fierceness in his clear
blue eyes.

"That will be my job," he said softly. "It is only right that I should
wear the robes of the *Spider*—I who have fought him so many times
and with such a sore heart. Perhaps, in that way, I can make amends."

His voice was desperate, but forlorn. It was as if he pledged himself to a cause lost before it was launched.

But Nita knew how great an effort that declaration cost him. Even in the battles as an outlaw, Kirkpatrick had done his best to uphold the law and order to which he had given a lifetime of service. If he were discovered in the *Spider*'s robes, not even the eventual triumph over the Master, the complete cleansing of the state, could ever restore him to his previous position. And yet, he was the man to lead!

Nita said quietly, "I agree."

Father Flower sighed, "I shall pray!"

He moved away to his room, and Kirkpatrick led Nita to the blazing fireplace. "Nita," he said slowly, "there was a hidden significance in your words that perhaps you didn't recognize yourself. You said that Dick had planned for himself to be captured. I've been afraid from the first of something close to that—that some of our own men planned it for him!"

"You mean. . . treachery!" Nita gasped. "Oh, no, none of these men would do that to Dick. They are too loyal!"

"Colonel Rice commanded the guard," Kirkpatrick said slowly. "The truck was rolling ahead and the road was blocked only by a barricade of cars. He could have rammed them aside. He didn't even try. He had machine guns but the attacking men suffered not a single casualty of any kind!"

"But Colonel Rice is being put on trial with Dick!" Nita cried. "Surely, he wouldn't do such a thing as that!"

Kirkpatrick shook his angular head bitterly. "I have been debating the possibility that Colonel Rice is the Master himself!" he said. "We know that it must be someone who has access to the Capitol. Rice has it. We know that once before the Master hid behind the identity of a minor official. He posed as the governor's secretary!"

"You may be right," Nita said slowly, "but if that's so, then the Master knows all the secrets of our camp! He may be, at this very moment, surrounding us here!"

Like an echo to her words, guns crashed suddenly outside the cabin and men shouted an alarm. A machine-gun chattered in a long, furious drum roll. Kirkpatrick and Nita stared at each other, then Kirkpatrick snatched his revolver from an under-arm holster and raced for the door.

"If we're attacked in force," he called back over his shoulder. "There's only one thing to do! We'll have to slip out by the crawlway Dick arranged. It's our only chance."

Even as he reached the door, there was a stunning blast and through its rumbling concussion, Nita heard the screams of a man and the roar of an airplane engine. Other explosions followed sharply on the heels of the first.

"We must retreat at once!" Nita called. "There's no time to delay. It does not matter how few men are outside, the camp has been discovered now and is useless!"

Kirkpatrick nodded brusquely, stepped outside the door. Nita heard his voice lifted in command and she ran to the trapdoor which opened into the basement beneath the cabin—and the crawlway which had been built by the idle men stationed here in the months of the Master's domination. It had been finished before Colonel Rice came to the camp, and there was a strong likelihood that he had not been told about it. If he had—Nita's lips twisted—then everything was lost, and Dick would never be rescued unless he could devise means to free himself!

Men began trooping into the cabin. Sailor Joe and Ram Singh hurried toward her, bringing Father Flower. "We got orders to take you out first, Miss Nita," Sailor Joe said hoarsely, "and we ain't got much time. Captain Kirkpatrick is going to blow up everything when the last man is through."

Nita drew in a slow, deep breath. Treachery and defeat, Dick a captive... They were beaten now, finally, permanently. She threw back her head and laughed, "Now, we begin to fight!" she cried. "I'll lead the way!" She went down in the darkness and damp gloom of the basement and moved toward the masked entrance of the crawlway.

RICHARD WENTWORTH learned of the disaster at the camp during the first day of his trial when the prosecutor made his opening address before the court.

"We are happy to announce," said the prosecutor, "that the last encampment of the outlaws has been annihilated. Men captured with the prisoner before the bar were glad to confess in greatest detail and to tell the secret of the camp where they had been virtually enslaved. . ."

Wentworth knew the helpless burn of fury. He had heard the evidence of those men who were "glad to confess." He had been a helpless prisoner in a dark, tiny cell at the main concentration camp when that had happened. He had heard the screams of men under torture. He could not blame them. Pain could loosen almost any tongue. His attention was drawn sharply to the prosecutor.

"We deliberately waited to allow them time to call in their reserves scattered all over the state," the man was saying. "Three flew in from New York City, two of them traitorously disguised as Black Police and bringing a woman with them who, we are reliably informed, is the inamorata of the prisoner before the bar. They were destroyed, all of them, in the attack!"

Wentworth found himself dazedly on his feet, felt the hard grip of hands upon his arms that dragged him to his chair again. But he scarcely heard the order that caused him to be chained down. Nita. . . Nita had flown to the camp and been. . . God, no, that couldn't happen to brave Nita!

So he consciously told himself, but there was a cold despair that told him this was truth. It was precisely what Nita would have done when she learned of his capture. She would have sped to the camp to organize rescue. If the blow had been intended to destroy Wentworth's morale, it had succeeded terribly. His spirit was not broken, but there was in him no will to live. Even if he escaped now, it would be a single-handed contest against overwhelming force. Kirkpatrick, Nita . . . gone.

During that day, he scarcely heard the procession of glib witnesses who confessed that they had helped Wentworth in his efforts to rob the state and put the blame upon the regularly elected officials. This was a cleverer plan than the Soviet government had thought out. Instead of permitting intimidated men to testify, they sent substitutes to court under the names of the accused. But when sentence was passed, it would be Wentworth's allies who were executed! On the stand, they confessed, too, that they had deliberately spread the plague through the state, under the guise of administering antitoxin!

When the long day was finished, the eve of election, Wentworth was led, still in chains, back across the armored bridge that had been built to connect with the jail. Through a high, bullet-proof window, he caught a glimpse of the street. It was filled with troops for two blocks around. Barricades fronted the jail building and the court and there were mounted machine guns upon it. Bewilderment touched Wentworth. If the last band of his men had been wiped out, why were all these precautions being taken against rescue? For a moment, he knew a gleam of hope, but it died quickly. It must all be intended merely to impress upon the people that revolt was useless.

One of the guards jostled him away from the window and sneered at him, "We're protecting you against the mob," he said hoarsely. "After they found out you spread the plague, they wanted to lynch you. We wouldn't want nothing like that to happen to you."

Only once during the election day, the second and last day of the Wentworth's trial, did he rouse from his lethargy. That was when Miller, the G-man who had taken Governor Whiting back to Albany from the Catskill camp made a brief appearance in court.

"This trial is completely irregular!" Miller shouted at the judge, his square face an angry red. "The prisoner has been given no chance to prepare his defense! I warn you that the federal government will take action!"

Miller was expelled from the court, and there were no further interruptions to the glib steadiness of the "confessions" that condemned him. The jury returned its verdict without leaving the box and the spectacled judge leaned toward Wentworth. He had been a political magistrate in New York City when the Whiting regime had begun but deaths and "resignations" had opened the way to the higher bench. He smiled thinly now.

"Does the prisoner have anything to say before sentence is passed upon him?" he asked and the question was like a threat.

Wentworth pushed heavily to his feet under the weight of his chains. Now that the travesty was ended, he found the remnants of his courage again. His head came up and the twist of his lips was mocking as of old. His friends were gone, his allies smashed, but he was still alive. He had begun his battles against the underworld alone long ago. Bereft of friends, he would be stronger than ever, because no longer were there any ties to hold him back.

"I'm afraid," he said dryly, "that truth would carry no weight in this court. Go ahead and sentence me, you hireling of crooks. God knows what name you put to the proceedings here, but they are a mockery to the name of justice!"

The judge's face turned angrily red, and a guard's fist smashed Wentworth back into his chair.

"Stand!" the judge shouted. "Stand while you are sentenced!"

Wentworth's bloodied lips still held their mocking smile as he pushed to his feet again. "That was well done," he said, "and typical of this court's justice!"

"Silence!" The judge was on his feet now. "Richard Wentworth, I sentence you to die by whatever means the state has decreed for the death of traitors! You will die tomorrow at sunrise!"

Wentworth started at the pronouncement. He had known he would be executed, but so soon! He flung back his head and clung to his smile. He was not yet dead!

"With you will die," the judge shouted on, "the nine men who have confessed you as their leader, in murder and crime!"

Wentworth's eyes swung toward the nine smiling men who had posed as his adherents and "confessed". Well, they knew that the men whose names they bore would die in their stead! Fury shook off every shred of Wentworth's despair. By God, somehow, he would break free and smash this corruption. . .

"Take the prisoner away, and do justice upon him," the judge finished hoarsely. As the guards gripped Wentworth's shoulders and thrust him once more toward the armored bridge that led to the jail and his double-barred cell, the prosecutor rose suavely to his feet.

"Thank you, your honor," he said pleasantly. "This completes our victory. I'm sure you will be glad to know, your honor, that the vote in the election today was ninety-eight percent for Governor Whiting. Next election, I think the other two percent will swing into line, too. It will be healthier!"

The court attendants broke into uproarious laughter and that was the sound that rang in Wentworth's ears as he was thrust into his cell, and the five men of the death watch took their stand outside. The chains were still on his ankles and wrists.

EXECUTION DAWN

HELPLESS in his chains, Wentworth sat out the long hours of the night. It was hard to cling to courage when the end was so near and so certain. He long ago had tested the strength of his tool-steel chains and found them beyond his strength. Under the constant vigilance of the five guards, there was certainly no hope. He tried to shape some plans. Would the execution take place here? Wentworth thought not. The nine men sentenced to die with him were still at the main concentration camp so far as he knew. If that were so, he would be moved some time during the night to the camp, or they would be brought here. . .

Wentworth schooled himself in patience to wait for that. Ten men were to be executed together. Even weighted with chains, ten men were a force to contend with. If he could stir them to action. . . It was past midnight when a file of men tramped down the hall and his cell door was thrown open. Without words, Wentworth was chained between two of the Black

Police who formed the guard and marched along echoing corridors.

Other prisoners sprang from their bunks to stare at him with white faces. They cursed him, heaped abuse upon his head. "The Plague-Bringer," they called him and the bitter words twisted a dull knife in Wentworth's heart. Even if he won freedom, what could he hope to accomplish against such madness as this? The people blaming him, fighting instead of helping him! He could look for no further action from Washington, since the election had failed. Before long, the Master might be stretching out his tentacles toward the nation's capitol itself!

Wentworth's thoughts were broken off short as he saw the arrangements that had been made for transporting him. An armored truck, such as was used to transport money, had been converted into a prison truck. He was wedged into a metal-lined cell barely large enough to receive him, the door slammed and locked. All around him was the roar of truck and motorcycle motors, and he had glimpsed machine guns mounted on them all.

Once more a transient doubt touched Wentworth. Were, all these precautions really necessary to guard against his being lynched? Or had the prosecutor lied about the complete destruction of his forces? The memory of the curses of the other prisoners came back to Wentworth and he deliberately killed his hope. No, escape must rest with him alone.

The truck lurched forward finally and, amid the clattering of a score of exhausts, got under way. Hours dragged past. It was only by a rigid exercise of his utmost will power that Wentworth resisted the inclination to fight against the close-pressing steel walls. They seemed to be strangling him, squeezing out his life. He controlled himself, but the effort left him exhausted. His knees sagged, but he could not even sit between the coffin-close walls.

The tapping must have been going on for minutes before Wentworth was even conscious of hearing it. He strained his ears then and caught, vibrating through the steel, a rhythmic series of barely audible sounds. Then he recognized Morse code and his heart leaped with hope—to die at once. It could not be any one except another prisoner. Nevertheless, when the Morse tapping stopped sig-

naling his name, Wentworth caught up a link of steel and began to
rasp out an answer.

"*Who are you?*" he signaled.

The reply came back deliberately. "*Miller. Sentenced to camp. Is
there any chance of rescue?*"

Wentworth smiled wryly in the darkness. Did Miller also think him
a miracle man? "*None,*" he tapped back. "*None at all.*" He hesitated
a moment then asked the question which had been gnawing at his heart
for days, "*Was my camp really destroyed?*"

Miller answered with a single word, "*Yes!*"

So that faint hope was finished! Miller proceeded to tap out some
of the details about the attack, about the election. Every word that
clicked out of the steel seemed to drive despair deeper into Wentworth's
soul. His control snapped and for a moment, he fought wildly against
the steel walls. His chains clattered, nearly deafened him in that narrow space. Finally, he sagged exhausted.

IT WAS perhaps an hour afterward that a series of hails signalized
their entrance into the concentration camp. Hauled finally from
his cell, Wentworth found himself scarcely able to walk, but he was
hustled along without mercy. He saw that the east was faintly grey.
Dawn. Execution dawn. Was it so close then to the time when he was
to die?

Wentworth threw back his head and sucked the crisp, cold air into
his lungs. Overhead the autumn sky was purple with increasing light.
The ground was iron hard with frost and rang under his heels. The
shackles were burning cold against the bare flesh of his wrists.
Wentworth stared hungrily about him. It was this hunger for life within
him which convinced him that he had not given up hope—not consciously. He would fight before he died, but what could it accomplish?

Men were stirring this early in the day. He could make out faintly the
blockhouses on the quadruple walls and fences that ringed the camp.
Over there near the guardhouse. Wentworth stared. It was a priest, all
right, but it couldn't possibly be Father Flower! The next instant,
Wentworth strangled his hopes again. Even if it were the gentle priest

of the outlaws, it could mean nothing except that he had come to offer final consolation.

Wentworth was on the point of asking for the priest, but restrained himself. So long as he did not talk with the man, he might in his secret heart hope that Nita had escaped the camp. It could not be Father Flower, of course. . .

Wentworth was hustled roughly across the quadrangle and thrust once more into a cell. At the sound of his entrance, other men stirred in their cells and pushed their pale faces against the bars. Wentworth realized that he was once more among his men, those who had been condemned without even the travesty of a trial—doomed by men who used their names, and lyingly confessed. At sight of him, they broke into a subdued cheer.

"The commander is back, men!" one cried softly. "Now we'll rip open this sardine can!"

Even in this moment of extremity, they counted on him! They could have faith that he would once more work one of those miracles which, time after time, had snatched them and himself from death. How vain it was now! Wentworth opened his lips to tell them, so—and could not. Let them hope. It would give them courage to the end. Let them even think he had a plan. . .

"Wait for my command," he whispered, "then strike! One of you ask for a priest!"

It had been an inspiration, that last. Let them think, too, that there was some chance of help from outside. Perhaps it was not vain. If they would all attack at his command, some might fight their way clear. . . Before the thoughts had coursed through his brain, armed guards were marching once more down the corridor. The cells were opened one by one and each man, as he was led out, had a steel collar locked about his neck—a collar whose chain linked him inescapably, before and after, to his companions. Their hands remained chained before them and short links coupled their ankles together.

Wentworth strangled down a mad impulse to wild laughter. Fight! Fight in chains that way? He stared despairingly at the faces of the men, but they were not downcast. There was in them instead a grim determination. One or two looked toward him, and there was a sly humor in their eyes, mingled with an almost idolatrous worship. Because he had bade them hope, not even these chains could daunt them.

WENTWORTH gripped the steel bars of his cell until his forearms burned with the pain of the tension. They counted on him. Could he let them down? By God, he would not. Somehow, before they were slaughtered, he would strike! It was his turn now. Men with drawn revolvers stood outside his cell and two men came in together with the last collar of the chain. It was clamped stranglingly tight about his throat. Outside, he could hear one of the men pleading for a priest, babbling, begging. . .

"How are we to die?" Wentworth asked quietly. "The court did not say."

The leader of the guard laughed hoarsely. "You'll find out soon enough. We got a neat new little gadget that ought to tickle your fancy."

One of the guards belched out a laugh. "Tickle his fancy! Gawd, that's good, chief! Tickle his fancy. . . Haw, haw, haw!"

There were guards at the head of the line and behind them now. Wentworth eyed their guns hungrily, but his heavy-manacled hands could not move swiftly enough to snatch one even if they came within reach. They had whips, too, and suddenly a lash bit through the clothing of his back and sent a stab of pain across his shoulders.

"March, you dogs!" the captain of the guard ordered. "March along. We got to kill you before we get to eat!"

Up ahead, the whips were cracking viciously and a man was still begging for a priest. They trooped along the concrete corridor dragging their chains, strangling against the steel collars, and debouched abruptly out into the quadrangle. It was dimly alight now with the increasing dawn and there was a faint redness to the clouds in the east. Sunrise. The prisoners of the camp were lined up in long lax ranks, their faces drawn and apathetic in the dim grey light. One group of men stood a little apart from the others. They seemed stronger, more alert than the others. Abruptly, with horror springing in his soul,

Wentworth swung back to the other men. He saw suddenly why they seemed so pale, why their lines and their manner was so listless and dull. They, too, were under sentence of death. Every man among them had the plague!

The man ahead of Wentworth in the chained line sagged suddenly back and began to cry out brokenly, fighting the forward pull of the chain about his throat. Guards were on him instantly, slashing him with whips. He sagged to his knees. "God, no!" he whimpered. "I don't want to die that way! Not that way!"

Wentworth stared ahead then and saw. . . how they were to die. A shudder tore at his soul and a fierce hot anger surged over him. In a glance, he saw the whole mechanism.

There was an electric winch with a chain fastened about the drum. . . a chain that would be hooked to their own and would draw them inescapably forward into the death machine. It was a circlet of stout, glittering steel blades like the chopping knives of a corn-fodder machine. As the chain drew them into those knives, they would be slashed to mincemeat—reduced to fragments of men while they still lived. No wonder the man ahead of him, brave fellow that he was, had collapsed in horror!

Now, he was staggering to his feet again under the bite of the whips. "A priest," he whimpered. "For the love of God, a *priest!*"

His voice wailed over the quadrangle. Wentworth saw a stir among those lines of doomed plague victims, and then, marching toward them; he saw again the black garbed priest. A feeling of utter incredulity shook him. *It was Father Flower!* If he had escaped from the Catskill camp, anything was possible. . .

Father Flower's gentle voice rang out clearly. "Peace, my children," he called. "If these men must die, let them make their peace with God!"

ONE of the guards whirled on the priest, and the whip lashed out. It licked about Father Flower's throat, and blood sprang in a thin, red trickle where the lash had cut. The violence of the blow threw Father Flower off balance a little, but the expression of his face did not change.

"For that, too, I forgive you," he said, still gently. "Let me go now to these poor men!"

A mutter stirred over the plague-ridden ranks as three trucks rolled abruptly out from behind the barracks buildings and leveled mounted machine guns at the prisoners. Father Flower ignored it all and came steadily on. The man who had struck him with the whip fell back, abashed, before the priest's unwavering courage.

"To hell with it!" the guard captain swore. "Get on with it." His whip swirled over the doomed men.

Father Flower's voice cracked out with a sharp anger. "Do you hope for mercy from God, you who show no mercy to others? Shall I call down the vengeance of heaven upon you, miserable sinner? Shall I curse the flesh from your bones and the fingers from your hands? Shall I curse the eyes from your sinner's face?"

The captain flinched before the barrage of the priest's suddenly stern voice. He looked about, but his men were quailing, too, and Father Flower marched on, his crucifix held before him.

The captain said, sullenly, "I guess it won't hurt none to let the priest mumble over them!"

Father Flower was moving along the line of men now, touching them with his hands. A man in uniform swung down from one of the machine-gun trucks, started toward them at a run.

"Stop that priest!" he shouted. "Get on with the execution!"

He caught up the end of the chain that was fastened to the winch in the slaughter machine. Dragging it forward, he fastened it with his own hands to the collar of the first man in the line.

"Start that winch!" he shouted.

Instantly, the slack of the chain was taken up and the slashing knives began to revolve. The sun pushed its red rim over the horizon, and its angry light fell upon the glistening blades, staining them as if already they were performing their butchery. The doomed men ahead of Wentworth braced themselves, fought frantically against that deathly chain, but their strength was not the equal of that machine-monster which dragged them to doom. Wentworth felt his own chain tighten and begin to drag him forward. "Say the word, commander!"

the man ahead of him pleaded. "Say the word, and let us strike now before it is too late!"

Father Flower was hurrying to keep pace with the line. He was abreast of Wentworth now, and Wentworth saw how pale his face was. His lips were moving in prayer. The first man was within a yard of those murderous, flashing knives!

"God help me," Father Flower was whispering. "God help me, I cannot permit this butchery! I. . ." Abruptly, his hand slid out of his robe and he held out a small, powerful revolver to Wentworth. "Do not kill, commander, unless you have to," he said. "It is my hand, which deals the bullets you fire!"

WENTWORTH'S weighted hands gripped the revolver as if it were his eternal salvation instead of the feeble thing it was. It might kill a few of these butchers, but no more. At least, they could go out fighting like men, not slaughtered like cattle! A guard saw the revolver and shrieked a warning, whirled his whip over Father Flower's head. Wentworth squeezed off a shot. His heavily weighted hands did not matter now. He had no need to aim. The guard pitched backward to the earth. . . but Wentworth had heeded the word of Father Flower and had not killed.

He fired again, and the man who gripped the lever of the winch staggered and fell backward. He clutched at the lever as he fell, and the clattering of the winch stopped suddenly as the first man in the line pitched forward into the very maw of the knives.

"Free yourself from that chain!" Wentworth cried. "And strike! Seize their weapons! Turn them on the guard, on the machine guns!"

The little revolver was cracking again in his hand. Ahead of him in line, the whip-lashed man surged sideways and dragged Wentworth and the man ahead of him along. He got the guard's revolver. "Flat on your faces!" Wentworth ordered. "Down for your lives!" With a sweep of his arm, he hurled Father Flower to the ground. Not an instant too soon! The machine guns burst into angry, hungry mirth.

"You prisoners!" Wentworth shouted at the plague-ridden men. "Do you love life so well? You are doomed anyway—dying! Kill some of the men who doomed you, before you die! Tear them to pieces with your hands. If you escape, I will cleanse you! I will cure your disease! It is the *Spider* who commands you! Fight!"

Like an echo of his words, guns began to hammer in the distance. There was the blast of a hand grenade, and he saw a machine-gun tower on the fence sag, riddled with the bursting shell fragments. Its gun was still.

"Help is coming!" Wentworth shouted. "My men are storming the walls! Fight, you dying men!"

It was a mad scene, a thing out of an insane man's dream. Men with palsied, disease ridden hands. Men without fingers and limping on the stubs of their feet, turned in sudden wrath on the guards about them. The machine guns stammered, and they fell in windrows of death, but even those who were wounded rose and shambled on to attack their murderers. And outside, guns hammered and there were more grenades. Wentworth's gun clicked empty in his hand, but he crawled to where a guard had fallen and found another revolver, and ammunition.

With deliberate, deadly aim, he opened on the machine gunners in the armored truck.

He could aim now, and the *Spider's* steady guns hammered with the skill and steadiness of years of practice on ranges and on the battlefields of crime. One by one the machine guns fell silent.

"Open the gates!" Wentworth ordered. "Smash open the gates!"

A few, a score or two, plunged toward the gates. The others were mad with slaughter, with wreaking upon these fiends in black uniform the agony of months of oppression and imprisonment, with avenging their withering bodies, stricken by the malignancy of man-spread disease.

Through the bedlam of death, one voice rose in clear, sweet majesty and, even in the midst of battle, Wentworth turned his head in amazement.

On his knees, his face turned toward the burning sun that thrust now wholly above the horizon, Father Flower was praying. . . praying for the souls of the men who thus paid the penalty of their crimes! It was over, even while Father Flower prayed. The gates burst open and a tight little group of Wentworth's men, following a striding figure in the black robes of the *Spider*, dashed in to complete the seizure of the camp. And from the mouth of that man in *Spider*'s garb came the crisp, ringing voice of. . . Stanley Kirkpatrick!

A great cry leaped from Wentworth's throat He stumbled to his feet and his chained hands reached out—for, stumbling blindly forward, running toward him with her arms outstretched, was Nita!

CHAPTER NINE

ARMY OF THE DYING

FOR a long moment, Wentworth gripped Nita's hands in his and his eyes blurred with tears, then her arms were locked tightly about his neck. Kirkpatrick's crisp voice was bringing order out of the chaos within the encampment. The last of the Black Police were being herded together, their machine-gun towers blown to bits. Even while he bent his head against Nita's fragrant hair, Wentworth's eyes were sweeping the enclosure.

There were many dead and dying upon the ground, but more than a thousand men were still on their feet. Most of them riddled with plague, yes, but frantic with hatred against the Black Police and the criminal over-lord of the state. He had promised to cleanse them of their disease. By God, if they would follow him, he would! There were supplies of antitoxin somewhere. . .

Now was the moment to strike—now while battle anger still shook them, while the state was rejoicing.

"Nita," he whispered. "Dear Nita. They told me you were dead!"

"Most of our camp was killed," Nita answered, her voice slow, heavy now with the relaxation of suspense. "A bomb collapsed the crawlway when only a few of us had broken through. But we gathered other men. . ."

"Do you know where there is a store of the antitoxin?" Wentworth interrupted. "These men must have it"

Nita told him swiftly what she knew of the concentration of the stores in New York City to protect it from their raids.

"New York City," Wentworth whispered. "Why with that in our hands again. . ." He broke into sharp laughter. "Free me of these chains, Nita," he cried. "There should be keys at the belt of the captain of the guard. Free me of these chains and we'll deliver New York City from the Black Police! Come on, hurry!" Minutes later, freed of the chains, Wentworth sprang to the hood of a machine-gun truck. "Listen to me, you men who are dying!" he cried. "I will bring you life and vengeance at the same time! A chance to avenge your families—or to rescue those who still live! Will you follow me? In New York, are all the stores of antitoxin which the Black Police possess. They are off-guard. They think we are finished forever. Will you follow me, to strike again a blow for liberty and your own lives? Will you follow me—you men who are dying—and form an army of death!"

For moments after his strong voice had rang out against the walls of the prison barracks, there was silence. Then a shout rose. A hoarse, formless shout from the throats of men who had despaired, and now were given a glimpse of life. Wentworth had his answer—an army that would follow him to hell itself!

Before that red sun, which had risen to see men slaughtered, had lifted itself an hour above the horizon, the army of death was organized and ready. Captained by the few men whom Wentworth had trained, armed from the arsenals of the Black Police, and riding in prison vans and machine-gun armed trucks, the army of death was pouring toward New York City.

In a car that raced at their head, Wentworth laid his plans with Kirkpatrick.

From him, he took the robes of the *Spider* and garbed himself in them. There was only one immediate cloud on the horizon, though it might well be that they rolled to their death. In all the prison, no one had been able to find a trace of G-man Miller.

"It's possible," Wentworth said slowly, "that they found he was signaling to me on the truck, and killed him. But I think not. Pass orders along the line that if G-man Miller is found, Kirk, he is to be brought to me. It is vitally important. Colonel Rice the Master, you say? No, he wasn't tried with me. And that is a little strange—more than a little."

Wentworth's grey-blue eyes stared emptily along the road ahead and, slowly, a smile began to tug at his lips. "I think," he said softly, "that I shall know the Master when I meet him! I think I shall know what to do!"

THE army of death was rolling through Westchester now. In other days, there would have been a thick line of traffic, of men bound to offices in the cities. Today there were almost none. The state was dying, was almost dead. Unless they could rescue it soon. . . But today, they would wrest New York City from the Master, perhaps slay the Master himself! Wentworth frowned. "Kirk, it's time to divide our force. You'll take a third of it and storm police headquarters. The radio will tell us when you have succeeded. There are two barracks of the Black Police. Sailor Joe will lead against one of them, in the Bronx. I'll take the force against the downtown armory where the antitoxin is stored."

He went on. "Once that is done, I'll go on the air, and appeal to the people. I think there will be small hesitancy on their part in deciding to help us, despite the propaganda of the Black Police and the Master against us. They couldn't really believe we would spread the plague. We have befriended too many of them!"

With those orders, Wentworth signaled a halt and the division of the forces was rapidly made. Father Flower, with Nita in the back of the car, was forlorn. It had been his hand, he felt, that had caused that slaughter in the city, and now more men were to die.

"It is the cause of heaven," he said, lifting his head now as the car was motionless. "If God had not intended it, he would not have let his servant prevail. I pray for you, Richard Wentworth."

Wentworth clasped the priest's hand warmly, "We'll try to deserve your prayers, father. Keep Nita safe with you."

Nita clung to Wentworth for a moment, then he was gone, striding to the car which would lead his contingent of the attack. . . Minutes later, the motorcade was under way again, but soon it divided and one line swung to the east behind Sailor Joe.

Presently, it divided again and Kirkpatrick parted with a swing of his hand. The cars filed past where Wentworth's column stood motionless and he saw the men's white, strained faces—the countenances of men who long had looked on death as their friend, and now hoped again. It was these men more than any other single factor, which would win the day. The Black Police would fight, but these men would be titans, without fear and without remorse.

WENTWORTH'S plans were fully laid for the attack upon the armory where the antitoxin had been stored. He did not intend to expend the strength of his men in useless fighting through the streets of New York.

At the first intersection of his course with that of the East Side subway, Wentworth flung his men from their machines and down the kiosks. People saw the traces of the plague and fled in panic. The train, which stopped at the station, quickly emptied itself of passengers in the same way, and Wentworth's men took it over. The guards were imprisoned and a man with a gun in his hand stood beside the motorman. The train swung on to the express tracks and bored at top-speed down beneath the city.

When it was necessary to slow down because of trains ahead, they delayed short of the stations and went past them at top speed. How long it would be before the police learned of the seizure, Wentworth could not guess, but they would not know his destination—and the train made far better speed than the motorcade could possibly have achieved through the city streets.

He remained on the front car and strained his eyes ahead along the dim corridors, of the subway. Station after station flashed past without an alarm. But it could not continue, Wentworth knew.

When the train reached the Thirty-third Street station, Wentworth abruptly halted it, disembarked his men and marched them at the double through crowds that parted hurriedly to give them passage. A squad of men, which Wentworth sent ahead, seized taxis on the street. And when his hundred and fifty men reached the surface, cars were waiting for most of them. Others were seized and, moments later, they were speeding southward again. Only a half dozen blocks to go now. Wentworth peered keenly ahead. As he watched, he saw a squad of Black Police dart from the entrance of the armory with a machine gun, and hurriedly set about rigging it up on a truck.

Calmly, Wentworth reached for the rifle of one of the men crowded into the cab behind him and took aim. At his first shot, a man was hurled bodily from the truck to the sidewalk. His second clipped the legs from under another policeman, and the balance bolted for the doors of the armory.

"On the sidewalk!" Wentworth snapped at his driver. "Right up the steps!"

The taxi hurdled the curb, bounced violently on the steps, but momentum carried them on. Just as the heavy metal doors were swinging shut, the taxi jammed in between, wedged them open, Wentworth was instantly out of the cab, revolver in each hand. He saw blurred, fugitive figures, and his guns spoke rhythmically. A rifle blasted close beside him and, up a flight of stairs, a man screamed. Wentworth whipped his head that way and, in the same instant, a grenade burst up there on the steps. There were more screams now. If that bomb had been thrown, the attack would have been blasted back in the same instant it began!

But more men were pouring past Wentworth now, coursing through the corridors with ready, hungry weapons, like hounds seeking a scent. Within two minutes, his entire force was within the armory. Wentworth ordered the taxi pushed out, the doors closed. Shots echoed from all sides within the building. Another bomb blasted, but the shouts that reached Wentworth's ears were cries of triumph. . . . His men were winning out! In fifteen minutes, the task was completed and the entire supply of antitoxin, cases of it in an emergency-rigged refrigeration room, were in Wentworth's hands. Rapidly, he instructed a half dozen men in the use of the needle, left a hundred men on guard in the armory and, with fifty others, raced farther downtown in the confiscated taxis.

No doubt that a counter-attack would be launched shortly on the armory, but he had left ample men for its protection and they would be on the alert. Machine guns were mounted now in all the turrets and on the roof of the building, and hand-grenades distributed. Wentworth knew that, except for the surprise of his own offensive, he could not possibly have forced the building.

But the armory was a minor objective, for all that it gave him the ammunition to fight the plague. Unless police headquarters itself was seized, they could not hope to conquer the city. The mass of the regular police force must still be ready to back Kirkpatrick, Wentworth believed. Without a leader, cowed by the swift vengeance of the Black Police if they erred, they had worn the Master's harness. They would be glad to throw it off—if headquarters could be wrested from the crew that held it!

AS WENTWORTH sped southward through the city, the sounds of heavy gunfire came to his ears, punctuated by the heavier thud of grenades. His face whitened with anxiety. Plainly, the battle was being fought in the streets, for otherwise he would not have been able to hear the sounds so clearly. That meant Kirkpatrick had been ambushed! With the reserves the Black Police could command, a simple reinforcement of Kirkpatrick's line would not help. He must plan something. . .

Even as the thought flashed across his mind, a scream of sirens heralded a column of motorcycle Black Police. Just ahead of his own motorcade, they flashed across Fourth Avenue. Each machine carried two men, and in the sidecar a machine gun was mounted. No doubt for what purpose they were intended! They would take Kirkpatrick on the flank!

With the thought, Wentworth flung his men to the attack. He whipped up his revolver and, with deliberate shots, picked off the drivers of motorcycles.

Three times, Wentworth's rifle spoke just as a machine gun was being aligned and three times the operators were hurled, lifeless, from their rests. Guns crashed interminably from the cabs. Motorcycles, rammed by the charging cars, were crippled and their men fled in frantic haste. One taxi caught a burst from a machine gun and ran wildly up the street. It smashed two of the cycles before it rammed a brick wall and came to rest. Within it, nothing stirred at all, and Wentworth's rifle silenced the gun.

Swiftly then, Wentworth reorganized his men. Under the leadership of one of his outlaw lieutenants, he organized a motorcycle squad. It was to circle far to the east and come at the police headquarters from the rear.

"Cover every window in sight," Wentworth ordered sharply, "then send your men inside under the barrage. I think three men working together might get one of the motorcycles in through the side door. You could command the entire first floor from that point. I'll strike from the west."

A half dozen of the machine guns were wrested from the motorcycles and thrust into the taxis. They could be wedged in place in the windows in place of solid mounting. Their accuracy would not be high, but should be sufficient to cover a charge. Wentworth sprang back to the leading taxi again and sent it racing at top speed down the street. The hammer of gunfire was continuing. At least, they had not succeeded in wiping out Kirkpatrick's force yet. . .

Two blocks away from headquarters, Wentworth flashed past on his race to take the police center from the west and south. He saw cars blockaded across the street and men firing from behind and through them. He frowned. It didn't look good. Kirkpatrick had been compelled to set up a siege of the building. By means of radio and telephone, the Black Police could summon reinforcements to attack from the rear. The offensive had to be pressed home at once, or all was lost!

ABRUPTLY, Wentworth halted the sweep of his cars, sent three men with messages to open the barricades. Then he divided his force into three parts, saving only three taxis, armed with machine guns, to go with him. Briefly, he outlined his plan.

"All three lines of cars will charge home at the same time," he directed. "Train your machine guns on the windows of police head-quarters and race past, firing as fast as you can. You will all turn to the right when you hit Centre Street, and hug the right hand curb. I'm going to circle and come up Centre Street from the south. While your barrage is hammering at them, I'm going into the building."

Protests lifted from the men, but Wentworth silenced them with a wave of his arm. "Either we take that building in the next five min-utes," he said quietly, "or the whole city is lost to us. That means death for all of us, of course, but it means much more. It means that we have lost all chance of ever reclaiming our state from these criminals! It means we are no longer free men, but slaves! It rests in your hands. Will you help?"

There was a rough, answering shout and the men raced back to their cabs. Wentworth, with his small force, tore off to the southward, cut across and back into Centre Street

An instant later the whole prospect opened up before him. At the door of police headquarters a dozen men's bodies lay sprawled, and they were the bodies of the attackers. Plainly, a machine gun had opened up from there on the instant when Kirkpatrick had thought victory within his grip. He had been forced to retreat behind barri-cades and attempt to shoot the Black Police out of their stronghold.

Flashes of gunfire came from the low-lying buildings opposite head-quarters, and Wentworth realized snipers were at work there. It was good work. Eventually it would succeed, but there was no time to waste. Wentworth knew that the troop of motorcycle machine-gunners he had intercepted was only the first of many relief forces that would be soon dispatched. Once they let them get inside the building. . .

His thoughts broke off as the first of the taxis, tires shrieking, cut into Centre Street. It was perfectly timed, for two other lines of taxis debouched from two other streets farther up at the same instant. Their guns opened as they entered the street and a heavy-concentration of lead blasted out the windows of headquarters.

For a space of moments, while Wentworth's own force raced nearer and nearer, there was no response at all. Then from within the building, a machine gun opened up. The second taxi in line slewed wildly and charged straight across the street at the headquarters building itself. Its guns were silent and it struck the wall of the building with crushing force, bounced, trundled a few feet down the sidewalk and nuzzled the bodies that littered the doorway. A grenade lobbed into the street and wrecked a second taxi, blocked the race of the cars—but their barrage kept up. Bullets laid a solid sheet of metal against the windows.

Under that screaming arch of death, Wentworth drove his own attack home.

Now machine guns were opening in the side street also, from the captured motorcycles. Wentworth raced for the door, flung himself flat as a machine gun opened inside. Two of his men went down before that scything murder-stream, but the others dropped prone beside him and opened a heavy revolver fire.

Then a second machinegun opened inside, farther back, and its lead did not scream out through the portal. The motorcycle attack had pressed home! With a shout and a wave of his arm to the men in the taxis, to Kirkpatrick's men at the barricades, Wentworth leaped for the doorway. A machine-gunner was dead across his barricaded weapon and, up the hall, a motorcycle was jammed half through a doorway, its machine gun commanding the approach.

FIERCELY, Wentworth caught up the machine gun of the slain Black Police. It was a heavy weapon, weighing seventy-five or eighty pounds, but in the fire of the attack Wentworth scarcely felt it. He moved toward the stairs with the gun kicking savagely in his arms.

There was a crouched squad of Black Police, a machine gun at the head of the steps. They scattered to the beat of Wentworth's bullets, were nailed screaming to the walls. Wentworth's men bounded up the stairs past him. Their shouts were hoarse with triumph.

There were screams of terror up there now as the disease-doomed men wreaked their vengeance on the Black Police whom they held accountable for all their misery. Wentworth dropped the hot machine gun, swung to others of the men pouring through the doors.

"Quickly!" he ordered. "Block the street with those taxis. Bring the machine guns in here and mount them on the first floor. Twenty of you take guns across the street and mount guns on the roofs of those buildings. Then let them try to drive us out of here!"

Wentworth sprang to the door. Kirkpatrick was already at work on the things he had just ordered and Wentworth laughed aloud at the sight. The armory was in their hands, and also police headquarters. If Sailor Joe had been able to drive home his attack in the Bronx. . .

"Quickly, Kirk!" Wentworth shouted. "Up to the radio room and let your old command hear your voice! Those men are loyal to you, personally! A few words will do it. . ." Kirkpatrick was beside him, and they were mounting the stairs to the radio room.

"Then order them to arrest all the Black Police they sight! Tell them to shoot if there is an instant's resistance! Give us an hour and we'll have this city cleaned out and ready to resist any attack the governor may send against us!"

Kirkpatrick nodded curtly. "Thank God you came in time, Dick. . . Hell, man, where are you going now?"

Wentworth was already bounding back toward the stairs.

"I'm taking twenty men, Kirk!" Wentworth shouted back. "I think this is a good time to take charge of city hall! If you need more forces, draw on the armory for them!"

VOLUNTEERS flocked to Wentworth at his call and he rapidly loaded them on a police emergency wagon and started a race toward city hall. As he swerved into Lafayette street, he flung on brakes frantically. From curb to curb the street was filled with marching people, thronging the way he was heading, Wentworth stared at them in amazement. Upon many were the ravages of disease and others bore the marks of torture at the hands of the Black Police. At their head. . . marched Nita and Father Flower, and the little priest bore aloft his crucifix.

It was a strange procession for a priest to lead and it was a strange song they sang. Wentworth caught the deep, hoarse vibrance of its rhythm before he could identify its words or tune, and it swelled to the heavens, filled the canyons between the buildings.

"Mine eyes have seen the Glory of the coming of the Lord,
He is trampling out the vintage where the grapes of wrath
*   are stored. . ."*

Old men marched with their heads flung back in a rejuvenation of spirit that swept their years aside. There were women who carried children in their arms and boys who strode along blindly, gazing on a dream. One and all they chanted the glorious paean of a war fought eighty years ago for freedom.

With a curt command, Wentworth sent the emergency wagon circling back and presently it rolled with the van of the procession. Cheers broke their song at the sight of the *Spider*'s black cape in their lead, the *Spider* marching beside the little priest with his upraised crucifix—beside the woman who led them with her glorious voice.

It was madness and it was wonder. A squad of Black Police ranged out into their path and, with lifted guns, ordered a halt. If the people heard them, they did not heed. They marched on, singing, singing. From the emergency wagon, a blast of gunfire rolled out. A few of the Black Police fell, but the others fled. And Wentworth knew it was not the bullets that had driven them into flight. It was the spirit of those marching people whom not death itself could stop.

As they marched, other scores and hundreds poured into their flanks and buildings trembled to the tread of their march. Now the city hall was in sight and, around it were lined deep ranks of Black Police. There were machine guns mounted behind barricades and armored cars loaded with rifle men. An officer on horseback galloped to meet the mob. His shouted words were drowned out in the deeper thunder of people's singing voices.

He yanked out a revolver and pointed it deliberately at Father Flower.

Wentworth's revolver spoke, and the man was hurled backward from the saddle. The people marched on.

Men were plucking up the priest now, catching hold of Wentworth, of Nita. Despite their violent efforts, they were passed back among the crowd, to safety from the threat of those guns. The marching people needed no leader now. The goal was in sight. Wentworth's shouted order to the men on the truck could not have been heard, but they, too, no longer needed a leader. Crowded behind the bullet-proof windshield of the truck, they opened fire. There were two Thompson submachine guns among them and, under the assault of bullets, men in black began to fall.

Now their machine guns, too, began to hammer. Swathes of blood were cut in those close-packed ranks, but they filled as soon as created, and never for an instant did the rolling chant of that battle hymn waver. The emergency truck crashed at full speed into the ranks of the Black Police. Many of them broke and fled, but others still hammered at the on pressing thousands. They might as well have tried to stop the march of the waves, the hurricane blast of a tempest. It was the sheer terror of the thing that could not be stopped—of men and women who marched singing to their certain death—that broke the spirit of the Black Police. Suddenly, the police were fleeing in every direction. . . and in no direction was there any escape. People fell upon them and slaughtered them with their bare hands, and all the while the song roared from their throats—the song of emancipation, of freedom and the triumph of the spirit over despair. The city hall was invested, overwhelmed.

Fighting to reach the mayor to force a surrender from him, Wentworth arrived minutes too late. He had been hanged from his own window by a score of willing hands.

WENTWORTH mounted then to the window from which the body of the mayor dangled and managed at last to make his voice heard. A great waiting quiet fell upon the multitude while their white faces turned upward to the man in the window, their savior from oppression. "Go to your homes now!" Wentworth called to them clearly. "Within three days an election will be held in which you shall name your new leaders! The police are in our hands. Antitoxin against the plague will be distributed. Governor Whiting will be forced to resign. All will be well. Go home now. You have done your job!"

The cheer that went up from the square made windows tremble in their frames then slowly the fringes of the crowd began to break up.

He was heavy with weariness and shaken with doubts. He had promised that Whiting would be forced out, and that the state would be honestly ruled again, but God knew that was far from accomplished. If they had caught the Master, yes—but with him at liberty; the rest of the state might still be turned against them. The federal government might intervene to put down an armed rebellion against a duly elected government. But if the Master were captured, the underlings would flee to cover, as the Black Police had scattered before the wrath of the aroused people.

Rapidly then, Wentworth put through a phone call to police headquarters. "Victory here Kirk," he reported steadily. "How did Sailor Joe fare in the Bronx?"

"Victory there, too," Kirkpatrick said briskly. "He has G-man Miller with him. Miller was locked up in a cell in the armory when Sailor Joe got in. . ."

Wentworth's voice leaped out. "Have a guard of fifty men thrown around Miller at once," he snapped, "and have him manacled hand and foot and locked in a cell!"

Kirkpatrick gasped, "Dick, have you gone mad? We need every friend at Washington we can get right now!"

"Mad?" Wentworth's voice rose. "Mad? No, I'm not mad! G-man Miller, so called, is the Master! I'm going after him at once!"

Wentworth raced down the stairs and caught up Nita at the door of the city hall. He raced with her to a car and sent it hurtling northward through the city. Crowds still blocked their way, but as they sped farther north, the people thinned out and he could go faster. He saw Black Police cornered and captured by men in blue, and everywhere the faces of people were beginning to smile again. Oppression was lifting. And at the armory in the Bronx would come the ultimate victory.

"No, I can't be wrong," Wentworth was saying rapidly to Nita. "This supposed Miller tried to get you to tell the secrets of the camp while you were prisoners in Albany. His credentials seemed all right, but I'm willing to swear that, when we investigate, well find that a G-man named Miller was murdered and his papers taken."

He pointed out, "When he came blindfolded to our camp in the hills, he told us nothing that every official in the state didn't know by that time—that the President had ordered an election. He came to make sure that Whiting was saved, and that he didn't talk. Whiting must have known more than he thought or else have known things the importance of which he didn't recognize."

"But he testified for you at your trial," Nita urged. "He tried to make them let you go."

"But he failed," Wentworth said, "and because he had protested, you and the rest figured that Washington must know the full details and didn't make any effort to communicate with federal authorities. That was what he accomplished, besides diverting suspicion from himself."

He explained. "In the prison van, driving to the camp, Miller tapped out messages to me, apparently as a prisoner trying to learn if I knew of any plans to liberate me. You notice that when we searched the camp for him, he was gone? That was because he was not really a prisoner. He didn't think there was any chance of my escape, so he had abandoned the role and left the camp. I realize that none of this evidence will stand in court, but it can be checked. . . as soon as we get the fingerprints of the real G-man from Washington."

HE BROKE off then as the armory came in sight over the crest of a hill. As he watched, men darted from the doorway and started off in all directions in cars and motorcycles. Nita's hand flew to Wentworth's arm, and he felt the elation suddenly go out of him. He did not need to ask the meaning of those suddenly dispersing men, but hoping against hope, he rushed into the building.

He found the cell where Miller had been prisoner. Lying in the corridor before it were the bodies of four men, terribly mangled by a bursting grenade. Two others had been shot, but the cell was empty. Miller was gone.

On the metal bench inside, Wentworth found a brief note addressed to him:

> *Greetings to the Spider. Sorry I can't remain for a more intimate converse with you, but I'm afraid this role has outlived its usefulness. Yours the victory, today. Mine, tomorrow!*
>
>   *The Master.*

On the bench lay the credentials of G-man Miller. That was all.

Sailor Joe came hurriedly into the cell. "I got orders from Captain Kirkpatrick, sir," he said, "and sent men to put the chains on Miller. Then I heard that explosion, and when I got here, Miller was gone! What the hell does it mean—begging your pardon, Miss, I'm sure."

Wentworth said heavily, "It means the Master has been too smart for us, once more, Joe. And while he's at large, we stand small chance of conquering the state and putting an end to the tyrannies of the Master and his men. We can look for trouble at once."

"But, Dick!" Nita cried. "You've won a splendid victory. If you work fast, you can beat him out."

"We will work fast," Wentworth said grimly. "And perhaps we'll win. It won't be for lack of trying." He looked down again at the note left by the Master, and his lips moved— *"Yours the victory today. Mine, tomorrow!"*

OVER NEW YORK
HAD SWEPT THE MASTER'S DREAD
BLACK POLICE—WIPING OUT
THE LAST ORGANIZED RESISTANCE
TO THEIR RUTHLESS UNDERWORLD
RULE OF THE EMPIRE STATE!

THE LITTLE CAMPS OF HONEST
FUGITIVE FIGHTING MEN,
BANDED TOGETHER UNDER
RICHARD WENTWORTH'S
DIRECTION, HAD
BEEN SCATTERED
FAR AND WIDE.

In one terrified, but loyal, town Wentworth was able to find a base for his final, desperate effort.

# BUT EVEN HERE, BECAUSE OF THE SINISTER SECRET ASSASSINATIONS OF THE MASTER, THERE WAS NOT MUCH AID.

NOWHERE WAS THERE RELIEF FOR THE THOUSANDS OF OPPRESSED, AND EVEN A DUPED FEDERAL GOVERNMENT WAS ARRAYED AGAINST THEM.

RICHARD WENTWORTH HAD REACHED TRAIL'S END!

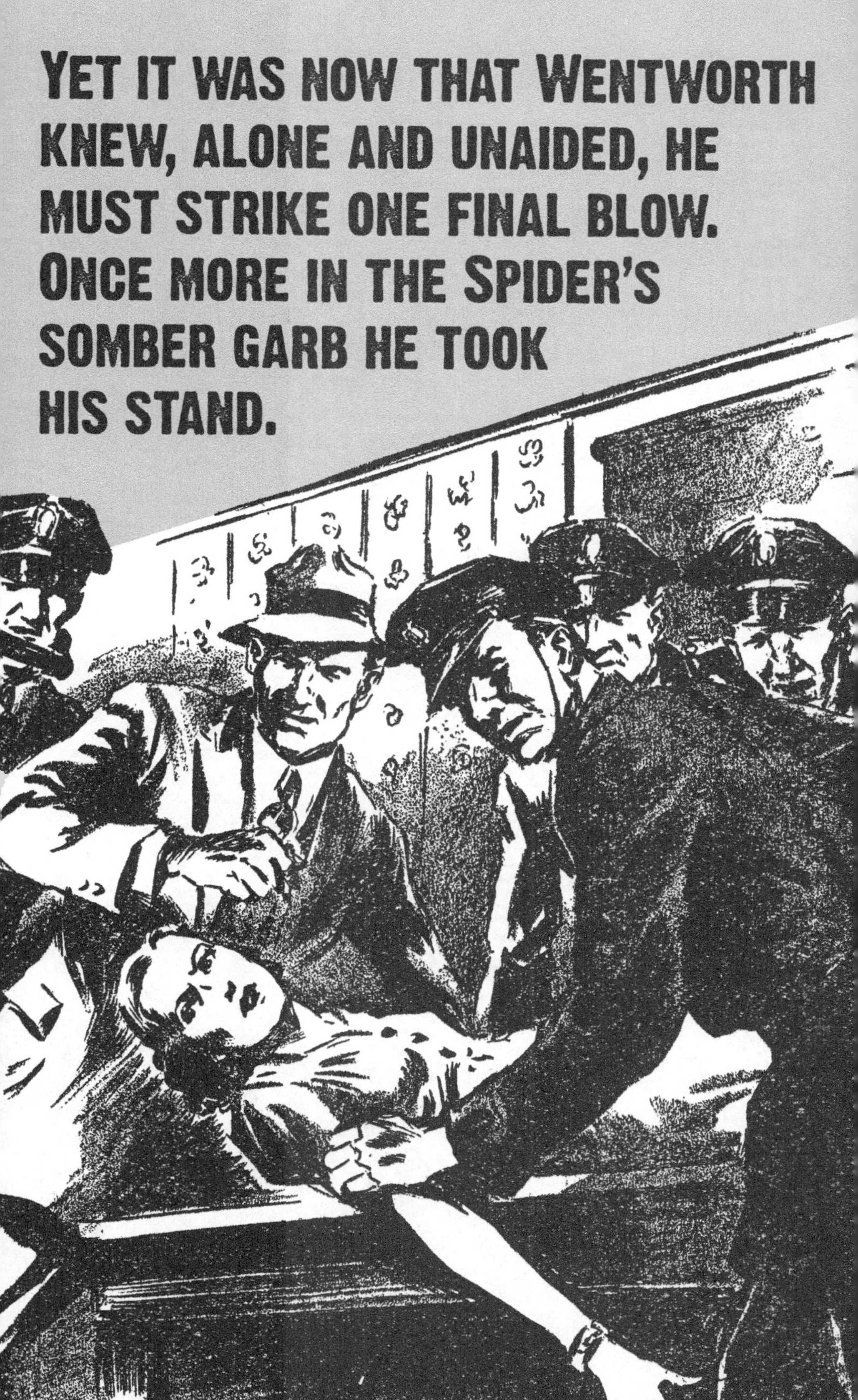

YET IT WAS NOW THAT WENTWORTH KNEW, ALONE AND UNAIDED, HE MUST STRIKE ONE FINAL BLOW. ONCE MORE IN THE SPIDER'S SOMBER GARB HE TOOK HIS STAND.

THE SPIDER STRUCK AGAIN AND AGAIN — TO RAISE THE EMPIRE STATE FROM THE DUST AND FREE AN ENTIRE DESPAIRING PEOPLE FROM THE SCOURGE OF LIVING DEATH!

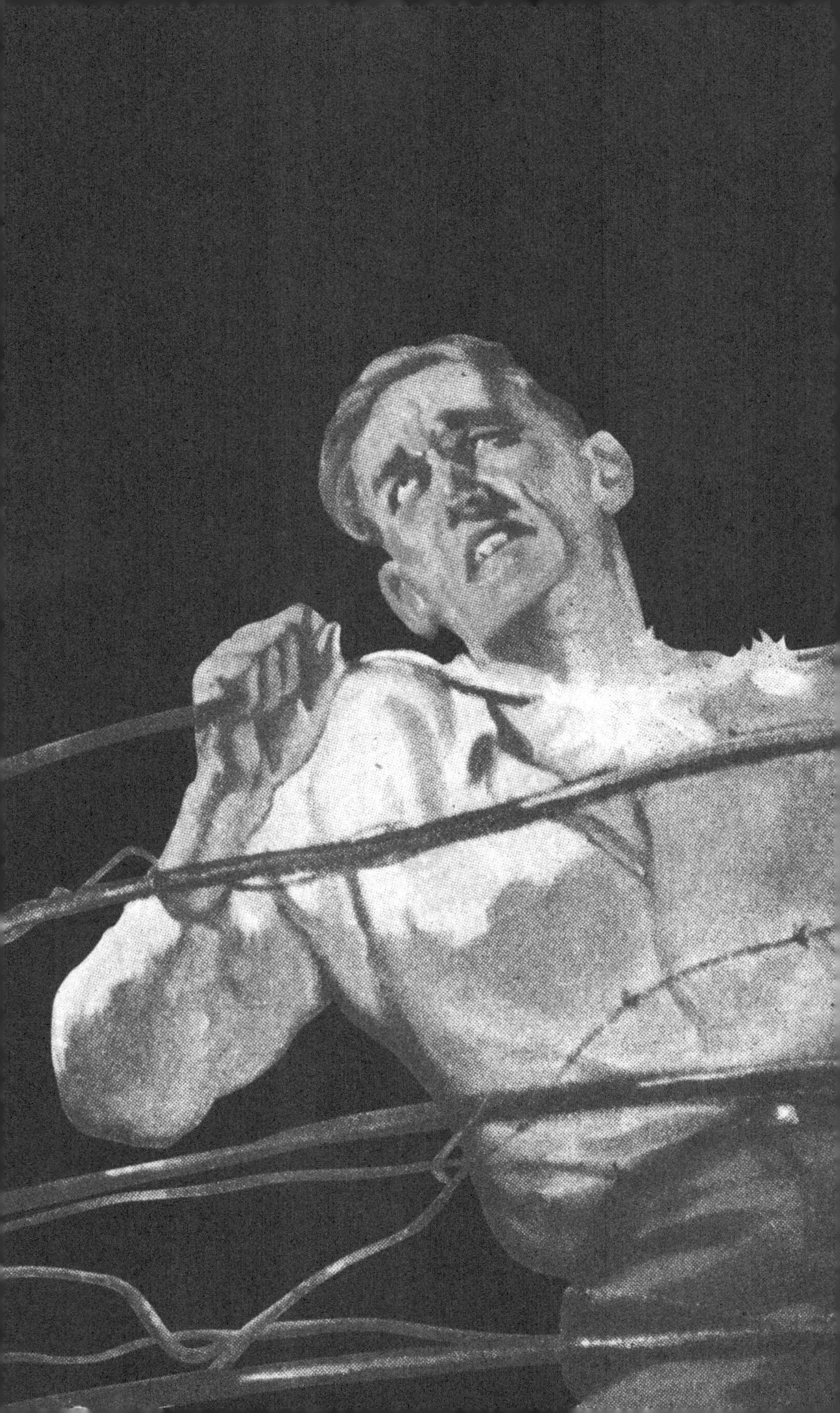

BOOK THREE

SCOURGE
OF THE
BLACK
LEGIONS

CHAPTER ONE

WHISPER OF DOOM

A DOUBLE file of policemen stood, back to back, and formed a narrow aisle from the doors of police headquarters to the powerful sedan waiting, with motor idling, at the curb. Each of the men held a revolver in his fist. On the buttresses, at either side of the doors, other men stood with machine guns. The eyes of all quested ceaselessly over the street, over the windows of the flanking buildings.

The doors whipped open and a chevroned sergeant barked an order at the police. "Close in!"

They narrowed the space between their backs so that a single man, with difficulty, could squeeze between them. The man in the doorway paused an instant. His face was lined with fatigue and his eyes, deep-set and shadowed, burned feverishly. He jerked his head impatiently at the tall, soldierly man beside him.

"Damn it, Kirk," he said irritably. "All this protection isn't necessary. If anyone wanted to kill me. . ."

"Someone apparently does," broke in the soldierly man—Stanley Kirkpatrick, revolutionary acting commissioner of police. His eyes swiftly swept the street and he nodded approval at the sergeant. "There have been two attempts on your life in the last forty-eight hours, Dick," he went on quietly. "It's madness for you even to leave headquarters."

"Let me be the judge of that, Kirk," the other man answered. "Those poor people are calling for Richard Wentworth and if I don't show myself, they're likely to get out of control. You don't want five thousand victims of the plague roaming the streets, spreading the disease. . ."

Wentworth's lips snapped grimly shut. Forty-eight hours before, he had led his small force of outlawed men against the criminals who ruled New York City and had managed to seize a partial control. Those criminals were the ones who had spread this horrible, leprosy-like disease among the populace. There had been only Wentworth and his small body of men to fight against the tyrants. Now the stricken were appealing to him for relief from the plague. Great armies of disease-ridden people were marching toward the city for the injections which would cure them. The supplies were here and, given time, they would be treated. But meantime, they must be held outside city limits less millions of others become infected. . .

"At least let me go in your place," Kirkpatrick made a final appeal. "Others can do my work, but we can't afford to lose you. Why, even this pilgrimage of plague victims may be a trick of the Black Police to capture you!"

Wentworth made no answer but went swiftly toward the car. There was scarcely room for him to walk between the policeâ€”every one of them was taller than his own six feet, and forming a flesh-and-blood shield between him and any assassins who might be lurking nearby. He was stepping into the sedan when a girl dodged past Kirkpatrick and ran toward the car. Kirkpatrick uttered a sharp cry and Wentworth whirled, hand leaping automatically to the gun beneath his armpit. He smiled then and let his hand drop. The girl caught his hands.

"There's no use in protesting, Dick!" she said swiftly. "I'm going with you! If there's any danger, my place is at your side. At least it can find us together!"

Wentworth looked down into her deep violet eyes, touched with gentle fingers the chestnut curls that softly framed her oval face. "No argument, Nita," he said gently, and handed her into the car. "Hurry, driver!" he called.

THE sedan lunged forward. The thin shriek of motorcycle sirens began and the thunder of their engines was all about them. Ahead and to the rear, sedans full of armed men formed a convoy. Wentworth disliked it, but conceded in his tired brain that it was perhaps necessary. The last forty-eight hours had taught him that the allies of the criminals he had ousted were still viciously active—and they knew well their business of murder!

Nor were the threats to his life and the impending invasion of the hordes of the plague his only concern. The criminals he had driven from office had been legally elected, and this placed Wentworth in the position of seemingly leading an armed rebellion against duly constituted authorities! It did not matter that hundreds of citizens had been tortured and killed; that outrageous taxes had been collected by racketeering methods and pocketed by the criminals and their myrmidons, the Black Police; or that it was the state government that had released the plague on the populace. None of these things could be proved in courts. . .

"Dick—" Nita's voice was low—"have you been able to get any word about what Governor Whiting is going to do in Albany?"

Wentworth, relaxed against the cushions with the enforced inertia which alone enabled him to continue for long hours without rest, opened his grey-blue eyes slowly. "No word at all," he said quietly. "We know that the Black Police hold all the rest of the state. He may lead them against us. I hope so."

"You hope so, Dick! Oh, you mean that then you might be able to take over the entire state!"

Wentworth smiled. "What I'm afraid of, Nita, is that Governor Whiting will call on Washington to send federal troops against us. After all, we are. . . insurgents."

"But, Dick, you couldn't fight them!"

"No," Wentworth said slowly, "we *wouldn't* fight them."

Wentworth was outside the law, but he had never turned his hand against the forces of the law, nor against any innocent person. As the *Spider*, that secret nemesis of all criminals, he had fought and killed criminals. Not even to save his own life, would he fight against federal troops. The state troops, the Black Police, were a different matter. They had been recruited from the underworld. Prison doors had been thrown open to flood their ranks. Not one of them but had been guilty of vile crimes under the crooked regime of Governor Whiting and the secret criminal power behind him whom Wentworth knew only by the name of the Master.

Wentworth sat more erectly and saw that the cars were rapidly nearing the outermost limits of the city. "You will stay in this car, Nita," he said crisply. "You'll be safer here, and I'll be safer since I can think only of myself."

Nita laughed, though there was tenderness in her eyes. "Dick, you never think of yourself!" she whispered.

Wentworth dropped his hand on hers, leaned forward to call to the driver. "Stop, and signal men from the other cars!" he ordered.

When the heavily armed men came toward him, Wentworth gave curt instructions in response to which his own car shot ahead of the others and they fell a hundred yards behind.

"Those poor devils with the plague trust me," he replied to Nita's protests. "Shall I show that I don't trust them by driving up with an armed escort like some European dictator?"

H E WAS peering ahead now and, from the crest of a rise, he caught his first glimpse of the thousands who had marched on New York City in the hope of relief from their awful disease. They had been stopped here by the police and, like dirty flood waters, they swelled out over the fields on each side of the highway.

They squatted on the ground in hopeless clusters—mothers with stricken children in their arms, listless aged men. But at the barricade the police had erected, there was another group. These were younger men and there was menace in their compact numbers. It was from them that the demand had come to see Wentworth. They had been lied to so much that their trust was worn thin. Yes, they had been promised help, but Wentworth. . .

Wentworth's lips set in a harsh line as the car rolled swiftly nearer and he saw more details of the horrors he had known he must find here. They believed in him, and by God, he would not fail them! It was for their sake that he had taken arms against the state government when he might so easily have fled to safety beyond its borders. It was for the sake of the people that he had so often risked his life as the *Spider* to fight their enemies. . .

"Stop here!" Wentworth ordered curtly, and punched open the door of the car.

"No, Dick!" Nita cried. "Let the car come closer, and. . ."

She stopped then, for already Wentworth was striding toward the close-packed group of men at the barricade. Resolutely, she drew an automatic from her handbag and held it ready in her hand, but her eyes were soft as she watched the steady swing of Wentworth's confident shoulders. They had borne so many burdens, but they never bowed even briefly in despair, such was the high courage of his heart. His head was high and there was no fatigue in the briskness of his stride, though he had not slept in forty-eight hours and more. . . Nita masked the gun in her hand and stepped to the running-board of the car. Dear God, let nothing happen to him. . .

The police at the barricade snapped to salute at Wentworth's approach, but he only acknowledged that briefly and mounted the barrier at once.

"You sent for me," he called out to the assembled thousands. "Here I am!"

White faces turned up to him incredulously. In the forefront of the crowd, a woman stared, and Wentworth saw her throat jerk convulsively. She dropped to her knees and her hands were lifted as if she prayed.

"It's Richard Wentworth!" Her cry ran thinly through the chill air of early winter. "Richard Wentworth, our commander, has come!"

Voice after voice took up that cry until it rang to the arch of the heavens, and Wentworth felt the hot stinging tears in his eyes. He felt humble before such trust. And Kirkpatrick had been afraid of trickery! Men and women were pressing forward with their up stretched, thin arms lifted to him. Wentworth lifted his hands.

"Please," he called. "Please, wait! Some medical supplies came with me and others will be sent as soon as possible. Also food. Quarters will be cleared for you on the northern boundaries of the city as rapidly as possible! You will be taken care of. I only ask that you wait for a little while—a few hours more, until people can be cleared out of the northern district of the city. You don't want others to fall ill of this accursed plague. I know you'll wait!"

His eyes quested everywhere over the people. They had left the meager fires they had built for warmth and were huddled before him like sheep, like children, frightened of the dark. The ambulance loaded with medical supplies, which had accompanied him, rolled up to the barricade, and Wentworth turned to the police.

"Break down this barricade!" he ordered. "These people have promised to wait!"

IF THERE was any hesitancy in the police in obeying that order, it faded before Wentworth's stern eyes. The barricade was breached and the ambulance backed closer. Interns made ready their injections and Wentworth stepped down among the plague-stricken people. He took off his overcoat and put it around the shoulders of an old woman. Her hands, gripping it, were twisted with the torture of the plague and her lips were dumb.

Wentworth turned from her—and from the thick-pressed ranks of the mob a man stepped forward. He had one arm in a sling. He pointed the cast of his arm at Wentworth and, at point-blank range, fired a hidden gun straight at Wentworth's breast!

Wentworth saw the movement of the man's arm, and the trick was old enough for him to be suspicious of a gun hidden in the cast. And yet he was not. He was overwhelmed with the misery of these people and for once his ever-alert guard was down. Richard Wentworth would have died in that instant, except for one thing.

His kindness saved him. The old woman about whose shoulders

he had placed his coat saw the movement and, with an inarticulate cry, she flung her body in the path of that bullet.

It tore cruelly into her worn back, and the impact of the brutal lead drove her into Wentworth's arms. He clasped her instinctively and fell with her to the ground. His hand belatedly leaped to his holstered gun. A moment before, there had been a thousand murmuring voices. Now they were stilled by the thunderclap of that shot. White faces stared in utter blank amazement at Wentworth, pitching to the ground with that aged woman clasped in his arms. But it endured only for a moment. Then a vast inchoate shout of rage lifted from a hundred throats. Before Wentworth could level his automatic and shoot down the assassin, a dozen men had thrown themselves between him and the killer!

Through the bedlam, Wentworth caught the angry shouts of the police; the hammer of engines as motorcycles and police cars raced forward. He sprang to his feet and, for a moment between the weaving heads of the crowd, he glimpsed the assassin. The man's face was bloodied and there were a score of fists beating at him. That much he saw before the assassin went down under the combined assault of an infuriated mob.

Wentworth sprang to the barricade and ordered the police back, then he leaped to the side of the old woman who had saved his life. He bent over her tenderly. . . and she was smiling. He bent close to her moving lips.

"My life," she whispered. "Nothing. You…you are the commander!"

Wentworth swung her into his arms and ran to the ambulance with her. "Quickly!" he rasped at the interns. "You must. . ."

He stopped then and something like a sob thrust hard and tearing into his throat. The old woman was already dead. Fury racked him. He sprang back to the barricade and flung a shout at the milling crowd beneath it. They could not hear him. He leaped down among them and fought his way to the midst of the brawling mob and finally they fell back. . . parted and let him gaze down on the thing that had been an assassin. He had been trampled into a shapeless mass upon the earth.

Wentworth's swift gaze brushed the faces of the men who stood around him. There was still fury in their eyes and horror. Wentworth said slowly, "It is well. I thank you. The relief work will proceed as rapidly as possible."

He turned heavily away and went back to the barricade and weariness weighted his heart. He had come to bring life—and death had followed him. It did not matter that this undoubtedly was an effort of the Black Police. To save him, that poor old woman. . . Nita was kneeling beside her, but it was futile. She rose as Wentworth came nearer and put her hand on his arm.

"Oh, Dick," she whispered. "I wanted to be with you!"

Wentworth shook his head. "I couldn't die with my work half done, Nita," he said gently. It was a rededication of his life to the service he had chosen. . .

The loud racketing of a motorcycle engine, the scream of its siren, jerked Wentworth about swiftly toward the road, and a policeman courier leaped from a machine, running to Wentworth with a written message.

"From the commissioner!"

Wentworth ripped it open, and his lips drew into harsh lines. He knotted the message into a tight wad, gestured sharply to the police. "Carry on here. I'll rush more supplies." He turned and strode toward the barricades. "I'll have to reassure them," he said aside to Nita. "We have to leave at once!"

"The Black Police!" Nita cried.

"It's worse than that," Wentworth clipped out his words harshly. "Washington has ordered federal troops out against us. I have one hour to surrender the city—and all my men!"

CHAPTER TWO

FLIGHT

BITTERNESS was in Wentworth's heart as he made his brief address to the plague victims, and rebellion sharpened his words. He had struck one shrewd blow at the Master who criminally ruled the state. From control of the city, his men might well move to an honest control of the entire state—and now in a single gesture the cup of success had been dashed from his lips. Oh, the Master played well!

There was one consolation. If the Master had found it necessary to appeal to federal troops against Wentworth and his men, it meant that his own control had been badly shaken. The Master would not want federal interference in the state. . . . Wentworth sprang down from the barricade and raced back to his sedan, sent it speeding toward police headquarters.

An hour was none too much time, but he could count on Kirkpatrick to assemble their men for a speedy retreat. He would know that there was no other course open to them.

Already, army planes were circling overhead. They

would not attack, of course, but at the first effort to escape from the city, they would give warning to headquarters. . .

As the sedan swept up to police headquarters, he saw the thick ranks of the men he had led to victory—barely a hundred of them left now. But they broke into cheers at sight of him, and Wentworth paused on the steps. A fierce resolve was forming in his mind.

"Men!" he called. "I have to lead you in retreat once more! But we will not lose everything we have gained here. The federal troops will take over New York City and it will be up to us to see that they stay here. I want a squad of volunteers to remain in the city and keep up an appearance of rebellion, stir the people to disorders—anything short of actual conflict with federal troops so that they will have an excuse to remain here. The probability is that you will be killed one by one. . ."

A sturdy man with a smiling, weathered face strode forward with the rolling stride of a seaman. "I'm your man, skipper," he touched his forelock. "We'll make them federals think there's a whole army hiding here."

Wentworth smiled in return. "Very well, Sailor Joe," he said quietly, but there was a choking in his throat. So many of his brave followers had died. Sailor Joe was almost the last of those who had first fled with him from New York City months ago when first the Master had shown his teeth.

"Ten men will do me, sir," Sailor Joe said and turned toward the bulk of the men. "Ten of you lubbers to die with Sailor Joe," he rasped out. "Stand forward!"

It was as if he had shouted, "Forward, march!" The entire company of men stepped forward, and Sailor Joe's deep laughter rolled out. He walked in front of the men and tallied them one by one to his side.

"The rest of you will have your chance at fighting," Wentworth assured them. "When we leave here, we march on Albany!"

He turned and strode into the headquarters with the eager shouts of the men ringing in his ears. Months of guerrilla warfare had made them wary and hard. And they would follow his lead into hell itself. With men such as these. . . Kirkpatrick rose grimly to his feet at Wentworth's entrance with Nita.

"I'm getting cars together for retreat," he said quietly. "Ready in ten minutes at the most." He knuckled the neatly waxed points of his mustache, a habit of his when he was worried. "I don't understand this demand for surrender without having made a demonstration in advance. You'd almost think they wanted us to escape."

"Either that or a trap!" Wentworth said quietly. "They may well throw out a force to the north of the city. A wise commander would prefer that to fighting through city streets."

Kirkpatrick's lips snapped together thinly. "That's it, then!" he said. "We'll send a police plane ahead. It can communicate with us by radio."

Wentworth shook his head again. "Not a chance. What makes me suspect a trap is the fact that there already are army planes overhead. They are there to prevent observation." He glanced at his watch. "Start the advance guard. We can move fast with our small force. Let the advance men take a two-way radio car."

Wentworth led the way presently to the same sedan in which he had raced to the barricades. The convoy waited, but he dismissed it curtly. "Federal troops will be here shortly. Until that time, it will be your business to hold this building and control of the police against the Black Police. They have no jurisdiction over you. If you'll phone the army headquarters on Governors' Island, I'm sure they'll authorize you for that."

One of the detectives, a grey-headed man with mild-seeming blue eyes, came forward and saluted. "We'd rather go with you, sir," he said. "There's plenty to hold headquarters."

Wentworth's smile was instant and warm, and he clapped a hand on the man's shoulder. "Sorry MacGregor," he said quietly. "You forget that we are insurgents—rebels. If we're caught, we'll be lucky to escape execution before a firing squad. And you can serve better here. See that every possible evidence of Black Police crookedness is placed before the federal authorities."

WITHOUT further words then, Wentworth climbed into the car and sent it racing toward the northern limits of the city. He was instantly relaxed against the cushions, conserving his energies for the action ahead. The need of sleep made a sick weight in his stomach, but his tired brain raced on with preparations for what lay ahead—trying to fathom federal plans and circumvent them. It was obvious that his best move would be to disband his men but he would not give up every hope of victory. If only they could reach Albany as a unit and smash the crooked government there when they were least expecting an attack. . .

That was it!

A shattering blast rocked the sedan, and Wentworth whipped erect in his seat to see a storm of earth settling a hundred yards to the right of the road where a bomb had been dropped. A second struck even nearer. The sedan swerved, then settled down to greater speed. The driver was hunched over the wheel. Wentworth's face was white, grimly set. They could make no answer to that attack. . .

"Smoke screen!" he snapped at the driver, saw the man's hand leap to a lever on the dashboard, and instants later black swirling smoke belched out behind the sedan. It made driving perilous, but at least it would mask the exact locations of the cars and make direct hits difficult.

The concussion of the bombs dropped behind, and Wentworth realized they were hammering through a small village. They would be safe here. . . safe only until troops could surround and smash them. That was the purpose of those planes overhead. Wentworth closed his lips thinly and did not speak. The sedan whipped through the close cluster of houses, and the bombing began again.

"Two cars hit," Kirkpatrick's voice came out thick and harsh.

Wentworth's hands were white, gripping his knees. This was complete madness. Under such an assault, they could never hope to break through to Albany. He was sacrificing his men needlessly.

Abruptly, an excited voice began to speak over the radio and, from the weak signals, Wentworth recognized that it came from the scout car ahead. "Road blocked by troops. Hundreds of them. We're surrounded. We. . ." The man's voice broke in a strangling gasp, and after that the radio's note sang on and on without interruption except that the scattered thin crepitation of rifle shots came to their ears.

Wentworth's face was strained and white. "There's a considerable woods ahead," he said, making his voice quiet only by stronger effort. "Turn off the road into them, driver, and sound three long blasts, three shorts on your horn."

The signal bellowed out from the horn, and Wentworth heard other automobile horns take it up behind him. An instant later, the car lurched into the ditch, charged up a gentle slope and lunged in among the trees.

"Disbandment?" Kirkpatrick asked quietly.

Wentworth lifted his shoulders heavily.

"There's nothing else. I can't have all the men killed. We can't defend ourselves."

Other cars were slamming into the woods and the men climbed out rapidly, began to form up under the low, swift orders of under officers. Abruptly, Wentworth bent close to the radio. There was a whisper coming from it, a faint whisper. . .

"Black Police," the whisper came.

"Looting town. Hundreds of them. Three companies are. . ." There was a thunderous blast of a shot, and the radio went dead.

Kirkpatrick and Wentworth stared at each other. Here was a faint hope. If it was only the Black Police who blocked their path, then the men could fight. And looting a town! That was a call the *Spider* could not ignore; his men would not. . . He strode rapidly toward them.

"Men," he began abruptly. "Our way is blocked by Black Police who are looting the town of Westphalian. The bombers are apparently army men. We can disband here and most of us win through, or we can attack. . ." He got no farther, for the voices of the men were drowning him out, and there was no mistaking the tenor of their shouts: "*Lead us!*" they shouted. "*Lead us! Attack!*"

Wentworth lifted his hands. "I expected no less," he said quietly. "If we can smash through the Black Police, we will rendezvous in Westphalian. After that, I hope to push on to Albany. It will be a fight to the finish there. All our camps are destroyed. . . but victory may be within our reach if we can strike. Here is our battle plan. . ."

SWIFTLY, Wentworth outlined it. He had no need to consult a map for he knew the territory perfectly. Two cars would dash along the road they had been following, until they established contact with the Black Police. Then they would retreat and attempt to draw the police with them.

The remaining eight cars would divide evenly and advance along parallel roads to attack the flanks.

"The idea is not to destroy the Black Police, but to reach Westphalian!" he finished. "If the people are being attacked there, we can count on recruiting more forces to wipe out the Black Police."

He swung back to the leading sedan and rapidly examined the motorcycle which was carried on a special rack behind it, found it in working order.

"The plan's good," Kirkpatrick said somberly. "It would be better if someone could reach the town and organize a sortie. . ."

Wentworth smiled, nodded, as he swung the motorcycle to the ground. "That's my job," he said. "No, Kirk, it's the barricades all over again. They'll follow. . . the *Spider!*"

As he spoke, he unlocked the trunk behind the sedan and took out a mirror, a shallow make-up tray and set to work on his face. "The *Spider* must be dead," he said quietly. "I can't see why else he would have remained idle during this fight with the Master. Since he has not shown himself, I'll have to substitute again. . ."

Kirkpatrick's face held its stiff, unyielding lines. He had long been convinced that Wentworth and the *Spider* were one, though he had never found the proof of that closely held secret. As police commissioner of New York City, it had been his duty—and he was not a man to swerve from duty at any cost—to track down the *Spider* because, in legal eyes, the *Spider's* executions of criminals could be regarded only as murder. It was for Kirkpatrick's sake—and in the hope that he would one day resume his post as commissioner—that Wentworth hid his double identity behind the subterfuge of "posing" as the *Spider*.

"Why not abandon this pretense, Dick?" Kirkpatrick demanded abruptly. "If your men know that you actually were the *Spider*, instead of merely pretending to be, their morale would be stronger."

Wentworth smiled and nodded toward the men. Standing loosely in formation, they were singing a marching song together, their faces bright, eager, dedicated. "Their morale couldn't be stronger," Wentworth said. "As to this masquerading as the *Spider*. I don't like it, but the people of Westphalian will need a more colorful leader than Richard Wentworth behind whom to rally. I only wish the *Spider* were active."

There was a touch of bitterness in Wentworth's voice as he rapidly daubed his face with a liquid that sallowed the skin and drew it tautly over the cheekbones. He blamed himself endlessly for his failures actually to identify and kill the Master. Twice he had trapped the man in clever disguises and each time the man had managed to elude the *Spider*'s swift justice. Now again the Master had disappeared into obscurity and, until he could be found out and destroyed, Wentworth knew that all his maneuvers against the Black Police must be merely temporary measures—a treatment of symptoms and their alleviation, instead of a cure for the disease that was destroying the state he loved.

And yet he could not abandon the people he served to the tyrannies and tortures of the Black Police. It was a fact that the Master had struck so often and so rapidly that it had taken all Wentworth's skill to contrive adequate defense of himself and his forces. There had been little time to track down the murderous Master.

Wentworth's hands rapidly fashioned his nose into a hawk-like predatory beak but the lipless gash they made of his mouth could not have been more grim than his thoughts. Once more the Master had him on the run; once more the man was hiding behind the swift and deadly progress of events. The man was a phantom—but none the less deadly.

Swiftly Wentworth finished the disguise of the *Spider*—bushy black brows over his own, a lank long wig. The face he had created was sinister, and it had carried terror to many a criminal. He drew on a black slouch hat, and swung a long cape from his shoulders. The cape was no longer the black, somber thing of other days when he had needed to have it merge with the background of furtive shadows. It was brilliant green.

"For visibility!" he explained with a short laugh. "I want people to notice me now!"

"But Dick," it was Nita at his side.

"It makes you a—a perfect target! At least a bullet-proof vest. . ."

"Too heavy," Wentworth said curtly.

"I'm off, Kirk. You know my plan. Give me ten minutes before you start the cars down the main road. By that time, you should be able to have your flanking cars in position, too. See you in Westphalian!"

He sprang to the saddle of the motorcycle and Nita clung to him, but only for a moment. She stepped bravely back then. Their lives were made up of such partings and well each of them knew that they might never meet again in this world.

Nita's hands were small, white fists at her sides.

"See you in Westphalian!" she cried gaily, and, while Wentworth could see her, she held her brave smile. But when his motorcycle had jounced out of sight on the race through the woods, tears were on her cheeks as she turned to Kirkpatrick.

"What's my job, Stanley?" she asked quietly then.

Kirkpatrick's frosty blue eyes rested kindly on her. "I need a machine-gunner in my car," he said. He glanced at his watch, waiting. Off to the northward, a bomb burst, and fragments clattered through the stripped limbs of the trees. A huge oak lifted bodily and climbed up thirty, forty feet into the air before it toppled and came crashing back.

Kirkpatrick waved a signal, and eight of the cars began to work their way off toward the parallel roads. It was characteristic of Kirkpatrick that he chose the most dangerous post for himself—in the two cars that were to draw the fire of the Black Police. He was very dapper, very straight as he stood—eyes returning now and again to his watch. There was, as always, a gardenia in his lapel. . .

Abruptly, he moved toward his car, climbed into the front beside the driver. "All ready, Frank," he said quietly. *"On to Westphalian!"*

T HROUGH the narrow lanes of the woods, Wentworth wheeled the motorcycle rapidly. The green cape billowed out from his shoulders like some knight's surplice. No knight ever had a more devoted sense of service than Wentworth, but there was nothing bright or eager about his grim-lined face. Battle lay ahead, and the risk of sudden death. Not that Wentworth feared death. They had been familiars on too many perilous expeditions, but he respected that universal antagonist—and Wentworth must not die. . . yet. He could not leave his task unfinished.

Thoughts of death rode coldly with him now. There was an icy bite to the wind that was not all the breath of December, and it irritated him. His eyes roved ceaselessly ahead, picking out the likeliest path for his race—watching, too, for ambush. The burst of a searching bomb thrust at him, and the concussion sucked at his clothing. Death. . . but it must not find him in any petty skirmish in the woods. It must not strike while the Master still lived and dominated all the state, twisting it into a private domain for his pilfering.

Wentworth burst from the cover of the woods and began a swift race across the fields. There were a half dozen planes in the air and, even as he spotted them, one wheeled in a swift bank and began a fierce swoop toward him. Wentworth had to school himself to caution. Fatigue was a perpetual goad to recklessness and he was feeling the drain of all those sleepless hours. He raced on—and checked between low stone walls that wandered along a farm lane.

He heard presently the splatting fury of machine-gun bullets shattered on the rocks; heard the angry snarl of malformed lead. A small bomb burst so close that his senses reeled, but the stone wall stood him in good stead. Presently, the plane had swooped on to other prey and he once more, reelingly, mounted his motorcycle to speed on.

Moments later, he crossed the parallel road to which he had assigned four of the automobiles, but he pushed on.

The Black Police patrols would have this covered and he must reach the town without interception. He must expect to find sentries, at least. . . His thoughts flew back to Nita, to Kirkpatrick, and he glanced at his watch. Ten minutes only had passed. They would be starting now on their dash down the central road. A renewed blasting of bombs told him grimly that the cars had left the cover of the woods. The battle was in the hands of the gods now—or in his own. He must hasten to the town and rouse the townspeople to a sortie that would smash the power of the police.

Hours seemed to dribble past while he wheeled the motorcycle at a terrific pace along the concrete road into which he had turned. Rifle fire came dimly to his ears through the hiss and hammer of the wind; through the flapping fury of his trailing cape. He wrenched the throttle open to the last notch, laid the machine far over on a curve—and spotted a picket of Black Police dead ahead! Three men were crouched in a covert of heaped-up brush—motorcycle and side-car mounted a machine gun. Even as Wentworth spotted them, they opened fire!

Only Wentworth's terrific speed saved him in that first instant. They had waited until they sighted him to open fire and in that brief heartbeat of time, his machine had covered many feet. Wentworth whipped one hand to an automatic beneath his armpit and emptied it in a swift drum roll of fire, as he swept past the machine gun. The men were struggling to wheel it about, to bring its sights to bear on Wentworth. High accuracy was impossible even for the *Spider's* unerring guns, but he saw one man hammered limply back across the gun; heard the hissing blast of a motorcycle tire let go. Then Wentworth was past and drilling on toward the city.

A belated blast of bullets hurricaned after him, but too late. The next instant, Wentworth swooped around another curve—and the town of Westphalian spread out below him.

UNDER the grey arch of the skies, it was neat and pleasant—homes set among trees that, though barren now, still held the grace of spring promise, a few parallel business streets were in its center. But Wentworth guessed at what loot the Black Police aimed. There was a powerful bank here and wealthy. They could sack that and lay the blame on "rebellion". . . . One long thoroughfare stretched out before Wentworth and he saw that it was blocked by barricades. Then he swooped down another hill and all the town was blotted out. Something wet spattered against his face and he was conscious of whirling black specks—it was snowing.

Wentworth felt a great lifting of his heart. If only the snow would thicken! It would blot out visibility from the skies above, render the planes useless. If it continued, his men might still escape! He skated the motorcycle around a corner and into the first street of Westphalian—

then a shout of anger leaped to his lips. The Black Police were being very thorough about their siege. It was their barricade Wentworth had spotted from above and it closed the street against escape from within. But the Black Police had not been content with barricading. There were upright posts atop the chest-high barrier, and to each post a woman had been bound!

One of the Black Police turned about leisurely at the sound of his motor. They were not expecting enemies from without! When he saw Wentworth, he stared for an incredulous moment before he could voice an alarm. Wentworth whipped his machine in between two buildings and was instantly on the ground. With steady, furious fingers he reloaded the emptied automatic and then, with a gun in each hand, he moved steadily toward the corner of the building.

There were a half dozen of the Black Police at the barricade. Others might be quartered in near-by houses. He would have to risk that. After all, he had fourteen bullets, and the range was less than fifty yards. The *Spider's* almost miraculous aim was equal to greater distances and long years had taught him the perfection of his test-barreled firearms. He stepped deliberately into the open. Three police were huddled together with the man who first had spotted him. So swift had been Wentworth's return that they had not yet decided on their course of action. Wentworth opened fire. . .

With the steadiness of a man on target-range, Wentworth's two guns rose and fell alternately. Three blasts, and those three men were down. One of the remaining three managed to get his rifle to his shoulder, but he was flustered and frightened. Brief seconds after the green-caped *Spider* stepped out from the shelter of the house, he was reloading his guns—and the Black Police were dead.

He walked swiftly forward. The women, bound to the posts, were straining white faces about toward him, but as yet he did not speak to them. He paused beside one of the dead police and, deliberately, pressed the base of a thin cigarette lighter to the man's forehead. Then he straightened, there was a glowing crimson mark on the whitening dead flesh, a thing of sprawling hairy legs and poison fangs—the *Seal of the Spider!*

Not until then did Wentworth face the women, and he saw tears of thanksgiving in their eyes. A girl, between joyous laughter and tears, lifted her face to the heavens.

"Thank God!" she cried. "Oh, thank God. Now we are saved! The *Spider* has come!"

Wentworth leaped to the barricade beside her and used a pocket knife on her bonds. For a moment, she shrank from him, for his face was the sinister countenance of the *Spider*. Then, as he finished freeing her, their eyes met and, swiftly, the girl smiled. She tossed the thick black hair that framed her face and laughed at him.

"If your enemies could see your eyes as I see them now," she said softly. "They would never fear you again! You are. . . *good!*"

Wentworth's gaze took in the firm strong line of her jaw and the determination in her mouth and nodded. He needed her help now.

"Take this knife," he ordered swiftly, "and cut all these other women free. Get everyone of them to a telephone and tell them to call numbers at random through the phone book. Tell the people the *Spider* has come to save them. His men are on the march. The people must meet me in the center of Westphalian. Pershing Square? Good! They are to bring every weapon they can lay their hands on! We'll destroy the Black Police!"

W ENTWORTH raced back to his motorcycle and, when he wheeled it into the street, all the women had disappeared save the black-haired girl. She was waiting calmly beside the barricade with a rifle slung across her shoulder and another, bayonet fixed, in her hands.

"Let the others do women's work," she said pleadingly to Wentworth, "I can use a rifle like a man. You'll need every good shot you can get!"

Wentworth smiled in spite of himself.

If he could only gain a following of such brave souls, they would wipe out the Black Police this day! Her words were the sort Nita would have uttered. . .

Wentworth's heart went cold for a moment, realizing the danger into which Nita must be moving with his men. He must hurry!

"On behind," he snapped at the girl. She sprang immediately to the rear fender of the motorcycle and he began a swift ride through the city streets, shouting as he went—shouting the news that the *Spider* had come to save them. Windows were flung wide, and white faces peered after him. The girl added her shouts to his. . .

"Must we women do your fighting for you?" she demanded scornfully. She brandished the rifle aloft at the white faces .

Men began to stream into the streets, and their shouts added to the din, drew others to the defense of their homes. They were brave enough. They needed only a leader and, God being willing, Wentworth would lead them! A mob of men followed him at a dead run toward Pershing Square. They brandished rifles and shotguns, revolvers, clubs. The battened door of a butcher shop flung open and the butcher, still in his white, stained apron, dashed out into the street waving a long knife and a cleaver. Wentworth heard his bellow above many others.

"Kill the Black Police! Kill them!" The air was suddenly alive with the clatter of gunshots that echoed in all directions as men, gathering their courage, attacked the barricades of the Black Police. Women were joining the march now, armed ludicrously with brooms, rolling pins. But it was their courage that counted, and the example they set their men. Ahead of him, Wentworth saw a woman with a baby in her arms. She ran into the middle of the street and stood almost in his path.

As he rolled past, he heard the woman speak to her child, "Look, Junior. Look, and don't forget this ever! You have seen him! The *Spider*! The greatest man. . ."

Wentworth felt his heart swell within him and his fatigue and despair were forgotten. How could any man fail when people would follow him like this! This single thing was worth all the years or risking death, of battling against hopeless odds. His lips tightened with resolution. No matter how futile the battle seemed, he would never stop until the Master was destroyed, or death. . . Wentworth did not complete the thought. He would defy even death to stop him!

The girl whispered in his ear, "We'll win! Oh, I know we'll win. Pershing Square is just ahead. See the people. Thousands of them!

But. . . if trouble comes! If you're hurt, come to the home of Maria Laplante! You'll be safe there!"

Wentworth said gently, "Thank you, Maria." He was to remember that. . .

Wentworth wheeled the motorcycle into Pershing Square and men already were jamming into it from every side. Wentworth sprang to the pedestal of Pershing's statue which stood in its midst and held up his arms for attention. He looked slowly over the white intent faces about him. The snow was falling with a slow dignity now, great white flakes that were gentle as a benediction. It clung to his hands before the warmth of his body melted it. And the sky was darkening, the menace of the planes gone. . .

"My men are already attacking the Black Police at three points to the south," he called clearly. "Will you let me lead you out to destroy the Black Police before it's too late?"

The shout that answered him rang up to the heavens, and a slow smile spread over Wentworth's grim-shaped lips. These men might know little of warfare, but they would be avenging a thousand indignities and crimes. They needed only a leader, and God willing. . .

"Southward then!" Wentworth shouted and pointed to the main road. "We will divide their forces in half, roll them up on themselves and. . . *destroy them!*"

"Destroy them!" the men echoed. Wentworth leaped to the ground and back to his motorcycle. He rolled it through the thick press of the men, and they opened an aisle for him. On every side, he saw whitely determined faces, heard their pledges and beheld the idolatry of their eyes as they rested on the green-caped figure of the *Spider*. Impossible to make any plan for battle; but equally impossible to envisage failure so long as he could lead these men!

BEFORE Wentworth reached the first barricade, men had swept the Black Police from the spot. More and more fighters were joining the ranks every moment. The hammering of heavy rifles reached Wentworth's ears now, coming from east and west. His men had joined battle and the Black Police before him were disconcerted. They could not know the strength of the forces behind them. For a few minutes, they maintained their fire, and around Wentworth men fell—but there was no faltering in the advance.

A half dozen of the Black Police jumped up from their hideouts and began to run. It was the beginning of the end. Panic shook them. Some even abandoned guns as they took to their heels. The citizens of Westphalian were everywhere. Guns blasted and, when there were no guns, the men raced eagerly ahead with clubs and brandished knives. Those Black Police who fell into their hands did not long survive— and each death brought a new weapon to the defenders of the city.

The charge had become a slaughter.

Here and there the Black Police attempted a stand, but were quickly wiped out. They were criminals and did not have the courage to stand in open battle. Theirs was the bravery that preyed on helpless people, but against such headlong, reckless morale as the citizens showed, they were terrified.

Finally, Wentworth called a halt and started the men back toward Westphalian. Dusk was beginning to fall and there was a wind that whirled the snow about him in eddying gusts. Already, some of the dead were beginning to find their shrouds of white. The victory had been won, but there was a tight, worried frown on Wentworth's forehead.

Though they had advanced ten miles from the city limits, and the road was entirely cleared, he had found no trace of the two cars which were to have pushed down that central way—the path that he knew Kirkpatrick and Nita would have chosen for their own. He hurried the return, racing for Pershing Square which was to be the rendezvous, too, of his men.

He sighted from afar the half dozen cars that stood there. Windows were shattered from them and a crude dressing station had been set up to care for the wounded. Wentworth raced ahead of the citizens on his motorcycle and flung his anxious inquiries at the men. There was no word of Nita or Kirkpatrick. All these had left Kirkpatrick in the wood and since then there had been nothing. Yes, there had been heavy firing on the central road, and several bombs. . .

Wentworth's face tautened at the news.

Nita had warned him that his green cape would make him a target, but he had ridden unscathed through a pitched battle, and she. . .

The rifle shot was not loud against the low whine of the mounting wind, and the bullet did not cause much pain, at first. It struck Wentworth somewhere in the back, he knew. The shock drove him forward to his knees. He was aware of his men's angry shouts, of them crowding about to shield him with their own bodies, from the assassins. Then he felt only a spreading numbness that seemed to reach to his very soul, and the grateful cool of the thin snow against his cheek.

He tried to arouse himself, to order the men to seek their own safety. Federal troops would press hard on their trail, he knew, and the Black Police would return in force. Without a leader, the citizens would be helpless again. He tried. . . but no sound came from his lips. His twilight faded almost instantly into night. . .

SOMETIME that first night, Wentworth recovered consciousness briefly and found himself in a low-roofed cellar with many of his men about him. The bullet had pierced his lung, a grave-faced doctor told him. It was a critical wound. He might live. . .

Wentworth's lips pulled back from his teeth with the effort the smile cost him. "I will live," he said faintly. "I still have work to do. I want my men here. All of them. At once!"

The doctor's clean-shaven cheeks drew in with gravity. "I can't allow it," he said sharply. "Any excitement. . . Didn't you understand me? The wound is very serious!"

Wentworth tried to push himself up on his elbows, but the effort was too much for him and a tearing cough brought the taste of blood to his lips. He lay quiet for a moment. "My men, doctor. All of them, and at once!"

From the shadows, a dark, bearded man with a white turban on his head stepped forward. His hand was on the hilt of a knife at his belt. "My master ordered his men!" he said sharply.

Relief flooded Wentworth's heart. This was his own trusty servitor, Ram Singh, who had been with one of the flanking actions. With him here to enforce his orders. . . Wentworth closed his eyes and rested.

He heard movement around him and knew that the men were assembling. There was a weight about his heart and breathing was a painful, draining effort. Presently, a hand touched Wentworth's arm and he opened his eyes to the concerned worshiping eyes of Ram Singh. Wentworth smiled faintly.

"I won't die, Ram Singh," he whispered. "I have work to do. Repeat my words to the men. . . These are orders. They are to hide their weapons, disperse, scatter at once over the state. When I can lead them again, I will recall them."

Ram Singh repeated the orders and sharp protests arose from the men. When presently, Wentworth whispered again, there was the silence of death in the low-ceilinged room.

"Federal troops are close," Wentworth said. "Black Police are coming, bent on revenge. I'm safe here. You would be sure to be found—and hanged! All our leaders are gone, Kirkpatrick, Miss van Sloan. . ." Pain stopped him then, and he could not guess whether it was the pain of the bullet, or of his own words. "You are thinking of me when you want to stay here. I know that. But so many of you hiding here will be more easily found than I would be, hiding alone. And there are not enough of us to resist a big force. You must go. At once! When I am well and the time is ripe, I'll call you together again. . ." A tearing cough broke in on his straining words, and Ram Singh's strong, nasal voice caught up his mandates and thundered them out.

A girl's voice joined with the Sikh's insistently and, for a wild hopeful moment, Wentworth thought that it was Nita. . . He forced himself up on his elbow. No, it was the black-haired girl of the barricades, Maria Laplante. Wentworth felt his senses slipping from him. He was bleeding again. . .

Apparently, Ram Singh had dominated. The men were filing past him one by one in leave-taking and there were tears on their faces. Wentworth's own eyes stung. God knew whether he would ever see these brave ones again, see Kirkpatrick and. . . and Nita. He tried to reassure the men, but the room whirled before him. . . his senses blacked out.

CHAPTER THREE

THE SPIDER IS DEAD!

NITA VAN SLOAN had recognized, at the beginning of Kirkpatrick's foray against the middle of the Black Police lines before Westphalian, that he had chosen the most dangerous post for himself. But even then she was not prepared for the fury of the attack which immediately manifested itself. Two machine guns concentrated their fire on the two cars, in which Kirkpatrick's small group moved forward, and wiped it out.

Somehow, Nita managed to grip the wheel of the car and wrench it from the road, send it crashing over among the trees. It was not until the thickness of the growth had cut off the storm of bullets that she realized she was alone in the car. The others were all dead and Kirkpatrick. . . She bent swiftly over him and found that he, at least, was still alive. The bullet had ploughed through his shoulder and driven him to the floor. Even as she examined the wound, he was stirring, forcing himself up.

She urged him to his feet, and, half carrying him,

led Kirkpatrick out into the winter-barren woods. Fortunately, the snow began to fall soon afterward and the darkening of the sky threw black shadows in the woods. It was during this breathing space that Nita found a thick clump of hemlock and, in its protection, bound up Kirkpatrick's shoulder. Afterward, they crouched in the thicket, guns in hand, and listened to the crescendo of gunfire, now near at hand and again thin with distance. Gradually, the tone of the crepitation changed, became steady and drew closer.

Nita drew in a slow breath and let it out again. It seemed to her that she had been holding her breath for hours. "Dick got the townspeople together," she said slowly. "He's driving the police back!"

Kirkpatrick's grim lips relaxed in a slight smile. "Did you ever doubt that he would? I can't think of Dick and failure at the same time. Just as I can never imagine death stopping him. It seems to me that Dick will live forever, ageless, fighting the people's battles. Sometimes. . ." He hesitated.

Kirkpatrick was not a demonstrative, nor an especially imaginative man, but there was a quiver of emotion in his voice as he went on. "Sometimes, I think that Dick must be the embodiment of all those ancient heroes—the saviors of mankind. Only they died, and Dick lives on and on. . ."

"Don't!" Nita cried. "Oh, don't! I. . . I'm superstitious." She laughed a little after she had said it, but her eyes were dark with fear.

A crashing in the underbrush jerked her suddenly tense and she peered out, gun ready. Three of the Black Police were dashing through the woods but Nita saw at once that she and Kirkpatrick were in no danger from them. They ran wildly, without weapons, their faces white with terror. Truly, Dick had won his battle!

It was long hours afterward that she and Kirkpatrick made their way into Westphalian and learned that Wentworth had been shot down in his moment of victory, but she could find no trace of him. The townspeople either were too suspicious to talk, or they honestly did not know where the *Spider* had been carried.

"His men took him away," a man told her in a whisper. "I don't know where. But if you're friends of his, you'd better get out of town.

The Black Police. . ." The man peered over his shoulder and suddenly took to his heels.

Nita stared where the man had glanced and saw a squad of Black Police marching grimly through the streets and, in their wake, rolled armored cars of the U.S. Army! Federal troops were taking over the city, and Nita knew that, as the ally of an armed rebel, she could expect no help there! She bundled Kirkpatrick into a hastily commandeered car and raced away toward the hill country to the northward. She escaped, but her heart was heavy within her. Dick wounded. . . and a fugitive from the combined forces of the army and the Black Police!

THE days that followed were frantic with worry. The radio carried notices of huge rewards for the capture of any rebel, and troops scoured the hill country. More than once, she and Kirkpatrick barely escaped them. It was a week after the disastrous victory at Westphalian that the radio brought Nita the news that turned her into a grief-stricken automaton.

She and Kirkpatrick were driving steadily northward over roads that were no more than rutted lanes over the mountains, picking a slow and perilous way by night, for they dared not move by day. The radio brought them news of a constantly widening search, of the capture of many of their allies, and then finally. . .

"Flash!" cried the announcer. "Here is the biggest news of the day and it means the rebellion is permanently crushed. The *Spider* is dead! His body, still attired in the green cape he wore when last seen in Westphalian, was brought into Albany today. It was riddled with bullets. . ."

Nita uttered a choked cry and covered her face with her hands, and Kirkpatrick wrenched the car to a halt on the verge of a cliff that would have meant death to them both. His face was dead white in the back-glow of light from the dashboard and his mouth was knife-thin. He did not turn off the radio.

"The *Spider*," the radio announcer rushed on, "was tracked to earth in a cellar in Westphalian where he had hidden, wounded, ever since the armed rebellion he stirred up in that city was crushed. In the face of overwhelming odds, he tried to shoot it out with the Black Police who found him, but this time there were too many for him. He was literally shot to pieces."

Nita whispered, "I can't stand any more, Stanley. I. . ."

Kirkpatrick's hand trembled as he shut off the radio. "It isn't necessarily true," he said, dull-voiced, but his apathy destroyed the optimistic tenor of his words. "The Black Police might put out a message like that to stop all resistance. It might be that the federal troops are in their way here in the state. In fact, we know they are. They keep the Master from going on with his looting. If Washington thought the *Spider* was dead, they would call off the troops. . ."

Nita's head came up slowly. "You don't believe any of that, Stanley," she said. "It sounded too—*true*. . ."

"The Master is clever, Nita."

"Yes," Nita whispered. "Yes—clever. I won't believe it, Stanley. Because I can't let myself! Stanley, we'll have to. . . keep on fighting, alone now. If the Master has killed Dick. . ." Her voice broke and strangling sobs shook her whole body.

Kirkpatrick sat by helplessly. There was so little anybody could do at a time like this. Finally, he persuaded Nita to let him drive and began to push on deeper into the hills. Dick Wentworth. . . *dead*.

It was hours before Nita's high courage lifted her from the utter despondency into which she had fallen.

"Stanley," she said, "I'm going to Albany!"

"It's certain capture, Nita!" Kirkpatrick protested. "What can you accomplish?"

Nita shook her head. "Perhaps nothing, but I'm going. Perhaps, I can make sure whether Dick is really dead. Regardless, I'm going to get together what men of ours are left alive and go on with the fight! Don't forget, Ram Singh was with us. He has not been reported dead. Somehow, he would have found his way to Dick, and. . ." She drew in a deep breath. "I'm going to Albany, to find the Master, and destroy him!"

"That's madness!" Kirkpatrick knew he was arguing in vain.

Nita got a small smile on her lips. "I'm going to Albany!" she said softly.

Kirkpatrick was silent but, when the road forked presently, he turned the car back toward Albany. Perhaps, when Nita was convinced of her plan's futility, he could persuade her to leave the state. Afterward. . . but God alone knew if there would be any "afterward" with which to concern himself! His frosty blue eyes were gentle as they rested on Nita.

NITA could find out nothing about the body identified as the *Spider*, when she reached Albany. It had been secretly buried, and even from that she garnered hope though she knew it was equally logical that the burial would be kept secret to prevent any disorders at the funeral.

She began to make her plans. Plainly, the best idea was for her to get stenographical work in some state office while Kirkpatrick traveled quietly over the state and assembled whatever men of theirs still were left alive. He would know at least where to find Jackson, Wentworth's chauffeur, who had been his sergeant during the war, the energetic and cheerful Sailor Joe, and perhaps Samuel Rice, the colonel of National Guard who had thrown in his lot with Wentworth.

With that force as a nucleus, something might be accomplished. Kirkpatrick fell in with her plans reluctantly. His hesitancy was not from fear, but out of sheer hopelessness of success. Since Wentworth had failed despite all his knowledge of such battles, what could they hope to accomplish? However, he yielded to Nita and started out to assemble the men.

In the lodging she had obtained, Nita attempted a slight disguise. She had learned the art under a master, Richard Wentworth, and she applied herself diligently. She straightened her crisp curls and donned glasses; masked her figure somewhat in misfit clothing. And she abandoned the usual erect, self-confident carriage of shoulders and head. Wentworth's precept was that a person was more often identified by manner of walking than by facial appearance. . . Apparently, her plan succeeded. In a surprisingly few days, she had landed a position, not only with the government, but in the outer office itself of the lieutenant-governor, Marvin Rixson!

Nita took this for an augury of success for her plans and drove herself strenuously forward in her self-appointed task of learning the plans of the Black Police, who were Rixson's especial charge. What she learned there drove her close to despair. The Black Police had completely reestablished their dominion, not only in New York City where Wentworth had so recently triumphed, but throughout the state. Since the invasion of federal troops and their withdrawal—since news of the *Spider*'s death had been broadcast, no one dared to resist their edicts. To be sure, a man now and then flew in the face of certain death to home or loved ones, but such outbreaks were sporadic, without plan— and utterly futile. Those who defied the Black Police merely died.

It was in her second week in the office that Nita began to get some inkling of the Master's plans. She copied over a series of orders for concentrations of the Black Police about three key cities in the state. What action would be taken against them, she did not know—but she could guess! When the black vultures, who wore the garb of the police, foregathered, there was looting and torture ahead! She would make sure that warnings were sent. This was the day Kirkpatrick had said he would return. Perhaps, they could work out some process for ferreting out the Master. Surely, in the presence of such a major operation, he would be somewhere near the center of action. . .

The winter night had fallen when Nita made her way out of the state office building and hurried toward the poor lodging she had taken. Even this early, the patrols of the Black Police were active, and five times before she reached her lodging she was stopped and ordered to show her papers. God, how could they hope to fight against such an organization as this! Nita's full lips tightened. If only Kirkpatrick had returned. . .

She hurried to her room, switched on her lights and her eyes flew to her mirror. There was a bit of red ribbon tied to the right side and, seeing that, Nita smiled for the first time in days. It meant that Kirkpatrick was back and would wait for her at the rendezvous! Nita had to force herself to eat and then once more she braved the police patrols. They seemed thicker tonight than ever before and a cold apprehension touched Nita's heart. What if her identity had been known all along, and she was being used to trap the rest of Wentworth's brave followers!

Nita fought down her fears and hurried on toward the meeting place they had fixed before Kirkpatrick's departure—the lobby of a motion picture theater. Three times she doubled on her trail, but she could find no evidence that she had been followed. Time and again she had to present her credentials to patrols of police. Finally, she entered the theater lobby and saw Kirkpatrick's lean form unfold itself from a chair. He looked shabby and was trying hard to hide the military erectness of his shoulders. He walked with a slight limp. There was no mistaking the gladness in his eyes.

"Maybe our luck has turned a little," he said softly. "You're safe—and I have found three men."

Nita's heart sank at the smallness of the results, but she kept her brave smile. "Good!" she whispered. "I have work for them."

THEY said no more during the hour they thought it necessary to remain in the theater. When they went out, Black Police were outside, examining the papers of every person who emerged at the exit.

"I have credentials," Kirkpatrick whispered.

They went past that obstacle without difficulty, but it seemed to Nita that the sergeant in charge peered harder at them than at the others. She said nothing until Kirkpatrick handed her into a taxi.

"I'm frightened," she whispered then. "I've never seen so many patrols, and did you see how that sergeant stared at us?"

"Imagination," Kirkpatrick assured her.

However, Nita saw that he glanced now and again at their back trail and, after they left the taxi, he moved circuitously toward the garage where he told her he had stationed the men.

"Jackson is with me," he said. "Colonel Rice, Sailor Joe. That's all. So many of our men have been captured."

"And there's still no trace of Ram Singh?"

"None, Nita. But that's a hopeful sign, if anything can be hopeful."

Nita made no answer and tried to drive her mind to some plans for using the small force they had. Instead, her thoughts persistently returned to the prevalence of the Black Police. She put a smile on her lips as Kirkpatrick led her through an echoing, black garage, up a ramp and to a small, windowless room on the third floor. In response to Kirkpatrick's signal, the door opened cautiously and then she was ushered rapidly inside.

A single dim candle burned on a rough table. There were a few chairs—nothing more in the room—and three men. They crowded around her and, at the sight of their familiar faces, Nita felt tears sting her eyes. She held out both her hands to the bluff Colonel Rice, to the still cheerful Sailor Joe and Jackson. Jackson's face was gaunt and the knotted muscles of his jaw, always prominent, seemed to have swollen his cheeks. His eyes were bleak.

"I'm not good for much, Miss Nita, but to take orders," he said flatly. "But I can promise you this. You point out the men who did for Major Wentworth and I. . . I'll do the rest!" His hands closed into white-hard knots.

Nita touched his fist with her own hand. "We'll do it together, Jackson," she promised. She swung to the others.

"None of you, then, has heard anything from Dick? Nothing that would indicate he was still alive?"

The silence of the men was answer enough. Nita had not known until that moment how much she had hoped. . . She shook her head to clear it of grief. Only in action could there be any relief. She swiftly began to outline what she had learned of the concentration of men about the three cities.

"Almost certainly, that means looting or action against some groups of people in those cities," she went on. "With our reduced force, we can only hope to warn them. What I want to devise is some means of forcing the Master out into the open, and then. . ."

Jackson's tense white face filled out her sentence. He, more than any of them save Nita, had built his life about Wentworth.

Kirkpatrick said slowly, "I once masqueraded as the *Spider*. I can do it again. Perhaps, if the Master thought the *Spider* was still alive. . ."

There was no warning of the attack. It came with the suddenness of a gunshot from the dark. The door slammed open and the opening was jammed with the Black Police, guns in hand, eyes alert and hard!

The voice that commanded surrender came from behind them and, as the Black Police pushed in through the doorway and slid along the walls to cover the prisoners completely, Nita saw the man who spoke. It was Lieutenant-governor Rixson. He stood braced in the doorway, a broad, a stubby man with a square-lined face that should have been honest, but missed somehow by the closeness of the eyes and meanness of the mouth.

"A nice bag of conspirators," he said cheerfully. "Did you think, Miss van Sloan, that you had really fooled us? Weren't you suspicious of all those patrols on the street, or hadn't it occurred to you that we could plot your movements perfectly by their reports? Yes, I think we'll wipe out the whole conspiracy tonight. . ."

His narrow, angry eyes swept over the men in the room. "Kirkpatrick, of course," he recognized them one by one. "Jackson, and this will be Sailor Joe. . . Colonel Rice." There was mockery as he called the colonel's name.

In Rice's face, Nita saw the dull, angry blood rising. The two men were strangely alike, save for that blot of dishonesty upon the face of the lieutenant-governor.

"A complete bag," Rixson said softly, "Complete except for one man, and we'll have him before the night is out if my men know anything about torture—which I fancy they do. You can save yourselves a lot of useless pain. . ." His face hardened and his voice snapped out, cold, incisive as a surgeon's scalpel. "*Where is the Spider?*"

NITA felt her senses reel under the impact of that question and its implication, but only for an instant. Then she laughed and her voice had the full throated gaiety of former days.

"You hear him, men?" She turned toward Kirkpatrick and the others. "You hear him? The *Spider* is still alive! Oh, now nothing matters! Now, we will win in spite of everything!"

Rixson took an angry stride forward, "You can't get away with any such pretense as that!" he said violently. "Wentworth has got in touch with you. We know that. All right, men, tie them up. We'll take the woman first!"

There was only a brief struggle before Kirkpatrick and the others were subdued, bound hand and foot and tossed like logs against the wall. Nita was left free, but now at Rixson's signal, two of the Black Police closed in on her. They seized her arms and, with a wrench, flung her supine upon the rough table. One of the men lighted up a cigarette.

"Now, damn you," Rixson said roughly. "You'll talk or I'll burn out those pretty eyes. *Where is the Spider?*"

Nita was afraid, but there was a warm courage in her heart that she knew nothing could touch.

"Go ahead and torture me," she said, as calmly as she could. "If I knew, I wouldn't tell you, but I swear to you that up to this minute, I, too, believed the *Spider* was dead!"

Rixson struck her heavily across the mouth. "Don't lie, woman," he said violently. "*Where is the Spider?*"

Nita's face went numb under the blow. Perhaps, it was the effect of that which made her think she heard laughter in the room, the flat, sinister and mocking laughter of the *Spider*! No, no, it was real. It had to be. . . No other man could make that taunting laughter; no other voice than Dick Wentworth's could speak so casually and yet with such cold menace. . .

"Ask me, Rixson," said the voice. "Ask me where the *Spider* is. . . and I'll answer you with the only kind of language you can understand. A bullet through your black heart!"

And into the doorway, a sub-machine gun cradled in his steady hands, stepped. . . the *Spider*!

CHAPTER FOUR

SIX AGAINST AN ARMY

NITA knew a joy that was like death itself in that instant as she thrust herself up from the table and gazed once more at the man she loved—whom she now admitted to herself that she had never hoped to see again in life. The face was the sinister face of the *Spider*, and she saw now how thin and wasted he was with illness—but it was Wentworth. Her heart told her that. . . Nothing could rob him of that arrogant poise of the head, those clear eyes that were made for command.

The Black Police and Rixson must have recognized, too, that there could be no doubt of the identity of the man who challenged them. Their hands lifted like the hands of one man—all save one. A sergeant of the Black Police whipped up his revolver. Nita saw it and uttered a gasping cry. She flung herself toward him, even as she realized that she must be too late.

Something flashed past before her eyes—a glittering line of steel—and there was a thud as it struck home into the throat of the sergeant!

Nita settled back then turned her eyes away from the dying man. Of course, Ram Singh would be there in the darkness.

It was his knife that had struck home so instantly to save his master.

Nita kept her head averted while she worked carefully around the table and began to untie Kirkpatrick. There was no need for Wentworth to give the order. But she was aware of his voice, speaking rapidly, urgently, behind her, ordering the Black Police to lie flat on their faces on the floor—all save Rixson.

His voice!

"There are a few things I want to learn from you, Rixson," Wentworth was saying. "Do you think you could stand some of your own medicine? Say, a spot of torture? Your men are experts at it, and I think I could *persuade* them to invent a few new tricks to use on you. How about it, Rixson?"

Rixson answered him with an obscene curse and Wentworth took a short stride forward and struck him heavily across the mouth. "You had that coming to you, Rixson," he said. "And there'll be more, Remember, there is a lady present!"

Behind Wentworth loomed the gaunt figure of Ram Singh with a big automatic in his right fist, a knife balanced in his left. His teeth gleamed white behind his black beard.

"*Salaam, missie sahib!*" he said resonantly.

Nita shook off the daze of her surprise and moved to Wentworth's side now. The glimmering of an idea was in her brain and she rested a hand softly on his arm, stood on tip-toe to whisper in his ear. Grief stabbed her at the thinness of that arm. God, what he must have suffered!

As she whispered, Wentworth's eyes went covertly from Rixson to Rice and back again. He nodded once. Kirkpatrick, freed by Nita, had cut the ropes of the others now and they were busy securing the Black Police. Kirkpatrick came forward and held out his hand silently. There was no need for words between them. His eyes told Wentworth of his rejoicing.

"Better take Jackson and keep watch downstairs, Kirk," Wentworth said rapidly. "The city is alive with the Black Police. Rixson can't make any noise under the torture—that a gag won't muffle."

Rixson said violently, "Damn you, Wentworth! You can't get away with this! I'll see you burned alive!"

Wentworth smiled mirthlessly. "You may. . . if you survive. *Ram Singh!*"

Ram Singh seized Rixson by the throat and bore him back on the table, twisted his arms down so that he could not move without exquisite pain, and held him there.

"Now, Colonel Rice," Wentworth said softly, "if you would get a cigarette going. . ."

Colonel Rice's hands trembled as he tucked a cigarette between his square-cut lips and touched a match to it. Wentworth watched him for a long moment, then he bent over Rixson.

"I've been playing with the idea, Rixson," he said, "that you may be the Master. That was why I followed you here tonight. Whether you are or not doesn't matter now. You're in charge of the Black Police and have ordered concentration at three cities. What's the plan?"

Rixson clamped his lips shut, and Wentworth shrugged, reached for the cigarette Rice had lighted. "I've been told," he said, "that a burning cigarette in the nostril is quite painful."

Rixson's forehead was beaded with sweat. "For God's sake, Samuel!" he cried, and rolled his head toward Rice. "For God's sake, you won't let them do this to your own brother! I saved your life. . ."

Wentworth straightened with a smile.

"I always wondered why Rice wasn't tried with me for rebellion," he said softly, "when the Master's men arrested him in my company some while ago. So that's the answer. You're twins, aren't you Rice?"

Colonel Rice's face was totally unrelenting. "Twin brothers, yes," he said coldly. "Marvin has been a crook since we were in grammar school together. I changed my name rather than be associated with him in any way. I don't believe he's the Master, but he's capable of his crimes. And he's master of the Black Police at least." He held out the cigarette and fought hard against the trembling of his hand.

Rixson uttered a despairing cry. "All right, all right, I'll talk! We're going to loot those three cities and blame it on rebels. Listen, if you'll let me go free, I'll tell you more! The Master is going to create a diversion in Pennsylvania at the same time, to distract the federal government's attention. They've been watching us too closely!"

"A diversion?" Wentworth said softly. "A diversion of what sort?"

Rixson's face was dead white. He twisted his head and stared at the captive Black Police, then whispered, "There's been a lot of rain, you know. Rivers flooded. He's going to blow up the dam at the Gap."

Wentworth felt the blood drain from his own face at the revelation. In order to divert attention from his looting, the Master intended to destroy hundreds, perhaps thousands of lives. There were cities in the valley below the Gap dam. The cold-bloodedness of the thing sent a tremor through his body.

"When?" he whispered. "In God's name, when?"

Rixson was watching him, narrow-eyed now. "At midnight," he said quietly. "I don't know the method. You'll have to move fast to stop that. I could get you out of the city and give you facilities for traveling. Without me. . ."

Wentworth was gazing at his watch. It was ten o'clock. If he could get a plane. . . He smiled thinly. "Yes, Rixson, you could do all of that, if I could trust you."

"Oh, you can! I swear it!" Wentworth shook his head, "That won't be necessary, Rixson," he said. "Colonel Rice, I think his clothes will come close to fitting you. Ram Singh will help you, if Rixson offers any objection. Nita, would you mind stepping outside. . ."

He closed the door of the small room on Rixson's indignant curses, and Nita was at once in his arms, "Oh, Dick!" she whispered.

WENTWORTH'S arms were tender about her. He held her hungrily to his heart, but there was no time even for this single stricken moment. "There was more to your idea of a relationship between Rice and Rixson, of course," he said rapidly. "I don't imagine Rice is much of an actor. He would have a hard time imitating his brother, but there's just a chance, if I had the time to coach him. . ."

"Then there might be a real chance of identifying the Master!" Nita whispered.

"More than that," Wentworth answered her softly. "It may enable us to take over the entire state. But that will develop later. Right now. . ."

"I'm not going to leave you again, Dick," Nita said firmly. "Every time we separate, something disastrous happens. I tremble to think how narrow your escape was. Your poor hands are so thin. . ." She drew his hand to her soft cheek, and Wentworth stooped to her lips.

"Poor child," he said gently. "You should never have met me."

Nita laughed up at him. "Oh, Grandpa, what funny ideas you have."

They stood for moments then in the half darkness of the garage, close together. For Nita, nothing now could be tragic since they were together, but she extracted the last atom of information about the days when they had been separated.

"I was hiding out the entire time in Westphalian," Wentworth told her. "The Black Police found one cellar hideout just after we'd abandoned it and that's when they faked my death. They picked up some poor devil off the street—he had a superficial resemblance to me—and murdered him!" His voice grew grim. "That's another tally against the Master to be repaid!"

"And Ram Singh nursed you back to health! He's wonderful, Dick."

"There was also a very lovely young lady named Maria Laplante," Wentworth said teasingly. "I cut her loose from a torture stake and she foolishly thought I had saved her life. She was most attentive."

"I'll scratch her eyes out!" Nita assured him savagely, and they were laughing when the sharp quick beat of feet, running through the darkness, whipped Wentworth about. He sent the light of his pocket flash reaching out, and picked up Jackson's figure.

Jackson jerked up stiffly to salute. He always used military form in addressing Wentworth, reminiscent of their years of service together.

"A company of Black Police in the street, sir!" he reported. "We're surrounded! They're not trying to get in. . . yet." Jackson broke off as the door of the small office opened and a man stood silhouetted against the light. Jackson's gun leaped to his hand. "Put them up, Rixson!" he snapped. "Major, the prisoner has escaped."

Wentworth laughed and the man in the doorway joined him

heartily. "Good," he said, "that was all I needed to give me confidence in my imposture. What are your orders, commander?"

Jackson said, uncertainly, "What the devil. . ."

Wentworth studied Colonel Rice, clad now in Rixson's clothing, and nodded his head slowly. Certainly, he could pass well enough at night. By daylight, the sober honesty of Rice's face might well betray him. Make-up might help that. . . Hope began to lift Wentworth's heart. With Nita and these brave men at his side, what couldn't he accomplish? But there was need for haste if he was to avert the breaching of the Gap dam, and the slaughter of hundreds of innocents. Wentworth spun toward Jackson.

"You and Kirkpatrick and Ram Singh will remain within the building when we get out," he ordered. "Take all the prisoners to the hideout in Westphalian. Ram Singh knows the place and the people are friendly. Colonel Rice will join you there later. Not one of the prisoners must be allowed to escape. Rixson will be held for ransom. Get word to the state, and be careful about the method, that we demand a hundred thousand dollars ransom. Colonel Rice—" Wentworth turned toward him—"you are Lieutenant-governor Rixson for the moment. There is a company of the Black Police at the door. We'll need them for an escort. . . to the flying field! Once there, I'll want you to commandeer a plane for me. Let's go!"

THERE was a tense moment when Wentworth, his cape carefully wound about his body beneath his coat, went out through the main doors of the garage behind Colonel Rice. Nita was at his side. But the Black Police snapped to attention at sight of Rice and there was no hitch. Within moments, they were racing toward the flying field with a police escort. Wentworth began to talk in a swift undertone to Rice.

"Thanks for supporting my bluff and making your brother talk, Colonel," he said softly. "Your brother's life is, of course, entirely safe. And the ransom is a pretext. While he is held a prisoner, I want you to study his every gesture and voice inflexion. I'll be back to help you with that presently. Then when his ransom is paid, we'll release. . . *you!*"

Rice's heavy jaw set solidly. "You mean," he said slowly, "you want me to go to Albany and usurp my brother's position as lieutenant-governor?"

"Exactly," Wentworth told him. "And at just about that time, Governor Whiting also will disappear. You will be acting governor—in complete control of the state under the Master!"

"My God!" Rice gasped. "If I only could! We could smash this thing wide open in twenty-four hours, take back the state. . ."

"We could try," Wentworth said softly. So much would depend on ferreting out the Master. If we could destroy him, the rest would be comparatively simple. It would depend on how thoroughly you can really play your brother's part."

Colonel Rice was staring straight before him, and Wentworth could see the working muscles in his jaw. The high red lights of the airport were just ahead, and the motorcycles were already shrieking out their siren warnings. Colonel Rice spoke in a voice that was strained and heavy.

"It's an enormous responsibility, commander," he said slowly. "I'll do my best!"

Wentworth said, "Good!" He clasped Rice's hand and their eyes met steadily. "I know you'll make good. I should be with you in Westphalian by morning. Good luck, Colonel."

"Good luck, commander!"

The car wheeled to a halt before the administration building of the field and one of the motorcycle police snapped open the door. Colonel Rice stepped down and, when he spoke, his voice had the harsh, arbitrary rasp of his brother.

"A fast plane, at once," he ordered.

"A two-seater and see that the machine guns are fully loaded."

An officer saluted him and ran off toward the administration building and Wentworth climbed to the ground, helped Nita to alight. One plan laid, his mind was already flashing to the job ahead. Rixson had not known what method would be employed to destroy the dam and loose the flood waters on the home-crowded valley below, but the hour. . . Wentworth glanced at his watch. Within ninety minutes, the Master would strike.

Time enough. . . if everything worked out precisely.

Lights sprang up in the hangar and Wentworth saw that its great open doors revealed only a few smaller ships in contrast to what he had expected. On the instant, certainty flashed into his mind that he knew the way in which the dam would be destroyed. He turned toward a nearby mechanic and waved toward the hangar.

"How long ago did the bombers take off?" he asked quietly.

"About fifteen minutes, sir," the man reported.

Wentworth swore under his breath.

Moments were precious now and he dared not rush the preparations of the plane for himself lest he attract undue attention to himself and Colonel Rice. But it was quite evident that Rixson had lied about the hour set for the destruction of the dam! The bombers would quickly reach the dam and, after that, a few well-placed high explosive bombs would loose catastrophe on the valley!

Wentworth turned sharply to Nita. "We'll have to separate, dear," he said swiftly. "You'll take a second plane and carry a warning to the people. Start the telephones working—send people by auto through the valley."

Nita's eyes strained wide and dark, but she uttered no protest. Only her hand closed tightly on Wentworth's arm, while Rice ordered out a second plane. "You're going to. . . fight the bombers, Dick?" she whispered.

Wentworth shook his head and a grim light touched his eyes. "I'm going to destroy them!" he said quietly.

FIVE minutes later, his plane was taxied forward and Wentworth saluted Colonel Rice, sprang to the cockpit and whipped the ship into the air—sent it streaking wide-open into the west toward the Gap dam. Flame streaked from the exhausts and for a few moments they were plain against the night sky, like strange, fading comets. Then the blackness swallowed up Wentworth's plane.

A short while later, Nita took off in his wake. She looked back once to see Colonel Rice already turning back to his car, then her eyes focused on the black, star-speckled arch of sky before her. Somewhere out there, Dick soon would be engaging the mighty bombers of the Black Police in a battle against fearful odds. And she could not help him, could not. . .

Wentworth was racing desperately with time. Under wide-open throttle, the plane shivered as it sliced through the air, and ever Wentworth's eyes strained ahead for the first tracery of exhaust flame against the night that would betray the presence of the bombers. Fifteen minutes start on a flight that would not take more than an hour might well be fatal, for all the greater speed of the ship he flew. Wentworth strained forward, searching—searching the skies. Minutes howled past, ticked off to the roaring revolutions of his motor.

Black country and the brief, clustered lights of cities flashed past beneath him. Soaring higher, he could finally catch in the distance the row of brilliant lights across Gap dam and, behind them the glitter of their white shadows on miles of pent-up flood waters. It was no more than fifteen miles away and still no trace of the bombers! Even as the thought flashed across his mind, he saw red fire vomit up from the earth below the dam, to be instantly blotted out in roiling smoke. The first bomb!

Wentworth hammered at his throttle to gain another fraction of speed from the ship. Now, dimly, he could catch the exhaust flame of the bombers. They were at about his own altitude and were swinging in a wide circle that would bring them directly over the dam. That first bomb apparently had been misdirected and they were shifting position. So precious few seconds between safety and the death of the hundreds in the valley below! Two or three direct hits by those bombs and the entire dam would be blown out, the flood waters sent tearing over the countryside on unsuspecting people. A few seconds. . . if he could reach them in time!

Wentworth thumbed his gun-trips to clear them, sent a handful of bullets clawing through the night. He could see the bombers more clearly now. Three of them in a tight formation, and they had straightened out for a straight sweep above the dam. They had only to dump their loads. . . How many miles? Hard to estimate against the blackness. Wentworth was hurtling through space at more than four miles a minute, but it was a matter of seconds. . .

Once more, pointing the nose of his ship high, Wentworth thumbed home on the gun-trips and sent lead leaping ahead of him through the night. They must be out of range, but there was just a bare chance. Ah! One of the huge bombers had wheeled out of the flight and was coming back to meet him! The pilot's intention was clear—to keep Wentworth away until the bombers had finished their task.

Wentworth laughed aloud and the hammering wind gagged his mouth. There was a trembling eagerness through all his body. Enemy machine guns were spitting their venomous red fire-tongues toward him now. He eased the stick forward and plummeted beneath the attacking bomber, made no attempt to attack but raced on after the other two. They were dangerously close now to the dam.

The lights below abruptly blacked out. That was wise but tardily done. Still it might have gained him a few seconds. The two bombers released flares which plummeted down for a few hundred feet, then caught on their parachutes and, with blazing lights, drifted toward the earth. The dam was visible once more and so were the scurrying black figures that were men. Wentworth whipped up the nose of his ship to bring his guns to bear on the foremost bomber, and thumbed the gun-trips.

Even above the hammer of his engine, he could hear the staccato coughing of the guns, saw the tracers streak the air with light. His first group struck squarely on the tail structure and, deliberately, he thrust the stick forward and sent the lead searching forward through the huge fuselage of the ship. A storm of lead clawed at his own plane, beating against the wings. Wentworth held his nose steady. . .

Then his plane was plucked up and tossed bodily through the air. Wentworth was dimly aware of a spinning instrument board. His plane was whirling through space like a top and his senses were reeling. The night was split wide open by a white and red flame. It seemed to stand out in the blackness for seconds before it died, before the overwhelming concussion of the blast struck Wentworth. Then even the lights were gone and he was a leaf spinning in unutterable cold space.

Through all that bewilderment and darkness, Wentworth was

conscious of a small sound that was like a sob. Ultimately he realized that it was himself laughing. Numbly, his senses came back. He knew then what had happened. One of his bullets had touched off a bomb in the leading ship and both of the great planes must have been blown out of the sky.

SHAKILY, Wentworth fumbled with his controls, and tried to orient himself. Sky and earth wheeled about him in bewildering succession. He was tail-spinning, and the earth was dangerously close. Mechanically, still dazed by the overwhelming blast, Wentworth reversed controls. With the lumbering slowness of a truck, the ship began to answer and he swished out of the spin with the trees almost brushing his undercarriage. Zooming back toward the arch of the sky, he spotted the third bomber. Even farther from the blast than himself, the ship had gone steadily on and now, once more, it was nearing a spot from which it could dump its bombs on the dam.

Wentworth fought to get more power out of his engine, to claw his way upward to enter the battle again. He knew, even while he struggled, that he would be too late. Desperately, he pointed his guns toward the far-off ship and squeezed the trips. Nothing happened. His guns were jammed! He fought the guns while he climbed skyward and his numbed ears caught the first shattering blast of a bomb!

Wentworth groaned aloud and struggled to clear his guns. Suddenly, he saw another small plane flash across the heavens straight at the bomber. Its guns were streaking fire and the multiple armament of the bomber was answering. A second bomb made a hollow ringing concussion—then the bomber staggered! Like a wounded bird, it wheeled off to the northward above the lake and two more bombs plowed up the waters futilely. Wentworth shouted a cheer into the night. Abruptly, he cleared the jam of his own guns and they were hurling lead into the night. He was within range now and saw the second small plane stoop past the bomber with spiteful guns streaking the night with tracer fire.

Wentworth pulled up the nose of his ship and raked the belly of the bomber with lead, leveled off and wheeled upward in an Immelmann turn—whipped about and ripped lead along its back. Still the bomber staggered on. It was making a gigantic, laboring turn now, back toward the dam. Its rear guns were silent, and Wentworth climbed to dive again as the second plane whipped past to renew the attack. He caught a glimpse of an intent small face in the lights of the dash, saw an arm flung aloft in greeting to him.

"Nita!" Wentworth shouted. "Nita…" Not that she could hear him.

Once more, and a second time, Wentworth and Nita dived on the laboring bomber and, suddenly, it was no longer flying, but spinning in a flat whirl toward the waters of the lake. A blob of white flung out from a doorway in its side, but the parachute had only started to open when the man struck the water. It was only then, when the victory had been won, that Wentworth became aware that his motor was limping badly and, despite a wide-open throttle, was sagging toward the lake also!

Wentworth whipped the nose of his ship toward the shore and fought for every inch of glide he could manage. Nita's plane was hovering above him, but helpless to assist. Above the faltering of his engine, Wentworth became aware of another deeper roar. The flood waters pouring over the dam! God, had he been too late then? Had those two bombs achieved the destruction of the dam? There were streaks of white in the black water—a break in the even line of the dam's top. Wentworth groaned, set his teeth grimly as he fought the ship.

He was only a few hundred yards from shore, but there was no landing place visible. The wooded shores rose steeply. Wentworth's lips straightened into a harsh line and, deliberately, he pointed for the shallows. It meant a crash landing, but it was the best he could hope for. He began to fumble out of the parachute harness, cut the motor. Overhead, Nita's plane was very close. Her motor sounded all right. He saw a flare break from its socket under the fuselage and a moment later its brilliant light picked out the trees and the waiting waters in dazzling white and utter black. Wentworth stood, loosening the safety strap, and swung his arm in a signal to Nita.

"Go warn the people!" he shouted. "Go warn the people!"

He pointed down valley and waved her that way. There was time for no more. He swung the plane about so that it slanted to the water parallel with the shore, deliberately pulled back the stick so that it pancaked down. The impact hurtled him fifty feet through the air, but he managed to ball and hit feet first. He split the water. Its icy cold seemed to strike instantly through to his heart and in an incredibly short time his lungs were aching with the need for air. It was deep, damnably deep. He flung out his arms, stroked upward to check his descent and at long last he began to rise.

Overhead, he could make out through the water the dazzle of the floating flare—then suddenly he broke the surface. He sucked in a deep breath and struck out for the shore a short distance away. He could still hear the circling beat of Nita's engine and rolled on his back so that his white face might shine up toward her. Once more he waved his arm in a signal. The flare blacked out an instant later and then a second one illumined the surface of the lake. Afterward, the engine sound began to dwindle down the valley.

IT WAS an eternity before Wentworth could drag himself, shivering with cold, up on the stony shore of the lake. He tried to fight to his feet, but for the moment he could not manage it. He lay panting heavily, shivering with weakness. Shock and cold, on top of his enfeebled condition, had taken their toll. Only his great will still was strong. It dragged him ultimately to his feet and sent him at a shambling run toward the dam itself. It was fully a half mile away. . . Gradually, as he ran, Wentworth's thoroughly chilled body warmed itself. The roar of the flood waters deepened as he drew near, and fear shook him.

It was clear that the bombs had not accomplished all that had been intended, but it might be enough—more than enough! The entire structure of the dam might be weakened. . . Wentworth burst from the woods and ran, more steadily now, toward the powerhouse at the near end of the dam. Inside, men were working frantically by the thin light of emergency dynamos. There was a great gaping hole in the roof.

Wentworth checked at the doorway, "Did you phone a warning to the valley?" he demanded harshly.

A man with a grease-smeared face turned toward him dazedly.

"Can't," he shouted. "They blew out the wires." Wentworth groaned and walked toward them. There were only three men. The shattered bodies of others lay about.

"We're trying to get these dynamos going again." the man said dully. "If we can get the flood gates open it may save the dam. It's. . . cracked."

"Aren't there any hand screws?" Wentworth demanded harshly.

The man shook his head again, "Takes two men to work one of them," he said slowly. "Only three of us. Never do it in time."

Wentworth ran to a window that showed the lower face of the dam and a shocked cry rose in his throat. One glance was enough to verify the man's words. The dam was doomed! He could see now the full damage of the bombs. The least of it was the half-moon of concrete scooped from the middle of the dam. Flood waters creamed through that break ten feet deep. It was perilous. It might close highways, but it would not doom the valley. The greater damage was below that—the crack the man had mentioned—and it was this that made the fate of the dam, of the people in the valley, so terribly sure.

That crack was already a half-foot across and, between its stone lips, a stream of water spurted straight out for fifty feet before the rising wind shattered it to spray. The pressure was tremendous. Even above the volume of the falls, he could hear the hissing of that wall of water that the lake spat out through the crack. Nothing could withstand it. Even if the flood-gates were opened at once, the dam would go, and the people below. . .

Wentworth wheeled from the window and broke into a run "A car!" he ordered thickly. "Give me a car. I'll go warn the people."

The three men stared dumbly. "You're nuts," one of them said. "Absolutely nuts. You wouldn't get a mile before the dam let go."

Wentworth whipped out an automatic and wrenched the man about by his collar, drove him toward the door. "A car, damn you, or you'll go out now!" he shouted.

The man moved at a shambling run before him, fumbling for keys in his pocket. Without words, he indicated a small sedan outside the powerhouse, and Wentworth sprang to the wheel. For a numb instant, he stared at the doomed dam. As he watched, a half-ton block of concrete broke off at the lip of the crack. Like a cannon ball, the stream hurled it through space, sent it crashing among thick trees on the bank. They snapped off like clay pipe-stems.

Wentworth whipped the car in a tight turn and sent it lunging down the valley. Almost immediately, the road swooped to the water's edge. Up here, the people would be comparatively safe. A short climb would take them to high ground, but the valley spread out a few miles below and that was where the towns were situated. Thousands of people lived in them along the banks of the river, secure in the thought of the great protective dam above them—secure until the Master needed to create a "diversion!"

A furious curse sprang to Wentworth's lips. That beast must be destroyed! Too long, he had evaded justice and thousands already had died so that he might satisfy his thirst for power and gold!

Wentworth jammed the horn button with a match so that its sound rocketed continuously ahead of him through the night. He spotted a cluster of buildings about a general store, whipped out his gun and fired three shots into the air. He glimpsed a white face at a window.

"Dam's going out!" Wentworth shouted. "Dam's going out! Phone the warning ahead! Get to high ground!"

The man echoed his shout and Wentworth drove the accelerator to the floor again! The people there would be safe, but the time was so short! He could save so few lives! He was aware of the cold wind that slashed like dull knives into his pain-thinned body; of the steady rising of the ice-rimmed river that growled its increasing menace beside the road.

Ahead of him, the highway dipped still lower and flood waters were swirling across it. Grimly, Wentworth shut his lips and sent the car lunging toward the water. If it was high enough to drown out his engine, or had already carried away the road, he was finished before he had started and the thousands in the valley below were doomed! The water splashed high across the windshield. Its bitter cold touched Wentworth's body. But he had to make it. He had to. . .

CHAPTER FIVE

THE DELUGE

THE lights blacked out in Greenhaven at 11:09 P.M. On the heels of that, a low rumbling sound, that was like distant thunder, rolled down from the hills, from the direction of the dam. But it couldn't be thunder, of course. Not in the middle of winter. A few nervous people called the telephone operator for information, but no word came through from the dam. No one took serious alarm. Why should they? The dam had held in much worse floods than these—in the days before the Master.

It was curious to see the dark city, illumed only by the head-lights of automobiles. The flicker of candles, lighted in the homes, was scarcely noticeable. Perhaps that was why, twenty minutes later, the plane that droned down the valley from the direction of the dam failed to spot the city and swept on past. It was about the time that its engine-beat faded out of hearing that Wentworth drove his car into the flood waters twenty miles to the north. . .

In the darkened Greenhaven Theater on Main Street,

an audience was still waiting in darkness for the show to go on. The manager came finally to the stage and focused a flashlight on his face.

"I don't know how long we'll have to wait for the power to go on," he said uncertainly. "We can't raise the powerhouse by phone. Meantime, we'll have a little music. . ."

A girl came out on the stage, dipped a curtsy, went to a piano and, by the light of the flash, began to hammer out a popular tune.

"All join in and sing!" the manager urged. "Come on, I'll lead you."

His voice was hoarse and tuneless and the audience laughed. . . and began to sing. Even if they could have heard it inside the theater, the song would have drowned out a more ominous mutter that rolled down the valley—more a disturbance of the air borne on the winter wind than an actual sound of furious waters. . .

"*The moon was bright and yellow*," sang the audience, "*When Carmen met young Manuela. . .*"

But there was no moon. Dark clouds blotted it out, and an airplane was still up there somewhere, searching for a doomed town. . .

Twenty miles away, the fierce stream of water, jutting through that crack, tore loose another chunk of concrete. The whole dam seemed to sag a little and a little wave of water—a little wave no more than three-feet high—went surging down the swollen river. Not much water, but enough to drown out a car already half submerged upon a sagging highway. It would be perhaps a half hour before that little wave reached the town of Greenhaven, but there were no lights. Perhaps, no one would notice. . .

The northern limits of Greenhaven were a series of small suburbs—cottage homes in the midst of friendly woods. The lights were out there, too, but in one home, the people scarcely noticed that. A fire crackled red and warm on the fireplace and a man and woman sat close together upon a davenport. In the next room, a baby fretted faintly. The woman stirred. . .

"That's three times now, Bob," she said. "Baby must be having a bad dream."

Bob laughed, "Silly, Sally," he whispered. "Baby is too young to have bad dreams—or any kind of dreams."

Sally shook her head and pushed to her feet. "What do you know about babies?" she demanded. "People say that sometimes babies feel things that grown-ups don't. You remember, the Jacksons' baby waked them up the night their house caught fire? If it hadn't been for that. . ."

"Our house isn't on fire!" Bob assured her, and stretched his long legs toward the fire.

The three-foot wave of water was pushing over the riverbanks nearby, but it wouldn't reach the snug little house of Sally and Bob. It wouldn't warn them. . . The baby fretted again.

Sally hummed to herself as she went into the baby's room and patted its back, whispered to it one of those soft little meaningless phrases that mothers say to their infants. She was still bending over it, when the doorbell pealed. Its jangling note hammered through the still house, and kept on and on. Sally ran to the front room where Bob was on his feet. They stared at the closed door, at each other. . .

Bob said, "What the devil?" He strode to the door and whipped it open.

A man staggered into the hallway, a man whose green cape was black with water that dripped and dripped to the polished floor.

"Quick!" he whispered hoarsely.

"Your phone! The dam is going out!"

Bob echoed his words without meaning. He peered past the man to the street and there came to his ears the distant mutter, the vibration of the air which perhaps the baby had felt. Somewhere in the distance, a dog threw a thin, wailing howl at the sky. The man in the doorway reeled, caught himself on the wall.

"The phone, you fool!" he snapped. "In here!" Sally called. "The phone is in here. Did you say. . . the dam. . ."

"Get out of here, fast!" the man said. "The dam is going out! It may have gone already."

As he staggered forward, the cape swung out and Sally uttered a low, small cry. "The *Spider!*" she whispered. "*It's the Spider!*"

WENTWORTH did not answer her. He was out on his feet, shuddering with cold. How long ago had his car foundered on the road? He had found a horse after that, killed it on the dash for Greenhaven. He could not feel the phone in his hand.

"Police headquarters," he said thickly.

"Quickly. . . and tell the chief operator, the dam is going out! Spread the alarm! Blow sirens, ring bells!. . . Police headquarters? I just got through from the dam. It's been dynamited. It's going out. If you'll listen, you can already hear the roar of the waters. For God's sake, get the people to high ground!"

He wheeled from the phone. Sally was wrapping up the baby in a blanket. "Get to high ground," the *Spider* said and ran toward the door. He staggered and his shoulder caught the wall. For an instant, he swayed there, then he bolted into the street. In the distance, a siren was beginning to wail, its note rising and falling. A church bell began a wild clangor. . . Wentworth began to run along the street, shouting hoarsely. He had reached the town ahead of the flood, but was there time enough?

There was a sudden, slight quaking of the ground under his feet. Even above the madness of bells and sirens, he could hear a new sullen rumble to the north. God! The dam had gone out! There could be no other reason for that sound! A motorcycle catapulted past the end of the street, siren shrill and terrible.

"The dam's going out!" the rider's hoarse voice sounded fiercely. "Get to high ground! Fast!"

A car hammered up the street, a white-faced man at the wheel. Beside him, a woman clutched a child in her arms. Wentworth saw the car stop and take on another couple at a corner, then race on. Wentworth tried to run and his feet got in their own way. He stumbled, clung to a tree, panting terribly. His eyes closed while he swayed there. His strength, drained by his long illness, had been completely used up.

Minutes dragged past while he hung on, unable to move. Children were crying somewhere near. The *Spider* forced open his weary eyes. A woman was running along the street, a baby in her arms. Two other children clung to the skirts of her coat. They turned in at the driveway of a house and at that moment, a car came roaring backward out of the garage. There was a man in it alone.

"Help!" the woman called to him. "For God's sake, Charlie. . ."

The car did not stop. It reached the street, straightened out. Wentworth fumbled an automatic from its holster, stepped into the path of the car.

"Halt!" he shouted.

He thought he shouted. His voice was no more than a whisper. The car roared toward him, unchecked. Wentworth squeezed the trigger and there was a shrill, rising scream, then the car's speed slackened. It jolted over the curb, nudged a tree and stopped.

"This way, madam!" Wentworth's voice was clearer now. "Here's a car for you!"

The woman hurried toward him with her children. "Oh," she whispered. "Oh, you. . . you killed him!"

"Get in the car," Wentworth said flatly.

"But I can't drive!"

Something like a groan squeezed from Wentworth's blue lips. He reeled toward the car. "Get in," he repeated.

He hauled the wounded man aside from the wheel. He was groaning, clutching a broken arm. "You murderer!" he whispered. "You murderer!"

The woman, driven by desperation, climbed into the back of the car, and Wentworth set it rolling forward along the street. Dozens of people were pouring from the houses now. Cars fled past like frightened animals before a forest fire but Wentworth stopped again and again, until the groaning auto labored and could carry no more. He found someone else who could drive, sent the car on its way. As it moved on, a woman's face showed white at the rear window for an instant and he caught the whisper of her voice.

"God bless you!" it cried. "God bless you, whoever you are!"

EVERYWHERE people were fleeing now, but the mutter of the river was damnably close. Wentworth broke into a shambling run. He had done his utmost. He must win to high ground somehow. He must return to New York. There were three cities under threat of death tonight at the hands of the Black Police. They would be warned, but they would not know how to resist. The Master might be there. He might for once come into the open. And the Master had to die. . . That was the thought that kept Wentworth moving one heavy foot before the other. He staggered as he ran. He fell, and there was not strength in him to rise. He got up and went on.

A baby's wail, then a woman's voice calling to him. Wentworth heard it, but there was no response in him, only a thought. He must get clear so that the Master could be slain. Hands touched his arms and he shook them off, and suddenly a man was in front of him.

"Get into the car!" the man shouted. Wentworth's fist knotted and somehow the words didn't make sense. He saw a fist flashed toward his jaw, felt the numbing shock of it. Only when he was falling did he realize who it was that stood before him. Somebody called Bob. . . He felt himself lifted and there was the hard hammer of a racing engine. People were crowded in close about him, on top of him. Wentworth tried to fight his way clear. He could get away under his own power. Someone else should have his place. . .

A rising scream, a scream of many voices blended together terribly, jerked him from his stupor of exhaustion. Wentworth lifted his head and found he could see out into the darkness through which they raced. He was looking at a black, high wall that was streaked with furious white. God, the flood! The wall of water from the dam! The car was laboring, was pounding under its terrific load, climbing a steep hill.

But the wall of water moved with the speed of death itself. It was reaching for them with hungry, foaming crest. It towered fifty feet high. It was upon them. It. . . The car seemed to leap forward. It lurched tremendously and struck, ground against a tree. Water battered against the side of the car, washed over the floor. There was a bedlam of frantic shouts, drowned out in the icy cold of the flood. Wentworth felt once more the frigid clutch of death. He fought to get his head above surface—and suddenly he was clear. He peered around, blindly.

The crest of the flood had hit and passed in an instant of mad destruction. The car vibrated against the tree where it had lodged and water still swirled above the level of the floor, but they were safe. . . safe. Wentworth pushed himself to his feet and climbed out. The flood sucked at him, waist-high.

"Out, you men," he ordered hoarsely.

"Pass the women and children to higher ground. That tree may go."

Slowly, men answered the note of command in his voice, recognizing even in the face of death the words of a leader. They made a chain, hand-to-hand, to higher ground and along that the women pulled their way with the children. There were voices on the hill crest above them, and Wentworth's little party found its way there, toward a gleam of fire already alight. Bitterness shook Wentworth. Because he had fought his way through the black night, a few had been saved. How many hundreds had perished in the town below, he dared not think. But the Master, in spite of him, had accomplished his purpose. He had his "diversion" and back home the slaughter would go on, the slaughter and the looting. . .

Wentworth turned from the fire and drove his weary body on through the night. He had done what he could here and the greater battle still lay ahead. Abruptly, he tipped back his head. A plane was droning overhead. There were fires ahead, a row of fires. As he peered upward, a landing dropped downward and burst into dazzling white light. By its illumination, he made out an open grain field ahead. He ran toward it. Nita, it might be Nita. . . The plane was circling lower. Before the flare blacked out, it was trundling to a halt in the field. He saw a woman's head. Thank God! Nita. . .

He called her name hoarsely as he ran and, moments later. Nita's arms were about him. "I warned the towns below," she said, in a dead, weary voice. "I think they got out all right. I couldn't find Greenhaven. The lights were out."

Other people were racing forward now. Wentworth heard the beat of their feet. He urged Nita toward the plane. "We've done all we can now," he said. "We'll radio a call for relief workers here, but I've got to get back to New York."

Nita let him urge her toward the plane, but she was holding back.

"Must you, Dick?" she whispered. "Oh, must you? You're worn to the bone. You're wet. . . A flight in the plane now in this bitter cold? Surely, you can wait until tomorrow. There's so little you can do back there, one man against an entire state."

Wentworth laughed, "One man, and one woman," he said softly. "With you, Nita, I'm a dozen men in one!" He urged her to the wing of the plane. With a sigh, Nita climbed up and Wentworth sprang to the forward cockpit.

"Home, James!" he cried. "Don't worry about the wet clothes, Nita. I'll skin out of them. There's a flying coat in here and boots. Get going!" He was shuddering violently with cold. The running of people's feet was very close. "Quickly, Nita! There might be police there. After all, the *Spider*. . ."

He heard Nita's gasp, then the engine drummed out more furiously.

A TAKE-OFF in the dark was incredibly dangerous, but the trees would show black against the dark sky. They would have to hope that there were no boulders, no ditches in the way. The plane began to move and, instants later, Nita jacked it into the air. It lifted heavily and the black line of the trees was dangerously close before they were flying easily. But they were clear now and headed home. . . Home! Bitterness surged through Wentworth's soul. When would this grueling struggle end. . .?

Wentworth crouched low in the cockpit and dragged off some of his wet clothing, his soggy shoes, drew on the flying coat and boots that were stuffed into the cockpit. Slowly, his body began to warm. His eyes were burning with fatigue, but he could not afford to sleep. He must plan. . . His numb brain refused to work. Reluctantly, he recognized that he must rest. How many hours had it been? He slid far down into the cockpit, fastened the safety-strap and let his eyelids close. Sleep hit him like a sledgehammer. . .

The slowing, uneven rhythm of the motor aroused him presently and the heavy jouncing, as the plane took the earth again, brought him wide awake. He hoisted himself stiffly in the cockpit, saw the barren rim of trees about a narrow field—saw the rose-tinted edge of the sun thrusting above a blue mountain. He twisted about and looked into Nita's fatigue-shadowed eyes.

"We're about a mile from Westphalian," she said, her voice loud and uncertain because of her motor-muted eardrums.

Wentworth dragged himself out of the cockpit. The smile on his lips was gentle and vigor stirred his heart again. "I'm a brute, Nita," he said. "I should have relieved you during the night."

Nita tore off a flying helmet and shook out her chestnut curls. "You needed more rest than you got," she said. "There's a farmhouse near. We might be able to get something to eat."

Wentworth was troubled by some elusive quality in her voice, by a heaviness that refused to allow her lips to smile, but he said nothing until he had helped her to the ground and they were stumbling along on stiff legs toward the farmhouse she had spotted.

"Something has gone wrong," he said gently then. "What is it?"

Nita shook her head, "I don't know," she said. "The radio brought reports of rebellion in three cities, crushed out, and something has happened in Westphalian. I don't know what. There were four fires scattered over the town when we landed."

Wentworth accepted the news with a grim tightening of his lips. Dashing off to save the people in the Gap valley, he had been too late to help the people in the cities the Master had selected for looting. And Westphalian. . . Fear touched him coldly. He had sent Rixson there a prisoner with all that remained of his gallant band. Had they walked into a trap? Unconsciously, his stride lengthened. God alone knew what new horrors the Master was perpetrating, but of this much he could be sure—that massacre of the dam had not been launched without commensurate for the Black Police.

"We've got to get back to Westphalian," Wentworth said quietly. "Rice has got to be taught how to analyze and copy Rixson's mannerisms—then I've got to go to Albany. Our plan to substitute Rice as lieutenant-governor is useless unless I can uncover the Master and destroy him."

"Yes, Dick," Nita's quiet voice was a sigh.

Wentworth glanced toward her quickly. Nita's head was bowed and her shoulders sagged with fatigue—or was it despair? He put his arm about her, tenderly.

"We'll win out, Nita," he said quietly. "We have to. Such criminals as the Master can't survive forever."

"Not forever," Nita acknowledged, "but long enough…Dick, we're in worse state than ever before. You had a small army to help you fight, now you have no more than a half dozen men. You're not even sure you have them until we learn what has happened in Westphalian.

"This plan of substituting Rice for Rixson is madness, and you know it. Suppose it did succeed for a little while? The trick would certainly be discovered within a few days, and after that, you'd be back where you started. We held New York for forty-eight hours. . . and the Master has it again, more tightly held than ever before. Dick, at last we've met our match. At least, we must go away until you have your strength again. Please, Dick!"

Wentworth didn't answer at once. His jaw thrust out grimly and his eyes were bleak. He realized the complete truth of what Nita said, but he would not give up. The farmhouse was before them now. A dog barked at them, backed under the porch and continued to howl his protests of their approach. A woman opened the door bruskly, ordered the dog to shut up and stood staring at them, suspiciously.

Wentworth called a greeting. "We made a forced landing in a field up on the hill," he said. "I wonder if you could give us something to eat. We'll pay you, of course."

The woman stood uncompromisingly in the doorway and continued to stare at them. "It depends," she said shortly. "People get in trouble for helping the wrong ones. Who are you?"

Wentworth laughed, "We're from Pennsylvania. There was a flood over there last night. We lost our way."

The woman stepped back and jerked her head for them to enter. "You picked a poor place to land," she said. "This is New York State."

THREE quarters of an hour later, Wentworth led Nita back to the plane, and now he answered the doubts she had voiced. "All that you say is true," he said quietly, "but this is also true. I received a wound that would have killed most men—and I lived. Without reason, I abandoned a hideout—and a few hours later the Black Police raided it. More times than I can count, my life was in danger last night, but each time I survived. There is a reason for that, Nita. I am being saved for the job I've given myself—and I believe I shall succeed. Somehow, somewhere, I will find the Master—and destroy him!"

Nita refused to be encouraged, but her hand rested gently on his arm. "So long as I am with you, Dick," she said. "It doesn't matter. I'll follow you and fight with you. . ."

She broke off at the sound of a footstep behind them in the wood. Wentworth whirled, his hand streaking toward his gun, but it was only the farm woman. She had a dour smile on her lips.

"You didn't fool me any," she said shortly. "You're some of the rebels that are against the Black Police. Don't be afraid I'll give you away. They shot my man a month ago. But I want to warn you. There was Black Police here last night. They say there ain't a road in the state they ain't watching—nor a hiding place you people can get to. They cleaned out a rebel bunch in Westphalian last night. Seems the lieutenant-governor, that murdering Rixson, was kidnapped. They got him back safe again, and bad luck to him!"

Wentworth said hoarsely, "You're sure of that?"

The woman lifted a bony shoulder.

"They said so. That's all I know."

Wentworth felt the lead of despair enter his heart. Nita clung to his arm. "Oh, now there's no hope at all, Dick," she said. "We've got to escape. That's all we can do."

"Aye," said the farm woman. "That's all you can do. You better climb in that contraption and go back to Pennsylvania." She held out a packet with an abrupt movement. "Here's some lunch I fixed for you."

Nita went toward the woman impulsively, put her arms around her. "You're kind!" she cried.

Wentworth turned away heavily toward the plane. What Nita said was true. Now, there was no hope at all. Wentworth's jaw tightened, stubbornly. He would not give up the fight! His eyes fell on his hand, resting on the wing of the plane, and its gaunt boniness startled him.

He touched his arms, felt their stringy weakness. In God's name, what could he do alone!

The hum of an airplane engine jerked his eyes aloft and he spotted a tight formation of fighting ships cruising high against the morning sky. Nita had thought to taxi her craft to the protection of trees before she stopped it and probably it would not be spotted. Still the planes laid emphasis on the woman's warning. All roads were closed to them— even the road to escape! With Rixson at liberty. . .

Wentworth swung about, "Nita, you'll have to stay here, if the lady will permit. I've got work to do."

Nita stared at him, her deep violet eyes wide. For a moment, protests hovered on her lips, but she did not utter them. Dick did what he must, and in her there could be only assent for his brave fight, however foredoomed she felt it to be.

"I'll go with you, Dick."

Wentworth shook his head. "I'm going into Westphalian. Your presence would only be an added danger."

Nita knew the reason Wentworth had given was not the true one and for a moment her jaw set in defiance. Then she softened. She must not complicate his difficulties. God knew they were strenuous enough. Presently, she watched Wentworth, in old clothing which had belonged to the farm woman's husband, drive off along the country road in a slattern car that was, literally, held together with bailing wire.

The women faced each other then; the older farm woman with her pursed lips and the scars of her years of struggle with the soil showing in her labor-bowed shoulders and her worn hands. Nita, softer, lovely in spite of fatigue and grief, but with kindness and humanity warming her face—and with her fate in her eyes. The fate of futile battles against hopeless odds, of her fruitless love for a man too chivalrous to bind her to him in marriage when disgrace and death stared him hourly in the face.

The women looked at each other and each knew the other's strength. "We'll hope it won't be a long wait," said the farm woman.

Nita smiled wistfully, "This wait, or another," she said. "What does it matter so long as he comes back at all. Oh, God help him!"

"Aye. Amen to that."

WENTWORTH blundered into the pickets of the Black Police at the very borders of Westphalian, but he had slipped into one of the disguises that never failed him—not a disguise of the face, but of the whole personality. He had become, in the interim of the drive to the town, a farmer of the rocky hills. His voice had a twang and his shoulders were stooped, his knuckles grimed.

"You going to stop us eating now?" he demanded harshly of the picket. "I just druv in to get some victuals."

The Black Police guffawed and let the old car rattle and thump its way through the streets. Lest they watch him, Wentworth actually stopped at a store and bought a supply of food stuffs. It was from a phone booth in the drugstore next door that he telephoned Maria Laplante, and, after an eternity of waiting, the black-haired girl came into the shop and made a minor purchase. She dropped a note to the floor beside Wentworth as she went out, but her eyes never touched him at all.

Wentworth stumped back to the car before he read the note and when his eyes had swept it swiftly, his face grew pale and his thin hands knotted despairingly upon the wheel.

"*All your men in Concentration Camp Seven,*" he read. "*I'm being watched. Rixson free. Three cities sacked last night. Twenty-four men arrested Westphalian last night, taken to camp. All our leaders. Seventy-five in Albany.*"

That was all, but such hell and hopelessness as those few words outlined! He was alone with a vengeance. Rice, Kirkpatrick, all of them in captivity. And the leaders. . . Wentworth knew well what that presaged. The Black Police were clamping the lid down all the way. Every man even suspected of subversive thoughts was being rounded up throughout the state. Twenty-four in Westphalian, seventy-five in Albany.

For a while, slumped there in the car, Wentworth fought out his bitter battle with himself. But there could be but one solution. Not resignation. . . but cold anger and determination to battle on until the very end!

How long the end could be staved off he could not know. While life was in him, he would not stop.

Wentworth kicked the old car into motion and rumbled once more through the almost deserted city streets. More plainly even than Maria Laplante's words, he read the history of the night's terror in the manner of the people. They moved along with the furtiveness of whipped dogs. A striding man in the gold-chevroned, black uniform of the Master's police walked straight down the middle of the sidewalk and, as he approached, men and women scuttled to the gutter to give him a wide berth. A child tumbled accidently into his path and a short stick the officer carried in his hand described a vicious arc. The child screamed once, then fled in silent terror.

Wentworth was hard put to resist striking down the cowardly officer of the Black Police. . . yet he dared not. It would accomplish no more than petty vengeance, and it might mean the end of the *Spider*. And the *Spider* must live now. If he failed to find and destroy the Master—if he was unable to free his men from the brutal concentration camp—all was lost forever. Freedom and liberty would become terms of which the people of this state no longer knew the meaning. . .

Wentworth gripped the jarring wheel of the car and drove past the same pickets who had laughingly admitted him to the town. . . They should have stopped him, if anything could stop the *Spider* now. For months, Wentworth had been fighting the Master with every faculty and man at his command, but he battled cautiously for there were those he must protect. Now, even that necessity was gone.

Wentworth felt a wild recklessness in his blood and anger was cold in his brain. His mouth was a lipless gash across his hard-set face.

Tonight, he moved on Albany. Tonight, the *Spider* went single-handed to war against the hidden Master. He would find him. God helping, the *Spider* would find its prey! And then. . . Wentworth's head wrenched back with the force of the harsh laughter that forced its way rasping from his throat. It was flat and mocking, that laughter, strangely sinister—the laughter of the *Spider* whose cape cloaked the wings of Death itself!

WHOM THE GODS DESTROY…

ON THE surface, Wentworth was calm when he returned to the farmhouse among the hills, but there was a nervous drive to his every movement that Nita recognized and which terrified her. She had seen the *Spider* before when cosmic anger poured its hot fire into his blood. Yet his voice was quiet enough as he told her the facts he had discovered in Westphalian.

"I want you to locate Camp Seven," he told her. "I don't know which one it is. Find out whatever you can about the locality, the time the guard changes, the number of guards and prisoners. . ."

"Dick!" Nita protested. "You're making excuses to protect me!"

Wentworth shook his head and his smile was almost cheerful. "Not at all. Tomorrow, or the next day at the latest, I intend to raid that camp."

"Alone?" Nita gasped.

Wentworth shrugged slightly. "Perhaps," he admitted. "There are certain preliminary steps I have to take in Albany tonight. After that, I can tell better."

Nita bowed to the mandate as everyone did when this high mood of exaltation sat upon the *Spider*, and he hurried off presently into the thin cold sunlight of the summer noon and sent their plane vaulting into the skies. The insignia the plane bore, stolen as it was from one of the Black Police hangars, got him past the aerial patrols, and he landed in a deserted field within a few miles of Albany. Then began the more perilous part of his trip. From here on, boldness would be his only protection. From here on, the *Spider* skulked no longer in back alleyways, discreetly trying to undermine the Master. Today, the *Spider* struck!

But first, as he had told Nita, there were certain preparations. He needed such a mirror as the Master used to transmit his commands. It was this process which had made the Master so difficult to identify. Wentworth had seized lieutenants of the Master, even the governor himself, in efforts to learn who the Master was. And all had failed because the criminal ruler of the state appeared to his underlings only as a white face in a concave mirror, speaking in a sepulchral and altered voice. Sometimes, Wentworth did not doubt, the Master himself spoke so from a mirror, but usually it was a mechanical trick of lights and phonographic attachments.

Wentworth had long ago recognized that in this device lay one of the Master's strong points—and one of his weaknesses. For others might use the same device to turn his own underlings against the Master! No doubt the Master guarded well against that weakness, but the *Spider* this night would break through that guard. And when he had. . . The Master would die! Tonight, the *Spider* intended to become the White Face in the Mirror and give orders in the Master's name!

Long ago, Wentworth had traced the glasses to their maker but though his men had kept ceaseless watch there, in the days when they could move freely about the state, they had never managed to ferret out the Master. Tonight, Wentworth was calling on the man, one Francis Kepler, for a different reason. . .

Once more, it was the toil-bowed farmer who trudged the last miles into Albany, but beneath his tattered clothes the folded cape of the *Spider* and the *Spider*'s guns were concealed. He was challenged by the

Black Police—and passed. It was close to the quick blue dusk of winter when he reached the remote and rather lonely section of Albany where Francis Kepler had his laboratory and dwelling. The faint warmth of the day already had faded and ice-rimed ground was iron-hard under foot.

The farmer that was Wentworth trudged past the house and into a thicket of scrubby trees beyond. From that hideout a while later, when darkness had fallen, there emerged a quite different figure—one that moved in swift, long strides, whose glittering eyes were masked beneath the broad brim of a black hat and from whose hunched and twisted shoulders swung a long, dark cape. His body merged with the shadows of the laboratory wall near a doorway. There was a brief, muted click of metal on metal and the door swung softly open.

Now. . .

Inside, there was darkness too, save where brilliant white light shafted out beneath a door, and it was here the *Spider* paused for a brief moment to listen. In the room, a man moved softly about to the constant tuneless whistling of a tone-deaf man. The *Spider* whipped out a pocket flash and shone its bright beam directly into his own eyes for a second so that the pupil became focused—then he flung open the door of the laboratory and stepped quietly inside.

"Good evening, Doctor Kepler," he said softly. "Pray don't trouble to reach for your gun. You couldn't possibly use it in time."

UNDER the menace of Wentworth's heavy automatic, Kepler let his hands fall useless at his side. He had the keen eyes of a scientist and the tight-pressed mouth of patience. His shoulders would have been wide and husky, but long labor at his benches had stooped them. His voice came out, thin and querulous.

"I've only got one more mirror ready," he said impatiently, "and there's no need to point that confounded gun at me."

Wentworth laughed softly, sibilantly. "One mirror will be quite enough for me, Doctor Kepler. I'll take it along." He did not put away the gun. Instead, it bore quite steadily on Kepler, as Wentworth followed him across the laboratory to a much-wrapped package against the wall.

"I'm sorry," Wentworth said then and struck Kepler lightly above the ear. The physicist pitched limply to the floor, and Wentworth stooped to bind his wrists and ankles tightly together. Afterward, he made a swift and thorough search of the laboratory in the hope of finding some clue to the Master. . . He failed.

Wentworth caught up the mirror and stole out into the darkness again, found Kepler's car and drove again into the concealment of the woods. There he set up the mirror and tested it, made a record for the phonographic attachment in imitation of the sepulchral voice used by the Master and then, once more, wrapped up the mirror carefully. He hid it in a thicket of shrubbery, took the record he had made and hurried across the city.

A dozen times in his swift progress, he was forced to double on his trail to avoid patrols of the Black Police and, at the delay, his anger mounted. Not exclusively because of the inconvenience to which he was put, but at thought of the terror and oppression such a patrol of the city streets indicated. Here, truly, liberty was dead! Well, it should be resurrected!

At last, Wentworth reached the house toward which he had been making his way—the home of Lieutenant-governor Rixson!

It was a curious home for a criminal—even for a criminal who was helping to loot an entire state. Set well back from the road among thick-planted and ancient shrubs and trees, it bespoke culture and family background. Strangely, it was Rixson's own and had been in the family for years. It should have belonged to such a man as his twin brother, Colonel Rice.

Wentworth had no need to spy out his surroundings. He knew them well, and knew, too, that the house would be well guarded by the Black Police. Later in the night, he would have had no trouble entering the place in safety, but to make his way inside at this hour, not only in safety, but utterly unseen, took all of even the *Spider's* superlative skill.

From beneath the low boughs of a spruce tree, Wentworth spied out the location of the guards. There were two of the Black Police at the front door, two at the back, and no others. They were not too alert.

Why should they be? Hadn't the last of the *Spider's* adherents been seized the night before and thrown into a concentration camp? What could one man do against the overwhelming force and organization of the Master? Wentworth's lips drew thin as he stole toward the glassed-in conservatory which covered one end of the house. His caped body merged with the black shadows against its wall and once more the slender lock pick of surgical steel did its work.

Moments later, he was in the humid, warm confines of the conservatory. He locked himself in, slipped toward the glass-paned door that gave on the house proper.

Through the curtained window, he made out a softly lighted library. Behind it, through a narrow arch, was Rixson's home office which was Wentworth's goal. There, he was sure, he would find the concave mirror through which the Master issued his orders—and through which the *Spider* would issue orders in the Master's name!

Once more a lock yielded to manipulation, and Wentworth slipped into the den. He heard a light footfall in the outer room and crouched behind a chair, gun snouting from his fist. Presently, a butler stood in the doorway. He looked about carefully, then shrugged and walked away. Probably, he had caught some half-heard sound or the scent of flower odors wafted through the temporarily opened door of the conservatory. Wentworth slowly straightened. Almost immediately, his eyes fell on the mirror he sought—set in a frame of wood built into the wall of the den itself.

WENTWORTH wasted no time in seeking for the secret spring that might swing the mirror open. More than likely, the phonographic records the Master used were placed in the machine by some secret passageway in the walls, such as Wentworth had once discovered in the home of Governor Whiting! As coolly as if every second did not increase his peril a hundred-fold, Wentworth set to work on the mirror. Using a small screwdriver, from a vertical pocket in a leather girdle about his waist, he rapidly loosened the frame. Now and again, he checked in his swift work to listen. He heard the measured footsteps of the butler occasionally in the hall—movements above stairs, but for long minutes he was undisturbed. Who would have suspected that the *Spider* labored in the very heart of the enemy forces?

Presently, the mirror panel came free in his hands, and Wentworth peered into a dark, narrow closet. Wentworth saw at once that a narrow door opened on one opposite side—either through a panel in the hallway or through some innocent seeming closet there. Abruptly, Wentworth stiffened in alarm. Those assured and striding footsteps he heard were no butler's subdued tread! Rixson himself must be in the hallway, entering the library! With a swiftly fluid movement, Wentworth hauled himself through the mirror opening and stood in the secret closet. Dexterously, he slid the glass panel into place beneath the moldings on three sides—secured it on the fourth by thrusting a knife blade snugly home against its edge. He was not a moment too soon. A light winked on in the den, and Wentworth found himself staring directly into the face of Lieutenant-governor Rixson!

It was several seconds before Wentworth realized that while he could see Rixson, the man could not possibly see him. What he gazed through plainly was Argus glass. . . Rixson was smoothing his hair neatly into place. He sauntered to a chair behind his desk.

A grim smile moved Wentworth's lips. This was even better than he had dared to hope. Not only would he have ample time to plant the phonograph record he had made, but he would be able to overhear whatever was said in the den tonight. That a conference of several persons was planned, Wentworth saw at once from the arrangement of the chairs. He saw Rixson's hand go to a call button and presently a girl entered with a stenographer's notebook in her hand. Wentworth barely repressed a violent start. There could be no mistaking the girl. It was Maria Laplante, who had befriended and protected him in Westphalian! But in God's name, what could she be doing in this house as the secretary of the commander of the Black Police?

Marvin Rixson leaned toward Maria, "Have you changed your mind, Maria?" he asked softly.

Maria's eyes met his directly and there was no smile on her lips. "Have you changed yours?" she demanded.

Rixson's mouth lost its meanness when he smiled. "You're stubborn,

Maria," he said, patiently. "I've got all the world in my hand, ready to lay it at your feet, and you want me to throw it away."

Maria settled herself and laid pencils in a row on the end of the desk. She frowned down at the blank pages of her notebook. "No, Marvin," she said quietly, "you're wrong. I don't care what you do with it. I'm only warning you that, sooner or later, you'll pay for your crimes. . ."

The butler stepped into the doorway of the den; "Governor Whiting, sir," he announced. "Mr. Daniel Oldham and Senator William MacFoulard."

Wentworth's interest quickened. He had not yet troubled to put his record upon the machine which, with a loudspeaker was attached to the wall below the mirror. Better to hear first what the record upon it would say. Rixson obviously already knew since he had not bothered to start the mechanism. . . The by-play between Rixson and Maria Laplante astonished him.

Obviously, during his brief incarceration in Westphalian, Rixson had become infatuated with the brave girl who had fought beside Wentworth there. Just as obviously, Marie Laplante would have nothing to do with him—unless he quit the Master!

But her presence here belied her pretended indifference. Wentworth's lips closed grimly as he reflected that he had lost one more trusted ally. After this, he dared not trust Maria. . .

A slight scraping sound behind him wrenched Wentworth about in the narrow confines of the secret closet, and his hand closed warily on his gun. Was someone about to open the hidden door? Was that someone. . . the Master? Wentworth felt tension rip through him. He had no thought for his own danger in that confined space, only for the fact that in a moment he might be face-to-face with the author of all this tyranny. He waited tautly, but the sound was not repeated and presently Wentworth turned again to the den. But he was conscious of that door at his back. It laid a coldness along his spine like the razor-edge of an assassin's knife. God, if his presence here should be discovered, he was as helpless as a fish in a barrel. Gunshots would rip through the panels like tissue paper. There was no room to dodge, scarcely space to draw a gun. . .

Resolutely, Wentworth crowded the peril of his situation into the background of his mind, for all that his senses kept constant watch. He focused his attention on the den.

The men had all taken their seats, and Rixson had resigned the seat behind the desk to Governor Whiting. Wentworth knew the timorous governor thoroughly and he scarcely gave the man a glance. Senator MacFoulard he recognized at once in the white-haired pompous hypocrite near the door. He was tilted back, smoking a black cigar, frowning with narrowed eyes up at the smoke. Boss Oldham looked like a small-town undertaker, dour and long of face, with a heavy watch chain across his vest. He sat bolt upright with an air of dauntless patience, while Whiting mumbled some preliminary words.

WENTWORTH'S keen eyes flashed from face to face. These were the four who ruled the state and were looting it, decimating its population for their own ends. Why not, right now, blast them out of their black lives? Surely, it would cripple the Master for a while! Damn it, one of them might well be the Master himself! The man was a master at disguise as well as murder. . .

Wentworth found that his automatic was in his hand, the muzzle questing like a hungry hound's muzzle over the men before him. It was a struggle to force that gun back into its holster. No, he must first be sure. These men deserved death a hundred times over, but it would be useless to remove them. He would only close the door to his one sure way of finding the Master!

Wentworth's eyes shifted beyond them to an officer of the Black Police who stood resolutely in the doorway, arms folded. There was something vaguely familiar about the man's piercing eyes. Wentworth frowned over it, then his attention was jerked violently back to Rixson. The lieutenant-governor was talking.

"The time has come for a final cleanup," he said, his pleasant orator's voice resonant. "We've got along longer than we had any right to expect, and the government can't keep its hands off much longer. We've been let alone, chiefly, because we threw up a clever smoke-screen—and because we left the big men alone. We won't any longer!"

Whiting said, worriedly, "Rixson, you're always stirring up trouble…"

"Oh, be quiet, Whiting," Rixson said shortly. "Listen. . ." With two long strides, he confronted the mirror behind which Wentworth stood and pitched his voice to a monotone. "White Face in the Mirror," he said, "what are your orders?"

There was a subdued clicking in the mechanism below the mirror. Lights were thrown upward and in from both sides on the concavity of the mirror and Wentworth knew that they were forming a shadow face there. From the loudspeaker, sepulchral and unearthly, came the voice of the Master!

"Clean out every man even suspected of having the brain to cause trouble," the Master ordered harshly. "Send them to concentration camps and kill them with the plague. Organize your forces and, in twenty-four hours, loot every bank and wealthy man in the state. The time has come for a final clean-up. Prepare your plans. I will name the hour within two days!"

Wentworth choked down the harsh oath that leaped to his lips as the voice ceased. The sheer enormity of the calm proposal for massacre was a profound shock even after these months of dealing with the merciless Master. Wentworth's fists knotted furiously at his side. By the heavens, these men should die now! No, no. Not yet. Not until he had set his own plans into operation.

Shuddering with the effort at control, Wentworth silently removed the played out record from the machine and substituted his own. Immediately, he knew that he had done something wrong. Scarcely had he slid the cylinder home when the lights blinked on again. The men in the room whirled tautly toward the mirror and Wentworth heard his own voice, in tones that matched those of the Master, issue new orders. . .

"I have received information," it said, "that a rebellion is planned here in Albany. Summon all Black Police here to the city at once at top speed. It is our only chance!"

For a moment, the men in the room stood in shocked tableau, then at the door, Wentworth caught a flash of movement. He saw the Black Police officer whip out his revolver and, even as Wentworth stared at him, the man drew a deliberate bead on the *Spider*! It was exactly as if, for him, the Argus glass offered no block to vision. His muzzle held unwaveringly on Wentworth's heart. The trigger finger was whitening with pressure. . .

Wentworth twisted frantically in the narrow closet and wedged himself toward the floor. He was not an instant too soon. The crash of the gun was an echo for the falling clatter of the bullet-smashed mirror. Wentworth had his gun in hand while he groped behind him for the fastening of the secret door. He must be swift. Within moments, the bullets would comb every inch of his narrow prison, and. . .

A jagged oath tore at Wentworth's throat! He was a fool! But it might not be too late! Wentworth held a gun in each hand, and he had not fired. He had seen the Black Police officer and felt his familiarity, and he had not killed him.

It was only now he realized that. . . the Black Police officer was the Master himself!

CHAPTER SEVEN

TO THE DEATH!

WENTWORTH started to straighten to the attack and, near his face, a heavy bullet punched through the wooden panel, gouged splinters into his cheek. Another plucked through his hat. Wentworth's face set in grim justice's mold, did not change. He should have recognized at once the meaning of the attack by the Black Police officer. Anyone of the men in the room might have known that the closet was there, but only the Master would know that he had never dictated the words uttered by one White Face in the Mirror. Or he must have figured that the *Spider* must be within the closet to change the records at that precise moment. Yes, it was typical of the Master's swift mental processes to figure matters out in such split-second style and to open fire at once!

Even as these thoughts went flashingly through his brain, Wentworth knew that he could stand no chance of shooting it out successfully with the Master unless he escaped from this closet that well might become his coffin. Only instants of time had elapsed since that first shot—only time enough to fire two more. And each of those had narrowly missed killing the *Spider*.

With the thought, Wentworth braced his shoulders against the small secret door, thrust violently with his powerful leg muscles—and crashed supine into the hall! He had a glimpse of a white-faced butler, rigid against the stair, saw plaster dust fly as bullets ranged through the closet and buried themselves in the wall. Then Wentworth was up and darting for the hallway's arch to the library and the den. It was one man against five, but one of the enemy was the Master! To reach him, Wentworth would gladly battle his way through an army!

There was a great bounding joy in Wentworth's heart. Nothing mattered save that, at last, he was to meet the Master face to face. He bounded into the library and gunshots streaked at him from the darkness of the den. He laid his bullets along those lances of flame and a man cursed in a thin, broken voice and afterward the fall of his body jarred the floor. Governor Whiting was pleading for protection. His whining was the only sound through a long dark moment while Wentworth crouched with his restless guns questing about him. He could plainly see the lighter squares of window doors. If anything moved against them. . .

A whistle skirled an alarm, or a command, and the building filled suddenly with the tramp of many running feet. The Black Police guards had been called in to exterminate him. Wentworth laughed silently. Before they could strike, his work would be finished. He straightened and went on soft, long-striding feet to the entrance of the den. His hand found the light switch! With one movement, he flicked it on and hurled himself aside, ready to shoot.

One man lay prone on the floor, a gun beside his hand. It was Senator MacFoulard. Governor Whiting was crouched behind desk and chair, still pleading for succor. There was no one else at all in the room! Anger shook Wentworth. He smacked out the light as bullets threshed across the den.

Whiting's pleading became screams but Wentworth was diving toward the mirror's opening and the closet. That way the Master, Rixson and Oldham must have fled. The feet of the charging Black

Police were tramping across the library. Their flashlights slashed the gloom. . . but the *Spider* was swift and silent. An instant before they entered the den, he was stepping quietly into the hallway. He closed the narrow secret door behind him, strode toward the butler.

"Where did they go?" he demanded harshly.

It was only then that he saw the man's arms doubled across his stomach. As Wentworth spoke, the man's eyes rolled up, his knees gave and he slid, twisting, to the floor! His arms fell aside and there were gaping red holes in the white vest. The curses of the Black Police, their running feet, were moving back toward the hallway now. Wentworth had a space of seconds to make his decision, but he reasoned coldly.

The Master and his allies had had no chance to get past him in the front hall. They could have only fled rearward. If they had left the house, they were beyond pursuit, but there was a cellar. . . Wentworth's lips moved in a hard smile. Even in their fear of the *Spider*, he doubted they would have fled from the house. They would be too anxious to make sure that their last potent enemy was slain! Surely, then, they were hiding in that basement!

Wentworth reached the doorway in two long bounds and whipped the door open. . . but did not stand in the opening. Silence and blackness below—no more. Wentworth lay prone on his stomach and made two, then three steps creak with the pressure of his hands as if a man crept down them, and still there was no response from the basement. Wentworth frowned, but did not doubt his reasoning.

He eased onto the steps, drew the door shut and, head-first, crawled down the stairway until cold concrete touched his palm. Wentworth was smiling now. The enemy was here. He could feel their presence, could almost hear their close, fast breathing. Softly, he moved around until he crouched behind the steps, his guns in hand. Then he settled himself to wait. . . to wait while overhead the wild search of the Black Police made the house shake, while their blood-thirsty shouts echoed about him. Let him find and slay the Master and he would take his chances with them!

ABRUPTLY, Wentworth caught his breath. He had heard a soft, metallic click that might be the cocking of a gun—or might be the closing of a door! He whipped out his flashlight, held it at arm's length above his lowered head and squeezed out a brilliant shaft of light.

In one swift sweep, it circled the basement—and found nothing! Yet they had been here. Wentworth knew it. Some secret door. . . Instantly, Wentworth was on his feet, questing over the cellar. There was not an opening of any kind that he could detect, not even a window. The walls were thick stone and gave back steadily the sound of solid masonry. . .

The voice that spoke to him was quiet, mocking. Wentworth whirled, his light questing, but found only a small loudspeaker placed high against the rafters.

"Congratulations, *Spider*," came the mocking voice of the Master. "You did well to escape the closet. Fortunately, the walls here are a bit more solid. But I won't risk my men to remove you. It isn't necessary in the least. If you'll listen carefully, you'll hear the hiss of gas. Phosgene, *Spider*. If you survive for five minutes, you will greatly surprise me. Still, you are intelligent. I conceded that. Say, five minutes. . . I shall miss you, *Spider*. You have made things. . . interesting. But I shall soon be through here. Good-by!"

Wentworth did not move until he heard the click which meant the microphone was dead. He flung a single swift glance up the stairs. There would be Black Police up there, but not the Master. He had spoken from whatever secret passage led out of the basement, and that was the way the *Spider* would flee! There was actually a smile on the *Spider*'s lips as he set swiftly to work.

He poured the contents of a tiny vial of fluid, drawn from a pocket of the girdle, upon a handkerchief and bound it tightly over nose and mouth. It was a gas neutralizer, designed chiefly for use against tear-gas but effective against others to some extent. Against phosgene. . . Wentworth's eyes were narrow and hard. He did not know what it would accomplish against phosgene, one of the most deadly gases contrived by man. Seconds were precious. . .

Wentworth closed his eyes and, in imagination, brought back that faint click he had heard in the darkness. He held his gun in his hand, for he knew that his instinctive pointing of the weapon, trained through long years of life-and-death struggle, would be more accurate than any logical placing of the sound by mental processes. He opened his eyes then and found the gun centered on the remote corner of the room. Wentworth swore under his breath—for it was from that corner, too, came the hiss of escaping gas! He was right, but any attempt to reach the wall might well prove fatal!

Wentworth's lips closed thinly. To hell with that! He was going through. . . Swiftly, he surveyed the wall. He tapped there with the gun butt and found it solid. Any opening of the wall then would be by means of counterbalance which meant, undoubtedly, that the section of wall which constituted the door would sink through the floor. He had to look then for a catch which would be released near the ceiling. Possibly the weight of his body, pressing down, would be sufficient to thrust the section of wall down. . .

With the thought, Wentworth sprang into action. There were water pipes overhead—cross-braces between the rafters—and phosgene was heavier than air though it took a very small admixture of the gas with air to make it lethal. The fact that the air of the basement was dead and would not circulate helped him some. If he were swift. . . With a lithe leap, Wentworth reached a water pipe and swung, hand over hand, along it, directly toward the corner where the gas escaped!

When he reached the corner, he swung up his knees and dangling by one hand only, flashed on his light. It swept minutely the juncture of floor and wall, and he smiled thinly. Figured logically, it was easy enough to locate the space where the door opened. The gas was escaping from the narrow crack beneath it. Wentworth turned his attention to the top of the wall to find the catch that would hold it in place against the counterbalance. With his screwdriver, he prodded into the cracks. . .

WENTWORTH'S eyes were burning and he was dizzy from the suppression of breath. He dared breathe only when he absolutely must, and then lightly. For long, dragging seconds, he forced himself to take in no air at all. The screwdriver grated on rock, slid from crack to crack, but nothing happened. No obstacle appeared that might be the catch. Wentworth found his movements becoming frenzied and deliberately stopped all action for a count of ten.

He peered at the wall then, thinking. . . thinking. He could not hope to accidentally find the catch. It must be done by reason. . . Abruptly, he reached out to the wall and threw his pressure upon a single rock. It did not yield. With the close white beam of his light, Wentworth studied the mortar between the rocks. His brain was reeling now from suffocation, his eyes starting from his head. And the gas. . . How long had the Master said. Five minutes? But probably, he had deliberately set the period long to lull the *Spider* into inactivity until too late.

Wentworth shook his head, stuck doggedly to his task. Finally, his searching eyes found what he wanted—not in the door itself, but in the wall beside it. A few flecks of mortar clinging to the rock-face, a slightly crumbled crack. . .

His fingers and knees were slipping from their grip on the pipes. He could scarcely see for the black pounding of suffocated blood behind his eyes. The hand he reached out to the rock trembled, but, by a supreme effort, he threw all his weight behind the thrust. He felt the rock yield fractionally, then it moved inward a half inch and he heard once more the faint click that had come to him through the darkness. Instantly, a section of the stone wall slid downward on smoothly oiled counterbalance and the next instant, Wentworth had hurled himself into the black passageway that was revealed!

A cool draft blew against Wentworth's face as he ran and there was a prayer of thanksgiving in his heart. That draft would hold back the awful gas that was filling the basement behind. The stone door already had slid back into place. . . Wentworth checked himself, listening intently. No sound reached him here—nothing at all stirred save the draft, cold against his face. He crept on more cautiously and now the gun was ready in his fist. Now and again, he sent the beam of his flashlight questing ahead. Only the narrow, dark walls of the tunnel showed, stretching ahead. He found the tank from which the gas issued and a microphone beside it. A dozen yards beyond, rough wooden steps led upward. A trap door was half-open.

For an instant longer, Wentworth crouched on the steps, listening. There was a mad urge in him to fling himself out into the open, to risk whatever bullets might fly in the mad hope of catching the Master. Reason dictated that the Master had long since fled the place. He was no more accustomed to revealing himself, in person, to his allies than to his enemies. . . Cautiously, Wentworth lifted the trap-door and found himself in an empty garage. A bitter curse fell from his lips, but only one. He had failed!

He had been face-to-face with the Master and had failed! His plan, too, to concentrate the Black Police, and hence weaken the guards of the prison camps, had gone awry. He could not delay for that reason. He must forge ahead more strongly than ever before. Within two days, the Master had said, he would order the wholesale massacre and looting of the state. Now that he knew his plans had been overheard, he would make every effort to speed the blow. And the *Spider* was alone, one man against an army.

It was time indeed for desperate measures! Wentworth drew in a deep, slow breath. Perhaps, desperation might win where long and faithful effort had failed. Perhaps. . . but Wentworth had only the hope that comes to men when death is near, the last frantic clutching at straws. Not that he would fight less hard because he realized how faint was his chance of success! That was not the way of the *Spider*!

Two paths only were open to him. He could remain in Albany and institute a *Spider*'s reign of terror—strike down the leaders of the criminals—or he could free his men from the concentration camp to which he had sent Nita as a spy, and put Rice in as the double of the lieutenant-governor. No man realized better than Wentworth the obstacles to both plans. His reign of terror could no more than begin before the massacre was launched. On the other hand, Rice could not hope to escape detection for long, even supposing Wentworth was fortunate enough to free him from the camp and to put him in Rixson's place without arousing suspicion. . .

Something very like a groan forced its way out between Wentworth's set teeth. Despite the difficulties, the plan that involved Rice was better. It alone offered any hope of permanent relief from the

Master and his hordes. If they could hold control of the state for a few hours and issue orders which would command the prompt obedience which the Master obtained through fear!

Slowly, Wentworth nodded. That was what he must do, and the first step was. . . to deliver Rice from a concentration camp. A small smile played around Wentworth's lips. Even with a body of armed men, that would be almost impossible now since Wentworth's previous raids had caused increased strength of fortifications and guards. Single-handed. . . The smile stiffened into a grimace of determination. They could not stop him now! They could not. . .

SWIFTLY, before the Master and his allies should discover the escape from the basement, Wentworth fled the neighborhood of Rixson's home. He went back to Dr. Kepler's stolen car and at various filling-stations, bought gallons of gasoline in cans to refuel the plane. He still had need of that. Wentworth's mind was working at top speed now. Already, he had a glimmering of an idea for forcing the camp, and he would need the plane for Rice's escape to Albany! So, two hours after his escape from the basement, Wentworth was winging his way back toward Westphalian again. A quick landing there and once more he was entering the beleaguered town. There were certain preparations to be made before he could raid the camp!

On a dark side-street, he waylaid one of the Black Police and swiftly donned his uniform. Then, carrying an order he had forged, he went to the central armory of Westphalian. Within another hour, he was driving from the city a huge truck loaded with mining supplies, among which were three boxes of dynamite! Back at the farmhouse in the hills, he found Nita just returning wearily from her survey of the camp. She flung herself into Wentworth's arms.

"Oh, Dick!" she cried. "I was sure you had met trouble in Albany!"

Wentworth laughed gently. "I met trouble. . . but it got away from me. The camp, Nita?"

"Impregnable," she said wearily.

"There are easily two hundred Black Police on guard with perhaps a thousand prisoners. There are five concentric fences around the camp, two of wood, three of barbed wire. The middlemost one is charged with electricity, a killing voltage."

Wentworth nodded, his eyes intent and eager. "When do they change guard, Nita?" he asked, "Say, at dinner hour at night and in the morning, are all the Black Police assembled?"

Nita nodded. "They certainly are at night. All the prisoners are lined up against one side of the camp. The guard changes on the opposite side, near the gates. They make the prisoners stand at salute almost an hour while some are disciplined. I. . . I heard a man flogged to death!"

"Sleep now, dearest," Wentworth admonished Nita. "At dawn, take the plane—it's been refueled—and fly to the most convenient hidden field near the camp. When you hear shooting, send up a rocket—I have some in the truck—so that I'll know where you are. I'll do the rest!"

Nita's tired face became more drawn, "You're going to try to deliver those prisoners," she said woodenly.

Wentworth bent to her lips, tenderly.

"No, darling, I'm *going* to deliver those prisoners. I must, or. . ." He let the sentence trail off. "Sleep until dawn, dearest."

"But you, Dick!"

Wentworth shook his head. "I have some supplies to deliver to Concentration Camp Seven. It's a longish drive!"

He gave Nita the supplies she needed, loaded down the farm woman with foodstuffs and, fifteen minutes later, was rolling off through the hills, still clad in the uniform of the Black Police. At dawn he stopped on the crest of a ridge and peered down into the wide, flat valley beyond. The concentration camp sprawled in its midst, without a tree, with only the rude hovels the prisoners had built themselves for protection against the bitter cold.

Wentworth himself was muffled in a heavy overcoat with thick gloves on his hands. In the frigid dawn, his breath made a white cloud like steam, as he labored over the boxes of dynamite and lengths of fuse and wire. When, presently, he heard the thin strains of a bugle in the camp, he climbed back to the driver's seat and started the truck lumbering downgrade. Its speed mounted steadily. . .

IN THE concentration camp, prisoners were being routed from their meager beds into the deathly cold. There were some, as every morning, who did not rise—who were beyond the cruelties of the Black guard, but the others rose, shivering, to stand in ragged lines at salute while the guard changed.

The Black Police were muffled to the ears in impressive uniform overcoats and even so there were men among them who grumbled as they took their places in line. The entire company was formed up save for those who kept watch from the machine-gun towers about the camp. One of these men caught up a phone that communicated with the gate.

"Supply truck coming," he said lazily, "and tell the cook to damn well hurry my breakfast up here. I'm hungry!"

The gate guard snarled back at him. "Starve, damn you! That watch tower is heated. I got to stand out in the cold."

The rumble of the truck was loud.

Plainly, the driver was in a hurry to reach shelter, too. He was driving with a wide-open throttle, and the heavy truck swayed as it hammered along the straightaway that ran directly to the gates through the multiple fences. Just inside the gates, the companies of the Black Police were formed up while the commander read out the orders for the day—and the punishment. One man was to be flogged before breakfast.

"God almighty," groaned one of the gate guards. "Now we got to wait until that damned punk dies. I hope be dies quick!"

The prisoner was marched out from solitary confinement in the cellar below the comfortable quarters of the troops. He was naked to the waist and shuddering with the cold. There was a bloody tear on his left bicep, an old wound, but his shoulders were well back and his soldier's head was carried erectly.

"Nuts," said the guard, "that one will be slow dying. It's that rebel, Kirkpatrick."

He was trussed up to a cruciform post, arms strained high, and the torturer stepped forward with his heavy whip. The roar of the truck was very close now. The gate guard turned that way sullenly, looking back over his shoulder as the whip swung through the air for the first slashing blow.

The guard touched his lips with his tongue, as the gashes cut by the thongs showed red against the white flesh. Then he looked toward the truck. . . His eyes stared abruptly wide.

He couldn't see anybody at the wheel and the truck was racing with tremendous speed straight for the gates, and less than a hundred feet away. The guard let out a strangled cry of amazement—and in the interim the truck covered the last hundred feet.

The steel gratings of the outer gate burst open with a report like a gunshot and were ripped bodily from their hinges. One of them caught a guard and tossed him, a broken thing, onto the barbed wire of the second barrier. The truck, with the huge momentum of its speed, the tons of weight of its body and load behind it, did not even hesitate.

It rammed through the second gate, the third, then whanged against the innermost barrier. This was a gate of steel, also, heavier than the outer portal, and strongly braced. Against it the truck lunged with an almost living fury. One of the gates ripped loose from its upper hinge and slammed flat down on the ground. A squad of men was caught beneath it. They did not have time even to scream before they were ground to pulp beneath it. The truck jounced up on the steel ramp the gate formed, trundled more slowly forward and rasped to a halt against the solid brick masonry of the gate post.

Inside the concentration camp, bedlam had broken loose. At the guard's first shout, the officers had stared toward him. Before they could even shout an order, the inner gate had fallen upon the close pressed ranks of the guard and killed a dozen. Men began to scatter, but the stern orders of the officers, the crack of a revolver that blew down a fugitive, whipped them back into line.

"Close the gates!" rang out the order of the commander. "Haul that truck inside!"

In response to his shouts, the Black guard converged on the truck while the prisoners still stood in ragged, shivering files. One of the Black Police reached the running-board and clambered on it. Other men swarmed up behind him. It was precisely sixty seconds since the truck, with a peculiar, wired contrivance on its bumper, had struck the first gate. Wentworth had done his timing well and he had calculated properly. As the last of sixty seconds dribbled past, the dynamite let go. It caught the Black Police at the time of maximum concentration about the truck. . .

FROM the ditch outside the camp into which he had thrown himself, Wentworth saw the up-thrust spires of scarlet and livid flame, saw the black whirling fragments of men tossed high against the sky. What remained of the gates and the posts beside them was blown outward, and Wentworth knew that the front end of the truck had exploded like a huge grenade, hurling jagged fragments among the close-packed police. Wentworth saw one wheel soar like a well thrown discus through the air and sail out beyond the confines of the camp. It bounced a full fifty feet into the air before it fell again and quivered to a halt like a spun coin.

The instant the concussion of the blast had swept past him, Wentworth was on his feet and running toward those shattered gates. An automatic was in each fist and his eyes swept the machine-gun towers. One of them had been shattered by a high-flung fragment of the truck. . . but there were three others. As soon as the men got over the stunning force of that explosion. . . *Ah!* Wentworth spotted movement inside the nearest tower and his guns blasted in unison. His deafened ears barely heard the shots, but he saw that the white face he had glimpsed, a moment since, was hammered out of sight.

Wentworth scrambled across the huge crater where the truck had stood and ripped off the overcoat and uniform cap. From his shoulders fluttered the green cape of the *Spider*.

"Citizens, arise!" he shouted clearly.

"Overthrow the tyrants! The *Spider* has come to save you!"

For an instant, those shivering ranks of men stared at him, motionless, as they had stood through even the terror of the blast. They had felt the iron hand of discipline so long! But at sight of Wentworth, a mutter stirred through them.

Then, as a wave breaks on the rocks, those lines shattered and the men charged forward. Some of the Black Police were still on their feet, though dazed by the enormity of the disaster that had struck them. They did not survive the charge. One of the machine guns stammered from a watch tower and cut a bloody swathe among the prisoners. Instantly, a dozen men were swarming up into the tower and soon the gun was still.

Wentworth spotted the tortured Kirkpatrick at once and ran to him with the overcoat he had discarded, laid it tenderly about the lacerated shoulders before he slashed loose the bonds. There was a thin, bitter smile on Kirkpatrick's lips.

"You didn't come too soon, Dick," he said crisply. "They were going to flog me to death before breakfast."

Wentworth cursed harshly. "Rice is still alive?" He scarcely dared voice the question.

"Alive, yes," Kirkpatrick said slowly.

He winced as he put arms into the coat-sleeves. "He got a bullet through the side when we were captured. I haven't seen him since. What now, Dick. . . Another march on New York?"

Kirkpatrick's voice sounded hopeless. God, if these camps could break the spirit of such men as Kirkpatrick! Wentworth peered at him, but did not voice his thought. And yet, he could not blame Kirkpatrick. He had been so hopeful when he had been restored to power in New York City as police commissioner, and nothing had come of it—nothing save flight and disaster.

"No march, no," Wentworth said shortly. "Take me to Rice and the others!"

The worshiping eyes of freed men followed Wentworth, as he strode toward the barracks building with Kirkpatrick. One man, thickly bearded, clad in rags, sprang into Wentworth's path. "I was your man, commander." he said hoarsely, "until the battle in Westphalian. They caught me after that, and by God they've made me suffer. With you to lead us. . .?"

Wentworth recognized the man with difficulty through the lines that suffering had gouged into his face. "You shall lead them Stevens," he said quietly. "You've seen how I smashed open this camp. There will be dynamite here. Steal trucks and attack the other camps, if the men will follow you—and I think they will. I have a job to do. If it succeeds. . ."

Stevens laughed hoarsely, "It will succeed, commander!" he cried. "You can't fail!"

Wentworth clasped the man's shoulder and strode on. He couldn't speak for the thickness that closed his throat. If only their faith in him was justified. "I can't fail," he muttered to Kirkpatrick.

Kirkpatrick looked at him curiously, "I don't believe you can, Dick," he said quietly. "Not in the end."

Wentworth laughed harshly and made no answer. Hadn't he had the Master under his gunpoint and let the man escape him? Never would he find the Master again in the identity he had assumed last night. No, it was all to do over again. If only Rice was strong enough. . . Cell doors clanged open under Wentworth's hand and he strode down the line of dark dungeons with their solid doors, throwing them wide open to free the wretches within. He found Jackson, Ram Singh, their faces haggard with starvation. Sailor Joe had almost lost his smile and Rice. . .

Wentworth stared down at the wreck of a man on a cot and saw the collapse of his plans. Rice managed a smile. "It's not as bad as it looks, commander," he said, "but the devils wouldn't patch up the wound—and they haven't fed me."

WENTWORTH permitted a single jagged oath to escape his lips. Rice's indomitable courage would undoubtedly pull him through, but there was no time to doctor up his strength. Already twelve of the maximum of forty-eight hours the Master had allowed were elapsed, and he had reason to know that the Master would rush his plans now. At most, twelve more hours remained to him. Wentworth swung from the cot.

"Ram Singh, cleanse and bandage the wound," he ordered. "Jackson, rustle food. Sailor Joe, Miss van Sloan has an airplane in the field a mile up the road and perhaps three hundred yards to the right. Take a car. Ask her to land as close to the fences as possible.

We'll take off in about an hour. Now, Colonel Rice. . ."

"Dick," Kirkpatrick interrupted, "If you don't need me, I'll get these poor devils upstairs organized and under way. They'll be slaughtered if they're caught here."

Wentworth nodded, his eyes never leaving those of Rice. Swiftly, he outlined to the prostrate soldier the details of the Master's plans. "Only one thing can stop them; only one man," Wentworth told him with slow emphasis. "If you can take Rixson's place and hold it for a few hours, we can disrupt their organization—perhaps disband the Black Police. If then, we could eliminate the Master, you might continue the masquerade until the entire state was on its feet again. I can't overemphasize the risk, but it's the only way open to us now."

Colonel Rice's gaunt face twitched at Ram Singh's ministrations to his wound, but he nodded. "You know, Wentworth, that anything I can do, I will. If you could stick with me and instruct me as we go along, I think perhaps we can do it. But how will you install me in Rixson's place?"

Wentworth said, "I have a plan!"

An hour later, the camp was cleared of men and with the pale, but strengthened Colonel Rice, Wentworth hurried to the two-seater plane which Nita had brought close against the fence. Nita's face was white, her eyes large and dark. "You let the prisoners go," she said. "I thought you'd use them as an army. . ."

Wentworth shook his head curtly. "We tried that once before—and the federal government chased us out. We're going to try what's known, in the banana republics, as a 'palace revolution'."

"And my job?" Nita asked quietly. Wentworth smiled at her, "Your job will be even more dangerous than mine, dear," he said softly. He turned to Kirkpatrick and threw his *Spider* cape about his friend's high shoulders. "You two must distract the attention of the Master, of the Black Police, and make them believe that the *Spider* freed his men only to harry them. Fight the Black Police at every turn, try to prevent them from taking prisoners, free chain-gangs and stop lootings. Go everywhere and sprinkle *Spider* seals over the face of the map."

"But you, Dick!" Kirkpatrick and Nita spoke together.

Wentworth still smiled. "Colonel Rice and I are flying to Albany. . . to stage our palace revolution!"

Moments later, Wentworth whipped the plane from the earth and sent it roaring toward Albany, and his eyes were bleak.

Those others, his friends and allies, were encouraged because of his feat at the camp, but Wentworth knew that this was nothing compared to the problem that lay ahead!

RED CHALLENGE

IN AN hour, Wentworth set the plane down on the official Black Police air field at Albany. He was once more in the uniform of an officer, of which there had been many at the concentration camp. Colonel Rice, unshaven, but otherwise well enough dressed, had his hands handcuffed before him and Wentworth kept a drawn gun in his hand.

"Special prisoner for the commander," he told men at the airport curtly. "Orders to take him directly to the commander's home."

He showed a written order which he had prepared and, within minutes, was roaring off to Rixson's home with a full police escort. He managed to get rid of them at the entrance of the grounds and then hurried, on foot, directly to the house itself. Colonel Rice kept his head bowed, his shoulders sagging with weakness as Wentworth directed. It was no part of his plan that the resemblance between Rice and Rixson should be detected, and he was gambling that Rixson would not be at home. . .

The butler opened the door to his peremptory ring, and Wentworth's eyes shot beyond him to the library and the den. They were empty, so far as he could see, and Wentworth checked a breath of relief.

"Prisoner for Commander Rixson," he snapped at the butler.

The man shook his head, "The lieutenant-governor isn't home," he said, "and. . ."

Wentworth thrust Colonel Rice forward into the hall. "Then we'll wait," he said shortly. "Give me a room for the prisoner and notify the commander. Important prisoner from New York City, by special order!"

Wentworth's heart was bounding with hope. He had calculated correctly so far. If Rixson was unsuspicious and came home at once without too many men. . . The butler bowed before his commanding manner and gestured him up the stairs. Wentworth thrust Rice that way with his ready gun, started up after him—and heard light quick footfalls in the hallway above. Wentworth's eyes jerked that way, and tautness raced over his body. Peering down at him was Maria Laplante!

Wentworth paid no attention to her, apparently, but he hurried Rice in his climb of the stairs and he made his own carriage a feigned swagger. There was a strong possibility that she would identify him, and there was no way of telling what her reaction would be. Though she had never betrayed the *Spider*, it was plain that she was very fond of Rixson and that fact made her damnably dangerous at this moment. One word of alarm from her now. . . The butler was calling up the information that Wentworth had given in answer to Maria Laplante's quick challenge.

"Stumble and fall!" Wentworth whispered to Rice.

Immediately, Colonel Rice tripped and pitched prone on the steps. Wentworth ripped out an oath and, apparently, drove his toe hard into the fallen man's side.

"No tricks!" he snapped. "One more like that, and I'll blow your spine in half!"

Maria Laplante came rapidly down the steps toward him and bent over the fallen man and, in that instant, Wentworth leaned close and jabbed the gun muzzle into her side.

"Not a sound, Maria," he whispered. "The *Spider* speaks!"

He felt Maria Laplante stiffen under the prod of the gun muzzle, but she was obedient. She helped Rice to his feet, "Oh, you poor man!" she said gently. "Are you hurt?"

Wentworth moved warily close to her as they climbed the steps and turned finally into a corner room. Wentworth whipped the door shut then, and Maria Laplante whirled toward him, her dark eyes angry and hurt.

"Do you have to hold a gun on me?" she demanded sharply. "Are you forgetting that I once saved your life at the risk of my own?"

Wentworth smiled at her, his eyes keen and searching. "No, Maria," he said gently, "but I'm not forgetting either that all this was before you met Marvin Rixson. It is a little. . . strange to find you here."

"Your cause was lost," the girl said with a toss of her thick black hair. "I tried to win by my own methods, to persuade Marvin Rixson to—" she glanced nervously about, changed to a whisper—"turn on the Master! Why are you here? I'll help you do anything, anything at all, except. . ."

"Except harm Marvin Rixson," Wentworth finished quietly. "Yes, I know. He won't be harmed, but I intend to hold him a prisoner in this room for a few days. After that—" he shrugged, "—we may all be dead."

Colonel Rice was watching the two of them keenly, "Your best guarantee that Marvin won't be harmed is this," he said to Maria. "Marvin is my brother."

Maria Laplante's eyes swung to him, probed keenly into his face. Abruptly, she sucked in her breath. "Oh, I understand now. I see the resemblance. You. . . you are going to be the lieutenant-governor!" Neither man answered, watching the girl closely. Maria began to smile, then laughed. "It's a good plan. You can count on me. Once Marvin is committed, I'm sure he'll help."

Wentworth made no reply to that. He had his own ideas about Marvin Rixson. It was quite apparent that he was the strong man under the Master; that it was he and not Whiting who commanded. If the *Spider* had not seen Rixson side by side with the Black Police officer whom he knew to be the Master, it would not be hard to believe that Rixson was the Master himself! He frowned. Could he be sure that Rixson had not ordered the officer to fire on the glass panel?

Slowly, Wentworth shook his head. He could not be sure. All that he knew was that only the Master could have known that the recorded voice which sounded was not his own. Anyone of the men in the den that day might have ordered the shot, by a single quick gesture.

"Colonel Rice has been wounded," Wentworth said rapidly. "Will you help him dress the wound, Maria? He has to shave also."

Maria Laplante nodded and turned toward an adjoining bath, and Wentworth whispered rapidly to Rice not to let the girl leave the room. Then Wentworth stepped out into the hall and clumped heavily down. "Have you called the commander?" he demanded of the butler. "Well, see that you do at once! A special prisoner from New York City, sent here on orders. Understand?"

The butler showed his distaste for the rough manner Wentworth assumed, but he bowed assent and moved, stiff-legged, to a phone. Wentworth heard the message given to Rixson, answer a few swift questions, then turn back toward him.

"The lieutenant-governor will be here in a few minutes," the butler reported.

Wentworth nodded casually, and fumbled out a cigarette. There were two Black guards outside the front door, huddled in overcoats against the cold. Undoubtedly, Rixson would bring others. If he were suspicious, if he were the Master. . . Wentworth closed his lips grimly. In that case, they had come to the end of the road!

WENTWORTH'S face was impassive as he waited with his automatic ready in an open holster on his hip. No man would have guessed that he knew the fate of the state, his own life and many others hinged on the next few moments. For if things went right—if he and Rice could act swiftly—they might save many men scheduled for death throughout New York, spare countless others who would be slain if the looting started. He had to succeed!

His keenly attuned ears caught the first faint wail of the sirens that heralded Rixson's approach. He was bringing a guard with him all right, but in itself it meant nothing—nothing at all. Wentworth stared out through the steam-clouded window panel of the door, waiting for the first glimpse of the escort Rixson had brought with him. He saw a motorcycle, with a sidecar that mounted a machine gun, skate to a halt at the entrance of the drive and wheel about so that its weapon covered the street. An instant later, another motorcycle raced up to the front door and took its position. Wentworth's hand strayed unconsciously toward his gun, but he held it in check. He still could not tell. These might be merely precautions. . .

Three automobiles raced up the driveway, and from two of them a dozen Black Police spilled, almost before they stopped, and spread out about the grounds with drawn revolvers in their hands. Then Rixson stepped from his sedan, face ruddy with cold, and came deliberately up the steps. There was a frown between his brows and two men, his bodyguards, marched at his heels. Just outside the door, Rixson paused and swung a slow scrutiny over the disposition of his men. He nodded curtly then and reached for the knob. The butler pushed past Wentworth to open the door for him and Wentworth got his shoulders close to the wall.

There was no longer any doubt that Rixson was suspicious. The multiple guard showed that more plainly than any words. Wentworth's grey-blue eyes took on a fierce glint and his lips felt cold and hard against his teeth. It would take more than this to foil his plans! If he had to kill Rixson, take all the police prisoner. . .

Rixson stepped through the doorway and his cold eyes swept over Wentworth. "Where is your prisoner?" he demanded.

"Upstairs, commander!" Wentworth made his voice respectful. "He's wounded and the lady is taking care of him."

"Wounded?" Rixson's voice rose.

"Who is he, your prisoner?"

Wentworth shook his head dumbly. "They didn't tell me in New York, commander. Only said I'd be shot if he got away." He grinned. "I didn't want to get shot, but the prisoner seemed to. It's not much of a wound."

Wentworth walked awkwardly ahead of Rixson toward the steps, in tune with the lack of precise discipline among the Black Police, and Rixson barked at him. Wentworth stepped aside then, to fall in immediately behind him and in front of the two bodyguards. That was what he had planned and he blocked their following Rixson too closely. Rice knew what to do. . .

Rixson stopped before the door of the room where Rice was, his eyes frowning and intent. He shrugged, opened the door and stepped inside. The door closed quickly and Wentworth, who had pretended to be about to follow inside, brought up sharply against it. He turned to the two guards.

"Guess he don't want us inside," he said. He stumbled as he took a step toward them, reaching for cigarettes, turned around and swore harshly at his own clumsiness. He had made a noise, and he thought it had successfully covered up the other noises inside—the noise that would be made by a man falling after being struck over the head!

FOR a half hour, Wentworth waited with the two guards outside the door and then Maria Laplante came out. "The commander says you two get your lunch downstairs," she told the bodyguards, then she turned to Wentworth. Her face was very pale and her hands trembled a little. "He wants you inside."

Wentworth thrust open the door for Maria Laplante to reenter, then followed her with hand close to his gun, ready for treachery. A man lay on the bed, gagged and tightly bound. Beside him stood another man in Rixson's clothing and with Rixson's haughty air. Wentworth's eyes swung jerkily from one to the other and the man in Rixson's clothing spoke.

"Everything proceeding according to schedule," he said, in a pleasant, resonant voice. "What are the orders, commander?"

Wentworth felt relief loosen all his muscles. It was Rice and his impersonation, even the voice tones, were a much better imitation of Rixson than he had dared to believe possible. Wentworth nodded curtly and reached the bed in a stride, met the angry glare of the captive lieutenant-governor.

"We are taking over the state by this little palace revolution," Wentworth told him quietly. "Help us, and when it's over, you'll be free so far as my men and I are concerned. I made Maria a promise that no harm would come to you."

Rixson turned his eyes haughtily to the ceiling and lay, rigid with his anger. Wentworth turned thoughtfully away.

His mind flashed to the heavy guard of Black Police outside the house. It was possible Rixson had given them some special orders as a precaution. but if Rice kept his head. . . Wentworth scrutinized the colonel, and Rice nodded, frowning.

"I think I can manage." he said.

"You'll have to," Wentworth agreed quietly, "and you will, I know. Come, Maria, we'll accompany Governor Rixson to his den. If we work furiously during the next hour, we will save literally thousands of lives and have a chance to reestablish orderly government."

The peremptory knock at the door whipped them all around, tense with anxiety. A man's voice called out hoarsely, "Hey, commander, you all right? Captain sent me to check up according to orders!"

Rice drew himself up slowly and, as the man shouted again outside the door, he moved steadily forward to meet the challenge. He whipped open the door.

"What the devil are you yelling about?" he demanded harshly. "Yes, yes, I'm all right. I'll be down presently." He turned his back on the Black guard. "Sergeant Whitfield. I'll hold you strictly responsible for the prisoner. He is to see no one, talk to no one. Understand?"

Wentworth saluted crisply while his eyes applauded. "Yes. commander!"

When Rice faced toward the hall again, the Black guard had gone. Wentworth strode forward and thrust Maria into the hall. They went rapidly down the stairs and into Rixson's office. With quick movements, Wentworth loosed the mirror panel. The recording mechanism held no disk and Wentworth rapidly inserted one he had prepared in advance. He whirled back to the others, speaking with rapid emphasis.

"We must get Governor Whiting here," he said. "He will be taken ill and you, Rixson, will be acting governor. You will issue instructions—

Maria will show us how it's done—to all the Black police, canceling all their previous orders and rushing them to Albany to put down a supposed rebellion. Meantime, for the same purpose, we will assemble the National Guard units to double the number of the Black Police. When the Blacks are all in one place, we will order them to disband, to turn in uniforms and arms at once. If they refuse. . .”

Rice's face was pale, his eyes brilliant with mounting excitement. "I didn't know the details of your plans," he said. "It should work! It *will* work!"

Wentworth shook his head. "That's only part of it. You must send out orders, removing every crooked official—mayor and sheriff, you have that power as governor—from office and substituting honest men. Guards of concentration camps must be greatly reduced and, as soon as possible, all the prisoners released. . .”

"It's wonderful." Maria whispered.

"I've been trying to get Marvin to do it, but he was afraid of. . . of the Master."

Wentworth said quietly, "I also am afraid of the Master! That is our big weakness. We don't know him, or from what point he will strike."

GOVERNOR WHITING protested weakly over the phone but Rice bullied him into coming promptly. He was led into the room where Rixson lay a prisoner, and then made a captive himself. Then Wentworth and Rice went swiftly to work, coding and shooting out orders to Black Police throughout the state, assembling the National Guard. This was the weakness of the Master, that he had always acted through underlings.

Even if he appeared in person and tried to block the orders, he would fail since no one would recognize his authority! The record Wentworth had made would help convince any recalcitrant officials. . .

Within two hours, the first of the companies of Black Police began to roll into town. They were directed straight to the massively fortified barracks the Master had built near Albany and there they found National Guardsmen in command. The men were instructed to turn in all arms for re-issue. . . Within an hour of their arrival, the first of these men, stripped of all weapons, was being shipped by truck to the concentration camp Wentworth had smashed earlier in the day, and under strong guards of soldiers.

Wentworth was constantly alert at Rice's elbow, awaiting the first hint of opposition. Every possible effort had been made to keep matters secret but with such widespread activity, it was inconceivable that the Master would not learn of it and strike back. Things were moving too swiftly, too smoothly for the *Spider* not to be apprehensive. Wentworth had little fear of a direct attack on Rixon's house, at least. He replaced the Black Police with an entire company of National Guards, drawn from the citizenry.

A second section of Black Police—three companies this time—was in the barracks being disarmed when the signal corps man Wentworth had installed within the building came into Rice's office at a run and thrust out a radio message.

Rice snatched the message and frowned over it, caught up a list which showed the disposal of Black Police troops over the state.

"Motorcade estimated at a thousand men coming in from the north," he told Wentworth with sharp excitement. "Speed, fifty miles an hour. No such outfit is shown on this list, and it's contrary to orders. My instructions were, specifically, that they come in small detachments without waiting to assemble."

Wentworth's grey-blue eyes glinted, "That's fully half the Black Police still at large in the state," he said swiftly. "There should be another thousand or so in the south, and. . ."

The radio operator darted back into the office. "Report from observer in scout plane to the south," he snapped and threw a sheet on the desk, rushed out again.

Wentworth bent over Rice's shoulder and drew in a slow breath. "It's come," he said. "The Master moved even faster than I had dreamed was possible. A unit of a thousand men coming from the south also means that all the rest of the Black Police have been organized for a frontal attack. If we can smash them. . ."

"They outnumber us heavily," Rice snapped. "We can't hold this house. Have to shift headquarters to the barracks."

Wentworth was smiling with thin, bitter lips.

"Carry on, Rice," he said softly. "Take the prisoners with you. It's open warfare now, but we've at least stripped the enemy of more than five hundred men. I think bombing attacks on the motorcades are indicated. You're in complete command."

Rice rose steadily to his feet, "And you, Wentworth?"

Wentworth's smile tightened. "The *Spider* will be busy," he said softly. "Carry on!" He strode from the office.

Wentworth slipped down into the basement and entered the secret passageway by which he had once escaped the death trap of the Master. There he set up his small make-up tray, the mirror. Under his deft hands his face rapidly changed its character and became the ominous and sinister countenance of the *Spider*. He wore the khaki uniform of a captain of the National Guard, but he carried a bundle under his arm that contained the brave green cape and the slouch black hat of the *Spider*.

This was the moment for which he had been maneuvering throughout all the months of battle against the Master and his Black killers. The Master would be fighting in the open, all his forces thrown into one final life-and-death struggle with the powers of law and order. There, in the forefront of battle, the *Spider* would find him.

CHAPTER NINE

DEATH SOUNDS THE BUGLES!

WENTWORTH left the passageway by the garage exit, entered a car and drove steadily in the direction of the fortress-barracks to the north of the city. Motorcycle couriers sped past him in the city streets, as Rice rushed his plans for meeting the power of the enemy. Wentworth had laid no plan of attack. He intended merely to place himself where he could catch a view of both forces of the Black Police and watch them through field-glasses. When he located the Master, he would know how to strike!

He saw that houses were being rapidly barricaded and windows jammed with furniture as protection and he nodded in agreement. Rice had done well to alarm the citizenry. Wentworth switched on the radio in his car and immediately caught the voice of an official announcer.

"Two regiments of the Black Police have rebelled," the man was saying rapidly. "They are bent on looting the city, on seizing control of the state government for themselves. All citizens are warned to lock and barricade their dwellings, to offer no help to the Black Police on pain of being declared rebels against the government, for which the penalty is death. . ."

Wentworth nodded in satisfaction. That was shrewd. Now, in extremity, the federal troops might be called in. No, it would never come to that. This effort would stand or fall on the results of the battle today—on the success of the *Spider*'s search for the Master!

He found a vantage point on a wooded knoll within a half mile to the west of the fortress and settled himself down to wait, his binoculars constantly scanning the terrain. He had not long to wait. Damnably soon, in spite of the harassment of bombers, the northern contingent of the Black Police poured over the crest of a wooded hill a mile away. Their cars were wrenched from the highway and, instantly, the men were spreading out in a long line of attack.

Planes were swinging high against the sky and, even while Wentworth watched, the first of them dived to the attack—but not against the Black Police! Instead, the swoop of the ships carried them over the fortress, bombs raining down upon the barracks buildings and the concrete walls which defended it! No wonder, the Black Police had come so soon! They had had aircraft to defend them against Rice's bombers!

Plane after plane swooped and dumped its deadly cargo of bombs into the fortification and the advancing lines of Black Police were opening fire. Wentworth sprang tautly to his feet, a curse on his lips. The southern force was already streaming out of the city streets to attack on the opposite side of the fort held by the National Guardsmen! Something had gone woefully wrong. All the rapid plans for blocking the attack—for delaying it—had misfired! In the swift precision of the Black attack, Wentworth saw the swift doom of all his efforts! If the Black Police won, not even the death of the Master would end this tyranny.

One last time, Wentworth's glasses swept the advancing battlefronts and then, behind the southern line, Wentworth's attention centered on an open truck that lumbered in the wake of the attack. A skeleton framework had been constructed over the open body and, from the ridgepole, human figures dangled and swayed with the rough lurching of the truck!

Wentworth focused his glasses narrowly, and saw that they were suspended by their thumbs from the framework. Then he saw who they were. Their suffering faces were brought into sharp delineation and a tortured cry was wrung from Wentworth's heart. He knew them all. . . Kirkpatrick, and Nita, his other remaining allies, Sailor Joe and Jackson and Ram Singh, swaying, lurching in that torture rack.

For a moment, Wentworth wavered on the point of hurling himself to the attack. But that was what was intended, wasn't it? Plainly, his allies were being tortured to bait him into the open. That meant the Master was nearby. . . *The Master!* Wentworth's lips were drawn back from his teeth in a grimace of pain, as he forced himself to continue the search for the commander of these butchers. And he found him— found what he least expected to see. . .

Within a car, whose heavily armored sides were easily identified, a man rode—one who sent orders ahead by swiftly running messengers, and plainly was the commander of this force. Wentworth's eyes widened incredulously at recognition of that face. It was not possible, and yet the image was there before his eyes, not to be denied.

The commander of the Black forces, the man who must be the Master—was *Marvin Rixon!*

HOW in God's name had Rixson escaped from the thick guard thrown about his home? But that was not the question now. The problem was to reach and kill him, before his superb generalship smashed the fort and once more loosed upon the people the fury of the aroused Black Police! Wentworth's heart was torn with pain for those tortured friends of his. Curses dripped steadily from his lips, but there was not the slightest chance that he could reach them successfully now—or kill the Master.

As he sent the car hurtling in a long circuit around the battle lines, Wentworth flung aside his uniform cap and dragged down over his head the black wig of the *Spider* and the wide-brimmed black hat. From the bundle, he fumbled out the long cape of brilliant green and flung it about his shoulders so that its fluttering skirt whipped in the cold wind like a battle flag. After that, he concentrated all his attention on driving.

A concrete strip opened whitely ahead and he sent the car skidding onto it, straightened out for the dash into Albany. A rifleman started from a hidden picket post and began to send bullets crashing at him. Wentworth wrenched out an automatic and laughter burst uncontrollably from his lips, the harsh, mocking laughter of the *Spider*. One man with a rifle? Did he think he could stop the *Spider* today?

Wentworth's automatic blasted and was thrust back into its holster. He scarcely needed to see the rifleman hurled, lifeless, back into his covert. Today, the *Spider* could not miss!

Frantically, he fought to wrench the last ounce of power from the roaring motor. He burst in among the first houses of Albany, without slackening speed. The barricaded entrances of houses frowned at him, but he had not yet reached his goal. He whirled on until he came to a place where homes jostled close together in the shadow of frowning factories, where men slunk like beaten dogs to the cover of slattern walls. These were the people who had suffered most at the hands of the Black Police—who had been torn and tortured to yield up their last dollar for the greedy pockets of the Master.

Where the houses were thickest, Wentworth wrenched the bucking car to a halt and, in one smooth movement, flung himself to the ground and then to the roof of the car. He stood there, both arms lifted against the sky, the green cape swirling and flapping in the winter wind, a banner for victory—or death.

"Now is your chance!" he shouted. "Oh, people, now is your chance to crush the Black Police; to destroy the men who have robbed you; to wipe out the tyrants who have tortured you; to wash out the insult these butchers have put upon free American citizens!"

A few men poked their heads out of their doors. He heard them calling excitedly to each other. Windows were flung open.

"The *Spider* summons you to battle!" Wentworth sent his deep, ringing voice through the streets. "Come! Every man of the Black Police in the entire state is here today! If you strike now, you can destroy them once and for all! You—" Wentworth singled out a man—"What have you lost to the Black Police!"

Anger suffused the man's face. "Everything, damn them!" he shouted. "My store! My home! My wife. . ."

"Here's your chance!" Wentworth cried. "Come and drive this car. Drive me through the city streets, slowly, while I call together the victims of the Black Police to rise and destroy them once and for all!"

The man came forward at a jolting run. "Hey you, Taylor!" he shouted. "What are you waiting for? Didn't they kill your boy? Didn't they rob you? Get your gun and come on!"

He sprang into Wentworth's car. "Slowly," Wentworth ordered him. "Slowly, so that people can hear me!"

He dropped to his knees on the roof to brace himself against the jolting of the ear, lifted his hands to the heavens. He was a man praying, a bitter Jeremiah summoning the people against the vices of murder and raping and looting. His voice keened above the rising wind, and everywhere men darted from their houses to stare and some to follow. A half hundred men were trotting behind the car now, grim-faced men with bitter determination in their eyes. Once, he had that nucleus, Wentworth knew the mob would grow.

"Americans!" he cried. "Free men! Will you be slaves? Slaves to the Black Police?"

A roar of wrath answered him. No singing for these men. Their hatred was too deep even for fierce hymns of slaughter. They marched in his wake, silent save for the heavy clumping of their feet.

SLOWLY, at Wentworth's orders, the car described a great circle through the northern limits of Albany. Once, a flying squad of Black Police came upon them and whirled to bring machine guns to bear. Wentworth was on his feet in a single bound and his two guns were in his hands, thundering out death. Four men, Wentworth's swift bullets struck. He had no need to do more. His followers were upon the Black Police, tearing them apart. . . Afterward, they moved on and they carried two machine guns with them! Small as the victory was, it gave the men courage and unity.

Wentworth halted the march finally and turned to face them from his vantage point on top the car. "To the north of the city," he said, "A thousand Black Police are storming the barracks which is held by the National Guardsmen—your friends and mine. If we attack them in the rear, they will crumple. Let nothing stop you until you can join your friends inside that fortress. Machine gunners, forward! Open fire as soon as you come in range of the enemy. Men, march! And the martyred souls of your kinspeople and your loved ones march with you!"

Wentworth sprang down from the roof of the car then and ran to the machine guns. Already, the furious men were in motion, a march as inevitable as the tides. They would follow now where he led. . . and he would lead them! Right to the Master, and then. . . Wentworth closed his mind to the memory of those poor helpless friends of his, of Nita, dangling from the ridgepole.

"Forward! Forward!" he shouted.

The light truck of the Black Police, which mounted the two machine guns, lumbered forward. Men were all about it, running, but in grim silence now. They would kill or be killed in that same way. Could the Black Police stand against them? Wentworth's lips twisted bitterly.

Swiftly, the men advanced and burst from the cover of the last houses. The battlefield was spread out before them now, the fortress crumbled in ruins from the blasts of the bombs, but its guns were still going. The Black Police were halfway up the last slope, at a fast charge. Wentworth ranged them with one of the machine guns, turned to face the men behind him.

He flung forward his arm. *"Charge!"*

His order was drowned out in the deep, roaring battle shout of the mob. Wentworth closed his finger on the machine gun's trigger and swung it as a reaper swings a scythe. His bullets sliced the line of the Black Police in half. He saw the white faces turn toward him an instant before they plunged into bloody death; saw the middle of the line ripped wide open as his men leaped forward in the wake of his shots. Whistles piped and swift orders were flung out. Black Police tried frantically to face both ways at once.

Just as the battle was joined, as men leaped with clutching, vengeful hands upon the Black Police—Wentworth heard a bugle blow, clearly and sweet, in the fortress; the rapid pulse of the command to charge and, forth from those crumbled walls poured a khaki column. It was rout for the Black Police. They threw down their arms and fled, and wherever they ran, men leaped and bounded in their wake, determined upon slaughter. Nor would they escape through the city, Wentworth knew. The very children would rise to wreak vengeance.

Nearly a hundred men still ran beside the truck and Wentworth flung them out to meet the Guardsmen. Their forces merged and, at Wentworth's shout, a young officer ran forward.

"Take the northern force on its flank!" Wentworth cried.

The man nodded, his face fierce and eager. "Colonel Rice's orders, sir!" he cried, and ran back to his men.

At a double, the united force started for the woods which flanked the Black Police. Wentworth had no longer any doubt of the issue, but his haunted eyes were searching the field. The armored car in which the Master had ridden was gone. The truck with the barren ridgepole was stalled in a ditch, but pitiful figures no longer dangled from its torture rack.

Heavily, Wentworth ran toward the spot, climbed into the abandoned truck. There were bloodstains on the floor. The ropes, that had strung the prisoners up, were severed—but of Kirkpatrick and Nita and the rest there was no trace at all!

A fury of savage futility burned in Wentworth's soul. He had saved the day for the Guardsmen, perhaps for the state if he could find and slay the Master, but Nita and Kirkpatrick! What could anything accomplish for him, if they were gone? He stood, shoulders sagging, while the crashing of guns mounted to sudden thunder in the north, continued for a long, long aching moment, and then began to die out. Not victory or death, though they had won. Not that. . . Victory and death; defeat in the hour of triumph. . .

WENTWORTH turned heavily away, started on slow feet toward the fort. The shouting of men turned his head, and he saw some of those he had led rushing toward him. For a moment, hope sprang up in him. Perhaps, they had found those poor prisoners! But it was not that. They babbled of triumph and victory and lifted Wentworth to their shoulders, bore him toward the fortress. They could sing now. Their tongues were loosened in a chant of victory. A sad smile stirred the corners of Wentworth's lips. Yes, he could lead men to triumph over their foes, but his own life was empty and stricken. And the Master still lived. God, yes, the Master still lived. . .

Wentworth's head lifted with the surge of bitter hatred through his body. He could still revenge! The men deposited him on the steps of the shattered barracks building and cheered him as he went steadily through the door. Here was no place for personal grief, nor time for its assuagement. He must organize an immediate hunt for the Master, and. . . He thrust wide the door of an office and, instantly, hard hands seized his throat from behind, a gun gouged into his spine!

Wentworth staggered, would have fallen, but for those strangling hands. They were eased when his guns had been taken, but still an automatic gouged into his spine. His wearied eyes swept the room, and something that might have been bitter laughter, or might have been a sob, thrust itself, rock-hard, up through his throat. And he had proclaimed the victory!

Nita was in the room, and Kirkpatrick and the rest. They were bound hand and foot, helpless prisoners against the wall. Colonel Rice was bound by stout ropes to a chair and over him stood two other men who might have been twins for resemblance. One, Wentworth knew, was the liberated Lieutenant Governor Rixson. The other. . . Wentworth's lips twisted bitterly The Master had chosen a new disguise, that was all. As Rixson, he had led the attacking force, had entered here of course by some secret way known to him alone. Black Police ringed the room with drawn guns.

Wentworth's eyes swept the room and centered at last on the other woman in the room, on Maria Laplante who stood at Rixson's side. Had she played them false at last, then? Was she the one who had accomplished their overthrow? The Master was talking, easily, softly...

"We meet at last, *Spider*," he said.

"We have met many times before, but never when you knew me.

You have fought well—very well indeed. Too bad you couldn't win. I shall have to reconstruct my machine, of course, but that won't be too difficult. . . when you are dead."

Wentworth was still staring fixedly at Maria Laplante. Her head was carried too proudly for traitor's blood. He swung his eyes from her to Rixson and back again. . .

"Yes," he said quietly to the Master, "you will be safe enough, once I am dead. There are good men in your force. Men almost good enough and brave enough to be honest, once they are shown the way. Men who might have been great leaders of the people, had they chosen the honest way, who still may lead. . ."

The Master's eyes sharpened. "Your talking will do you no good, *Spider*," he said softly, "but I think you'd better be quiet. Other criminals have held you in their power, but because they paused to gloat or to torture you, you have always escaped. You won't this time. I won't even torture you by killing your adherents first. They are but underlings. You the leader. . ."

The Master's gun lifted steadily and he took deliberate aim at Wentworth's face. "Hold him steadily, men," he said. "Give him no chance to dodge. Goodbye *Spider*! Too bad to lose so worthy an enemy!" He began to squeeze the trigger deliberately, his eyes tight and hard and steady.

"Rixson," Wentworth said quietly.

"Now is your chance. Maria. . ."

The Master wavered. Wentworth dared not look toward Rixson. He held the Master's eyes with his own. "That's right, Rixson," he said. "You can still be the savior of the state. Don't forget that every good reform we have put through has been in your name. The credit can still be yours!"

The Master swore harshly and pulled the trigger. He had delayed an instant too long. In the moment that he squeezed the trigger, Maria LaPlante and Rixson both leaped forward. Their clutching hands wrenched the muzzle of the gun aside. The bullet burned across Wentworth's shoulder and the man who gripped his arm uttered a choked cry as his hands relaxed. Wentworth spun on a heel, his fist striking upward into the face of the Black Police who had held him. Guns were blasting in the room, and there were the shouts of the Black Police. The Master shouted a hoarse command. . .

WENTWORTH saw the widening eyes of the man who held him at gun point, felt, more than saw, the blast of the revolver and felt lead tear through his side. But not death itself could have stopped his fist. It jarred home to the man's throat, drove him, already unconscious against the wall. Wentworth sagged to a knee, but he had the revolver now. He twisted about. . .

In the middle of the room, the Master fought frantically with Rixson and the girl. One of the Black Police stepped forward, as Wentworth watched, and jerked up a gun to smash Rixson's skull. Wentworth's gun blasted, and the Master's man was hurled backward, already dead with a bullet through his skull.

"Maria!" Wentworth shouted. "Cut the prisoners loose!"

The Master's head wrenched toward him, and Wentworth whipped up his and fired in the same moment. And yet, he was too late. The Master ducked and the next moment, Maria held before him as a shield, was backing toward the door. He cleared the way for two more of the Black Police and they threw down on Wentworth frantically. A bullet plucked at his cape and another scored a lock of hair from his wig. They had time for no more than that before the *Spider's* lead cut them down.

Nita's voice cut sharp across the bedlam in frantic warning, and Wentworth hurled himself face down on the floor. Lead whined past his ear. He twisted. . . and Maria LaPlante stumbled toward him, pitched across his body. Wentworth wrenched an arm, his head out from beneath her. Down the hall, he saw the Master just ducking through another doorway. He fired without aiming, without thought, saw the Master stagger and heard him shout hoarsely as he vanished through the opening.

Wentworth fought to be free of Maria's weight, but it was inert across his shoulders, and he was weak. . . weak. There was a fury in his side where the bullet had struck. He clawed at the floor and, suddenly, the weight was lifted from him. He flung a single swift glance around the room. Rice was free. There were no more Black Police. Reeling, scarcely able to stand, Wentworth fought his way down the hallway toward that door through which the Master had vanished. The fiend could not elude him now. . .

Wentworth staggered through the door, gun ready, and stared about him in dazed bewilderment. The room was empty! Hell! The secret passageway which Wentworth had deduced must have its exit in this room. If he could find it. . . Wentworth took a staggering step forward and was suddenly on his hands and knees on the floor. An instant later, warm arms closed about his neck and Nita's lips brushed his cheek.

"He's gone, dear," she whispered. "Lie down. I must bind that wound!"

Wentworth tried to fight to his feet, but he had not the strength. "Be quick!" he whispered. "Be quick. He must die."

He caught his breath then, as Nita set to work on his wound with swift, efficient hands. He was aware of movement in the room, but did not open his eyes. He was thinking swiftly. Something familiar about the movements of the Master in that last swift retreat. He knew the man. He must know him! If only he could think. . .

Iodine stung his side fiercely, then a bandage tightened about him. The Master. He must know him, must. . . Abruptly, a great cry sprung from Wentworth's lips. He thrust himself up on an arm, scrambled to his knees. He staggered to his feet, almost fell.

"Some brandy!" he said hoarsely. "Whisky, ammonia. Anything! I must be fast!"

Someone thrust a flask into his hand and he tipped it. The stuff was fiery in his throat. His heart began to hammer with fierce throbs and a false strength touched his limbs. Wentworth laughed, tossed the flask aside. He ran through the door. Men shouted behind him. They were following, but he could not wait. The Master would waste no time. He would make a quick clean-up and fly—or he would return to his own identity and seek to hide under it. . .

There was a motorcycle in the quadrangle, and Wentworth seized it, ran, stumbling, with it. The motor caught and its forward surge fairly threw him into the saddle. The cold bite of the wind in Wentworth's face helped, but he was reeling. Weak, so damned weak! But he had the Master! He could not escape now!

ACROSS the jumbled battlefield with its heaped dead, he sped, his green cape kiting out behind him. . . through littered streets. Everywhere about him were the tokens of victory. Flags flaunted from the windows and women were marching, singing. There were grimmer fruits, too, that dangled from the lampposts—the Black Police who had thought they could escape the wrath of an aroused people.

Cheers. . .

Wentworth scarcely heard these things. Men were cheering him as he rode, crouched low over the handlebars of the machine. Wentworth drove almost blindly, his eyes strained wide, searching ahead, ever ahead. Finally, he wrenched the motorcycle to a halt and ran at a low flight of steps, pounded up them. The reloaded gun in his hand crashed twice, and the shattered lock yielded under the thrust of his shoulder, He ran along a short hall, blundered in through a door—and then a gun blasted at him from behind a chair.

Wentworth laughed. He did not dodge, nor attempt to charge. He had not the strength. But the gun in his hand leaped and leaped again. Bullets clawed through the flimsy back of the chair. He heard a man scream, saw arms and legs floundering, but the gun in the *Spider*'s hand never ceased to hammer until it gave forth a dry, empty clicking that meant the last bullet was sped. Wentworth went forward then, stumbling, uncertain of his tread, and gazed down on the dead man behind the chair.

The Master had had just time to remove the make-up from his face. His shoulder was roughly bandaged and it. . .

Wentworth stooped over him and ground against the paling forehead the base of his cigarette lighter. The crimson seal of the *Spider* sprang vividly to life there. Wentworth straightened, turned heavily away. The strength was going out of him now. He staggered, managed to catch the wall with his hand and leaned there, panting, sobbing for breath. His slow, heavy feet took him to the street, somehow to the motorcycle.

A boy was standing on the sidewalk, staring at him with dilated eyes. "Geez!" he gasped. "Geez! The *Spider*!"

The *Spider* managed a smile. "Where's the nearest hospital, son?" he asked hoarsely. . .

WENTWORTH said easily, as he tilted back in a chair in the office of the police commissioner in New York, "Of course, I'd like the claim credit for that kill in Albany—the Master, I mean. The doctors will tell you, I was found unconscious in the streets, and there was no green cape, no face of the *Spider*, nothing. No, I guess the *Spider* put one over on us after all, Kirkpatrick. But he still left plenty for you to do. . ."

Kirkpatrick smiled grimly. "I have plenty to do all right, putting the lid back on the underworld. Rixson is going to make a good man there in Albany, with Maria LaPlante to help him. He'll never turn crook again."

Wentworth shook his head. "If he should," he said softly, "I think some ghosts might well haunt him to his grave. Many ghosts. . . But seriously. Kirk, we were fools not to have suspected the Master's identity all along. The nub of the whole affair from its beginning was this White Face in the Mirror. That was what sold the plan to its original backers—the fact that the Mirror concealed them absolutely. So the Master had to be a man who could contrive a thing like that, and who better fitted to do that than the man who openly made the mirrors for the Master! That was the cleverest subterfuge of all—and Doctor Kepler almost got away with it. Doctor Kepler, who was the Master in disguise!"

Kirkpatrick was scrutinizing papers on his desk, scarcely listening to his friend, Wentworth. There were so many problems. Suddenly, he uttered a sharp oath and surged to his feet. Wentworth stared at him, saw the white gravity of his friend's face.

"In heaven's name, Kirk?" he demanded. "What is it?"

Kirkpatrick said heavily, "I'll resign! By the heavens, I'll resign first! The damned fools! As if all the world didn't know what a debt of gratitude it owes. . . Listen, Dick. . .

"'We, the undersigned, respectfully submit, that no drive to wipe out crime can be complete, no citizenry can hold respect for the law, until the greatest criminal of all is brought to justice and made to pay for his many crimes. We submit that this is your task and we urge and, in fact, demand, that you throw every resource at your command into an immediate and thorough effort to find and destroy the criminal who calls himself the *Spider!*' "

Wentworth broke into laughter, but Kirkpatrick's gravity did not lighten.

"The names on that list command respect, Dick," he said. "I'll either have to do what they demand. . . or resign. And, by God, they can have my resignation right now!"

Wentworth continued to laugh. He picked up the gardenia from the thin vase on Kirkpatrick's desk and wafted its scent to his nostrils. "Why be so disturbed, Kirk?" he said pleasantly. "You've been trying for a great many years to catch the *Spider*, or find some proof against him—and you haven't succeeded yet!"

Kirkpatrick stared at Wentworth and gradually his mouth corners quirked in a smile. It broadened and he burst into a laugh, and Wentworth joined with him. It was loud and hearty, their laughter. In the outer office, one cop looked at another and grinned.

"Hell, you can't blame them for laughing," he said. "They've won the right to keep on laughing all their lives—after what they've done for this state."

THE END

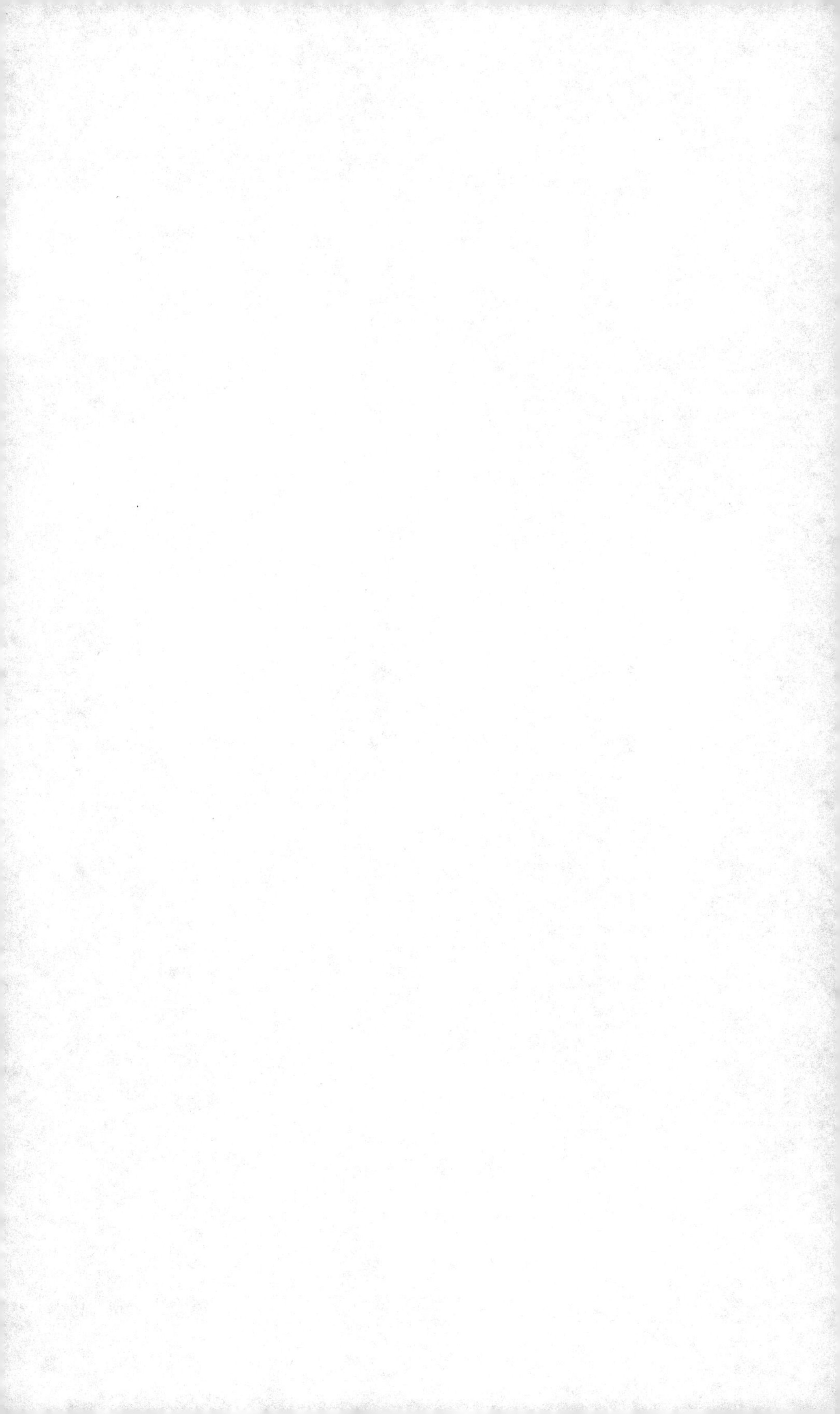

Cover of the September 1938 issue of The Spider magazine
Artwork by John Newton Howitt

ABOUT THE AUTHOR

Norvell W. Page (1906-1961) grew up in Richmond, Virginia, the son of an executive at the Wurlitzer Music Company, and the great-grandson of the Governor of Williamsburg. He attended William & Mary College in Virginia, where he met his future wife, Audrey Rohr. He had already started his career as a newspaperman at 18, working for *The Cincinnati Post*, then *The Norfolk Virginia-Pilot*. After college he moved to New York where he worked for the *Herald Tribune*, the *Times*, and finally the *World Telegraph* (until 1934).

In order to help support his family which was ruined in the stock market crash, he needed to supplement his newspaper salary, so he turned to pulp writing in 1930. He was soon writing for *Western Trails, Black Mask, Dime Mystery,* and *Ten Detective Aces* (where he memorably contributed the Ken Carter character). In 1933, with Arthur J. Burks, he founded the American Fiction Guild, a national association of pulp authors, and became president of the New York chapter.

It was also in 1933, at the age of 27, that he was picked to write The Spider under the house name "Grant Stockbridge," starting with the third issue. Page was selected for one important reason: He wrote really quickly. It's estimated that he churned out between 100,000 and 120,000 words a month for the pulps, approximately 60,000 going to *The Spider*. He received $500 for each Spider story at first, then later $600, and $700 by the end of the series.

Page also wrote under two other pseudonyms: As "Randolf Craig" he wrote the "Dr. Skull" stories in the single-issue *The Octopus* and *The Scorpion* pulps; As "N. Wooten Poge" he contributed to *Spicy Detective Stories* and *Detective-Dragnet*.

When *The Spider* ended its run in 1943, Page left the pulps behind and joined the war effort, copywriting for the Office of War Information in Washington, DC. After the war, he continued in government work, ending up at the Atomic Energy Commission's Public Information Division in 1949, where he worked until he died in 1961 at the age of 57 due to complications from an earlier surgery.

Cover of the October 1938 issue of The Spider magazine
Artwork by John Newton Howitt

ABOUT THE ILLUSTRATOR

John Fleming Gould (1906-1996) was born in Worcester, Massachusetts, and grew up in Brooklyn, where he was childhood friends with Walter Baumhofer, future *Doc Savage* cover artist. In fact, when he failed to get into any engineering programs, he went to Pratt Art Institute a year behind Baumhofer. After college they rented studio space together along with seven other guys, at 161 West 23rd Street, New York. (Rent was $90 a month for the whole top floor of the building.)

John Gould started illustrating pulp magazines in 1927. The first thing he did was add the "Fleming" (his mother's maiden name), in an effort to sound classier. *Danger Trails* was his first assignment. Soon he was working for *Cowboy Stories, Astounding Stories,* and *Blue Book,* and in those days was receiving $10-15 per illustration.

Gould worked with Harry Steeger when he was an editor at Dell Publications. After Steeger struck out on his own in 1930 to form Popular Publications, he offered Gould a deal he couldn't refuse: $8 per illustration, but all the work he wanted. At Popular, Gould did all the illustrations for every issue of *The Spider, G-8 and His Battle Aces,* and *Operator 5,* among others, until he left the Pulps behind in 1942.

With many top artists drafted for the war, Gould (now with a family) finally got his shot at the "slick" magazines. He became the top illustrator at the *Saturday Evening Post* for the next eight years, then moved to *Redbook.* He expanded into advertising art in 1946, working for General Electric and other top corporations. In later years he also did fine art.

Gould was also a teacher and lecturer. Starting in his pulp days, he taught night school at Pratt for 22 years. In 1957 he opened the Bethlehem Art Gallery and Art School near Newburgh, NY.

Cover of the November 1938 issue of The Spider magazine
Artwork by John Newton Howitt

ABOUT THE PULP COVER ARTIST

John Newton Howitt (1885-1958), a graduate of the Art Students League (other grads: Homer, Gibson, Pyle), started working professionally in 1907 as a painter of portraits, landscapes, and covers, and an illustrator of interior artwork for many "slick" magazines as well. Howitt had a parallel career as a fine artist, even exhibiting his work in major galleries in the 1920s. He produced a huge volume of work despite crippling polio for which he wore an iron brace on his right leg.

After the stock market crash of 1929, Howitt supplemented his work for the likes of *The Saturday Evening Post* and *Country Gentleman* (where he signed his full name) with work in the pulp field (where he signed his covers simply with an "H"). He painted for *Top Notch, Adventure, Street & Smith Love Story, Clues, Detective Story* and *The Whisperer*. For Popular Publications he created covers for *Operator 5, Dime Detective, Horror Stories,* and *Terror Tales,* as well as *The Spider* (beginning with the second issue in 1933, when he was 48). At his most prolific, he painted as many as seven pulp covers in a single month, and is estimated to have done over 300 total. Howitt put many devils in these details, and became known as the Dean of Weird Menace Cover Art commanding top-dollar ($900) for his work.

Howitt disappeared from the pulp field following the September 1939 issue of *The Spider* and the September/October 1939 issue of *Operator 5*. Howitt had moved back to the "slick" magazines exclusively, along with his advertising art; he also painted wartime posters for the Red Cross. He continued, as he started, painting commercial and fine art—obsessively, every day—until his death in 1958 at the age of 72, even winning awards in later years for his landscapes.

It is believed that Howitt ultimately looked down on his career in the pulps despite the effort he put into it. His wife, Bertha (1880-1975), definitely did, preferring her husband to be remembered as a fine artist and teacher. There are very few known existing original pulp paintings by Howitt, and this appears to be intentional on the part of the artist or his widow.

While the Black Police trilogy was being devoured by pulp readers, the first of two 15-chapter Spider movie serials was being filmed in California by Columbia Pictures. (Principal photography took place from August 29 to September 29, 1938.) Many of the staged publicity photos for **The Spider's Web** were taken in the final days of August 1938 (by A.L. Schafer) and the then-current issue of the magazine, "The Spider at Bay," figures in five different cast shots. This same issue then made its way into publicity materials as well. Pictured here is Kenneth Duncan as Ram Singh. Warren Hull starred as Wentworth, and *Web* proved so popular that Hull and Duncan reprised their roles in *The Spider Returns,* released in 1941. (*The Spider's Web* photography copyright © 2009 Columbia Pictures Corporation. All rights reserved.)

FURTHER READING

More adventures of The Spider

Trade and mass-market paperbacks from Baen Books:
THE SPIDER: ROBOT TITANS OF GOTHAM, THE SPIDER: CITY OF DOOM
three-story reprint collections available whereever books are sold.

PULP DOUBLES from Girasol Collectables:
12 two-story trade paperbacks, with new books published four times
a year. Available in comic shops or from GirasolCollectables.com.

PULP REPLICAS from Girasol Collectables:
High-end cover-to-cover recreations of the first 44 issues of The
Spider magazine are available, with new editions being released
eight times a year. Available from GirasolCollectables.com.

New stories from Moonstone Books:
THE SPIDER CHRONICLES is an omnibus of 19 new short stories by
contemporary writers. THE SPIDER: JUDGEMENT KNIGHT is an ongo-
ing series of "wide-vision" graphic novels. Available in comic shops.

Also by Norvell Page

CITY OF CORPSES: THE COLLECTED WEIRD MYSTERIES OF KEN
CARTER, published by Black Dog Books. Available from online
retailers such as AdventureHouse.com.

Also published by Age of Aces Books

SKY DEVIL: HELL'S SKIPPER by Harold F. Cruickshank
MURDER OF THE ADMIRAL/MURDER OF THE PIGBOAT SKIPPER
a flip-book of two Sheridan Doome mysteries by Steve Fisher
CAPTAIN BABYFACE: THE COMPLETE ADVENTURES by Steve Fisher
THE RED FALCON: THE DARE-DEVIL ACES YEARS (Vol 1-4) and
THE ADVENTURES OF SMOKE WADE (Vol 1) by Robert J. Hogan
CHINESE BRADY: THE COMPLETE ADVENTURES by C.M. Miller
THE BLACK SHEEP OF BELOGUE: THE BEST OF O.B. MYERS
THE ADVENTURES OF THE THREE MOSQUITOES: THE WIZARD ACE
and THE MAGIC INFERNO by Ralph Oppenheim
Available from Amazon.com.

FURTHER READING

Information available on life in America during the 1930s is enormous. For readers interested in the events of the period or in the pulp magazines, and particularly *The Spider*, themselves, the following are good places to start:

America in the 1930s:

Allen, Frederick Lewis. 1940. SINCE YESTERDAY: THE NINETEEN-THIRTIES IN AMERICA, SEPTEMBER 3, 1929-SEPTEMBER 3, 1939. New York: Harper & Brothers.

Manchester, William. 1974. THE GLORY AND THE DREAM: A NARRATIVE HISTORY OF AMERICA, 1932-1972. Boston: Little, Brown.

Hamby, Alonzo. 2004. FOR THE SURVIVAL OF DEMOCRACY: FRANKLIN ROOSEVELT AND THE WORLD CRISIS OF THE 1930S. New York: Free Press.

Zalampas, Michael. 1989. ADOLPH HITLER AND THE THIRD REICH IN AMERICAN MAGAZINES, 1923-1939. Bowling Green, OH: Bowling Green State University Popular Press.

The Pulp Magazines and The Spider:

Hardin, Nils. 1977. "Interview with Harry Steeger." XENOPHILE #33 (July 1977).

Sampson, Robert. 1987. SPIDER. Bowling Green, OH: Bowling Green State University Popular Press.

Server, Lee. 1993. DANGER IS MY BUSINESS: AN ILLUSTRATED HISTORY OF THE FABULOUS PULP MAGAZINES. San Francisco: Chronicle Books.

Information on The Spider is also available at SpiderReturns.com

Made in the USA
Coppell, TX
19 February 2025

46141809R00249